THE
CREEPER

THE
CREEPER

Tania Carver

SPHERE

First published in Great Britain as a paperback original
in 2010 by Sphere
Reprinted 2010 (twice)

A CIP catalogue record for this book
is available from the British Library.

Printed and bound in Great Britain by
Clays Ltd, St Ives plc

Papers used by Sphere are natural renewable and
recyclable products sourced from well-managed forests and certified
in accordance with the rules of the Forest Stewardship Council.

Mixed Sources
Product group from well-managed
forests and other controlled sources
www.fsc.org Cert no. SGS-COC-004081
© 1996 Forest Stewardship Council

FSC

Sphere
An imprint of
Little, Brown Book Group
100 Victoria Embankment
London EC4Y 0DY

An Hachette UK Company
www.hachette.co.uk

www.littlebrown.co.uk

Once again thank you to David, Dan, Thalia, Andy and the rest of the team at Little, Brown. And to my agent Jane Gregory and everyone at Gregory and Company. Huge thanks to Joan Medland for her expert advice.

The version of Colchester General Hospital as imagined in this novel is entirely my own. As is Colchester, for that matter.

PART ONE

1

It was the little things she had noticed first.

Ornaments slightly out of place, a mug on the draining board that she thought she had put back in the cupboard, a damp towel in the bathroom that should have been dry.

Little things. Puzzling things.

Unsettling things.

But not enough to be worried about.

If Suzanne Perry had known then how far it would go, what kind of nightmare her life would become, she would have been more than worried. She would have run as fast and as far away as possible.

Suzanne was twenty-six. She lived alone in a flat on the Maldon Road in Colchester. She worked as a speech therapist at the General Hospital. She had broken up with her boyfriend a few months ago and, while she had dated since then, she wasn't looking for anything serious.

She just wanted to enjoy herself.

Suzanne went out with her friends once a week, to a few bars in town, maybe a club. She liked dancing. She liked whatever was popular. She played Little Boots and Lady

Gaga in the car and sang along. She enjoyed movies, especially comedies. And eating out, when she could afford it. Some nights she wished she had a boyfriend, some nights she liked nothing better than curling up on the sofa with a chick-lit novel, a bar of chocolate and a glass of white wine.

She was attractive and friendly and she didn't think she was anything special.

But someone did.

Someone thought Suzanne Perry was very special indeed.

The nightmare started in early June. Suzanne was asleep in her bed, in her room, in her flat. The doors locked and bolted, the windows secured. She thought she was safe.

She was wrong.

The thick, heavy drapes were pulled close at the window, the wooden blinds tight shut. As always. Since she had been a child she was a light sleeper, needing total darkness and silence. So her bedroom was like a sensory deprivation chamber. She loved that.

But this night was different. This darkness was different. Not comforting or secure but cold and deep, as if the safety of her womb-like room had been breached. She didn't know if she was dreaming or awake. The room was hers and not hers.

She lay on her back in her bed, her eyes wide open, her head propped up on pillows, stared straight ahead into a nightmare-black darkness of deep, dank shadows in which huge, hulking shapes could be glimpsed. She blinked, tried to move. Couldn't. Blinked again. Her head, full of imagined whispers and screams, ached.

A shadow detached itself from the darkness, moved towards her. Her heart raced, she tried to roll over, pull away. Couldn't. Her body wouldn't respond.

The shadow took shape. An outline against the blackness. A human shape, bulky, with two huge, glowing eyes at the front of its head. Bright, like car headlights. Suzanne tried to shield her face, but her arm wouldn't respond. She closed her eyes. The shadow moved in closer. Suzanne, her heart hammering, kept her eyes closed. Her brain sent a signal to her mouth: open, scream. Nothing happened.

She kept her eyes screwed tight shut, tried not to breathe. Pretended she wasn't there. Willed herself to waken.

Nothing happened.

She opened her eyes. The dream room was spinning, a pitch-black kaleidoscope. She pulled it into focus. The shadow was right beside her, its bright eyes by the side of her head. She could feel its dream breath on her dream cheek.

She closed her eyes again, tried to move her lips, a mantra running through her head: *It's only a dream . . . it's only a dream . . . it's only a dream . . .*

Then the shadow spoke. Low, burbling and monotonous, a rattle and rasp like a pan of water boiling dry. Crooned, painful words she didn't understand.

She tried to understand, form those words into sentences. There was something familiar about the sound, carried over from her waking life if only she could understand it. But the words shivered away into the recesses of her dream, lost and irretrievable.

Then the shadow moved, flowed over her body; it smelled of dark, oily, toxic smoke.

Then it wasn't smoke. It became hard, rough, unyielding.

She held her breath once more, tried to call out. Nothing. She tried to pull her legs away, stand up. Nothing. Bring her hands up clenched as fists, fight the shadow off. Nothing.

Cold, hard hands touched her, ran down her sides. Her dream body recoiled, but stayed where it was. The hands slowly moved down to her thighs, to the hem of her T-shirt.

It's only a dream . . . only a dream . . .

The hands moved her T-shirt up, over her thighs.

Only a dream . . . a dream . . .

She screwed her eyes closed once more.

The shadow started talking again. The wounded, twisted crooning.

Wake up . . . wake up . . .

The crooning building, getting louder . . .

Only a dream . . . wake up, please . . . wake up . . .

Then flash of light. A scream. Not Suzanne's.

Then silence.

Suzanne opened her eyes. The shadow had gone. She was alone in the darkness once more.

Her heart was still hammering, her breathing harsh and ragged. She kept her eyes closed. Willed herself to go to another area of sleep. A safer, kinder one.

Suzanne slept.

A harsh, shrill noise crashed in Suzanne's ears.

She jumped, opened her eyes. Blinked. Looked around. Sighed. Her womb-like bedroom. She closed her eyes again.

But the noise wouldn't let her sleep: Chris Moyles' voice blaring out, telling her in his own unlovable way that it was time to get up.

She opened her eyes again. Something wasn't right. It took her a few moments but she worked out what it was. Sunlight was streaming round the edges of the blackout curtains.

Suzanne sighed again. Normally she liked to lie after the alarm woke her, cherish the last few foggy tendrils of sleep that had wrapped themselves round her. Leave it as late as possible before throwing the duvet back and reluctantly trudging off to the shower.

But not this morning. Not with the nightmare she'd had. She didn't want to stay in bed a second longer than she had to.

Now she threw the duvet back, felt pins and needles all down her arms. She swung her legs round and down to the floor. They ached, felt heavier than usual, stiffer. She tried to sit up, felt her head spin. Blinked as the room refused to stay still. She flopped back on the bed again.

Her body felt as if she had done a particularly strenuous workout in the gym followed by a huge session in the pub with Zoe and Rosie then had just collapsed into bed and not moved all night. But she knew that wasn't true.

She'd had a night in, watching *Corrie*, eating a bar of Fruit and Nut. Couple of phone calls then a long bubble bath and an early night with a Kate Atkinson novel. No workout. Only a small glass of wine, what was left in the bottle.

Suzanne tried once more to stand and made it, her legs shaking, the room spinning. Maybe I'm coming down with something, she thought. Swine flu, probably. She stumbled towards the window, placing one hand on the sill to steady herself, pulled back the drapes, ready to see what kind of day it was.

She didn't get as far as looking out of the window.

The blinds were up, which explained the extra light in the room, and there was something stuck to the pane of glass. She frowned, not quite understanding what it was doing there, why the blinds were up. Then she pulled the object off, scrutinised it more closely.

And felt her heart lurch.

It was a photo. Of herself, sleeping. The oversize T-shirt she wore for bed – the one she was wearing now – had been pulled up, revealing her trimmed pubic hair, the tops of her thighs.

Blood sped round her system. Her chest pumped, as if she couldn't get enough air into her body. Her legs shook even more.

She turned the photo over. Gasped as fear shuddered through her. There were words on the back. Neatly printed block capitals. She read them.

I'M WATCHING OVER YOU

The nightmares punched back into her head. The shadows. The lights. The voice.

The hands on her body.

Suzanne's head spun rapidly, her legs gave way, her eyes closed.

It was no nightmare. It had been real.

She fainted.

2

'Well,' said Detective Sergeant Mickey Philips, trying to give a cocky smile, 'someone didn't like her . . .' The smile then disappeared as his face rapidly changed colour, draining to a shade of mildewed putty. He then heaved his head over the side and was sick into the river.

'Do it in the bag . . .' Detective Inspector Phil Brennan's words came too late.

'Sorry . . .' The apology came accompanied by gasps and spitting.

Phil Brennan shook his head, turned away from his new DS and back to what was before him. New or not, he couldn't blame the man. Not really. In his years with the Major Incident Squad – MIS – he had seen plenty of unpleasant things but the sight before him was definitely one of the worst.

The body had once been female. Now, it more resembled something from a butcher's shop or a horror film. Abattoir leavings. The woman had been stripped naked and severely mutilated. Tortured. Her torso, arms, legs and head were criss-crossed by a lattice of scars, most of them deep. Whip marks, Phil guessed. Knife marks. Chain marks, even.

But amongst all that devastation two things stood out for Phil. The first was that her vagina had been savagely mutilated, even more so than the rest of her body, and her legs spread open at the base of the light tower. The second was that a word had been carved into her forehead:

WHORE

'I think,' said Phil, 'someone's trying to send a message . . .'

He was standing on the deck of an old lightship moored to King Edward Quay on the River Colne in Colchester. A banner along the front railing proclaimed it to be used by the Sea Cadets. Each side of the river seemed to host two separate worlds. The quay held a ribbon of single-storey buildings, all fenced off businesses and none of them looking too prosperous: a scrapyard, a garage, a couple of small manufacturing units. Brightly coloured billboards loudly proclaimed urban redevelopment.

On the opposite side of the river apartment blocks in glass, metal and wood, some cool and minimal, some gaudy and primary-coloured, lined the bank side. Creating a mini Docklands skyline, they demonstrated the redevelopment along the Hythe. The past on one side, the future on the other, thought Phil. Old and decaying versus shiny and new. And in the middle, a dead woman on a lightship.

Phil shook his head, tried to clear away the thoughts that had preoccupied him on his way to work. About his personal life. Shove them to one side, get on with his job.

DS Mickey Philips hauled himself back upright. Phil looked at him. 'Better?'

He nodded, cheeks now flushed with exertion and embarrassment. 'Sorry. Suppose it'll get easier . . .'

Phil's features were tight. 'If it does, it's God's way of telling you to go and work security in M & S.'

'Right. Yes, boss.' Mickey Philips risked a glance at the body. 'Is it . . . d'you think it's her, boss?'

Phil looked down also. Flies were beginning to gather. He batted them away, knowing they would return. 'I hope so,' he said. 'I mean . . . I hope not, but yes, because I'd hate to think there was another . . .'

Mickey Philips nodded, understood.

Phil turned away, looked upwards. The sun was up already, the sky a vivid robin's egg blue. The air alive with warmth and possibility. But for Phil, the brightest light cast the darkest shadows. He saw the scene with cop's eyes because he saw the world with cop's eyes. He couldn't help it; it was the job. Instead of the living he saw the dead. And the ghosts of the dead spoke to him all the time, asked him for justice, for peace. The gentle creak and maw of the boat giving the dead woman a voice, seeming to whisper to him, plead with him. Find who did this. Let me rest.

Julie Miller had disappeared a week last Thursday. Twelve days ago.

Phil hadn't dealt with the case directly, an ordinary missing persons not falling under the MIS remit unless foul play was suspected. But he had heard about it.

In her late twenties, regular boyfriend, worked as an occupational therapist at the Colchester General Hospital. Own flat, own car. And then one night she disappeared. The police investigated, found no signs of a struggle, forcible abduction or murder. The distraught boyfriend had been thoroughly questioned and released. Uniforms had checked hours of CCTV footage following Julie to and from work. Nothing. It was as if she had completely vanished.

Julie Miler was young, pretty, white and middle class. The media's favourite profile. They got involved, issuing appeals, showing photos. Julie's parents and boyfriend had given a press conference, made tearful pleas to her to return home. And still no sign of her.

People do that all the time. Disappear. The words no comfort or consolation for Julie's parents but they heard them over and over, a mantra of no explanation. *She'll either come back on her own,* people said, *or she won't.* No one knew what to do next, apart from hope Julie sent a postcard from somewhere hot and far away.

'This our runaway, then?'

Phil turned at the voice. Detective Chief Inspector Ben Fenwick was walking up the gangplank, his blue suit, gloves, boots and hood somehow not obscuring his smugness.

'I think so, sir,' said Phil, knowing that 'sir' gave the pretence of deference Fenwick liked. 'I mean, I hope so.'

Fenwick nodded, his face a mask of professional concern. 'Yes. Right,' he said, standing beside Phil and looking down at the body, wincing. 'Wouldn't want there to be another one, would we?'

Phil had voiced the same sentiment out of concern for the victim. Fenwick, he knew from experience, had expressed concern at keeping his stats down.

There was no love lost between the pair of them. But they had called a temporary truce in order to get their jobs done. Since Phil was hardworking, inspired and always got results, Fenwick, as his superior, endured him as a necessary evil. Phil, for his part, thought Fenwick was a phoney; trotting out whatever the latest politically correct management-speak jargon happened to be, paying lip service to ideas of progressiveness and equality in the police force, but underneath his tailored suit and expensive haircut he was as reactionary and scheming as any old department dinosaur.

Phil noticed Fenwick had brought with him a similarly blue-suited sidekick who stopped walking when he did. Fenwick turned to the newcomer.

'This is Detective Sergeant Martin. Rose. She was in charge of the original missing person's case.' Fenwick smiled. 'She's here to give her expert opinion.'

DS Rose Martin stepped forward, shared a small smile with Phil and Mickey, looked down at the body. She flinched, looked away. Phil feared her response was going to be the same as Mickey's but she composed herself, looked again, bending down getting in closer. Phil admired her for that. Mickey, Phil noticed, seemed slightly put out at her reaction.

'What d'you think?' asked Phil. 'You've got a better idea than us. Is it her?'

Rose Martin straightened up. Keeping her eyes on the body she nodded. 'I think so. Yes, I think this is Julie Miller.'

Phil nodded. Looked at the body again.

Definitely no time for personal stuff now.

3

Phil looked at the other three, all of them sweating inside their blue paper suits. He was aware what they must look like standing there, hoods up, feet and hands covered. A twenty-first century gathering of druids at a contemporary sacrificial altar.

'Clearly not natural causes, then,' said Fenwick, trying for a feeble joke.

No one laughed.

'Her heart stopped,' said Mickey Philips, wiping his mouth with the back of his hand, 'how natural d'you want?'

Phil turned to his new DS, the comment leading him to believe the man had regained his cocky composure after the vomiting incident. But the look in his eyes said something different. His words had been a genuine response to Fenwick's weak joke. There was nothing funny or flippant about them. Phil began to warm to him a little.

'Phil,' said Fenwick, making a stab at some kind of authority, 'I'd like you heading up the team for this case.'

Phil nodded.

'And I think it would be a good idea if Rose, DS Martin,

14

that is, joined your team. She's had nearly a week working on this already. Knows the lay of the land.'

The lay of the land, thought Phil. King Cliché rides again.

'OK.' Normally Phil liked to choose his own team members, make sure he could trust them, but he could see the sense in Fenwick's words.

'Good. I'll handle the media and leave you to it. You report directly to both me and the Super in Chelmsford as per usual.'

'What about the media? We going public with this?'

Fenwick frowned. 'Let's get a definite confirmation before we release any names. Don't want to jump the gun, do we?'

Jump the gun. 'Of course not.'

'Good. Well, I'll leave you to it.'

Fenwick turned and moved away. As he did so, Phil noticed that his hand lingered on the small of Rose Martin's back for a few seconds longer than it should have done.

'Right,' Phil said and made introductions. 'Looks like you're my team on this one. We may get Anni back but we can't count on that so let's get cracking. Gather.'

Phil always had his team group at the site of an incident, pool thoughts, ideas.

'Before we do anything else, let's see what this scene tells us. What's important here?'

'You mean was she placed here deliberately, that kind of thing?' Rose Martin frowned as she said it.

'That kind of thing, yes,' said Phil. He looked again at the body. 'Her head's facing towards the front end of the boat—'

'Bow,' said Mickey Philips. Phil looked at him. The DS blushed. 'Front end. Bow. My old man. Used to take me sailing.'

Phil surprised himself and smiled. 'Really?'

Mickey shrugged. 'Yeah. Hated it. Always threw up.' He gave a self-deprecating smile. 'No change there.'

'Concentrate,' said Phil. They did so. 'So her head is at the bow, her body in a straight line towards the cabin and the light tower. Her legs are apart.' He looked at the other two. 'Is that deliberate? Did whoever did this want us to find her like that? Or is it just accidental, the way it turned out?'

'Looks deliberate to me,' said Rose. 'I mean, the body could just have been dumped and left. He took the time to arrange her, place her like that.'

Mickey pointed to the wooden deck. 'There's the scuff marks. Could they be from who ever left her here?'

'Could be,' said Phil. 'Might have taken a while to get her the way he wanted her. There's blood on the floor too, smudged where he's moved her.'

'Just one bloke, boss? Or d'you think there was more than one?'

Phil shrugged. 'Hard to say. She doesn't look that big. One guy would have struggled, two could have handled her easily.'

'Killers working in tandem?' said Rose. 'Rapist-killers?'

'We don't know she's been raped yet, Rose.'

'It's a fair assumption,' said Mickey, pointing at her mutilated vagina, swallowing hard.

'Sexually motivated, you think?' said Phil.

Rose looked around the boat. 'Legs apart with a huge tower of light between them? That's Freud for Beginners, isn't it?'

'It looks that way but let's not jump to conclusions. Wait till Nick Lines has his say. What we do know is she wasn't killed here. Not enough blood. But she was left here for a reason.'

'Her flat,' said Rose.

Phil looked at her, waited.

She pointed over the river to the apartment blocks. 'She lived there. In one of those flats. In fact, I think you can see this ship from her window.'

Phil felt a familiar tingle inside him. Information was coalescing, forming patterns. He didn't know what it meant but he was sure it was significant. He nodded. 'Deliberate, then.'

'And I think it's safe to say he hates women,' said Rose, trying not to look at the carving on the body's forehead.

'I'd say that was a given.' Phil looked at his watch. 'CSI on the way?' Phil hated saying that. But since the TV franchise had conquered the world the department insisted.

Rose nodded. 'Ben called them on the way here.'

Ben, thought Phil.

'Probably stopped for an ice cream,' said Mickey Philips, wiping sweat off his forehead with the back of his gloved hand.

Phil ignored him.

'No one touch anything,' Phil said then looked pointedly at his DS. 'No sweat and certainly no more vomit. Let's get this crime scene sealed off.'

The three of them left the boat as the uniforms stepped in and did their job. The roads were cordoned off, blue and white tape stretched across all access routes, traffic stopped down the road and turned back. The CSIs would assume the largest possible area for a crime scene then circle inwards, blue-suited birds of prey, narrowing their scope of reference down to just the body. Then, using their painstaking, occult sciences, hopefully recreate the path it took to reach there. And, more importantly, tell Phil and his team who put it there. And maybe even how to catch them.

There was a man sitting on a wood and concrete bench in front of an urban regeneration mural. Middle-aged and balding, in a blue polo shirt with an exercise-free stomach spilling over the complaining waistband of work trousers. He looked visibly shaken. A uniformed officer who had been sitting with him stood up, crossed towards Phil.

'That the guy who phoned it in?' said Phil.

She nodded.

'Made a statement?'

She nodded. 'Came to open the garage as usual. Saw some seagulls – an unusual amount, he said – congregating on the deck of the boat. Crossed over to shoo them away, saw the body.'

'He see anything else? Hear anything? Vans? People acting suspiciously?'

She looked down the length of the quay. 'You know what some of these firms are like down here, boss. If it wasn't for suspicious characters they'd have gone out of business long ago.'

Phil sighed. 'Point taken. But take him through it again. You never know, something might trigger a memory. Thanks.'

The officer nodded, turned her attention back to the seated man. Phil turned back to the boat. He couldn't see the body for the lip of the boat's side but he knew it was there.

Mickey Philips came and stood alongside him, his eyes as focused as Phil's, his hood pulled down. The departure of Phil's previous DS had been traumatic, murdered in the course of work, an act which had devastated the whole team. He knew Mickey Philips was aware of that, knew his attempts at humour, however misplaced, his strained bonhomie, were just his way of trying to fit in.

Phil gave him a quick glance. The DS was unzipping his blue suit, pulling his shirt away from his chest to allow air to circulate. Mickey Philips was a burly, rugby-playing type. Stocky and muscled, like a shaved and domesticated bull. He was dressed like every policeman was supposed to be. Well-cut – but not flashy – suit. Polished shoes. Short, spiky haircut. Cufflinks, even. Under his paper suit, Phil looked the opposite. And deliberately so. Jeans. Superdry trainers. An untucked, flowered shirt with a suit jacket over the top. Hair spiked and quiffed. When he had graduated from uniform and joined the Major Incident Squad he had been adamant he wouldn't be swapping one uniform for another. And he had stuck to his word. In fact, he was well dressed by his usual standards.

DS Rose Martin came over to join them, her paper suit dispensed with altogether. Phil got his first real look at her. Tall and big-boned yet fit and lean, her straight black hair was cut into a long bob with a fringe resting below her eyebrows. And with her jeans, T-shirt, boots and designer-looking, collarless leather bike jacket, she looked like she fitted Phil's work ethos better than Mickey Philips. But appearances, he knew, were deceptive.

Phil hoped there wouldn't be tension between these two. He already had trouble with another of his DCs, Anni Hepburn. She had put herself in for promotion when the DS position needed filling, been unsuccessful and was consequently harbouring resentment about it. He had tried to call her, get her to join him this morning, but she had already been called out on another matter. He wondered whether she had arranged that deliberately.

He just hoped his team could put aside whatever differences they had and work together. They had to. It was his job to ensure that.

'Right,' said Phil, 'before we start, any questions?'

'Boss . . .' said Mickey.

'Yes, Mickey?'

'Well . . .' He glanced round at the boat, back to Phil. 'I'm just wondering. I know I'm new here, coming from the drugs squad an' that, but this looks pretty serious. Less like a one-off and more like a serial in the making, you know what I mean?'

'What are you getting at?'

'Well, shouldn't we think about getting a profiler in?'

'It's a possibility,' said Phil.

'D'you know any good ones?' said Rose.

'One or two,' said Phil. 'One in particular.'

'Worth a call?' said Mickey.

Phil became thoughtful. Marina Esposito was the best profiler he had ever worked with. She was also his partner. His soulmate. The mother of his child. And the cause of his problems he had tried not to bring to work with him that morning. Right now she was distant. Hard to read, to talk to. Secretive, even. About where she went, what she did. Something wasn't right. He would have to sort it out, talk to her. Work it out between them. It had taken so much to get them together, he wasn't going to let anything pull them apart.

'Not at the moment,' said Phil. 'She's . . . busy. Anything else?'

They both shook their heads.

'Good. Oh, and one more thing.'

They looked at him expectantly.

'Welcome to MIS,' Phil said.

4

'**H**i.'
Marina Esposito sat down in the chair provided, looked at the man opposite her. He was still, his face, his posture serene, in an attitude of listening. She gave him a small, tentative smile.

'Traffic was awful,' she said. 'Murder coming up past the station. Everything rerouted, for some reason.' She sighed. It covered up the awkwardness she was feeling. 'But I made it. Wouldn't want to miss our session.'

She was dressed in a long, black linen skirt, white linen top, jewellery. Large-lensed sunglasses pushed up on the top of her thick, dark, curly hair. It felt good to be out of the house. To get dressed up for something. For anything. Even to come here.

Marina pulled the chair round, positioned it the way she wanted. The windows were open, the late spring/early summer air and morning sunshine giving the institution-alised room a warmth and life it didn't often have.

'Right then . . .' She sighed again. Then found things that

needed doing before she could next speak. Physical actions that helped to compose her mind. She switched her phone to silent, rearranged the contents of her bag prior to placing it on the floor. Marvelled at some of the things she found there. Pushed her hair behind her ears, arranged her neckline. Pulled her top away from her chest, allowed air to travel down there, stop it sticking. Eventually, with nothing more to occupy them, her hands came to rest in her lap like grounded birds. The signal that she was finally ready to talk.

'So . . .' She glanced at him. His face was immobile. Waiting. 'I'll start. It's been . . . OK. Yeah,' she said, as if convincing herself, 'OK. Josephina's doing well. I've left her with her . . . with Eileen and Don. They love her. So that's . . . that's where she is this morning.'

Marina sighed. Words were tumbling through her brain. She grasped for them, clutching them, hoped she settled on the right ones. 'I'm . . . things are going all right. Since we last . . . since our . . . since the last time I came to see you. All right.' She nodded. 'Yeah.'

She sighed again and a cloud covered the sun. The summer brightness was leached from the walls as they became grey and bleak and the room became what it was – an institutionalised, dying room.

'No,' she said, as if the change in the light had also stripped away her false brightness, leaving just a grim honesty. 'Things are not all right. I mean, Phil and I are good. You know, good. We've got the new baby who's just gorgeous, and the new house. So that's all positive. That's good. But there's . . . you know. The other stuff.'

She waited for the sunlight to return. It didn't. She went on.

'The fear. That's what they never tell you about. The fear. You've got this tiny little infant, this . . . human life . . .' She clasped her hands, looked down at them as if they held her invisible daughter. 'And you've got to, you've got to look after her. You're responsible for her. You've given her life, now you have to help her to live.'

She unclasped her hands. Looked up. Back at him.

'Sorry. You don't need to hear that. I'm sure.' Another sigh. 'Because there's all the other stuff too. All of . . . this.' The words were starting to tumble out now. This was what she had wanted to say. Came here to say. 'I can't . . . can't . . . enjoy it. Any of it. There's this shadow. This . . . spectre at the feast, elephant in the room. Call it what you like, you know what I mean. And sometimes I forget, and I'm happy for a moment. Just a moment. And I can relax. And laugh. And then I remember. And it starts again. And I just . . .' Her hands were out in front of her, fingers twisted, as if grasping in the air for an invisible, intangible solution. Her voice dropped. 'Sometimes I don't think it'll ever change. I think that this is it. This is the way it'll always be.'

She looked round. The sunlight had returned and with it warmth, but Marina didn't notice. To her, it seemed suddenly cold. Not light, but dark.

'And . . . I can't live with that.'

She stopped talking. She waited for a reply. None came. Took his silence as listening, as encouragement to keep talking.

'It's my fault. I know that. Mine. And . . .' Her hands started grasping once more, fingers wriggling as if to be free. 'I don't know. I don't know, I don't know what to do . . .'

She paused, looked down at her hands once more.

'I just feel so . . . guilty . . . And I am. It's my fault. Everything that happened, everything that went wrong. My fault. But I don't know what to do for the best. I need . . . I want this hurt to stop. I need to know what to do for the best . . .'

The tears came, as they always did at this time. She bent her head forward, reached out. Took his hand. He let her. She sat like that until it was time for her to leave.

She wiped her cheeks, took a tissue from her bag, dabbed her eyes, blew her nose. 'I'll be . . . I'll be back soon. Thanks. For listening.'

She opened her mouth as if to speak once more, closed it again, her thoughts unvoiced, her words unspoken. She shook her head, placed the sunglasses over her eyes, turned, left the room.

'Ms Esposito . . .' A voice down the corridor. Footsteps accompanying it.

Marina stopped, turned. A nursing official was making her way towards her. She knew the woman, didn't have anything against her, but still felt an irrational irritation bordering on anger at the sight of her. Marina waited until she was level. She looked at her. Made no attempt to remove her sunglasses.

The nursing official looked at the door Marina had just come out of. 'How was . . .'

Marina took a deep breath, expelled it. Said nothing. She was glad the nurse couldn't see her eyes.

The woman's voice dropped. 'I don't mean to . . . you've been coming here for quite some time now. Longer than we would normally allow.'

'I know.' Marina's voice was like old, rusted gears.

'You have to . . . I'll be blunt. This situation can't continue. You must reach a decision. Very soon.'

Marina nodded, not trusting her voice this time.

'If you'd like to, we can talk—'

'No. No. I'll . . . I'll do it.'

The nurse looked relieved. 'If you're sure. But we'll—'

Marina turned away. 'I know. I have to go. I have to pick up my daughter.' Her voice caught on the words.

She hurried down the corridor and out of the building.

The sunlight hit her but didn't reach her. Without looking back, she hurried away.

To pick up Josephina.

To make her decision.

To try and get on with her life.

5

'So . . . is that it, then?'

'Nearly.' DC Anni Hepburn glanced down at her notes. 'Just a couple of things. Can you just take me through it again from waking up, check there's nothing I've missed . . .'

Suzanne Perry sat opposite her on the sofa in the living room of her apartment. She was still dressed in the T-shirt she had slept in, a dressing gown over it, pulled tight round her body. The mug of coffee she was holding was down to cold dregs. She swirled the gritty liquid around, her eyes following its progress, clamped to the mug as if scared to look anywhere else. She sighed.

'But I've already . . .'

'Please. Just once more.' Anni's voice sounded compassionate, tender yet laced with steel, showing she was used to having her requests carried out. It wasn't something she had consciously worked on, just a skill that had naturally evolved with the job until it was an everyday part of her working identity.

Suzanne's eyes slowly closed, her head lolling forward.

Then she gave a start, her eyes wide and staring, darting round the room as if searching for anything – or anyone – hidden in the shadows. Anni caught the look, tried to reassure her.

'It's OK. Just me here.'

A two-person CSI team had painstakingly examined Suzanne's bedroom, hallway and any potential entrances and exits for possible clues to the identity of her supposed intruder. From the tone of their voices and the expressions on their faces, they didn't seem to regard those chances as high.

Anni checked her notes. Looked at the woman before her. Suzanne Perry was a speech therapist, working at the General Hospital, first job after graduating from Essex University. She was tall to medium height, with a good figure, dark hair and a slight Mediterranean cast to her skin. But it was her eyes that you noticed first, Anni thought. Beautiful, clear brown eyes. Even through all the tears and redness, the beauty of those eyes came through.

The flat was on the top floor of an old Edwardian house that had been divided up, on Maldon Road. Quite spacious with good period fittings, but with its primary coloured bookshelves, beanbags, throws and sub-Bridget Riley prints on the walls, it had been furnished predominantly in a kind of Ikea version of sixties pop art. But already there were other touches creeping in that suggested the garishness would soon go, to be replaced by a more mature style. Anni had seen this kind of thing before. The first tentative steps taken between student and wage earner. It felt like that had been her, not so long ago.

This case was a natural fit for Anni. A reactive DC working with the Major Incident Squad, she specialised in rape cases, abused children, had been trained for any situation where a male presence might be a barrier to uncovering the truth. This case was clearly one for her. Plus, it would keep her away from Phil, which, given the way things had been between them lately, wasn't a bad thing.

'So,' Anni said, concentrating once more, 'you woke up . . .'

'No, before that.' Suzanne Perry placed her coffee mug down on a nearby shelf but still kept her eyes on it as if it was a talisman giving out a protective aura. 'While I was asleep . . . I thought, I felt . . . someone in the room with me.'

'When you were asleep.'

'I don't know . . . I think I was asleep. But then . . . then . . . I felt it . . .'

'It?'

'Him. I felt him. His hands on me, his . . .' She shuddered.

Anni waited.

'And I couldn't . . . I couldn't move . . .'

Another shudder. Anni feared she might cry again. It had happened twice already. She pressed on.

'You felt his hands on you.'

Suzanne nodded.

'Do you remember whereabouts on your body?'

Suzanne looked to the floor, her cheeks red.

Anni had to be careful what she said. Traumatic experiences often left a victim open to suggestion. She didn't want to say anything that could later, in court, be seen as leading Suzanne on. 'Where did he touch you, Suzanne?'

Suzanne turned her face even further away, closed her eyes like she was anticipating a punch.

'Suzanne.' Steel in Anni's voice once more. Suzanne's head snapped back round. Now she had her attention again she allowed her voice to drop once more. 'Suzanne . . . where did he touch you?'

Suzanne's eyes closed once more, her lower lip began to tremble. 'He . . . he moved my T-shirt up . . . I couldn't stop him, I . . .' The tears started again. 'And . . . and he . . .'

Anni sat back. 'OK. OK . . .' Her voice was soothing once

28

more. 'Take a moment.' Anni waited until Suzanne had composed herself. 'You said he spoke to you. Can you remember any of the words he said?'

Suzanne shook her head.

'What did he look like? Can you describe him?'

Another shake of her head. 'Just . . . a shape. And those eyes, shining, staring . . . like, like devils' eyes . . . And his hands, touching me. And I, I couldn't move . . .'

Anni didn't press her any more. She decided to move on. 'And then you, what? Slept?'

Suzanne shrugged. 'Must have done.'

'Then got up, opened the curtains . . .'

Suzanne nodded. 'Yes. And then . . .' Her head dropped once more.

Anni kept looking at her. Scrutinising her. Something was gnawing at her. 'Were the blinds closed or open?'

'Open. That's how I saw the photo.'

'You said earlier you like your bedroom dark. Is it possible you could have left them open?'

Suzanne shook her head. 'I'm a light sleeper. I need the room dark as possible. Specially in the summer . . .' Her voice trailed off.

'So you couldn't have opened the blinds yourself?'

'No. I never open them.' Her voice emphatic.

'Do you open the window to sleep? When it's warm?'

'No.' But her voice wasn't so emphatic this time.

Anni saw the opening, jumped in. 'Could you have left the window open and someone got in? Is it possible?'

Suzanne looked up at her, those brown eyes looking suddenly lost. 'I . . . I . . . does it matter?'

Anni shrugged. 'I don't know, Suzanne. When something like this happens, we think everything matters.'

She sighed. 'I don't know . . . I didn't . . . I can't . . . I don't know . . .' She looked once more at the coffee mug.

'What about the people downstairs?' Anni had spoken to

29

her neighbours, got nothing from them, ruled them out. But she had to ask. 'Could they have access?'

'I don't see how . . .'

'Can you remember going to bed last night?'

'I . . .' Suzanne seemed about to answer in the affirmative but stopped herself. 'No. I . . . I woke up this morning feeling really bad, shaky, like I was hungover or something.' She screwed her face up, thinking back. 'I can't . . . I can't remember going to bed . . .'

'Had you been drinking? Were you hungover?'

She shook her head. 'No. I just had a bath. Then some chocolate. A glass of wine. Red. Just one. With the chocolate. While I sat on the sofa. Red.'

'Small glass?'

Suzanne nodded. 'It's . . . on the draining board. The wine bottle is there, too. With the, the cork in it. And then this morning I felt terrible.'

'Maybe you're coming down with something.'

'Maybe. Swine flu. Great. Just what I need.'

'So, the blind. If you can't remember going to bed, you might have left it up by mistake. The window open.'

Suzanne frowned. 'Up? No. The blind's never up. It might have been open, but it's never up . . . and the window . . . no. No . . . I didn't, no . . .'

Anni looked at her face, checking for truth.

'Never,' she said. 'Never . . .'

The fear was back in Suzanne's eyes.

30

6

The Creeper loved being close.

It was what thrilled him.

Not that he didn't enjoy the planning – he did. All the following, the strategising. The courtship. The anticipation. It was all good, but it was all for an end result. Being close.

That was what really did it for him. Being in a relationship. Half of a couple. In someone else's life. That was the part he loved most. It topped the lot, made everything else worthwhile.

And now he had found her. The one.

He smiled to himself.

He had been searching for her for so long. Everywhere. The town, the countryside. Here and . . . and there. Waiting to hear her voice, a sign, any of the things that would let him know that she was the one.

His star-crossed lover.

His Rani.

And he had her.

And that made him happy.

There had been false starts. Times when he thought he

had her, was sure he had her, only for her to disappear once more, leaving only a husk behind. A husk to be disposed of.

And he had been stupid, been a fool for love. But this one was real. He knew it. Could feel it.

And there she was now, so close to him, a few metres away. He could even reach out, touch her . . . like he had last night.

But he wouldn't. Not while that policewoman was there. He would just wait, be patient.

He lay back, stretched out. Listened to the sound of Rani's voice coming through the boards.

Waiting for another chance to be alone with his lover.

7

Phil looked along the quay, checked to see how well his instructions had been implemented.

The road was completely sealed off from the roundabout. Nothing and no one could get in or out. Workers in businesses along the quay had been given a few hours of enforced leisure and gawping. Phil didn't think they'd mind.

Over the other side of the river and on the bridge, gawkers were gathering. Phil had ordered the erection of a white tent over the body, both to preserve the crime scene and to deter onlookers. As always, he wasn't sure if doing that didn't just make them even more curious.

A full team of CSIs was scrutinising the deck of the boat and working their way out to the quay and the road. Taking impressions left on the ground, scraping surfaces, bagging and cataloguing anything that struck them as potentially interesting. Not for the first time, and definitely not for the last, the blue-suited, booted, masked and gloved figures reminded Phil of a haz-mat team stopping the spread of a lethal virus. Which in a sense, he supposed, was what they were.

As Phil watched, his hand instinctively went to his ribs. Nothing. No pain. It had been absent for months but it still surprised him.

He had been victim of panic attacks since he was a boy. He knew what had caused them originally – the children's homes he had grown up in weren't known for their nurturing atmosphere. In fact, they were at the cutting edge of Darwinism. They were bound to leave some scars, whether physical, mental, emotional or all three. When he had finally settled down with Don and Eileen Brennan, his foster-parents, later his adoptive ones and, ultimately, the only people he dared call Mum and Dad, the panic attacks had ceased. But during his police career they had made return visits. Usually mild, but sometimes crippling. Always at moments of great stress. Like a huge iron fist was wrapping itself round his ribs and squeezing as hard as it could. Squeezing the life out of him.

He knew some officers who would have milked the situation, seen a doctor, taken paid sick leave with union backing. But Phil wasn't like that. He had told no one, preferring to cope himself.

But he hadn't had one in months. Not since . . .

Not since he and Marina had set up home together. Not since he'd became a father.

But he still felt his body for the attacks. Braced himself for their return. Because it was only a matter of time until something happened, some dark trigger tripped and that iron fist would have him in its grip once more. Only a matter of time.

But not today. And not now. Or at least not yet.

Nick Lines, the pathologist, was examining the body in place. He called to Phil.

'I'm about to turn her. Want to see?'

Phil hurried back up the gangplank, on to the boat.

Nick Lines was only slightly more animated and lifelike than the corpses he worked with. Stripped of his paper suit, and despite the warmth, he stood dressed in a three-piece suit, pointed shoes, his tie loosened at the neck. He was tall, thin and bald; his glasses, perched on the end of his nose, might have looked fashionable on someone else. He wore the kind of expression that might have got him a part-time job either as a professional mourner or the kind of character actor in horror films who warned teenagers not to stray off the path into the woods. This expression, Phil knew from years of experience, hid a razor-sharp intellect and an even sharper – and dryer – wit.

Nick, together with a CSI, turned the body over.

'Oh God . . .'

'Hmm . . .' Nick was masking any revulsion he may have felt by appearing to be professionally interested. For all Phil knew, he might have been.

Phil pointed. 'Are those . . . hook marks?'

Nick peered at the back of the woman's body. There were two huge wounds underneath her shoulder blades where something large and sharp had been gouged into her flesh.

'Looks that way. By the way the flesh has torn, she must have been hung up to be tortured.'

'Great.' Phil felt his own stomach pitch. Emotions hurled themselves around inside him. Anger at what had been done. Revulsion. Sorrow. And a hard, burning flame in the pit of his stomach that made him want to catch the person who had done this. He stood up, turned away from the body. 'So what have we got to go on, Nick?'

Nick stood also. 'Not a lot. Female, mid-twenties. Tortured, sexually mutilated, murdered.'

'In that order?'

Nick glanced at the body. 'Your guess is as good as mine at the moment. But if I had to stick my neck out I'd say, judging by blood pooling and lividity, the sexual mutilation was carried out after the killing.'

Mickey Philips and Rose Martin came onboard. Rose had her notebook in hand, open.

'You'd better stand near the side, Mickey,' said Phil. 'In case you go again.'

Mickey Philips was about to argue then got a look at the body. He moved over to the side.

'Cause of death?' asked Rose, her face rigidly composed.

Nick shrugged. 'Take your pick. Knife wounds, chain wounds . . . she was comprehensively worked over.' He sighed and, for the first time that day, Phil saw genuine concern break through the man's brittle mask. 'And from the looks of it, whatever the weapons were, they'd been . . . augmented.'

Phil fell silent, contemplative. He knew what that meant. Hammers. Nails. Razors. Blades. Julie Miller, if it was her, hadn't died easily.

Phil swallowed. 'Time of death?'

Nick looked round at the sky, back to Phil, a gesture that made him look like he was thinking but was more about regaining his composure. 'It's a hot day, Phil. Clearly, she was killed elsewhere and brought here. From what I can make out of the internal blood pooling and lividity in her body she was lying on her back for some time. Best I can do at the moment.'

Phil turned away, walked down the gangplank. The image of the dead woman seared on his retinas. The hatred someone must have felt to do that . . .

Nick called out to him. 'I'll let you know when I've got anything.'

'Thanks, Nick.'

Phil called Mickey and Rose to him. Looked at the pair of them. His new team. He hoped they were as good as . . . Just hoped they were good. 'Right,' he said, 'this is it. I should imagine this case is going to be high priority so I need you to be on top of your game here. Pool information. Support each other. No mavericking, right?'

They both nodded.

'Right,' said Phil. 'Here's what needs to happen. The Birdies should be here soon. They can—'

Mickey Philips laughed. 'The what?'

'Birdies,' said Phil, impatient at the interruption. 'DC Adrian Wren and DS Jane Gosling. Hence, the Birdies. Adrian can follow Nick to the mortuary, do chain of evidence. Jane can get started with you, Mickey, on the door-to-door.'

Mickey Philips looked around. 'Over there?'

'Start with the businesses here. Someone might have been in early, seen something. Then after that . . .' He looked across the river. 'The flats over there. Coordinate with uniforms. Rose, you handle that. You've done it before, see what Julie Miller's neighbours have to say.'

Rose nodded. Phil looked saw the eagerness in her eyes. Ready, burning to go. He hoped that energy wasn't misplaced. He didn't want her making mistakes. Either of them, for that matter.

'I'll get Milhouse to set up the incident room back at Southway, get a mobile one put here, couple of uniforms manning it. Bit of presence, you never know.' He looked between the two of them.

'What about where she was killed, boss?' said Mickey. 'Should we be looking for that?'

'Initiative is good,' said Phil, 'and I approve, but, as our esteemed leader DCI Fenwick would say, that would be creating a needle/haystack interface.'

Mickey, surprised at Phil criticising his superior, smiled. Phil also noticed that Rose's attention sharpened at the mention of Fenwick's name. He caught the look, filed it away with the other stuff.

Phil continued. 'We think we know who she is. Once that's confirmed, hopefully the where and the why will follow.' He looked at his watch. 'Anni should be joining us soon, so that's one more body.' He looked between the pair of them. 'Any questions?'

If they had, they were keeping them to themselves.

Phil breathed in, out. No pain. His ribs felt fine.

'Good. Right. Let's—'

'What the hell's going on with my boat?'

The three of them turned. A middle-aged man, red-faced and sweating, was running towards them, a uniform in pursuit.

'Ah,' said Phil, smiling. 'I think this may be the boat's owner.' He turned to the other two. 'I'll deal with him. You go catch a killer.'

8

Anni's questions had kept Suzanne's tears at bay. She pressed on.

'Suzanne, your flat. The CSIs are checking everything now. They say the lock on the door hasn't been forced. Same with the window. Is there any other way someone could have got in?'

She shook her head.

'Anyone else have a key?'

Something flitted across her face. Dark and swift, an evil fairy-tale sprite. 'No.'

Anni leaned forward, surprised by the response. 'You sure about that?'

'Just . . .' Suzanne kept her eyes averted from Anni. 'Zoe. My friend Zoe.'

The look hadn't been for her friend Zoe. 'No one else?'

Suzanne looked away, shook her head.

'Suzanne, I'm trying to help you here. If there's someone who could have had a key then please tell me. It could be important.'

Another sigh from Suzanne. 'I think Mark might still have one.'

'Who's Mark?'

'Mark Turner. My old boyfriend. But he's . . . It's not important. We're not seeing each other any more.'

'Could he have done this?'

'I doubt it.'

'Why?'

'Because . . . because we're not . . . he's just not that into me any more.' The American accent was an attempted joke but the bitterness of the words cancelled it out.

'Oh,' said Anni. 'Right.'

Suzanne looked at her once more. 'These things happen.' Her voice reedy, unconvincing.

'But he still has a key.'

'Yeah.' Suzanne frowned, as if the thought had just entered her head. 'Not because he still wanted to see me. Just . . .' She shrugged. '. . . because . . .'

'Never gave it back.' Anni took his details. 'So you got a new boyfriend?'

Suzanne shook her head. Picked up the mug once more, toying with it, swirling the dregs round and round, staring.

Anni sensed there was something more. 'Have you had trouble like this before, Suzanne? With men?'

She answered without taking her eyes off the mug. 'I . . . no. Never. Nothing like this.'

'Nothing at all? No intruders? Stalkers?'

The last word hit a nerve. Suzanne said nothing.

'Suzanne?'

'No.' She shook her head with a finality that told Anni she wouldn't be getting anything further from that line of questioning.

'This photo . . .' Anni gestured to it, sitting alongside her in a clear plastic evidence bag.

Suzanne braced herself once more, as if she was expecting a physical assault.

'Are you sure it was taken last night?'

She nodded. 'Yes.'

'There's no chance it might have been older?'

She shook her head.

'You sure?'

'I'm sure.'

'Why?'

'Because . . .' Suzanne began turning the coffee mug once more. Cold, brown liquid spilled over the sides, splashed out on to the floor. She didn't notice.

'Suzanne?' Anni reached out a hand. She placed it over Suzanne's, stopping her agitated movements. Suzanne looked up at her. Anni held the eye contact. 'Why are you so sure it was taken last night?'

'I . . . it was. I had . . . in the bathroom last night, I . . . did my . . . my bikini line.' She swallowed the words in embarrassment. 'With a razor. I . . . cut myself. It's . . . on the photo. You can, you can see the, the cut . . .'

Anni looked at the photo. It clearly showed Suzanne asleep with her T-shirt pulled up to her breasts, exposing her body. Her legs were open. She leaned in closer, squinting. The cut was clearly visible.

She looked back to Suzanne. The mug fell to the floor, the remaining liquid spilling out. Suzanne looked at it as if not understanding what it was. Then her head dropped, her shoulders moved rhythmically back and forwards.

Anni had no option but to let her cry.

Eventually, Suzanne found her voice. 'I'm not – not lying . . .'

'I didn't –'

'I'm not making it up.'

'I didn't say you were.'

Suzanne looked up, an angry fire fighting through the tears. 'I wasn't then and I'm not now. Right?'

'You weren't doing what then?'

Suzanne looked away, regained composure. 'Nothing.'

'What did you mean, Suzanne? Was it something to do with your ex-boyfriend Mark?'

She wiped her face with the sleeve of her dressing gown. Sat back, exhausted. 'I can't talk any more . . .'

Anni knew that was all she would be getting. For now. She leaned forward once more. 'Suzanne, I'd like you to come with me.'

Suzanne sat back, fear and distrust on her face. 'Where? Why?'

'To the station.' Anni's voice was all calmness and reason once more. 'I'd like you to be seen by a doctor.'

Anni nodded. 'It'll be sensitively handled. It won't hurt. And I'd also like your consent to a blood test on top of that.'

'Why?'

'To see if you've got anything in your system that could have made you feel bad this morning. Other than a glass of red wine and chocolate, of course.' She smiled. Suzanne didn't return it.

'OK?'

Suzanne nodded, her face slack, empty, like she was still in a dream. She stood up, her body moving like a somnambulist's.

Anni told her to come as she was and bring a change of clothing to go home in. Suzanne numbly walked to the bedroom to do so. Anni watched her go. As Suzanne reached the doorway, she turned.

'Do you . . . The door, I'll, I'll . . . keep it open.'

'I'll be here.'

Suzanne took a bag from the wardrobe, began to throw clothes into it. She was clearly traumatised, thought Anni, but something was off. Suzanne Perry was holding something back, hiding something. Never mind. While Suzanne was in the rape suite Anni would be at her computer running background checks.

Whatever it was, it wouldn't stay hidden for long.

42

9

The Creeper was missing Rani.

She had gone out. Left the flat with that black girl, the police officer. Left him alone. He didn't mind. As long as she wasn't too long. He would get lonely if she was away too long. Miss her. That wouldn't do. And if she was away too long he would be angry with her.

And she really didn't want that.

But he knew what to do. How to fill in the time until she returned, make it feel as if she was there with him.

The door clicked shut. He waited, counted to a thousand, then came out. Looked round. Felt anger rise within him. The police had left the place in a real mess. That wasn't fair. Wasn't fair at all. Maybe he should tidy up. A treat for Rani coming home. Or maybe not. Might make her cry again.

He smiled. He liked it when she cried. Made him feel like his love was working, like she wanted him.

He went into the kitchen. Thought about making himself a cup of tea. Decided not to. He wasn't in the mood. He looked across the hall to the bedroom. Smiled.

He knew what he was in the mood for.

He went into the bedroom. It was only a few hours since he had been in here with her, his beautiful Rani, but it felt longer. So much longer. He closed his eyes, took a deep breath. Held it as long as he could. Let it go. Smiled. He could smell her. Her perfume, her skin, her clothes ... everything. He opened the wardrobe door, looked at her clothes hanging there. Traced his fingers along, felt the fabric of her skirts, her jeans, her dresses. Slowly caressing, imagining being next to her skin ...

Then away from the wardrobe. He knew what was coming next. Could feel it. He went to the sideboard, opened the second drawer down on the right. Rani's underwear drawer. He smiled. Put his hands in.

He ignored the everyday stuff. The boring cotton drip catchers. Went straight for the flimsy, filmy gossamers. Rubbed the sheer fabric between his fingers. Imagined her in them ...

The Creeper was getting hard. He knew what was coming next.

He chose the pair of knickers he wanted. Black and dirty-pink, all sheer and see-through, lace and bows. Then lay down on the bed, undid his flies. Got comfortable, in the right position. And with her knickers in his hand, he closed his eyes, summoned her.

And there she was before him. Vividly alive, realer than real, better than life. His fingers moved slowly. He felt the fabric against his skin, whispered her name.

'Rani . . .' Sighed again. Smiled again. His heart pumping, butterflies fluttering in his stomach from just hearing it said aloud. 'Rani . . .'

And she answered him. As she always did. *I'm here . . . for you . . .*

Rani was her real name. Her secret name. He didn't care what name she went by, what she called herself day to day. Because he knew what she really looked like, who she really was. She had told him. Revealed herself to him.

He sighed. His fingers moved faster, heart picking up speed.

'Rani . . .'

Yes, my love?

'I've been with you all day . . . did you see me?'

I did . . .

'I was with you this morning, there when you opened your eyes.' He paused, gave a small laugh. 'You looked funny. When you got up you could hardly walk.'

She laughed also. *I'm glad I make you laugh.*

He felt a thrill course through him at her words. Quickened his pace. 'Last night . . . I felt so close to you . . .'

And I you . . .

'Did you like my present?'

Loved it . . .

His little valentine. His declaration of love and intent.

I'M WATCHING OVER YOU

He'd spent a long time working on that sentence, trying to find words that expressed not only his love for her, but also his devotion. Her own personal guardian angel. And he thought he had achieved it. Proud of it.

'You cried when you saw it . . .'

I did . . .

His fingers moved faster at the thought, no longer butterflies in his stomach, more like finches trapped in a barn.

But then . . .

That thing caught inside him. That niggle, that thought, working away at him like a worm in an apple . . .

'Oh Rani . . .'

Sadness overwhelmed him. Like he hadn't felt for ages, not since . . . before. He tried not to think of it, let his mind go back there. Concentrate on the present. On Rani. On his love. But it was difficult.

Other memories, other voices, would fill his head and the butterflies, the swallows, would leave his stomach, and something else, something more dangerous, would take their place. A serpent, hard, cold and coiled in the depths of his guts, hissing acid inside him, poisoning him with fear and hate.

And its voice . . . all that anger, that hate . . . *All women are whores . . . every one . . . use them like whores . . . that's all they're good for . . .*

'No . . . no . . .'

Cut them, slice them . . .

It wasn't him. Not now. Not any more. He had to do something, drive the voice out, repeat his mantra, defeat the snake. 'Out of the cleansing fire I was born and he was lost . . .' Keep going . . . 'Out of the cleansing fire her soul was freed when her body was lost . . .' Keep going . . . 'Out of the cleansing fire was born my search and love to be found . . .'

The snake slithered away, back to the darkness. He heard Rani's voice once more.

I'm still here . . .

Joy flooded his heart. He was hard again. His fingers moved faster, a smile spreading across his face.

His fingers increased speed, his breathing became heavier. His love's voice was in his head once more, her face before him.

Then, gasping and whispering her name, it was all over.

'I love you, I love you, I love you . . .' Over and over, gasping and whispering. Sighing and smiling.

'Rani . . . Rani . . .'

And I love you . . . He voice faded as it always did in these moments. But she would be back. He had no doubt.

He opened his eyes. Wiped himself off on her knickers, pocketed them for later. He had an idea what to do with them.

Rani needed another present, another token of his love for her . . .

He looked round the room, getting dreamy. He could lie here all day. But he had things to do. So he got up, left the bedroom.

He stood in the hall, looked up at the hatch to the loft. Time to go back. Assume his position watching over Rani, her own guardian angel. But not just yet.

Down the hall and into the bathroom. Just time for a quick shower.

Then leave his present where she would find it.

The Creeper couldn't wait until Rani came home.

He had such plans for her . . .

10

Mickey Philips flipped his notebook shut, put it in his jacket pocket and crossed the road, walking away from the river.

The businesses along the quay hadn't yielded up anything of value. Mickey hadn't been made welcome. When he approached with the uniforms, orders were shouted in languages other than English and bodies dissolved into shadows. Rags were thrown over number plates in workshops, objects were put hastily into desk drawers or beneath counters. He was met with too-wide smiles and helpless shrugs, and eyes that looked anywhere but at him. Even when he told them it was a murder inquiry and that he didn't care what else they had going on, the smiles dropped but the shrugs continued. No one had seen anything, no one knew anything. He heard it so many times that eventually he thought it might even be the truth. Eventually he left the uniforms to it, instructing them to take extra notice of anyone giving them a particularly hard time, and walked off down the road.

He preferred working alone, in spite of what DI Brennan had said about mavericking. It was when he could drop the persona and be himself, not have to be one of the lads, play the game. Remember he was a university graduate and not just a *Nuts* mag cookie-cutter copper. He'd been there, done that. And seen what it had almost cost him.

The job wasn't for the weak-willed, he knew that when he signed up, but the Drugs Squad was one of the most full-on outfits in the force. He had gone into it looking for glory, for collars, for headlines. Knowing the rewards could be big, ignoring the fact that the failures could be bigger.

As a DC he had thrown himself into the life. One of the gang, never missed a night out whether it was playing pool or poker, off for a curry or out to a strip club. Bonding, he told himself. Helping to make them a team, a unit.

And what a unit they had been. What a force on the street. Cocks of the walk, the Met's finest, like *The Sweeney* reborn, with Danny Dyer playing him in the film version. And with a clean-up rate second to none. And if some of their haul never made it to evidence, so what? Bit of charlie never hurt anyone. Perks of the job. And if one drug dealer was allowed to flourish at the expense of another because he kept the boys supplied with both information and product, how was that wrong? And if they made a little cash looking the other way occasionally, so what? No harm done in the great scheme of things.

Except there was. As his girlfriend pointed out one day when, blood running down his nose and the backs of his eyes feeling like they were pincushions for burning needles, he pulled his fist back and screamed that she didn't have a fucking clue what she was talking about. And not for the first time. She made him see his life ahead of him. The ghost of Christmas yet to come. And it wasn't pretty.

So that was it. Fix-up time. Get straight, ship out.

And he had. Narcotics Anonymous. Alcoholics Anonymous, too, just to be on the safe side. Even thought about church. But not very seriously. Took the sergeant's exam, filled an opening up in Colchester, Essex. Played up the arrests, played down the rest. His girlfriend didn't hang around, though, she'd had enough. But that was OK. He deserved it.

So, Colchester. Clean slate, new start.

He made a mental note not to keep trying too hard with his new squad members and checked his watch. Gone eleven. And he hadn't eaten since God knows when. Well before he'd thrown up. Not even a cup of tea. As if on cue, his stomach rumbled.

He looked ahead. And smiled. A burger van was parked at the side of the road. He quickened his pace.

'Bacon sandwich and cup of tea, please, mate,' he said to the guy behind the counter. He was big, fat and greasy-looking. A bad advert for getting high on your own supply, thought Mickey.

'You with that lot over there?' the bloke said, slapping a couple of rashers of bacon down on the grill, standing back as they started to spit.

'Yeah,' said Mickey, staring at the bacon hungrily.

'Looks pretty bad,' the bloke said.

'It is,' said Mickey. 'Very bad.'

'If you're gonna be here long,' the bloke said, 'send them over here. I'll do discount.'

'Cheers. You not busy, then?'

'Been here since crack of dawn. Same as usual. Those places along the river start early. But the recession . . .' He sniffed. 'Customer's a customer, innit?' The bloke moved the bacon round the griddle, picking up old, black grease but still looking tasty.

'It is,' said Mickey, hoping the bacon wouldn't take long.

'What is it then, murder? Body or somethin'?

Mickey nodded. 'Yeah. Awful.' A thought struck him. 'Hey, you've been here all hours. See any activity on the quay this morning?'

'Like what?'

'Dunno.' He shrugged, tried to keep it light. 'Vans, people coming and going. Maybe quickly, maybe acting like they shouldn't have been there. That kind of thing.'

He stared at the grill, kept the bacon moving. 'Don't know nothin' about that.'

At the bloke's reaction, Mickey felt that thrill. The copper's thrill, the one that meant a breakthrough.

'You did, didn't you?'

The bloke said nothing, just became intensely interested in the grill, willing the bacon to cook quicker, prodding it with his spatula.

'What did you see?'

'I . . . nothin'. Didn't see nothin'. Keep me out o' this.'

'Listen. Someone's been murdered over there. A young woman. It was the worst thing I've ever seen. In my life. Now, if you've seen something, you'd better tell me.'

He took the bacon off the grill, stuck it on a slice of white bread, slapped another one on top of it, put it on the counter. 'On the house.'

Mickey sighed. 'I didn't want to do this, but . . .' He shrugged. 'Like you said, over there is swarming with coppers. Now, I can either direct them across to here when they get a bit hungry and thirsty or I can get this van impounded and off the road.'

The man held his spatula in the air. 'What for?'

'I'll think of something. Health and safety's a godsend for stuff like that.'

'Bastard.'

'Or . . .'

The man looked around the inside of his van like it was his own little kingdom, one he would never see again. He sighed. 'All right, then. I'll tell you.'

He did.

And Mickey got that tingle again, that frisson that said he

51

was on to something. And it felt so damned good. He had forgotten just how good. In fact, he was in such a hurry to get back to the quay he almost forgot his bacon sandwich.

Almost.

11

Suzanne closed the door, put the bolts in place, the chain across, flattened herself against it. Sighed like she had been holding her breath underwater.

She looked down the hall of her flat. At first glance, everything looked the same as it always did, but, looking more closely, she noticed differences. Things had been moved out of place and not put back. Doors and drawers left open that she would usually have shut. And vice versa.

The police. She hoped.

This should have been the place she felt safe, could take refuge in. Not any more. There was nowhere she could feel safe in now. Not even her own body. Not after today. What she had just been through.

The rape suite had been what she expected. White, tiled, functional.

So had the feelings inside her: apprehension, fear, terror.

The detective had taken her into the station, insisting Suzanne call her by her first name of Anni. Taking her straight through to this white room, waving away the paperwork until afterwards. Then pulling up two stiff-backed chairs, sitting opposite each other, talking and maintaining eye contact all the while.

'You can have counselling, you know. We can arrange it.'

Suzanne couldn't reply. There were no words in her mouth.

Anni continued. 'If, you know, you need it. If things . . .'

Suzanne's head was still spinning. It was like she had stepped out of her normal life into something surreal. A waking dream or some absurdist theatre play. In the car on the way to the station she had looked out of the window, watched people moving around, going in and out of shops, coffee houses. Carrying shopping, talking on phones, wheeling pushchairs. Normal people doing normal things. Leading normal lives. And there was her. Watching that life through the window, like a TV documentary on an alien tribe.

Suzanne found a nod for Anni. Anni returned it, gave her knee a squeeze. Suzanne's first instinct was to place her own hand over it, keep it there, pressing hard, her only communication to that normal world. But she didn't. She just sat there numbly, allowing Anni's hand to stay where it was. Anni stood up.

'We need you to undress,' she said.

Suzanne was still wearing the T-shirt she had slept in the previous night, her dressing gown over the top of it. Anni left the room, gave her privacy, waited until she was in the cotton hospital gown. She sat on the examining table, against the wall, the loose ties at the back of the gown making her feel even more naked.

Anni returned and, with gloved hands, held out a plastic bag for Suzanne to deposit her T-shirt into. She did so. Anni smiled. Suzanne couldn't return it.

'Right,' Anni said, sitting down next to her on the table. 'I've got to nip upstairs to get some paperwork done. You won't be alone for long. Will you be OK for a couple of minutes?'

Suzanne nodded, her head down, hair wafting back and forth like curtains in a slow breeze.

'Good. The doctor'll not be long.' She placed her hand on Suzanne's shoulder, gave another small squeeze.

Eventually, with another small squeeze, Anni removed her hand, stood up and left the room.

Now it was just Suzanne. Alone, but with a whole new world in her head for company.

Her mind slipped back to the night before. The dream that might not have been a dream. Her moods, her responses to it, had clicked backwards and forwards all day like a metronome: I'm making it all up. Imagining things. Wasting their time. Then: no. I'm not. It was real and there was someone with me. Someone in my room. In my bed. In my—

She tried to balance her thoughts, still her racing heart. Her hands clamped between her thighs, her ankles crossed. She closed her eyes, attempted to calm her breathing. The same thoughts tumbling over and over in her head.

I'm not giving in to this . . . I'm not giving in to this . . . I'm going to be strong, be strong . . . this bastard isn't going to win . . .

And then the door opened.

Suzanne gave a start as a woman in a white coat entered. Overweight, hair a functional bob, clothes muted shades of grey and beige. She held a file, looked at it.

'Suzanne . . . Perry?' She looked at Suzanne with eyes that had a calculated, professional deadness about them, a shield between herself and the wreckage of women she must confront daily.

'Yes.' Suzanne's voice was small, rusty, as if shrunken from disuse. She cleared her throat, spoke again. 'Yes.' Stronger this time.

The doctor gave a smile that penetrated the shield and reached her eyes, showed that, no matter how much she tried not to become involved with her patients, she was still a human being.

'I'm Doctor Winter,' she said, still smiling, trying to reassure her. She took another look at the file in her hands, then looked back at Suzanne. 'Right,' she said, her voice warm and comforting, like a children's storybook reader. 'The first thing I want you to do is to provide a urine sample.'

Doctor Winter sent her into a cubicle with two small pots to fill. Suzanne did as she was asked, returned with the pots, put them on the desk as instructed.

'OK,' said Doctor Winter, snapping on latex gloves, 'if you could just pop yourself on the table . . .'

Suzanne did as she was told. 'Legs apart, knees bent, please. I'll try to make this as painless as possible . . .'

Suzanne put her head back, closed her eyes. She had been fine up until then. This was the part she had been dreading.

12

It was afternoon, the sun was shining and Castle Park seemed to have been specially designed as the perfect place to enjoy the perfect day.

The castle had stood for two thousand years and looked like it was ready to stand for another couple of thousand. Flowers bloomed from the perfectly maintained beds and borders surrounding it, people strolled along the neat walkways. Even those who were hurrying to weekday work or business appointments slowed down to enjoy the surroundings. It felt to Marina like a small vacation in another world.

The parkland behind the castle sloped down towards the small lake and the children's play areas. For Marina, sitting on a bench, taking in the view, the castle always brought to mind images of Boudica and her army, blazing around in their chariots. But where once the warrior-queen would have whipped her horses to get up the hill, attacking the castle while dodging arrows and spears, now the grounds were full of school children on educational day trips, young mothers, nannies and au pairs pushing their baby buggies round. The only kind of sustained assault on the castle came from busloads of primary school children running riot or the occasional Lycra-wearing, stroller-pushing mother taking on the hill as part of her jogging route.

One was running past Marina now. She looked up, smiled. The woman, thin, tanned, her blonde hair pulled away from her sweating face in a severe ponytail, saw Marina sitting with one hand resting on Josephina's buggy, returned the smile.

'Got to keep going,' the woman gasped, passing, 'get my shape back . . .' And off she went.

Marina watched her go. What did she mean, get her shape back? The woman looked in perfect condition. Thin, fit-looking, her stomach didn't even have the slightest bit of sag to it.

Despite the sunshine, Marina felt suddenly cold, like the black cloud from earlier was following her. Was that the kind of thing she was expected to do? Run to get back in shape? To have her new mother's body scrutinised and deemed either acceptable or unacceptable? She didn't want that. She couldn't have that.

Marina thought back to her pregnancy. Before Phil. While Tony was still – was still around. That was hard enough. She felt like she was the first person ever to experience what she was feeling. There was no elation about it, none of the joy she had been told to expect. Just terror. Abject terror.

And then there was Phil. Getting together had been trau-matic enough, and she had hoped that, once he was there, Josephina's real father, then things would be OK. She would calm down. Enjoy the changes her life was going through.

But.

It felt like every time she looked at Josephina she was reminded of what happened. Of the real, dark world, not this sunny, colourful one before her. She saw not a baby but a living slab of guilt.

And that was it. She felt like she could never relax, never

58

enjoy the life she ought to be having with her partner and daughter the way she should be. The way all the other mothers around her in the park seemed to be doing.

Or maybe they didn't. Maybe they were just pretending, putting on a public face. Maybe they were shrivelled with terror inside.

She looked round. No. They didn't seem to be. The mothers around her seemed to be as happy as their children in the play area. She looked down at Josephina. The baby was lying asleep, arms up as if in surrender, tiny fists at the sides of her head. Completely unaware of this world – or any world – and anything in it.

And Marina felt another layer of guilt. For the baby. She should be happy, enjoying herself for Josephina's sake. She was with the man she loved, Phil, the baby's real father. She tried to imagine what it would have been like the other way round, what she would have felt if they hadn't all been together. But that didn't work.

So she tried to wish herself happy. Tried. And failed.

Marina pushed the baby buggy backwards and forwards. Josephina stirred slightly, kept on sleeping. She had tried to talk to the other mothers in the park but they seemed to have their own circles of friends. None of her old friends from teaching had small children so she couldn't talk to them. And she couldn't talk to Phil either, no matter how much she loved him.

Sitting there in the sunshine, with children playing all around her, the flowers in bloom and what she usually regarded as the comforting presence of the castle, she felt alone. Completely alone.

Her phone rang. She jumped. Her first response was to check the baby, see if it had woken her, if she was upset in any way. But Josephina just kept on sleeping. Good. Relieved, she checked the display, answered it. She knew who it was.

'Hey,' she said.

'Hey yourself.'

Phil.

Then couldn't think of anything more to say to him.

'You OK?' he said.

'Fine. Just in Castle Park. Pushing Josephina. Letting her see the sunshine.' She bit her lip.

'Wish I was with you.' He gave a small, brittle laugh that died away. 'You've probably heard on the news, there's been a murder.'

She hadn't heard. She was barely aware of anything or anyone but herself at the moment. Still, the old, dark familiar shiver ran through her. 'So that means . . .'

'I'll be late.' He sighed. 'Sorry. You know . . . you know what it's like.'

That shiver again. 'Yes. I know what it's like. Is it . . .' she said, knowing she should say something. '. . . is it bad?'

'Like there are good ones?' An old phrase he always used. 'Yeah. Worse than . . . yeah.' There were some other voices on the line, the sound of Phil covering the mouthpiece to talk to them. 'Look,' he said, coming back to her, 'I've got to go. I'll call you later, OK? Let you know what's happening.'

'OK.'

She rang off, looked at the phone. Only then realising he had still been talking to her, telling her he loved her.

She stood up. Looked around, saw nothing to keep her in the park, her vacation over. Started walking. She reached the top of the hill, the main road. Looked down the hill towards East Hill, upwards towards the town centre. Set off walking.

It was only when she found herself down by the bridge over the River Colne then she realised she had no idea where she had been or where she was going.

13

Suzanne stood with her back against her front door, wondering when she would ever feel safe again, hoping the locks and chains would be enough to keep out any intruder.

She could still feel the ghost of the cold metal inside her. See the screw-top pots with her different bodily fluids and samples taken on cotton buds all in a line. And Doctor Winter checking her notes, looking her in the eye:

'*You haven't been raped.*'

There would be more tests, but that was the conclusion. Suzanne should have felt relieved. But . . .

Before her was the phone table. Her landline handset lying across her hard-back address book. Had she left it that way? At that angle? Down the hall she could see into her bedroom, see the duvet pulled back, the open curtains, the raised, wooden blind . . .

'Oh God . . .'

She sank to the floor, her back against the front door, covered her face with her hands. Tears came. Great, wracking sobs. She pulled her hands in tighter, her fingernails digging into her skin.

'No . . . no . . .'

Her legs kicked out, impotent with rage and frustration. Felt herself caving in to the emotion, being weakened by it like acid eating away at her, destroying her from the inside . . . Then she opened her eyes. Willed the tears to stop.

'No . . .' Shouting. 'No . . . you're not going to win . . . No . . .'

Suzanne felt something rise within her. Hot. Fiery. Angry. She stood up.

'No, no, you bastard . . .'

She looked around the hallway for something – anything – to hold. Saw the phone. Picked it up. 'You hear me?' Turning round on the spot, shouting at the walls. 'You're not . . . going to . . . fucking . . . win . . .'

She hurled the phone as hard as she could. It hit the far wall, fell to the floor.

She stared at it, sighed. Light-headed but the emotion subsiding, breathing like she had just run a marathon. Or run for her life.

And she hadn't mentioned Anthony. Surely they would find out soon enough. They had records, they would check them. And then they would think she was lying. Making it up for whatever reason, to get attention.

Well, she wasn't lying. Wasn't making it up. And if the bastards thought that . . .

She wiped the tears away, her cheeks burning. Sat back on the floor.

The photo of her lying semi-naked would now be in some forensic lab. She could just imagine it being passed round by strangers, objectified like some porn image. Being commented on, judged, rated. It felt like a second violation. She tried to tell herself that they were professionals, that it was only a piece of evidence from which clues could be removed. But she wasn't convinced. She began to tremble, from anger or pity she didn't know. Didn't want to know.

She breathed deeply, tried to focus. Concentrate. Her fingers picking at the plaster in the crook of her arm where she had given a blood sample. She looked down the hall again, into the rooms. Everything that she had built up, the place she regarded as safe, had been violated. No other word for it. Burglary victims talked of the same thing, but this, thought Suzanne, was something more. Something deeper and crueller. A kind of rape.

'Bastard . . .' Her jaw ached. She was grinding her teeth.

Then the doorbell sounded.

And Suzanne screamed.

14

Anni Hepburn lifted the phone, keyed in a number, waited. It was answered.

'DS Gosling.'

'Jane? It's Anni. You busy?'

'Doing door-to-door. You going to be long?'

Door-to-door. The Birdies were working with Phil, of course they were. Well, good luck to them. And him.

A shudder of guilt ran through her. No. Bitterness wasn't healthy. She should ignore it. But it had been happening more and more since Clayton's death. The team had been shaken after that and, she told herself, they all had different ways of coping. As Phil had told her, grieve all you like, but get on with the job.

And she would. Just as far away from Phil as possible.

Anni leaned back at her desk, the phone cradled in the crook of her neck. 'This won't take long, Jane, thanks. Just a case you once worked on. See if you can remember it.'

'I'll try.'

Anni had left Suzanne in the rape suite of Southway station, come into the office to do a bit of checking. She had run Suzanne Perry's name through the computer and was surprised to find a hit. She had come to their attention before. She had checked the case notes.

Two years previously Suzanne had been a student at Essex University on a post-graduate course in speech therapy. She claimed that one of her tutors, Anthony Howe, had offered her a first in exchange for sex. She had turned him down and reported him for sexual harassment. It came down to her word against his and, with no evidence to back up the claim, it was dismissed.

But that wasn't the end of it. Anthony Howe, Suzanne said, began stalking her. Standing outside her flat at night, sending her obscene texts, leaving messages on the phone or just not speaking at all. Her claims were investigated. No further action taken.

Strange, thought Anni. Why no further action? She had picked up the phone.

'Suzanne Perry,' said Anni into the phone. 'University student, couple of years back. You were the investigating officer. Ring any bells?'

'Not offhand.' Anni could hear traffic, voices in the background. Jane Gosling wasn't giving her full attention. She would have to help her.

Anni filled her in on what the file said. The harassment claim, the stalking. 'Any clearer?'

'Student . . .' said Jane. 'Flat on Maldon Road?'

'That's her. Teacher was stalking her. Anthony Howe.'

'Right. Except he wasn't.'

Anni leaned forward, interested now. 'Really?'

'Yeah. Let me just . . .' Another pause while she brought up the memory. 'Phone calls, wasn't it? Texts?'

'What it says here.'

'Only there weren't any. We checked her landline. No messages. Her mobile. No texts. Said she'd deleted them. Made her feel violated. Same with her answerphone. This

65

teacher said she'd been nothing but trouble the whole course, looked like she was going to fail, made the whole thing up to get a higher mark. He was furious, going to sue her for defamation of character, if she kept going. And that was that. We heard no more.'

'You reckon she was making it up?'

'Probably. I thought it was just a bit of a fling that went wrong and she was trying to get revenge.'

'Did she mention a boyfriend? Mark Turner?'

Jane Gosling gave a laugh of irritation. 'Two years ago, Anni. Can barely remember what I had for dinner last night.'

They both laughed.

'She back in the news, then?' said Jane.

'Another stalker. Inside the flat this time.'

Jane's turn to laugh. 'Good luck with that.'

'Another? What was it Oscar Wilde sort of said? To get one stalker is a misfortune. To get two is just carelessness.'

Anni laughed. 'Oscar Wilde?'

'Amateur dramatics. I was a very good Miss Prism. Got all the laughs.'

'I don't doubt it.'

'Look, I'd better go. Listen, get your paperwork done and get down here. We could use a bit of help.'

'I'll see.'

They made their goodbyes, Anni rang off. She sat back once more, considering her options. Polish off the paperwork of what looked like a fantasist wasting police time and go join Phil, or investigate Suzanne Perry's claims thoroughly.

She checked her notes, moved her fingers over the keyboard.

Looked for Anthony Howe's contact details.

15

Phil felt like a ghost hunter.

Julie Miller's flat held a kind of terminal emptiness, a sense of a life interrupted, never to be finished. Sadness and loss hung heavier in the air than dust.

This was one of the things he hated most about the job. He could face down a knife-wielding drunk or tackle a two-fisted husband using his wife for target practice, no problem. He could hold his own in court against some defence barrister trying to provoke him and belittle him. He could even write up a whole barrage of arse-covering reports and attend box-ticking diversity training sessions. But to stand in the ruins of someone's life and be expected to make sense of their absence just depressed him to the core. And left him with no answers.

Phil closed his eyes, blinked the thoughts away. They wouldn't help him to find out what had happened, to catch Julie Miller's killer. To do his job.

'So Julie Miller went missing a week past Thursday,' he said.

'*Reported* missing a week last Thursday,' said Rose Martin.

'By her mother. Lives in Stanway. Julie hadn't been at work the day before. Missed some appointments. Parents were down as contacts. Work called them, asked if she was ill. No reply. Quick call, and there we were.'

'And everything was checked? The doors, the windows—'

'Yes.' Exasperation in her voice. 'CCTV. Door-to-door. Statements taken from neighbours. I am a professional, you know.'

Phil reddened. 'Sorry. I didn't mean it to sound that way. I have to check.'

Rose nodded. Waited a few seconds before speaking. 'I know. We couldn't understand it either. It was like she had just . . . vanished.'

Phil looked all round the room as if the walls would answer him. 'And no one saw her?'

'No one.'

'Upstairs? Downstairs? Heard nothing?'

'Downstairs said they heard nothing. Concierge says upstairs are away on holiday.'

He sighed. 'Let's look round. See if anything stands out.'

They were in the living room. Phil tried not to acknowledge the cruel irony in that. It was sparsely furnished, what furniture there was chosen as if not to upset the bland, beige colour scheme on the walls and ceiling. A sofa in a darker shade of beige had a brightly coloured throw over it. A multi-coloured rug covered the fitted beige carpet. A small, flatscreen TV and DVD recorder was on a glass stand against one wall, a small hi-fi unit with a docked iPod next to it. A blond wood bookcase stood in the corner of the room, the shelves mostly empty of books and ornaments, as if a life was just being acquired and collected.

The heavy-handed remains of a police presence also contributed to a sense of a life interrupted. Windowsills and door frames held residues of silver, black and white powder where prints had been lifted. Furniture and possessions had

68

clearly been moved and not returned properly to their original positions. Drawn curtains added to the gloom.

'Check the shelves,' said Phil. 'See if there's a diary, anything like that. A photo album, anything.'

'We did that,' said Rose.

'I know,' said Phil. 'But you were looking for a misper. I'm looking for a killer. And open those curtains, let some light in here.'

Phil went into the kitchen. It was clean and tidy for the most part. A single mug stood on the draining board, coffee stained dry inside it. He checked the dishwasher. A small number of dirty dishes in it, ready to be washed.

He went looking for other rooms. Found the bedroom. Bedrooms, in cases like this, were even worse for Phil than living rooms. Living rooms were for show. There were no secrets in bedrooms. No hiding.

He looked round. It was hard to tell whether it had been left in a mess by Julie Miller or by the investigators. The bed was unmade. Underwear and jeans were piled at the bottom. A pair of trainers that looked liked they had been kicked off. Drawers pulled open, their contents spilling out.

Phil looked at the bedside cabinet. A Jodi Picoult novel lay there, the bookmark about a third of the way in. He opened the bedside cabinet door. Another couple of books, some prescription blister packs of contraceptive pills. Nothing else.

He knelt down, looked under the bed. Saw something silhouetted against the light on the other side. He stretched his arm in, made contact, pulled it out. A laptop wearing a thin coat of dust. Phil took it out, opened it, booted it up.

'You missed this,' he called out.

Rose Martin entered the bedroom, stopped when she saw what he had. 'Where did you find that?'

'Under the bed. Right under the bed, mind.'

Rose nodded, her features tight. 'As you say, we were looking for a missing person. Whoever searched this room wouldn't have thought she'd be able to fit under there.'

Phil, eyes on the laptop, didn't rise to her words. He just hoped it wouldn't be password protected. It wasn't. Desktop wallpaper appeared, a shaggy-haired dog, its tongue lolling from the corner of its mouth.

'What about the boyfriend?'

'Clean. And, believe me, we looked at him from every angle.'

His fingers moved over the keys, searching for anything that would give him a clue as to Julie Miller's life. He established Wi-Fi connection, clicked on Facebook. Julie Miller's homepage appeared. In the corner was a photo of a dark-haired woman in her twenties, lying on a bed, her hand in her hair, smiling shyly for the camera, her mouth open as if she was in mid-sentence to the photographer. The photo looked both innocent and intimate at the same time.

'That her?'

Rose sat down next to him. 'From the other photos I've seen, yes. Do you agree with me that it's her down there?'

Phil tried to imagine the smiling, pretty face before him superimposed on to the body on the boat. It was depressingly easy to match the two. 'I . . . it's looking that way.' He kept looking at the photo. 'Why did she put this one on? Out of all of them she could pick, why this one?'

Rose looked at it too. 'Because it's flattering, a good like-ness . . . Maybe her boyfriend liked it.'

'Maybe.'

He sighed, kept looking through the Facebook profile. She had her place of work as Colchester General Hospital, her schooling as the local secondary in Stanway, her university as Essex in Colchester. She hadn't moved far away from home.

She didn't have an enormous number of friends, which was good news for the officers who would have to trawl through them, but there were enough. He started to look through them but didn't get far.

'Phil?'

He hadn't noticed Rose get up and move away. Her voice came from the living room. He got up, followed her. She was standing by the window, the drawn curtains slightly parted, looking downwards.

'I was right,' she said. 'Look.'

Phil looked. Down below them was the River Colne. And the lightship.

He looked at her. 'Coincidence?'

'No such thing,' she said. 'Not in cases like this.'

Phil looked at his new junior officer. Saw only sadness and concern in her eyes. And a copper's hunger for answers. Good, thought Phil. The right stuff. Then looked again out of the window.

The white tent had been erected on the boat, a temporary barrier placed along the road. A small crowd of print journalists, photographers and TV cameras had gathered behind the barrier and Detective Chief Inspector Ben Fenwick was still down there giving an address. Or practising his clichés, thought Phil.

'There he is,' said Phil. 'King Cliché rides again.'

Without looking at her, Phil felt Rose bridle and stiffen beside him. He had said that deliberately to see what her reaction would be. He knew now. She was sleeping with his boss. And no doubt telling him everything he said. Phil would have to watch himself. Or make sure he only said things he wanted to get back to Fenwick.

Phil sighed. 'Time to pay the parents a visit, I think.'

'We don't know for definite it's her, do we? Shouldn't we wait?'

Phil gestured to the crowd of reporters below them. 'And let one of them do it instead? I think we should at least talk to them.'

Rose nodded.

They would move in a moment. But for now they just stood there. The room still and tomb-like behind them.

16

The bell rang again.

Suzanne stayed where she was, slumped against the front door.

Was it him? Back again? Had he hidden himself outside, waiting for the police to leave, to see Suzanne return alone? Was it?

The doorbell rang again.

Suzanne stared at the door, at the chains across, at the lock. Hoped it would be strong enough. She reached out a hand to open it, pulled it back. Just stared at it.

'Leave me alone . . . *leave me alone . . .*'

The angry resolve of a few moments ago was dissipating. Panic was again threatening to overwhelm her. Her heart began pumping like sports car pistons, pounding the blood round her body. She stretched out her hand.

Her third-floor flat in the old Edwardian house had no entry phone or intercom system. If someone rang, they had to be let in manually. Down three flights of stairs to the front of the house.

No. Opening the door was one thing. Going down all

those stairs – alone – was another. So she stayed where she was. Waited.

The bell didn't sound again.

They had gone, left her in peace. Suzanne sighed.

Then her phone rang.

She jumped again. Looked around. The handset lay on the floor, the plastic and metal flashing and bleating.

'No, just . . . just fuck off . . .'

It kept ringing, an insistent, piercing, metallic clang. She stayed where she was, eyes screwed tight shut. Wanting it to end, wanting to be somewhere – anywhere – else.

The phone kept ringing.

Until the answerphone kicked in, her voice telling the caller to leave a message, then the tone.

Then: 'Hey, Suzanne, it's me. I'm outside now, you—'

Zoe. Her best friend. She got to her knees, made her way into the living room, grabbed the phone.

'Zoe?' She was breathing heavily, like the last few minutes had given her an hour's worth of gym workout.

'You OK? What's the matter?'

'Oh . . . oh . . .' Struggling to get her breath.

Zoe's voice was full of concern. 'What's happened?'

'It's started again, Zoe, it's started again . . .'

Suzanne stared into her coffee mug. It was one of her favourites, an Indian design in various swirling shades of turquoise, bought from The Pier before the shop crashed and disappeared.

Before her life did the same.

'C'mon, then.' Zoe sat in the same place Anni Hepburn had occupied earlier. She placed her mug on a side table and stray strands of perfectly coloured blonde hair fell, as if by design, around her face, framing her pretty features. Zoe seemed to find the business of looking beautiful effortless. It made Suzanne feel even worse.

'You told me to come over. I've had to throw a sicky so tell all.'

Suzanne sighed, held the mug in front of her once more like a shield, told her everything.

'So . . .' Her account didn't actually conclude, she just seemed to lose the energy to make words. 'That's, that's it . . .'

Zoe stared at Suzanne, eyes wide, lips parted. Even her look of horror seemed perfect. Suzanne felt suddenly tired once more.

'God, Suzanne, that's, that's really horrible . . .'

Suzanne closed her eyes, said nothing. She knew that already.

Zoe leaned forward. 'Was it . . .'

Suzanne opened her eyes again. 'Couldn't have been. I . . . No.' She sighed. 'No.' Her head dropped. 'No.'

Zoe leaned back, said nothing.

Suzanne looked up. 'Why would it be him? Why now?' Emotion was building inside her once more. 'Why?'

'It can't be him, not Anthony . . .'

'You weren't there, Zoe. You didn't see the photo, you didn't have the dream.' Her mind slipped back to the previous night. 'The dream, oh God, Zoe . . .'

'Suzanne.' Zoe's eyes locked on to Suzanne's. Clear and bright and blue, not like Suzanne's muddy-brown ones. Her hands reached out, took Suzanne's.

'You being a therapist, now?' Suzanne's smile was as weak as her voice.

'Bringing my work home with me,' said Zoe. 'Now take a deep breath. Be calm. It can't be Anthony. You know that.'

Suzanne said nothing, just concentrated on breathing, waited for Zoe to continue.

'What happened with Anthony, Suzanne . . . that's all done with.'

Suzanne said nothing, kept her eyes averted from her friend.

Zoe tried to make eye contact, frowned. 'Suzanne, it is finished, isn't it?'

Suzanne said nothing.

Zoe sat back, dropped Suzanne's hands. 'Oh, you're not. Suzanne, tell me you're not . . .'

Suzanne looked up. 'No. I'm not.'

'Sure?'

'Yes,' Suzanne said, looking at the carpet. 'I'm sure.'

'Good.' Zoe smiled. 'Well, you needn't worry. I'll stay tonight.'

Suzanne looked up. 'You can't do that.'

'Why not? You can't stay on your own. I'll be with you. We can go to work together tomorrow. You *are* going in tomorrow?'

'Well, yes, I hope so, but . . .' Suzanne tried to find some objection. This was typical of Zoe. Good-looking and good-hearted. Sometimes she didn't feel worthy of her friendship. 'What about Russell? He'll—'

'—be fine for a couple of days. He can cope.' Zoe smiled. 'Might give him a chance to miss me. Appreciate me all the more when I go home.'

'But—' Suzanne felt tears well within once more.

'Stop it. None of that.' Zoe stood up. 'I'll just nip home and get a few things. Will you be OK on your own for an hour or so or d'you want to come with me?'

'I'll be fine.'

'Lock the door after me.'

Suzanne did so, triple-checking the locks. Then walked back into the living room, sat down. Her coffee was cold. She looked round for something to do, something to distract her. Take her mind off things until Zoe returned. Saw the phone.

No.

No. She shouldn't.

She knew what she was going to do. Who she was going to call. No.

She picked it up. Put it on the table.

Kept looking at it.

No.

Picked it up again. Her hand a claw, holding the receiver like an eagle would its prey.

Dialled a number she knew by heart. A number she had never forgotten.

17

Anni Hepburn stared at the painting on the wall and wondered what to make of it and also the person who owned it.

It took centre stage in a very small, cramped office, a narrow, shelf-lined room that could have doubled as a store cupboard or a corridor to nowhere. The shelves were full of books: textbooks, novels, old, new, with no particular order to them that she could work out. Shoved in around the books were magazines, folders, papers. A few ornaments and nick-nacks sat on what space there was. Small and disparate, things that probably had a story or at least a joke behind them when first placed there, but were now dust-heavy and sun-faded. Opposite the shelves a desk dominated the rest of the room. A computer in the centre surrounded by a mini cityscape of piles of books. Around the painting on the wall was a timetable, a wall planner, a few postcards, a couple of yellowed cartoon strips cut from newspapers. But it was the painting that drew the eye. Anni was sure that was the intention.

Mounted in an elaborate, yet old and chipped gold frame, it showed a man, tall, young and handsome, head back, chin up, standing in some marbled hall, his hands grasping the lapels of his jacket, gazing out with, on first viewing, a look of untouchable arrogance and haughtiness that bordered on contempt. On closer viewing, however, it showed the skill of the painter. The arrogance that informed the handsome features never reached the eyes. They held a mirth, a mockery, saying that the whole thing was a sham and that the man was going to burst out laughing at any moment.

A smaller piece of artwork was pinned up next to the painting. Superman, all massive chest, huge arms and tiny underpants, was soaring above the Earth, an American flag fluttering behind him.

The man has a serious ego problem, thought Anni.

She sat in a gap between the desk and the doorway in a chair, ancient and wooden, dark and worn, with a tired tapestry cushion on the seat. It seemed to be at odds with the rest of the room, more like something found by the fire in an old, wood-beamed pub rather than in a functional 1960s office, all breeze-block walls and cast-iron windows, of a university professor.

The subject of the painting was now sitting in front of Anni, at the book-covered desk, and he was no superman. His appearance showed, even more than the damaged frame, the dust collected on it or the fading of the oils, just how long ago it had been painted. He was still tall, but the black hair was largely grey and thinning slightly at the temples. The arrogant, haughty set of his features had deepened to become a set of permanent lines, like a mask worn for so long and so often it had become the wearer's real face. The eyes, though, were what had changed the most. Rather than the self-mocking dancing in the painting, they just showed a weariness. And, once Anni had announced who she was, a wariness.

'You're lucky to catch me,' he said. 'I was about to go home.'

She smiled. 'So, Professor—'

'Just Anthony, please,' he said, offering a tentative smile. 'No need for formality.'

'Right.'

Professor Anthony Howe had been easy to track down. Anni had made one phone call to the university to find him in his office. He had finished teaching for the day and was catching up on his marking. He would be in for a few hours, he said, if she wanted to drop by, but what was it concerning? Once she mentioned Suzanne Perry's name, however, he hurriedly said he had to leave for home. When she suggested she meet him there he claimed to be on his way to a pressing engagement. No problem, she would catch him in the morning. But she would talk to him. It was important.

And he had sighed and, realising she was going nowhere and that it would be best to get it over with as soon as possible, had relented. So there she was.

'I must say,' he said, still working on his smile, 'you're not what I was expecting.'

'Really.' Anni raised an eyebrow. Almost stifled a yawn. 'Because I'm black?'

He nodded, then realised what Anni must have been thinking. 'Oh no, not because you're . . . because of that. No. Just . . . when I spoke to you on the phone I got quite a different impression of you.'

'In what way?'

He tried for a smile. 'You sounded like a police officer. Now, sitting here, you could pass for a student. That's all.'

Anni thought of what had happened with Suzanne Perry and was glad she wasn't. She smiled politely.

He returned it.

He was trying, she thought. To be polite, to be at ease. But he hadn't offered her tea.

'Nice painting, by the way.'

The smile became slightly more genuine. 'Thank you. I like it, something a bit different. Got used to it, really.

Forget it's there until someone points it out to me.'

'Must have cost a bit to have done.'

A small laugh. 'Had a friend, aspiring artist. She wanted subjects, models. Cost me nothing.' He couldn't hide the pride in his voice. 'But . . .' He waved his hand as if dismissing it. 'All in the past. A long time ago.'

Anni kept her attention on the wall. She pointed at Superman. 'What about the guy next to him?'

'Oh. Him.' He smiled again, and this time he looked like a university teacher about to address a class. 'What do you think he sounds like?'

'Pardon?'

'Superman. His voice. What do you think he sounds like? Timid? Shy? Does he stutter?'

'I doubt it,' Anni said, wondering where this was leading, 'Authoritative. In command. That kind of thing. American.'

He nodded. 'And Clark Kent?'

'What?'

'His alter ego. Clark Kent. How does he talk?'

'Erm . . .' Anni had never given the matter much thought. 'Like . . . a normal bloke?'

Anthony Howe nodded, as if she had just confirmed a thesis he had personally created. 'Exactly. If he spoke like Superman he would never fit in, would he? Not at the *Daily Planet*. Not bumbling, mild-mannered Clark Kent, would he?'

'No.'

Anthony Howe sat back, folded his arms. Thesis proven. 'We change. We don't have just one voice. We have several. Depending where we are, who we're talking to at the time, how we want to be seen, to come across. Different voices for different situations.' A smug smile. 'One of the first things I teach my students. If you're going to be a speech therapist, find out which voice – which persona – the patient needs to use most.'

She couldn't resist the next line. His arrogant statement set him up for it.

'And which persona did you use with Suzanne Perry?'

His expression – his demeanour – changed. The set of his mouth hardened. His eyes narrowed, were lit by a dark, ugly light. He moved his body towards her.

And in that moment, Anni wasn't so ready to believe that Suzanne had been making it all up.

18

The death knock. The bit Phil hated most.

It made him think of his own parents, Don and Eileen. What it would be like if one of his colleagues turned up on their doorstep with news of him. And now, of course, there was Marina. And their daughter Josephina.

Everything had changed when she was born. He had been there at the birth, holding Marina's hand as she screamed the baby out. Afterwards, he kept trying to understand the conflicting emotions he had gone through. It was a polarising experience. On the one hand there was his child, his daughter, coming into the world. Joyful, yes, but also terrifying. Another life. A huge responsibility. And there was Marina. Screaming out, her body twisted with pain. And the blood . . . he hadn't expected there to be so much blood. It came gushing out of her, the weight of it pooling in the sheet underneath her. He had hated to see her suffering, and also hated the fact that he was helpless to do anything about it. But then there was the baby . . . And she more than made up for it.

But it was the responsibility that hit him most. A parent.

A father. He had noticed himself do different things. Not take chances at red lights. Drive more carefully. Look both ways before crossing the road. Cut down his alcohol and takeaway food intake. Start running again. Because it wasn't just him any more, or him and Marina. It was their daughter, and he had to be there for her. Because if something happened to him or Marina, Josephina might end up having the kind of upbringing he had. And he didn't wish that on anyone.

Phil stood on the doorstep, hesitated. Rose Martin was beside him, along with Cheryl Bland, the Family Liaison Officer. She was a small, blonde woman, mid- to late twenties, Phil guessed, but difficult to place with any accuracy as she looked even younger. Soft eyes. Phil imagined that was a bonus in her area of work.

His Audi was parked in the gravel driveway. The house was detached, the plasterwork decorative, all fleur-de-lis and faux-heraldic roses. Pots of flowers lined the drive like herbaceous sentries. Twin potted bay trees flanked the heavy wooden front door.

'What can we expect, then?' he asked Cheryl.

'They're a nice couple. Decent. He might get a bit angry, wanting action, she'll talk. About Julie.'

Phil nodded. Thought once more of Eileen and Don. 'Any brothers or sisters?'

'One brother. Works out in the Middle East. Supertankers, something like that.' Cheryl smiled. 'She did tell me.'

'And their names?'

'Colin and Brenda.'

Phil thanked her, rang the bell. Waited.

A woman opened it, middle-aged and in good shape, but tired looking. She looked at Phil, then Rose, hope rising in her eyes. Then she saw Cheryl Bland and the hope died.

'Mrs Miller?' Phil said. 'Brenda?'

She nodded. Her mouth moved but no words emerged.

'Can we come in?'

'What's happened? What have you got to tell me?' She clung on to the edge of the door, her knuckles white.

'I think it's better if we come in.' Cheryl moved forward, placed her hand on Brenda Miller's arm.

She jerked the door backwards, stood aside, her breathing increasing.

They went in, Phil and Rose first, to the living room. Cheryl Bland, her hand still on Brenda Miller's arm, steered her to the sofa. Cheryl sat, Brenda refused, staying standing. She looked at Rose and Phil as if only registering them now.

'Who . . .'

'I'm Detective Inspector Brennan and this is Detective Sergeant Martin.'

'I know you,' Brenda said. 'You're the one who was in charge of the . . .' Her mouth hung open. 'Oh God . . . you've . . . oh God . . .'

The three police officers shared a look between each other. Phil nodded. He would take it.

'Mrs Miller . . . Brenda . . . I've got something to tell you.'

Brenda Miller's breathing increased, her chest rising and falling, her hand to her neck.

'We've discovered a body.'

'Oh God . . . oh God . . .'

'We can't say for certain at this stage that it is Julie, however we strongly suspect it may be.'

But Brenda Miller wasn't listening.

Because, like her world, she had collapsed.

19

'Well, that went as well as expected.'

Rose Martin was sitting on the Millers' front doorstep, a Silk Cut clamped between her lips. She was drawing the smoke down deep, as if reinflating her lungs after giving the kiss of life.

Phil closed the front door behind him, sat down next to her.

Brenda Miller had been helped to the sofa and brought round. Cheryl Bland had made tea and Phil, as tactfully as possible, had told her what had happened. She had sat there blank-faced, her mouth slightly open, as if punch-drunk from a twelve-round heavyweight fight.

Rose drew in more smoke, put her head back, let it out in a huge, grey fountain, an artificial cloud against the blue sky. She turned to Phil.

'It was a good investigation.'

'I don't doubt it.'

'We did everything we could.' There was a hardness in her eyes, almost an anger.

'I'm sure you did.'

'We had no leads. None at all. It was, literally, like she had vanished. We tried everything. We . . .' She stubbed the cigarette out on the gravel, so hard the filter snapped off.

'We'll reinterview,' said Phil. 'Old boyfriends, work colleagues, family. Everyone. Go back to the beginning.'

She was nodding, not hearing his words, just waiting for him to finish so she could start speaking. 'Back to the beginning. Start again. So that's it, is it? You come in and take it away from me.'

'That's not the way it works. You know that.' Phil's voice calm and even, trying to talk down her anger.

'MIS comes in and we just roll over. And you glory boys get your collar and make us ordinary CID plods look like brainless shits.'

Phil managed not to rise to her words. He knew she was upset and angry and looking for someone to lash out at. 'You're part of the team. We need you here. I need you here.'

'Yeah.'

'Why don't you take a couple of hours off? Get your head together. Because you're no use to me like this. And you're no use to Julie Miller either.'

Rose didn't get the chance to answer as two men came hurrying round the corner, up the drive. One of them trailing behind the other, weighed down by camera equipment.

'Shit,' said Phil, standing up.

Rose joined him. 'You know them?'

'Dave Terry and Adrian Macintyre. Freelancers. Both obnoxious twats.'

Rose smiled. 'Is that your professional opinion?'

'On every level. They're local but they sell to the nationals. Trying to beat the competition to it. Wondered who'd be the first to work out where we were. Come on.'

Phil stepped in front of the two journalists, stopping their progress. The one with the camera, Adrian Macintyre, tried to dodge round him. Rose grabbed him.

'Whoa there,' she said.

'Look, we're just doing our jobs,' said Dave Terry. 'We've got as much right to be here as you two.'

'No, you don't,' said Phil. 'We haven't confirmed that the body is Julie Miller so the last thing the family needs is you two pestering them. There's no story here.'

'Yeah?' said Terry, a snide grin appearing on his face, 'then what are you two doin' here?'

'Stopping people like you harassing innocent citizens,' said Rose. 'Now back off.'

'Sorry, darlin'.' Macintyre slipped Rose's grasp and was round her.

'Hey . . .' She turned, gave chase up the drive, grabbed him easily. She turned him to face her.

'Get your hands off me or I'll do you for assault . . .' He slid the camera bag from his arm, struggled to free himself. His face twisted with anger.

'Want to get arrested? Yeah?' Rose's voice was rising.

'Get your fuckin' hands off me!' Camera down, his fists were raised to reply.

'Rose . . .' Phil turned, made to go to her, but didn't get that far.

From out of her pocket she produced a small canister and sprayed it in Macintyre's face. His hands went immediately to his eyes and he fell to his knees, screaming.

Phil stared. She looked at him, anger still dancing in her eyes. 'You saw what happened,' she shouted. 'He assaulted me. I was within my limits and defending myself. Right?'

Terry was standing open-mouthed. A smile crept over his features, his eyes still glassy. Phil could see the journalist's mind working. Terry knew as well as Phil that DS Rose Martin had been not only out of order but also out of control. And that meant money.

Phil had to take action. He couldn't give Rose a bollocking in front of the two journalists but he couldn't let them get away to tell what had happened. He turned to Terry. 'There's no story here, right?'

Terry looked at him as if he was breaking a spell.

'Right?'

He gave an ugly laugh. 'Really? You don't think so?'

Phil's eyes hardened, his body language became tense, threatening. 'At the moment your little mate is looking at assaulting a police officer and trespassing. What about you? Want to join him?'

'There was only one person doing any assaulting here.' Terry's eyes were lit by a nasty light. He had found an even better story. 'That's how it's going to read.'

Phil sighed. 'I'm warning you . . .'

Terry laughed. 'What you gonna do, Officer? Hit me as well?'

Phil sighed. 'Here we go . . .' He grabbed hold of Terry, turning him round and thrusting his arm up his back, reading him his rights as he did so.

Terry cried out in pain. 'What . . . what you doin'?'

'Arresting you.' He turned to Rose. 'Get the other one.'

She didn't need to be told. Macintyre had slipped to his knees, hands rubbing his eyes and whimpering, kicking out his legs in pain. She roughly pulled his hands behind him, cuffed him.

They had the two journalists in armlocks and were preparing to take them to Phil's Audi when the front door opened. Brenda Miller stood there, Cheryl Bland behind her.

'What . . . what's happening?' she said, her voice distant and small as if trying to wake from a stubborn dream.

'Journalists,' said Rose Martin. 'Trying to make your life hell. We stopped them.' She couldn't keep the triumph from her voice.

'My life is already hell . . .' the words screamed, her voice cresting before breaking down into sobs. Cheryl Bland put her arm around her, led her away from the door.

But not before she had fixed Phil with a look that spoke of pain and disappointment. At everything and everyone. At him.

He didn't blame her. Pushing Terry inside the back of the Audi he felt the same way himself.

He got behind the steering wheel, started the car. Rose got into the passenger seat, eyes blazing with righteous anger. She was smiling. There was no sense of victory inside Phil. Only a hollowness.

Not trusting himself to speak, Phil drove to the station in silence. He put a CD into the player, wanting something to fill the empty space.

Doves: *Lost Souls*.

It felt appropriate.

20

There was a knock at the door.

The tension was broken. Anthony Howe straightened up, looked at the door, frowning as if emerging from sleep. His features changed, his eyes no longer darkly lit.

'Come in,' he called.

The door opened. A young man, dark-haired, tall, dressed in regulation student-issue jeans and sloganed T-shirt, stood there. He was about to speak but saw Anni sitting there, stopped.

'Yes, Jake,' Anthony Howe said.

The student looked between the two of them, uneasily. 'Um . . . we had a meeting?'

'Did we? Thought I was . . .' Howe looked at his watch. 'Right. Sorry. Just a few more minutes. Not be long.'

Jake pointed towards the corridor. 'Shall I . . .'

'Please.'

He left, closing the door behind him. The silence in the room was like the inside of a human heart; Anni could hear, feel, the blood rushing round her body.

'Right,' said Howe, finding a pen on his desk suddenly

fascinating enough to lift up and toy with in his fingers, 'you mentioned Suzanne Perry?' His voice had changed. Softer, reasoned. Back in control.

'Yes, I did.'

'Why? That subject, as far as I'm concerned, is closed.'

'Perhaps.' Anni crossed her legs, looked down at her notepad, pen poised over the page. 'Can I just ask you where you were last night?'

'I was—' He pulled his eyes off the pen, back to her. 'Can I ask why you need to know that?'

'If you could just answer the question, please.'

He sighed. Anni watched his eyes. He seemed to be deciding how best to answer the question, what tone to take, what information to give. 'I . . . was at home.'

'Alone?'

'Yes.'

'You live alone?'

'I . . . we're separated. My wife and I.'

'And there was no one with you?'

'Please tell me what this is concerning.'

His voice was rising. Anni kept hers steady, her gaze level.

'In a moment. If you could just answer the question, please.'

'As I said, I was at home.'

'And what did you do there?'

'I . . . made dinner. Then I read for a while. Watched some TV.'

'What did you watch?'

He looked startled by the question. 'Why do you need to know that? Are you making, making some kind of value judgements about me?'

'No. I just wanted to know what you watched.'

'A soap opera. *Coronation Street*. Then . . .' He put his head back, thinking. Or, thought Anni, pretending to think. 'I don't know. Something on BBC4. A documentary.'

'About what?'

'Byzantine art.'

'That something you're interested in?'

'Not particularly. It was on and I, I . . . can you tell me what this is about, please?'

'And what did you do after that?'

'Had a whisky. Went to bed. What I normally do.'

'And that was it for the night?'

He nodded. Anni didn't reply.

'Am I supposed to have done something? Does this involve Suzanne?'

The dark fire returned to his eyes when he mentioned her name. Dark. Nasty, Anni would have said.

'It does,' she said. 'Suzanne Perry was attacked last night.'

He recoiled, as if the news had hit him in a physical way.

'Attacked . . . where?'

'In her flat.'

'How?'

'Someone came in while she was sleeping, into her bedroom.'

'My God . . .' He looked again at the pen, thought of picking it up once more, then decided against it. 'Did he . . . what happened?' And then, before she could answer, almost as if he didn't want to hear the answer to his question, he said, 'Was she hurt?'

'We don't think so.'

Anthony Howe shook his head. 'Oh dear . . .' Then a realisation seemed to dawn on his face. He looked directly at Anni. 'You think I did it?'

She said nothing.

His anger rose. 'You think I did it? I . . . somehow . . . made my way into her flat and, and . . . you think that was me, that I could do that?'

Anni kept her voice professionally calm and even. 'We don't know, Mr Howe. There was no sign of forced entry.

Whoever it was must have been known to Suzanne. Probably had a key.'

Howe sat there, staring at the wall, saying nothing.

'And since you and Suzanne have, shall we say, a history, I thought I should pay you a visit.'

Still nothing.

'What did happen between you and Suzanne, Mr Howe?'

'Professor.'

'Professor.' So much for informality, she thought. 'What happened?'

He sighed. 'She destroyed my marriage.' His voice was small, fragile. 'I . . . We had an affair. That was that.' He looked at Anni. No trace of any anger in his eyes now. No trace of anything but sadness. 'That was that.'

'And the stalking? The phone calls?'

'It ended badly. Animosity. Accusations.'

'But was there any—'

'It ended badly. That's all I'm saying.'

Anni didn't press him. 'So,' she said instead, 'last night—'

'I was at home. All night.'

'No one to vouch for that?'

Bitterness entered his voice. 'I didn't know I would need anyone to.'

'Do you still have a key to Suzanne's flat?'

'I never had one in the first place.'

'But you're still in touch with her.'

'No.' Said very quickly.

'But you're—'

'I said no. She destroyed my marriage. Offered me her body if I gave her a first. Then, when it all went wrong, went to the police, to you lot, told them lie after lie about me. I'm lucky to still have a job here.' He leaned towards her once more, anger informing his features. 'So after all that, would I really stay in touch with her? Really?'

The mobile on his desk rang, stopping Anni from giving an answer.

'Excuse me.' He leaned forward, picked it up ready to answer. Checked the read-out. Stopped.

It kept ringing.

Anni put her pen down. 'Don't mind me.'

He kept staring at it, his eyes widening. His fingers began to shake.

Anni looked at the phone, back to Howe. 'I said, don't mind me.'

He kept staring, then, as if breaking from a trance, glanced at Anni, back to his phone. He hit the red button, silencing it.

'They can leave a message if it's important.' He pocketed the phone, turned back to her. 'And that's all I have to say. So if you'll excuse me, Detective, I have work to do.' He picked up a sheet of paper from his desk, pretended to look at it. His hands were still shaking.

Anni stood up, saw herself out.

She passed the student, waiting patiently outside the door, made her way down the corridor.

She had seen the read-out on the screen. The name.

Suzanne.

The blood was pounding in her ears, her wrists.

Anni left the building.

21

'**D**on't you ever do that again.'

Phil had parked the car at the station with the two reporters still in the back, gestured for Rose to join him at the other side of the car park.

She looked up at him, eyes still dancing with a defiant adrenalin rush. 'Why? They were out of order. It's a damned good job I stepped in.'

'Is it? Really?'

'I was within my rights on everything. You'll back me on it.'

'You were angry. At me, at the case, at not finding Julie Miller. You allowed that anger to cloud your professional judgement.'

'You backed me up.' Her voice was petulant but still defiant.

Phil leaned into her, face to face. 'I had no choice, did I? But don't you ever do that again. No mavericking, I told you. You pull something like that again and you're off this case.'

'You need me. I was in charge of the original investigation.'

'I don't need an officer who behaves like that.'

'Make a complaint against me, then.' There was an ugly smile twitching at the corners of her mouth.

Phil knew what that smile meant. Fenwick, his boss, was her protector. *Let's see who he believes*, she was thinking.

Phil stepped back. 'You can take them in, you can get them processed, you can handle the paperwork. Good luck.' He turned to walk away, stopped, turned back to her. 'This is your last chance with me. I mean it. And I don't care who you think's protecting your back.'

He watched the shock register on her face as she realised who he was talking about.

'Yeah,' he said, 'I know.'

And this time walked away.

Suzanne heard his phone switch to voicemail. She started speaking but stopped herself. She didn't know what to say. How to say it. Instead she ended the call.

She put the phone down on the table, sighed.

She would try again later.

The building was low-level with a brown sloping roof and nicotine-yellow brick walls. An anonymous piece of eighties architecture, this beige palace could have been anything from a prison to a hospital to a provincial budget motel. But it was none of those things. It was the main police station for the town.

Phil stood back and let Rose march their charges through the main door and up to the desk. She could deal with the Duty Sergeant and the processing. Good luck to her.

Phil crossed to the door at the side of the reception desk, punched in the code on the keypad. The lock clicked.

'Excuse me . . .'

Phil opened the door, didn't realise the voice was addressing him.

'Excuse me . . .'

Phil turned. A woman had stood up from the sofa, was standing directly in front of him. She looked tired, her eyes red-rimmed, her face creased into worry-heavy frown lines. No make-up and her clothes weren't good quality and they hadn't been selected with care. She looked like she had slept in them. Her hair was uncombed and he couldn't place her age. Possibly mid-forties but it could have been ten years either side of that.

Rose took the two journalists through the door without looking back. The pneumatic hinges pulled the door shut, leaving him behind. He had to talk to the woman now.

'Yes?'

She looked him up and down. 'You're a police detective, aren't you?'

The uniform on the desk had seen what was happening. 'Just a minute, please,' he said.

Phil held up a hand. 'It's OK, Darren.' He turned back to the woman. 'Detective Inspector Brennan. Major Incident Squad. What can I do for you?'

Her eyes held his, unblinking. Like sci-fi tractor beams. 'There's been a body found, hasn't there?'

Phil said nothing.

Her hand gripped his sleeve like a vulture on carrion. 'Hasn't there? A young woman. In her twenties. Hasn't there?'

'There . . .' No point in lying, he thought. 'Yes. We've found a body answering that description, yes.'

The woman's hand slipped from his arm. She gave a rough gasp, like she'd taken in more than she could swallow. She recovered quickly, her eyes locking on his once more. 'Is it . . . is it my daughter?'

'I don't know,' he said and she gasped again. 'Have you informed us that your daughter is missing?'

She gave a bitter laugh. 'Over a week ago.'

'What's her name?'

'Adele. Adele Harrison. I'm her mother, Paula.'

'Paula Harrison.'

'OK. What does she look like?'

''Bout my height, bit big, dark hair—'

'Dark?'

She nodded once more, eyes still on his, waiting for the next words out of his mouth.

'We think we have an identification for the body we've found, Ms Hamilton. I can't say too much about an ongoing investigation, I'm afraid. But if there are any changes we'll be in touch.'

The air seemed to sag out of her, her legs buckled. Phil knew the signs. Not dead but not safe. The tyranny of hope, Marina had called it.

Marina. He hadn't thought about her or the baby for hours. But he couldn't feel guilty now, while he was working. He would leave that luxury for later.

'So where's my Adele, then?'

'I . . . don't know. It's not my case, I'm afraid.'

'That other girl, the one who's on the news all the time, I bet you're working on her case, aren't you?'

Phil couldn't answer.

'I bet she's gettin' all the attention. An' my Adele gets nothin'. No one'll take any responsibility. My daughter just disappears, vanishes, and there's nothin' any of you can do—'

Her voice was tightroping on hysteria. When she spoke Phil saw the bite marks on her lips, anxiety kisses. She was attracting an audience in the reception area. Phil put his hands on her shoulders, looked into her eyes. 'Please don't shout. I don't know anything about your daughter's case. But if you give me the details I'll get someone to look into it.'

'Get someone. Yeah, right.'

Phil sighed. 'Who's your FLO?'

'What?'

'Family Liaison Officer. You must have been assigned one.'

'Some kid. Cheryl Bland. Some kid.'

Busy woman, thought Phil. 'Couldn't you speak to her?'

'Worse than useless. Looks about twelve.'

'Right. Who's the CIO, the Chief Investigating Officer?'

'Farrell. Detective Sergeant. But I never get to talk to him. They fob me off with this Cheryl Bland.'

'OK. I'll see what I can do. Have a word with DS Farrell, if he's here. See if there's any news.'

She gave a bitter laugh. Twisted the corners of her mouth into a cruel parody of a smile. 'No you won't. You'll get behind that door and you'll forget all about me. About Adele. You might speak to him and say I'm here. Then you'll laugh about the stupid woman sittin' there. And walk away and forget me.'

'No I won't.'

'Yes you will. You'll just forget. But I'll still be here. I'll still be waitin'.'

'Look, Paula.' He held her gaze again, returning her stare. 'I appreciate you must be going through a considerable amount of pain. But I'm sure DS Farrell will be doing everything he can. And I will talk to him.'

Her gaze wavered slightly, his words connecting with her.

'If he's in the building I'll talk to him and ask him to come down to talk to you. Give you an update.'

'Thank you.'

'OK?'

She nodded. Bowed her head quickly as her eyes became glassy and moist. 'Thank you.'

'No problem.'

Phil looked at the woman standing before him. Her anger now dissipated by his words, she seemed to have shrunk. He put his hands on her forearms, gave her a reassuring squeeze.

'I'll go find him now.'

She nodded, not raising her head.

Phil punched the numbers in, let the hydraulic door swallow him up.

22

The Creeper was irritated. And when he got irritated he became unhappy. And when he became unhappy he became angry.

And that wasn't good. For any one.

Rani was back home. Which was good. He was looking forward to spending some quality time with her. Just the pair of them. The way it should be. But that wouldn't be happening. Because she'd brought her friend with her. Without asking.

This was *their* place. Didn't she understand that? If she wanted to bring people back she should ask him first.

Or accept the consequences.

But no, there she sat, in the living room, the blonde one who thought she was really pretty, drinking, not going anywhere in a hurry. In fact, she had brought a bag with her. Looked like she was going to stay.

The Creeper's irritation tripped over into anger. That wasn't right. Not right at all.

He had only just found her again. After all this time. There was so much they had to say to each other, so much catching up to do. So much time to spend together, just the pair of them.

That coiled snake began to writhe and twist inside him once more. Zoe shouldn't be there. It should be Rani and him. Only him. They didn't need her. They didn't need anyone.

He watched, shaking, as Zoe went into the kitchen, began to prepare food for her and Rani.

The snake slithered, spat. That's where he had left his present. And now this whore was going to find it. Not Rani.

Poison spread through him. His hands flexed and unflexed. Saliva foamed and frothed round his mouth, as he breathed through clenched teeth.

Not for her . . . not for her . . .

But there was nothing he could do, just watch.

Zoe went into Suzanne's kitchen, filled the kettle. Tea. That was what was needed now. Not coffee, tea. It was warming, soothing. It destressed you, brought back happy associations from when you were younger, made you feel like you were curled in a chair, safe and warm. And if you had chocolate HobNobs to go with it, so much the better.

Zoe took the biscuits from the canvas carrier she had brought with her. When she had gone home to grab some clothes, she had popped into Sainsbury's on the way, put a few essentials together, the makings of a meal for the pair of them, something for them to share in the hope it would take Suzanne's mind off what had happened.

She arrayed the food on the counter. Looked at the biscuits and felt immediately hungry. She wanted to open the packet, start in on them right now. But she wouldn't. She would take them in to Suzanne, open them in front of her and allow herself only one. Or perhaps even a half. And make sure Suzanne took them and put them away. Somewhere Zoe couldn't find them.

Her stomach felt like a ravenous, cavernous space. But then it always did.

She loved food. Loved the sheer sensuality of eating, the feel of it in her mouth, the smells, the tastes, the textures. The way it slipped down her throat and into her stomach. The act of putting something inside her body, satisfying herself, her hungers and cravings, feeling it gradually fill her out. Wonderful. Nothing to touch it in the world. For Zoe, food was her sex.

But like so many of Zoe's early sexual encounters, she ended up feeling bad about it afterwards. Guilt-ridden, hating herself and what her hungers had led her to do.

And that's when her problems had started.

She'd never been anorexic, never been one to starve herself. That was something, she supposed. But sticking her fingers down her throat to bring it all back up again . . . to let her body feel cleansed, guilt-free and empty . . . that made perfect sense to her.

University for her had been about secrets and lies and double lives. The happy, extrovert – even exhibitionist at times – Zoe who was never short on friends or boyfriends. And the self-loathing, toilet bowl-hugging wreck that she really saw herself as.

Thank God she wasn't like that any more. Thank God for her friends – or rather Suzanne. She had been there for her, helped her out, shown strength when Zoe didn't have any of her own. She had picked her up, made her feel worthwhile, turned her life around. Been there for her when she needed her.

And thank God for therapy. It had been Suzanne's idea and she couldn't thank her enough for it. She hadn't wanted to go at first but had to admit it was the best thing she had ever done. It gave her a new life, new confidence.

And a new boyfriend. Not as good-looking as the others but he loved her. She had felt he was different and she was right. She thought she could trust him with the truth so she told him all about her trouble. It was the best thing she had ever done. He said he didn't care, would love her whatever size she was. And that filled her with something else, so rich and full and nourishing that her hungry heart no longer needed to binge any more.

But those HobNobs still looked good, though.

The kettle boiled and Zoe went about making tea in two of Suzanne's fanciest mugs. A little thing, but hopefully it might help to cheer her up.

She opened the fridge door, looking for milk.

And stopped dead, her heart skipping a beat.

'Suzanne . . .' Her voice was small, wavering. Her heart skipped, a shiver of real dread passed through her. 'I think . . . can you come here . . .'

Bitch.

Fucking Bitch. Why did she have to find it first? It wasn't for her. It was for Rani. It was all for Rani. The blonde bitch was unworthy of it. Like she was unworthy of everything to do with Rani.

The snake was writhing and hissing inside him, coiling and uncoiling, baring its fangs, spitting poison. The voice had returned. *Whores . . . the whole fucking lot of them . . . whores . . . that's all they're good for . . . don't trust them . . . any of them . . .*

He hated the blonde bitch. Wanted her gone. She'd come between them, she had no future.

Rani entered the kitchen. The snake calmed itself.

He watched.

Listened.

Hung on her every word, her every action and gesture.

Spotting the secret ones she made just for him.

Breathing fast. Excited, because even if the blonde bitch was there, Rani was going to see his present.

His valentine.

*

'Oh my God . . .'

'Is . . . is that what . . . what I think it is . . .?'

Suzanne had taken one look inside the fridge and stumbled backwards. Her legs were shaking, about to collapse beneath her, her heart hammering, thudding against her ribcage. Zoe was still looking, fascinated yet repelled.

'Oh God . . .' Suzanne's eyes were screwed tight shut, willing it all to be a dream, herself to be somewhere else, somewhere safe.

Zoe reached out a hand. Suzanne opened her eyes.

'Don't touch . . .'

Zoe turned, stared eyes wide at her friend.

'Please, don't . . . don't touch . . .'

'Leave it for the police, you mean?'

'Just, just leave it. Leave it . . .' Suzanne wanted just to slump down on to a kitchen chair, her head in her hands. Give in. Not hold back any longer. Let those huge, great, wracking sobs out of her body. And tell him: you win. Whoever you are, you win.

But she didn't.

Instead she stood there, felt that heat rise once more, that anger. Clenched her fists. 'I'm not giving in, you bastard. You hear me? I'm not . . .'

'Suzanne?' Zoe crossed to her, put her arms round her.

'He's been here again, Zoe, here . . .'

'Or the police missed it. Bloody useless.'

Zoe looked at the open fridge door. On the top shelf was a pair of her knickers. With something unmistakeable on them.

Semen.

'Oh God . . . what a fucking nightmare . . .'

Zoe held her, said nothing. There was nothing she could find to say.

*

The Creeper smiled. Watched. Rani was sitting down, over-come with emotion. Weeping with joy at his present.

'Oh, Rani . . .'

He felt himself hardening as he stared at her.

Touching himself.

Smiling.

Blonde bitch or not, it couldn't have gone any better.

'What d'you want to do?'

'I want to find him.' Suzanne didn't recognise her own voice. 'I want to find him, Zoe, and I want to take the biggest knife I can find and stick it in him. Right in him. And watch him suffer. Like he's made me suffer. And watch him die. That's what I want to do, Zoe.'

Zoe was sitting next to her. Her arm tightened round her. 'I know you do. I know. What about the police? D'you want me to phone them? D'you want to go somewhere else?' No reply. Suzanne stared at the wall. 'Just tell me and we can do it.'

She spoke eventually. 'I want . . .'

Zoe waited.

'I want . . .' She sighed. 'I want my life back . . .'

Zoe kept holding her.

Suzanne started sobbing. She didn't know if they were tears of anger or pain or pity or what.

She just sobbed her heart out.

The Creeper kept watching.

Smiling.

Waiting.

23

'She still down there, then? Heard she was in, poor cow. Don't know what I can do, though. Part from slap an ASBO on her, restraining order, or something.' He snorted. 'Probably not the first.'

Detective Sergeant John Farrell leaned back in his chair, stretched out his legs, hands behind his head. He was a small man, round and bald. His suit looked like he had been wrestled into it, collar open, tie askew. Tired shoes on his feet. His words contained the usual amount of copper's front and bluster, but his eyes showed a genuine care. Or at least Phil hoped that was what he saw there.

'She says you're not updating her on the investigation.'

Farrell looked at Phil, eyes narrowed. 'FLO not good enough for her?'

Phil held up his hands. 'I'm only repeating what she said. She's concerned. Wants to know what's happening.'

Farrell sighed. 'Nothing. That's what. Her daughter ran off a couple of weeks ago, we've been trying to find her. Exhausted all the avenues, boyfriends, ex-boyfriends, work colleagues, family, the lot.' He reeled off his achievements –

or lack of them – on his fingers. 'Tried all the usual stuff, TV, the papers, internet, radio, National Missing Persons Helpline. Nada. Blank.'

'No sign of abduction? Nothing like that?'

'If it was it must have been Derren bloody Brown.'

'Right.'

'But between you an' me . . .' Farrell removed his hands from behind his head, leaned forward. 'Typical mispers case, I reckon. Done a bunk. She's got previous.'

'For what?'

'Runnin' away. Works as a barmaid, pub in New Town. Part-time. Got history of bein' a bit loose, if you catch my drift.'

Phil frowned. 'You mean, what? She's a prostitute?'

Farrell shrugged. 'Part-time, like I said. Used to go off with blokes, not come back for days. Mother says she's changed, havin' a kid an' that, but . . . dunno. Leopards an' spots, you know.'

'So what you're saying is,' said Phil, 'she's not a priority.'

Another shrug. 'You know what it's like. When they don't want to be found they don't want to be found. They'll come home when they want to.' He sat back once more, replacing his hands behind his head. 'When the bloke's money runs out.'

Phil was more than a little annoyed at his colleague's attitude but he had to admit he did know what that was like. He'd been on enough cases that didn't come to a conclusion but just petered out, faded away. But that still didn't excuse his attitude.

'And you don't think there's any connection between Adele Harrison going missing and the body we found this morning by the Hythe?'

Farrell sat forward again. 'It's not her, is it?'

'We think it might be Julie Miller, the girl who disappeared last week.'

Farrell sat back again, satisfied. 'There you go, then. Different case entirely.'

'You don't think there's a connection? Two young women disappear within days of each other?'

'What, that posh bird that's all over the news and my case? Doubt it.'

Phil sighed. 'Her mother's downstairs. Go and see her.'

Farrell looked to Phil as if he was about to say something but changed his mind. Instead he said, 'You've just had a kid, haven't you?'

Phil nodded. 'Daughter.'

Farrell nodded as if that explained everything. 'Right.' He unclasped his hands from behind his head. 'All right, then. I'll go down and see her. Tell her again her part-time prossie daughter's off with some bloke an' that she'll come home when he gets bored of her.' He looked at Phil, saw the look he was giving. 'In the nicest possible terms, of course.'

'Thank you.'

'Welcome.' Farrell didn't move. 'Then maybe she'll go home, give us all a bit of peace.'

Phil walked away from him, glad Farrell wasn't on his team.

And peace was the last thing he wished on him.

Phil tried to use the time spent walking down the corridor productively. He called Nick Lines to see if there was any news from the autopsy. Nothing new as yet, was the reply. Adrian would present the full findings in the morning. No DNA results yet, so no positive match could be made. But he was fairly sure it was Julie Miller. Unless there was another missing girl he didn't know about. Phil said nothing and rang off. Thinking.

His mobile went before he could put it in his pocket.

'Boss? Mickey.'

Phil could tell by the tone of his DS's voice that it was important. 'What you got?'

'Sighting of a van.' There was the sound of scrabbling on the line. Mickey getting his notepad ready. 'Early this morning. Black, small. Not a Transit, he said, something with back doors. Came down to the quay at about five this morning.'

'Who told you this?'

'Guy in the food van. Gets down there early.'

Excitement rose within Phil's chest. 'Number plate?'

'Nah, sorry. He didn't see. Didn't think it would be important. Says he only remembered when he saw us all down there.'

'What made him remember?'

'The speed it was doing. Came off the quay like Jensen Button, he said.'

'Driver's description?'

'Two of them, he thinks. That's all he can remember. Came out, turned left. Sped off.'

'Thanks, Mickey. The first solid lead. We've got something to go on.'

He broke the connection, after telling Mickey there wasn't much more he could do for the day but to start looking into it first thing in the morning.

Thought of Marina. Of Josephina. Felt something tugging at him from deep inside.

He wanted to go home. *Needed to go home*.

But there was business to attend to first.

24

Marina signed, sat down in the armchair, took a sip from the Californian Shiraz at her side, sighed, closed her eyes.

Josephina had gone down peacefully. Her regular feed, already snuggled up in her Babygro, eyes fluttering as she drank. Now she was asleep in her cot at the side of their bed, lying on her back, her eyes closed, her face peaceful, fingers curled in like tiny woodlice.

Marina had set up the baby intercom, crept downstairs, sank into an armchair with a book and a large glass of wine. Tried to tune everything out, relax while Midlake played on low volume in the background, singing about heading home.

Home.

The new house she had bought with Phil. It was part of a new waterfront development in the west side of Wivenhoe, not far from where she used to live. Wivenhoe was an old fishing village full of old, character-filled houses, independent shops, good pubs and interesting people. The university where Marina had worked was just down the road and consequently the town had a distinctly liberal, corduroy feel to the place. It was comfortable, homely, vaguely bohemian and a little self-consciously arty. Martina used to feel very at home there.

But not any more.

The new house was at the opposite side to the cottage she used to live in. Designed to fit in and complement the ambience of the old waterfront, the development consisted of tall, red-brick houses in a small development with an aged, nautical feel, arranged round a lock gate that flowed out to the River Colne. It was a compromise. Phil, she knew, might not have felt comfortable in such an old house, but there was no way Marina could stay where she had been living.

Her first instinct had been to move as far away as possible, not be anywhere that would remind her of what had happened in her old house; the nightmares were getting less frequent, but were still bad enough. Phil, knowing her state of mind and understanding entirely, had left the decision up to her and they had looked at property all over Colchester. But when it came to it, she couldn't move. It was like something was still holding her there, drawing her back. So she'd relented. And they'd bought the new house.

And now she wasn't so sure.

Another mouthful of wine. She looked round. The room, like the rest of the house, wasn't fully hers yet, or Phil's. They had put out what they needed – furniture, TV, hi-fi – but the bookshelves were still empty, the walls still bare and there were boxes everywhere. It wasn't a home. Not yet. But hopefully it would be.

Hopefully.

She checked her watch, wondered what time Phil would be back. She had eaten and was planning on an early night since she knew she'd be up with Josephina at some point. She might not get to see him. She didn't know if that was a good or bad thing.

Phil was her soulmate. She knew that. When she and him

met, she had never felt a connection like it. They understood each other perfectly, seeing the damage and sense of loss in each of them reflected in the other, knowing that apart they would be incomplete individuals but together they would make a complete whole.

His childhood spent in brutal institutions and uncaring foster homes mirrored hers spent with a violent, abusive father, an emotionally absent mother and brothers she never wanted to see again. Phil's adoptive parents had saved him. Marina's mind had saved her. University, leading to a job as a practising psychologist, meant she never had to go home again.

Marina hated using pop psychology greetings card analogies but in this case it was true. Phil completed her. And she him.

If only it was that simple. If only it was just the pair of them.

It wasn't even Josephina. They were both thrilled about their daughter. Thrilled and terrified. She should have been a proud, public acknowledgement of their love for one another, their sense of commitment to each other, their contentment.

She should have been. And if it was just the three of them, even that would be fine.

But . . .

She picked the book up from the arm of the chair, tried to tune everything out of her head, just get into it, slip away. James M. Cain's *Double Indemnity*. She had found it in one of the boxes, not picked it up since she'd studied it as part of her MA at university and had now decided to reread it.

The story of a couple who recognise something damaged and kindred in each other and fall madly, passionately, in love. The only obstacle is the woman's husband so they murder him in order to be together. But once they do that they find their guilt has bound them together in a fearful, destructive state and killed any future happiness between them. At least that was the way Marina was reading it.

She put the book down, tears beginning to form in the corners of her eyes.

Another mouthful of wine. Then another.

Another look round the room in the house that wasn't hers, the home that wouldn't be.

'Oh God . . .'

The words of the nurse that morning came back to her, about how things couldn't continue as they were, how she had to make a decision.

Midlake playing, Tim Smith singing that there was no one else so kind, no one else to find and that it was hard for him, but he was trying.

Marina sighed, took another mouthful of wine.

Not knowing how much more of this she could bear, forcing herself to come to a decision.

Not noticing the tears rolling down her cheeks.

25

The main MIS office was busy, even though it was time for most people to leave for the day. Milhouse was working at his computer terminal, looking for clues in the virtual world. It wasn't his real name but no one used that. His resemblance to the *Simpsons* character was uncanny, even down to his level of social skills, so it had stuck. When he was referred to officially as DC Pecknold, Phil often had to take a few seconds to realise who was being addressed.

Rose Martin had been given a desk and a computer and now sat before it, writing up reports and looking thoroughly, angrily, unhappy. She saw Phil enter, looked immediately back to her work.

And then Anni entered. There was no way the two of them could avoid each other as he was standing right beside the door and she literally bumped into him.

'Hi,' he said.

'Boss,' she said, and tried to dodge round him.

But Phil wasn't about to let her go so quickly. 'Haven't seen you for a while, what you working on?'

Anni shrugged. 'Stalking case. Maybe breaking and entering.'

Phil frowned. 'That's not MIS. That's just bog-standard CID, isn't it?'

Anni's turn to shrug now. 'It came in, there was no one else to take it.'

Silence fell between them. Like a heavy wool blanket, uncomfortable and irritating.

Phil's voice dropped. He led her to one side. 'Look, I know you're still pissed off that you put in for promotion and didn't get it. Especially after the last big case we did.'

Anni said nothing.

'I put your name forward. I wanted you.'

She looked at him as if about to argue.

'I know you think I didn't—'

'I was *told* you didn't.' Her eyes were angry dots.

'And I know who told you.' Phil glanced over towards Fenwick's office. The DCI was behind his desk, on the phone. Phil noticed that, by a strange coincidence, Rose was also on the phone, her hand over the receiver.

Anni looked at Fenwick's office, looked back at him. Her eyes dropped. 'Why would he lie, then? Why would he say that?'

Phil gave a small smile. 'You're asking that? Of Fenwick? Because he's a twat, that's why.'

Anni smiled too. She nodded.

'Now, d'you think you can put your case to bed and come and join me?' Another quick glance at Rose Martin, who, putting the phone down, got up from her desk and came towards them. 'I need your help. Soon as.'

'I just have one more person to see, an old boyfriend, then I'm done. For now.'

'Good.'

'I've done the reports and got the two journalists ready for processing.' Rose Martin came to halt before the pair of them, started talking. 'They're in an interview room waiting to be spoken to.'

Phil was annoyed at being interrupted but didn't think confrontation would be the best way to go. 'Good work, DS Martin. Now let them go.'

Her face flushed red. 'What?'

'Insufficient evidence, whatever you want to call it. We've kept them away from the Miller home for a while, given them a scare. Let them go.'

Her voice was rising. 'After all I've done—'

Phil squared up to her. 'You made the play. You carry it through. Maybe you'll think twice next time, before you go all Dirty Harry on me.'

Rose clamped her mouth shut, swallowing whatever it was she had been about to say. She took a deep breath. Another. Phil waited.

'So that's that, is it? I've learnt my lesson and I'm back on active duty, right?' Her voice was heavy with sarcasm.

Phil didn't rise to it, kept his voice calm and level. 'Just about.' Then he glanced at Anni, back to Rose. A smile played on his lips. 'One more thing,' he said. 'DC Hepburn here, I don't know if you've met, is coming to join us but needs a bit of help in wrapping up her case. If you wouldn't mind . . .'

Phil led Anni and Rose over to Anni's desk. Both women looked surprised. 'Anni'll give you the details. Just one last thing before home time and then the slate's clean and tomorrow is another day. OK?'

He left them to it, crossing the floor to Fenwick's office.

Unable to keep the smile off his face.

117

26

Phil knocked on the door, entered. Fenwick looked like he was expecting him. He sat down before the desk. Fenwick leaned back on the other side, scrutinising Phil. He was sure it was meant to be intimidating but one thought went through Phil's head:

David Brent.

'So how's it coming, then? The Julie Miller murder inquiry?'

'We're making progress. But we don't know for a fact that it's Julie Miller yet. Let's not call it that until we know for certain.'

Fenwick sat back, a smile playing at the corners of his mouth. 'Well, no one else has gone missing recently from Colchester, have they?'

'Well . . .' Phil told him about Adele Harrison. Watched the expression on his face change, the smile disappear. Concern – or something like it – crept into his eyes.

'Oh. Shit.'

'Indeed. Does that change things?'

'John Farrell doesn't think so.'

'John Farrell's an arsehole.' Fenwick stared at him. 'Sir.'

Fenwick seemed happy with that.

'I just think we should be aware. If Adele Harrison's body turns up and we haven't done all we could have done . . .' Phil left the threat hanging in the air. Fenwick stared at him, deciding whether Phil was trying to start a fight.

There was animosity between himself and his superior. Phil thought Fenwick insincere, two-faced. Paying lip service to progressive ideas, hiding his reactionary soul in management-speak so he could advance up the political police ladder. Mostly they managed to work together but occasionally there was conflict. Sometimes huge.

'Just covering ourselves, sir,' said Phil, using a phrase Fenwick would understand.

Fenwick nodded. 'Covering. Yes. In case it does, you know . . .' He made what Phil assumed was a thoughtful face. 'Perhaps we should call in a profiler.'

'Marina's on maternity leave.'

'Of course. Congratulations, by the way.'

Was there relief in Fenwick's features? Phil had met Marina when she had been brought in to work a case with him as a profiler. Fenwick had shouted her down, humiliated her, derided her input. Then gone crawling to her afterwards when he realised that her help had been invaluable in bringing the case to a successful conclusion.

Fenwick then frowned, spoke as if arguing with himself. 'But the expense . . . Budgets are already being cut, overtime slashed . . . Plus we don't know for certain that this is a serial. Not yet.'

Phil said nothing, waited to see how Fenwick's dialogue with himself played out.

He sighed, nodded. 'I'll make some calls,' he said. 'See what we can get. Still got contacts at the university. The hospital. And a lot of incoming officers are of the new breed, Phil. Trained in behavioural science and profiling. Much better able to make informed judgements. Might not be as expensive as we think, eh?'

'Well, if you're getting one we need them to start as soon as possible. And be good.' Fenwick was still looking at him. 'And cheap, of course. Sir.'

Fenwick narrowed his eyes, wary. Was Phil being cheeky again?

'Covering ourselves, sir, remember?'

Fenwick, sensing no threat this time, agreed. He looked at his watch. 'Well, time to be off. Early start tomorrow, briefing eight thirty. No overtime for now, but let's see if the powers that be upgrade this case.'

They will if there's another murder, thought Phil, but again didn't voice it.

'Oh, by the way,' said Fenwick, a slight glint in his eye, 'what d'you think of your new team, Phil? Working out all right?'

Phil again kept his face blank. 'OK so far. We'll see.'

'DS Martin comes highly recommended.'

'You'd know more about that than me, sir.'

Fenwick reddened immediately, his mouth opened, about to say something, but he was too late.

Phil had already left the office.

27

Rose's temper was flaming.

It was bad enough that Phil Brennan was punishing her by sending her out when everyone else was going home, but spending over a quarter of an hour driving up and down Greenstead Road trying to find a parking space just made it worse.

If it wasn't permit parking it was double yellow lines. She could have just parked anywhere, flashed her warrant card and claimed official police business if hassled. Fine in theory, but it still didn't make a space appear.

She eventually found one at the far end from where she wanted to be. Took a quick look at the notes, familiarised herself with the case, and, still fuming, set off to walk.

The houses on Greenstead Road were small. Red-brick terraces with minuscule gardens slabbed over for car parking. The only remaining greenery weeds poking between the cracks. From the lack of both upkeep and pride in the exteriors, most of the houses looked rented. Those that weren't seemed to belong to people who were either starting out on the property ladder or whose progression had stalled.

Rose walked along to the far end of the road, the second to

last house before a Chinese takeaway and a patch of waste ground. The day still held residual warmth as she pulled her top away from her chest, checked the address. The brickwork had been plastered over and painted a pale herb green, now darkened from road dirt. The windows were white casement, paint peeling, panes dirty. The front door, dark-stained with flaking varnish, led directly on to the pavement.

She raised her hand to knock but stopped as a sound ripped through the air. Like a car or burglar alarm turned up to eleven. The level crossing at the side of the road. The houses backed on to the main line to London. Lovely, thought Rose. And wished she wasn't there.

Rose Martin was ambitious. She had made no secret of it. Married for two years to a solicitor and with a comfortable-sized Edwardian house in the Old Heath area of town, they had a good life. No kids – she was adamant – or at least not until her career had gone as far as she felt it could.

Her husband, Tim, was a good man. Dependable, honest, stoical. Taciturn, even. All manly traits she admired. And, yes, she loved him, sure. But that hadn't stopped her having an affair with Ben Fenwick.

It had started, the way these things often do, with a few drinks after work. All the gang together, then the pair of them had got talking, found a spark, started to see each other separately. Before too long they were both telling their spouses they had to work late and booking hotel rooms where they could indulge in levels of lust that Rose found surprisingly animalistic but very cathartic.

The affair wasn't anything she had thought about greatly. Just a mutual attraction acted upon. Easily compartmentalised and coped with. Ben had something that Tim hadn't, provided her with something Tim couldn't. She couldn't specifically say what it was but it was fun finding out. But nothing serious, at least not as far as she was concerned. She didn't want to leave Tim and she didn't want Ben to leave his wife and kids. Just a bit of fun. Filthy, flirty, secret fun. Well, possibly career-related. Ben was a DCI, two steps above her. And it was always handy to have someone higher up to be able to put in a good word for her, to help with advancement. She certainly wouldn't have dreamed of having an affair with anyone ranked lower than her.

But now Phil Brennan knew about it. A higher ranking officer who seemed to be developing a grudge against her. Not good. He had leverage against her now and that could make him a threat. An affair like this could halt her progress if it was discovered. And she didn't want that. She would have to tread carefully. Do something about him, even get something on him if she could. Or get Ben to.

But that was for tomorrow. She cleared all that from her mind, concentrated on the job in hand. Waited for the noise of the level crossing and the train passing to subsist, then knocked on the door.

No reply. She knocked again.

Eventually she heard someone making their way to the door. It opened. A man stood there, tall, dark, greasy, messed-up hair, young. He wore a T-shirt with a logo on that Rose didn't recognise or understand, jeans, glasses. His eyes behind the glasses were red-rimmed, like he had been staring at a screen for too long. He blinked at her. Said nothing. Like voice production involved a different part of the brain to the one he'd been using.

'Mark Turner?'

He nodded.

She held up her warrant card. 'Detective Sergeant Martin. Can I come in?'

Mark Turner blinked again. Eyes narrowing, focusing, as if understanding that something was catching up with him. 'What?'

She tried a smile, not wanting him to catch any trace of her earlier temper or irritation, all professional now. 'Just need to talk to you about something. Might be better to do it inside.' She gestured behind him. 'Shall we?'

Mark Turner blinked again, stood out of the way, allowing her entry.

She went in.

The curtains were closed, the house in near darkness. It felt odd, a complete contrast to the early evening sunshine outside. Dust motes danced and jumped, caught in the beams of light that crept in through the chinks. She made the outlines of furniture, square and heavy looking. Covered with sheets or throws. The room was cold. It felt remote, cut off from the world, Dickensian almost. Rose half expected to find Miss Haversham lurking in some corner.

'Sorry,' said Mark Turner, 'I was ... working upstairs. I ... My Ph.D.' He looked round as if seeing the room through her eyes. Then turned back to her, remembering who she was. 'Why are you here, please?'

'Is there somewhere we could sit?'

Mark Turner found the light switch. An old three-bulb chandelier lit up the room. Rose saw that the house was small, living room and dining room all in one. Stairs in the centre. A kitchen at the back of the house. A brick chimney breast with a gas fire in front of it. Shelves on both sides, crammed with books. A TV and DVD player underneath the window. CD system beside it. Throws covered the furniture. It looked functional, nothing more. A student or academic house. Except for one thing. Halfway down the room was a tree. The trunk against the wall, the branches spreading out along the ceiling, separating the one room into two areas.

'Nice feature,' said Rose. 'Still alive?'

Mark Turner looked at it, frowned, as if it was the first time he had noticed it. 'What? Oh. Here before me. Dead. Think it's just for ornamentation.'

'Right.' She sat down in a covered armchair. Took out her notepad and pen.

He sat also, on the sofa. 'So . . . what's happened?'

'You used to be involved with . . .' She checked the notebook. 'Suzanne Perry.'

A wariness came into his eyes, as if whatever answer he gave would lead him into a trap. 'Yes . . .'

'You and her were an item?'

'Yes . . . why?'

A quick check of the notes again. Concentrate. Into the groove, get the answers quickly, then off home. 'She was attacked at home last night.'

He reeled backwards as if a sudden gust had taken him by surprise. 'What? She . . .'

'Was attacked.' She dropped her voice, calm and authoritative. 'So we're talking to anyone who knew her and who may have a key to her flat.'

'Well, I . . .' Mark Turner's eyes widened. 'You think I . . . you mean, I . . .'

Three 'I's in one breath, thought Rose. He might look innocuous enough, but that was a sure sign he had an ego on him. 'When you and her split up, was it harmonious?'

He shrugged. 'Is any break-up easy?'

'You didn't want anything more to do with her.'

His voice raised slightly. 'Right. No. I didn't. Had enough of her.'

'But you kept her key.'

His eyes widened. 'What?'

'Her key. To her flat. You kept it.'

Mark Turner said nothing.

'Any reason?'

'I . . .' His eyes darted all round the room as if looking for something or someone to answer for him. Eventually, finding nothing, he answered for himself. 'I don't know.'

'Didn't leave any of your stuff there to pick up later?'

He shook his head.

'You still in touch with Suzanne?'

125

'No.'

Rose looked at her notepad, read back something she had just written. 'You'd had enough of her.' She looked up at Turner. He was perched on the edge of the sofa, looking like he wanted to run. 'What do you mean by that?'

He ran his hand through his greasy, unkempt hair, searching for inspiration, playing for time. 'I'd just . . .' He sighed, his whole body deflating. 'She wasn't an easy person to get on with.'

'Why not?'

'She . . .' He shook his head. 'I couldn't trust her.'

Rose leaned forward, interested now. 'You mean with other men?'

'Not . . . really. Just . . . well, she'd tell me things, right? Little things. Plays or films she'd seen, who she'd been there with. Or people she'd met. And then we'd all be out together, the rest of the people from her course, and they wouldn't know anything about it.'

Rose said nothing, made notes, encouraged him to continue.

'Then we'd go and meet people for a drink and beforehand she would tell me about things that I was supposed to have done. You know, if anyone asked me.'

'Why did she do that, d'you think?'

He shrugged. 'Dunno. Wanted to seem more popular? She didn't think she was well liked, I don't think. Felt she had to do something to attract attention to herself. Make herself stand out.'

Rose said nothing, just took notes.

He sighed. As he did so, there came the creak of floorboards from upstairs. He glanced up quickly, Rose's eyes following him.

'Someone else here?' she said.

'No,' he said quickly, his eyes darting down to the right.

He's lying, thought Rose.

28

Phil opened the door quietly, slowly, like he would at a crime scene when he didn't want to disturb anything.

The house was in darkness apart from one table light, its crackled, mirrored mosaic base casting out a spider-web glow into the room. An empty wine glass and bottle next to it on the table, a paperback book left face down and open, like a bird refusing, or unable, to fly.

Marina must have been sitting there. Ever the detective, he thought, then castigated himself for the thought. Loosen up. You're at home now.

He listened. No sound. Josephina would be sleeping. He put his car keys on the table, went into the kitchen, took a bottle of beer from the fridge, opened it, returned to the living room and sat down in the seat Marina had recently occupied. Took a long drink, sighed, closed his eyes and put his head back, tried to work the tension of the day out of his body.

Phil opened his eyes, looked round. So unlike his old, comfortable house, things here were unfamiliar and out of place. Still trying to think of the new house as home, of

Marina and Josephina as family. Knowing they were both things he would have to work at.

He got up, checked the CD in the hi-fi. Midlake. Thought of putting it on himself but didn't want to wake his partner and daughter. So he took another mouthful of beer, sat back.

He felt restless, agitated. Tried to tell himself it was because of the case. But he knew it wasn't. Knew there were other reasons.

Knew that wherever he went in this house there were invisible walls that he couldn't see, couldn't go round, couldn't climb over.

It was an early summer's evening, still light, still sunny. A beautiful, tranquil view just outside his front door, a promenade by the river. The three of them could have gone for a walk, put Josephina in her buggy, set off along the front. Maybe stopped for a drink at the Rose and Crown, sat out on the front and watched the boats bob in the low tide, the sun go down.

Enjoying life. Enjoying one another in each other's lives. Living.

Irritation rose with him. Strong irritation. That was what he saw himself doing when he moved to Wivenhoe. That's what he should have been doing. With Marina and Josephina. Relaxing, having fun. Enjoying each other's company. As a family.

Instead Marina was living an almost separate life from him, like she was in a hermetically sealed glass box. He could see her and even hear her but not reach her, touch her. It wouldn't have mattered so much if it had been someone else doing it. Someone who didn't mean as much to him as she did. Didn't mean everything to him. But it was her. She was excluding him from something – from her life – and it hurt. Badly.

He drained the bottle of beer, went into the kitchen to get another one. Stopped himself. No, he thought. This isn't the answer.

Instead he turned, made his way upstairs. Slowly, so as not to wake them.

Marina had done the same thing the night before. Been asleep when he came in. Or claimed to be asleep. He was sure she was faking, lying as still as possible until he put the light out, fell asleep himself.

He wished he knew why.

He opened the bedroom door. Again, slowly, carefully. Looked in, expecting to see Josephina, with her tiny, perfect face, lying in her cot, Marina next to her.

But saw nothing.

He opened the door all the way, not bothering about making a noise now.

The cot was empty, as was the bed.

He checked the other rooms, called for her. No reply.

Downstairs, in all the rooms. No reply.

She must have taken Josephina for a walk, he thought, an angry envy working its way into his brain. Taking her for the kind of walk he wanted them to take as a family.

He checked for the baby buggy. Gone.

Then back into the living room, looking round again. And he saw the book on the table, the paperback Marina had been reading. Noticed there was something sticking out from underneath it. He crossed the room, picked the book up. Underneath was a folded piece of paper with his name written on it. He unfolded it, saw the first word.

Sorry . . .

Read the rest.

And sank into the chair.

'Oh no . . . oh God, no . . .'

They were gone. Marina, Josephina. His family.

Gone.

129

29

'S ure?' Rose Martin looked carefully at Mark Turner. 'Sure there's no one here?'

He shrugged. 'My girlfriend. New girlfriend. Having a . . . a lie in.' His voice trailed away.

Rose stifled a smile. 'Right,' she said. 'So, back to Suzanne. You were together for . . .' She checked Anni's notes.

'Two years.'

'Happy?'

He shrugged. 'Yeah. Mostly. You know. Ups and downs.'

'D'you miss her?'

He didn't answer straight away. Instead, he glanced towards the stairs. 'It . . . had run its course.'

Rose nodded. As he spoke, Mark Turner sat back, settled into the chair. He seemed to relax, become less bookish, more socialised. Growing in confidence as he dealt with questions he knew the answers to. Everything seemed fine, she thought. Couple more questions then she could go home. She checked the notes.

'What about Anthony Howe? Where does he come into this?'

Turner's mood changed instantly. He became tense, sat upright. 'He . . . ask Suzanne.' His lip curled. The words sounded unpleasant in his mouth. 'Ask her.'

The way he said *her* sounded to Rose like he was saying *whore*. 'I'm asking you.'

Mark Turner's fingers became agitated, restless, like a jonesing drummer denied his kit. 'That's . . .' His breathing became heavier. It looked like he was fighting to stop himself from saying what he really wanted to. He sat back. 'No. There's lying and lying. Ask her.'

Rose knew that was all she would be getting from him on the subject. 'Where were you last night, Mr Turner?'

'Here.' He frowned. 'When last night?'

Rose tried not to smile. 'Wrong order.'

'What?'

'You're supposed to ask what time I'm talking about before you say where you were.'

His features tightened. His eyes became lit by a cruel, angry light. Again, he seemed to be stopping himself from saying what he wanted to. 'I didn't break into her flat. I didn't beat her up, or whatever. I was here. All night.'

'Alone?'

He hesitated. 'No.'

'With . . .'

'My girlfriend.'

'Who would be . . .?'

'She doesn't need to be involved. I don't want her . . . not with Suzanne. Please.'

'She does if she's your alibi. Is that her upstairs?'

He nodded. 'She's . . . asleep. I don't want to bother her.'

'Noisy sleeper.'

'Yes,' he said weakly, 'she is.'

'Right. And you and her were here all night. What did you do?'

'I . . . I don't know.' He cast a look towards the stairs as if

131

willing her to answer the questions for him, beckoning her with the power of his mind.

'Read? Watch TV? A DVD?'

Turner looked from Rose to the stairs and back again. 'We . . . I . . .'

His phone rang. They both jumped.

He looked at Rose apologetically, pulled it from his pocket, answered it. After the initial greeting he turned away from Rose. He didn't say much, just nodded his head, made a few affirmative noises. He rang off, turned back to her. There was a new kind of light in his eyes. Shining, more confident.

'We were working,' he said.

'Sorry?'

'Last night. We were working. Late. Here.' He made the statement sound like scientific fact.

Whoever had been on the phone had given Mark Turner strength. Sitting there erect, he seemed to have grown taller, his eyes bright, alert. A small smile danced at the corners of his mouth. There was a kind of cruel triumph in the smile – like an habitual victim suddenly being gifted the power of the bully.

'And I . . . I think, I think it's time for you to leave now, Detective, Detective Sergeant Martin.' His voice became clearer, stronger as the sentence went on. He stood up at the end to emphasise his words.

Rose stood also, flipped her notebook closed. 'Thank you for your time.' She made her way to the door. She could feel his eyes on her all the way.

Weirdo, she thought. And his ex-girlfriend sounded like she made stuff up all the time. There was a feel of that from the case notes. And that's what her report would say.

She left the house and went to find her car.

Outside on the street, the level crossing siren was broadcasting at air raid pitch once again.

She blocked it from her mind, thought about the first gin and tonic waiting for her at home.

30

The Creeper closed his eyes, willed the night to wrap itself around him.

He had learned to love the dark. The time of hunters. Of secrets. Of lovers. It made him feel truly alive, let him move, flow like a living shadow. His vision was at its strongest. The world was at its truest. And Rani would talk to him the most.

Whisper her secrets. Tell him what to do.

He smiled at the thought.

He used to hate the dark. Hate and fear it. It was where the demons lived. Waiting until nightfall when they would emerge, come hunting for him. Canvas-covered, smelling of sweat and drink, of secrets and lies. Of pain and fear.

He hid at first but that never fooled them. They knew all his secret places. They would find him. And hurt him.

But that wasn't him any more. That boy died in the fire. Now he was the Creeper. And he could fight back. And the demons couldn't hurt, couldn't scare him any more.

His eyes were screwed tight shut but darkness refused to fall quick enough.

He thought again of the previous night. Kneeling beside

Rani, his head next to hers, smelling along her arms, the soft, downy hair tickling his nostrils.

Then later, moving her T-shirt up and licking her stomach. One long line from the top of her trimmed hair to her belly button. He had savoured the taste. Relived it now . . . Smiled at the memory.

The smile stopped. There would be nothing like that tonight. Not with the blonde bitch there.

Rani had found her present. It had moved her to tears once more. He enjoyed seeing that. Afterwards, he was sure she would have sent the blonde bitch home, let the pair of them be alone. Together. But she hadn't. They had drunk a bottle of wine between them and it looked like they were embarking on another. And sometimes Rani had cried and the blonde bitch had consoled her. Sitting where he should have been. Her arm round his love.

Him bringing the smile back to her face. Him. *Him.*

His hands begin to shake. Not a good sign. He had always been angry. Like that kids cartoon character, the Tasmanian Devil, spinning and punching and kicking his way through life. Until Rani appeared. And he had learnt how to harness it. Use it, don't let *it* use *him.* Difficult at first, but he had managed it. But it was still there, slithering underneath his skin, threatening to return him to how he used be, threatening to take control.

He watched them again. Rani thanking the blonde bitch for staying, the bitch saying it was the least she could do. Control the shake. Keep breathing.

And still, he hadn't heard her voice.

He closed his eyes, tried to concentrate. He could see his lover better that way.

He felt himself stiffening. Felt that curling and writhing in the pit of his stomach. His hand moved down his body, found the waistband of his trousers. He sighed. Kept his eyes closed. Kept touching.

What are you doing now?

He took his hand away quickly. Tried to control his breathing. 'Nothing . . .'

You sure?

'Yes, yes, I'm . . . Sorry, sorry, Rani . . .'

Don't be sorry. It's nice you make tributes to me. Shows you love me, doesn't it?

'Oh, I do, Rani, I do, you know I do. That's why I left you the present . . .'

She was silent for a few seconds. He heard her breathing, thought she was going to disappear again. Then she was back. Her voice less playful, angry even. *You've been naughty again, have you?*

He froze. She knew. The police, everything. She knew. He had to be careful, not lose her again. He said nothing.

You just had to touch, didn't you? You just had to touch me . . .

He said nothing.

Didn't you?

'Yes . . . yes . . .'

You came into my room . . . touched me while I was asleep. Didn't you?

He nodded.

Can't hear you . . .

'Yes . . . I'm sorry . . .'

You've caused a lot of trouble, you know.

'I know. And I'm sorry . . .'

Lot of trouble. The police, everything.

'I know . . . I'm sorry . . .'

I might have to disappear.

Fear suddenly grabbed him, a childhood demon, its claw round his throat. 'No, no, you can't, please no . . .' Life without Rani. Wasn't worth living.

You've made things very difficult . . .

'No, no, please, don't go, I'll do anything, anything . . .'

She sent silent. He thought she had disappeared.

135

'Rani . . .'

I'm here. I'm thinking.

Relief washed over him. Flooded through to his nerve ends. 'Whatever you want. I'll do it.'

I know you will. Let me think.

He waited, hardly daring to breathe.

I think . . . it's time for me to change.

'What? Again? But you've just . . .'

Doesn't matter. You know what to do. Don't worry. You'll see me again.

'Yes. I will. I never doubt you.'

Good. I'll tell you where I'll be soon.

'I know you will, but . . .'

But what?

He looked at Rani again, sitting there on the sofa, the blonde bitch with her arm around her, her mouth moving but different words coming out to the ones the blonde bitch was hearing. Words for him and him alone. The truth. The blonde bitch getting any old lies.

He smiled.

But what?

He heard the sharpness in her voice, jumped. 'The blonde bitch,' he said quickly. 'What about that blonde bitch?'

What about her?

'She's sitting there, talking to you . . .'

I'm only pretending to be interested. You know that, don't you?

'Yes . . .'

It's you I want to be with.

'So . . . what should I do?'

I don't want her. You decide.

'Right . . .' He smiled.

You know what you're doing?

He nodded. 'Yeah.'

Good. Then do it. For me.

And she was gone.

He kept looking at her. Rani was alone now. The blonde bitch had got up, gone into the kitchen for another bottle of wine. Rani looked up. Right at him.

His heart jumped, he pulled a breath quickly into his body. Smiled at her.

'For you . . .'

Stretched his fingers out. He could feel her, stroked her.

'Soon,' he said to her. 'Soon, it'll just be you and me . . .'

31

Zoe couldn't sleep.

There should have been no problem, given the amount of wine she and Suzanne had put away. Not to mention the stress of the day. And if there was an intruder, the huge kitchen knife she'd placed under her side of the bed would offer plenty of protection. So she had expected to just drop straight off. But she hadn't. She couldn't.

Suzanne, lying next to her in bed, was spark out, but that may have been a combination of wine, exhaustion and sleeping pills. For Suzanne every little creak and groan from the old house, every car or lorry that went past the window was an intruder.

They should never have stayed. She knew that. As soon as they found that disgusting thing in the fridge they should have upped and left. Zoe should have insisted. But no, she had given in to Suzanne who didn't want to be driven out of her own home. So they had stayed, tried to be comfort for one another, draw strength. And now, in what must have been the middle of the night, it seemed like a very stupid idea.

And, to make matters worse, she was hungry.

Another car went past, another jump and involuntary tug on the duvet. Another sigh, once it had gone.

'This is ridiculous,' said Zoe.

Zoe had made a decision. She wasn't going to be scared any more. There was no one else in the flat but herself and Suzanne. She had checked, double-checked and rechecked the locks on the doors and windows. No way anyone could get through them. At least, not without making a hell of a racket in doing so. So they were alone. They were safe.

And she was still hungry.

She flung the duvet back, got out of bed. Her head spinning slightly from the wine. Suzanne didn't wake, didn't even move.

She padded to the kitchen, checked her watch as she went. Just after three a.m. What was that quote? Something about in the real dark night of the soul it's always three a.m.? Was that it? And who said it? Scott Fitzgerald, wasn't it? Well, she thought, looking round the kitchen, seeing yellow sodium streaks of street light and shadow snaking round the window blind, he had a point.

She crossed to the fridge, opened it, glad of the unapologetically bright light that shone out, looked inside. Suzanne didn't have much. Cheese, milk, some leftover pasta, a bit of salad. A couple of bottles of white wine. Cheese gives you nightmares, she thought. She doubted that. You had to be asleep to have nightmares. That would do her.

Taking out a lump of cheddar, she stood up, closed the door, turned.

And stopped dead.

Was that a shadow flitting across the doorway? Someone moving in the hall?

Her heart tripped. 'Suzanne?'

No response.

Zoe looked round. It was impossible. She had locked the

doors and windows, checked and double-checked them. No one could have got in. She would have heard them.

She stood still. Listened.

Nothing.

Must have been a trick of the light. Seeing things out of the corner of her eye. Her imagination working overtime. Yes. That's what it was.

But still . . .

The knife. She had left it in the bedroom. It was the only sharp thing in the kitchen, Suzanne being domestically useless. She should get it, just in case. She would feel safer with it in her hand.

The cheese forgotten, she put her head slowly round the kitchen door, checked both ways up and down the hall. Nothing. She hurried across to the bedroom. Suzanne was still lying there, sound asleep, mouth open, snoring slightly.

Zoe knelt down at the side of the bed, felt for the knife.

It was gone.

Her heart hammered once more.

The rational side of her brain kicked in. She must have pushed it underneath, knocked it with her foot, sent it further in than she had realised. She felt around, arm extended as far as she could.

Nothing.

Quickly, she straightened up. Thought of waking Suzanne, decided against it. She was too out of it. Instead, she ran across the hall to the kitchen, pulled out drawers, frantically searched for another knife, anything she could use as a weapon.

Nothing.

Then, a noise. From behind her. Zoe turned.

A figure moved forwards. Big, dark, like a living shadow had detached itself from the corner of the room and come to life. It seemed to flow towards her.

Zoe didn't have time to cry out, to scream.

She barely had time to feel the knife – the missing knife from underneath the bed – slice quickly across her throat, push into her neck.

She knocked the lump of cheese from the worktop to the floor as her hand went to her throat.

Thoughts spat, rapid fire, through her head.

Cheese gives you nightmares – that was quick, haven't even eaten it yet . . .

The real dark night of the soul is always three a.m . . .

Sodium yellow streetlights and living shadows . . .

I checked all the locks, I double-checked . . .

The knife . . .

Hungry . . .

She fell to her knees, her hands feeling hot and wet at her throat.

Nightmare . . .

She saw the shadow flow out of the room, head towards Suzanne's bedroom. She tried to call out but no sound would leave her lips, just more hot redness.

Darkness began to grow before Zoe's eyes, a darkness more than night, untouched by streetlights or shadows.

Then her eyes closed and she felt hungry and sad and anxious.

And scared.

Very scared.

Her head hit the floor, her body shuddered and vibrated like it was trying to expel its last few atoms of air and there was no more time to think or feel anything.

Nothing.

PART TWO

PART TWO

32

Phil stood once more on the threshold. The gateway to another world.

There is a darker world, Phil knew, that lives alongside the everyday one. This secret world was unpleasant and depressing, a world of pain and hurt and sudden, senseless death, loss and despair. It turned homes, places of refuge and safety, into cold, abattoir death scenes. Destroyed lives both by what it took and what it left behind.

It was a place most people were aware of but chose to ignore, hoping that entry would only be for others, something that only happened to someone else. Not them. Never them.

But it didn't work like that. The doorway to the secret world could be opened at any time, anywhere by anyone. This was the silently acknowledged truth. Its worst kept secret.

And here it was again, on Maldon Road in Colchester.

Suzanne Perry's flat was now the latest gateway to the secret world.

Dead bodies in homes were the worst of all, Phil thought.

Finding the body of the woman he presumed to be Julie Miller was horrific enough. But that had been outdoors with the possibility of looking away. A dead body in a domestic environment was much more upsetting to him. There, it was impossible to look away. Everywhere he looked he ended up looking back at the body.

'Oh God, not again . . .'

Phil didn't realise he had spoken aloud until everyone else turned to look at him. But they knew he was just voicing what the rest of them were thinking.

He stood in the kitchen doorway. Or it had once been a kitchen, now it was a killing room. Blood sprayed on the walls, the ceiling, the floor. On every surface, in every nook and cranny. Blood. Everywhere.

He looked down at the body of a blonde-haired woman. Her head was right back, at an angle that would have been impossible during life. The gash in her throat was so deep, wide and scarlet it was a parody of an extra smile. Her hands were at her throat as if trying to stop the spray of blood and her legs were splayed out at awkward angles to the rest of her body as if she had been kicking violently against death. Her eyes were wide, staring, her mouth open, as if she didn't understand what had happened to her. Phil's heart went out to her.

Mickey Philips appeared alongside him. 'Morning, boss.'

'Mickey,' said Phil, his eyes still on the body. 'What we got?'

Mickey opened his notepad. 'Name's Zoe Herriot. Speech therapist at the General. Boyfriend called it in.'

Phil frowned. 'Boyfriend?'

'Friend's been having trouble, apparently. She stayed over.'

Phil nodded, still not looking at his DS. He became aware, however, that his DS was looking at him. He looked at Mickey. 'What?'

Mickey quickly looked away. 'Nothing, boss. Just . . . nothing.'

Phil knew what he must look like. But he didn't care. He had read Marina's letter the previous evening. All about needing space to make decisions. Wanting time to think things through. She had taken Josephina with her, was promising to look after her. Don't call her, don't contact her. Just give her time and space. To get her head straight.

To sort out my love.

He had no idea what that meant. But it scared him.

Putting the letter down he had felt the murmurings of a panic attack begin to grip him. He had stood up, walked round the house breathing deeply, trying to shake it off. But he kept going back to the letter, reading it and rereading it, looking for clues, hidden meanings, anything that might tell him where she had gone, what she was doing. She was the love of his life. He had gone through too much to have her in his life for her to leave it again.

It was too much for him. Eventually he had broken down, cried. Then picked up the phone.

He knew that wasn't a good idea, going directly against Marina's wishes, but he couldn't help it. Couldn't help himself. He rang her mobile. Waited, hands shaking. Nothing. Voicemail. Left a message. Short, together. *Call me. Let me know you're OK.* Nothing. Then another call. Nothing. Then another. Nothing, every time.

Eventually he ended up sitting on the side of the bed – Marina's side of the bed – staring at the cot, unable to move. He had stayed that way for most of the night, the phone next to him, his hand on it, just in case she called.

But there had been nothing. No call, no text. Nothing.

At some point he must have fallen asleep fully clothed, curled up on Marina's side of the bed. He was woken by his mobile. Thinking it was Marina he scrambled to the floor, grabbed it from where it had fallen, put it straight to his ear. Chest pounding, hoping it was Marina.

It had been Mickey. Telling him of a murder at a flat on Maldon Road and to get down as quickly as possible.

He had got straight up, had only a cursory wash and teeth brush, tried to pull himself together, compartmentalise and made his way straight there. He knew what he must look like. He didn't care.

'The boyfriend's called Adrian Murphy. Apparently' – he gave a quick glance at the body on the floor, not too long, remembering what had happened with the last one – 'Zoe said her friend was having a bit of trouble. Ex-boyfriend, or something. Zoe phoned him last night, said she couldn't sleep. He said he'd come over but she didn't think that was such a good idea. Said to phone her first thing and if she didn't answer, then come over. That's what he did.'

'And where is he now?'

'Down the station. Giving a statement. Didn't think it was too healthy to keep him here.'

'Right.'

Mickey kept looking at him. 'We better get suited up, boss. CSI'll be here soon.'

Phil nodded, looked up. Saw Anni making her way down the narrow hall towards him. Her eyes were almost as wide as the blonde corpse's on the floor.

'You all right?'

She nodded absently. 'This was my case, boss. The one I told you about yesterday.'

Phil looked once more at the body then at his DC. 'This is her? Your stalking victim?'

Anni shook her head. 'This is the friend that was staying with her.'

Phil looked about. 'So where is she, then? Your girl?'

'I don't know,' said Anni. 'Gone . . .'

33

Suzanne opened her eyes. And it was still dark.

She tried to move. Couldn't.

Panic welled within her and she started to kick. She didn't get very far.

Tears sprang into the corners of her eyes. She screamed. Nothing. No response. Just her muffled cries dying away.

She lay still, breathing hard, breathing heavy. Trying to work out where she was, what had happened to her. She closed her eyes, cast her mind back to how she got there, what had happened.

There was that figure. The one from her dream. Back in her bedroom again, looming over her, lights at the side of its head, sharp, white demon eyes staring right down at her. Had she screamed? She thought she had but it had happened so quickly. One second it was at the end of the bed, the next on her. Hand clamped over her mouth, tight and hard, cutting off her words, her breath.

She remembered being lifted up, carried. Trying to kick and scream and making no impact, her hands and feet held firmly. And then . . .

Oh God.

Zoe. Lying there, on the kitchen floor. Blood all over the place. So much blood, it seemed more than one body could hold . . .

And the gash across her best friend's throat. The way her legs lay, her arms, her face.

Oh God, her face . . .

She screamed again, kicked again. Kept screaming and kicking until her body rode out the wave of fear and anger, leaving her still, panting. She looked round, willed her eyes to grow accustomed to the dark, make something out of her surroundings.

She was in a box of some kind. She breathed in, deeply. Smelled wood. A wooden box. Big, big enough for her.

Oh God, she thought. A coffin.

She held her hysteria down, tried to think.

The box was sealed. Tight. But she was breathing so there must be some air holes somewhere, some kind of contact with outside. She looked around. Blinked. Looked away, tried to see out of the corners of her eyes, like looking for stars on a dark, cloudless night.

There were some holes, just above her head. Round, like they'd been drilled. Still dark, but different. She couldn't tell if it was day or night.

And her hands were tied together in front of her body. She tried pulling them apart, felt nothing but pain around her wrists. Either sharp plastic or wire. Something that would only make things worse for her the more she pulled. The same for her ankles. Her feet were bare and she was cold. There was a blanket wrapped round her, old and itchy. But she still felt cold. Not uncomfortably so, just not warm.

Suzanne lay still, listened. Tried to take in sounds beyond the box, make out where she was. Nothing. Silence.

She sighed. Tried not to let her fear overwhelm her once

more. Because she had always been claustrophobic, that was bad enough. But there was something else.

There had been a film out years ago, *Boxing Helena*. About an obsessed doctor who keeps a young woman captive and gradually removes her arms and legs, ending up with just her torso and head, alive and in a box. Her friends and her had watched it late one drunken night at uni. And they had laughed at it, said what rubbish it was. But Suzanne hadn't laughed. Because for Suzanne it was, quite literally, her worst nightmare.

Ever since she was a child she had had a recurring dream. Her arms and legs would stop moving, stop responding. Her dreaming mind would tell her that she had to run, escape. And she would try. But she could never move. Not an arm, not a leg. Nothing, until she woke up.

And when she did the dream was always so vivid and terrifying, she would spend the next day trying to shake it away. But it was harder to get rid of than tattoos.

And now the dream was back again.

Except this time it was real.

The fear, the panic, welled up inside Suzanne once more and she screamed. As loud and as hard as she could. And when the scream subsided she started it up again. Accompanied by kicks from her tied feet, punches from her tied wrists. She hit the wood, felt the blows bounce harmlessly off. She may as well have been trying to break into Fort Knox with a toffee hammer.

She lay back panting for breath, sweat on her face, trickling down her body. Let her pulse rate fall back, gather her strength.

Try to keep the panic down.

Soon, all she heard was her own breathing, all she could see was the different coloured blackness of the air holes.

She lay as still as she could, waiting to see what would happen next.

'Be quiet . . . just be quiet . . .'

Suzanne's heart skipped a beat. Then another. Was that her voice? Was she speaking aloud or imagining she was speaking aloud?

'Hello?'

'Please, be quiet . . .'

No. It was definitely a voice. Coming from outside her box. Not her own.

Suzanne looked round but of course she couldn't see anything or anyone. Hope rose within her. There was someone there, someone else besides herself. They could help her, get her out. She should talk, communicate. Let them know she was here.

Then another thought struck her. Maybe this was her captor. What had the voice said? Be quiet. Maybe if she made more noise the voice would open the box. Do to her what it had done to Zoe.

She lay in the darkness, heart thudding, terrified. Waiting.

The voice spoke again. 'There's no point in shouting . . . or trying to get out. There's no one here to hear you. But me.'

'What . . . what . . . who are you?'

Nothing. Suzanne waited. Nothing.

'Just, please . . . who are you? How do you know you can't get out?'

The voice sighed. 'Because I tried . . .'

34

'So,' said Phil, pulling the hood of his blue paper suit round his face, 'Suzanne Perry had been stalked before?'

Anni nodded. 'Anthony Howe, one of her lecturers at university. Apparently they had an affair and he couldn't let go. Apparently. There was some doubt.'

Phil looked round the flat. The CSIs were moving through, sifting, numbering, examining, analysing. 'Someone couldn't let go . . .'

Anni had brought him up to speed about Suzanne Perry. The intruder of the night before, the rape examination. Also the lack of physical evidence for a break-in and the previous trouble with Anthony Howe, including the unsubstantiated allegations Suzanne made against him. Plus her subsequent scepticism about Suzanne's claims.

Phil saw the look on her face, the guilt-ridden, haunted look in her eyes. She wasn't sceptical now.

'What about the ex-boyfriend?' said Phil.

'I don't know till I talk to Rose Martin. She spoke to him last night.'

Phil nodded. Perhaps punishing the errant DS by giving her unpaid overtime on a case that wasn't hers hadn't been, in retrospect, such a good idea.

Mickey had suited up, come to join them. 'So where do we go from here, boss?'

'Out, I think,' said Phil. It was another hot day and the small flat couldn't take the press of extra bodies. Plus they were getting in the way of the CSIs.

They moved out to the landing, which wasn't much bigger but was slightly cooler. Outside, the whole of the old Edwardian house had been cordoned off, the street outside swathed in yellow and black tape as if it had been gift wrapped by a wasp.

'So what do we think?' said Phil.

'You mean is this connected with Julie Miller?' said Mickey.

Anni joined Mickey in looking at Phil, waiting expectantly for him to answer.

'Well, in a way I hope so. Two dead bodies in two days. Both young women . . .' He shrugged. 'Big coincidence.'

'You're right. Anni, what does Suzanne Perry look like?'

'Tall, long dark hair, pretty.' She looked between the two men. 'Why?'

'Because that's a description of Julie Miller,' said Mickey.

'And Adele Harrison,' said Phil. The other two looked at him. 'She went missing last week, hasn't been found. There may be a connection.' Phil sighed. Tall, long dark hair, pretty. *Marina*. His mind slipped, jumped its professional groove to a personal one. He felt a constricting band round his chest . . .

'You OK, boss?'

Anni was looking at him, concern in her eyes.

'Fine, yeah,' he said, regaining control. 'Come on, let's think. If there's a connection, what is it? Why is it there?'

'Maybe we need a profiler, boss,' said Mickey.

Phil nodded, trying not to think of Marina. 'Maybe. Let's see what Fenwick can come up with.'

'Speak of the devil,' said Anni.

She was looking down the stairs. The two men followed her eyes. Fenwick was making his way up towards them, suit and hair immaculate. Rose Martin was behind him with another woman next to her.

'Charlie and his Angels,' said Anni quietly, but loudly enough for the other two to catch and smile at.

Fenwick arrived on the landing. 'Phil. You and the team here already. Good man.'

'Sir,' said Phil. He was aware of Rose Martin looking at him. A strange look on her face: a mix of sly smile and barely disguised loathing. He smiled at her. 'Rose. How you doing?'

She didn't reply.

Neither did Fenwick. Instead he turned and ushered forward the woman standing behind him. 'Allow me to introduce the answer to your prayers,' he said with what Phil would call his typical modesty. 'Fiona Welch.'

The woman was small, compact. She stood with her clasped hands before her body, handbag hanging from them. Her mousey hair was cut into a short bob and she wore glasses and little make-up and she was wearing a flowery summer frock in the manner of someone who didn't get the opportunity to dress up much.

'Hello,' she said, giving a little wave of her hand, nearly dropping her oversized handbag in the process.

Phil returned the greeting then looked quizzically at Fenwick.

'Remember we discussed getting a profiler in?' he said by way of explanation, then gestured to her with a flourish. 'This is her.'

'Welcome aboard,' said Phil, then turned to Anni and Mickey.

'She's got both a B.Sc. and an M.Sc. in Forensic

Psychology,' said Fenwick as if reciting. 'She's working at the hospital and teaches at Essex University.'

'I'm studying there for my Ph.D. in Victimology,' she said in voice that looked surprisingly stronger than her frame. 'Part-time.'

Fenwick beamed as if she was his puppet and he was operating her from behind.

'Right,' said Phil. 'Good.' He introduced her to Anni and Mickey. She smiled shyly at both of them, her eyes perhaps staying on Mickey for a beat longer than was professional, Phil thought. Mickey didn't seem to have noticed.

'Right. I think we have to assume,' said Fenwick, looking round to see if they were alone, 'that these two murders are connected.'

'We don't have to assume anything,' said Phil, looking round also. 'There's a strong possibility but given a lack of similarities so far it's not a certainty.'

'Can I . . . Can I say something?' said Fiona Welch.

The two men stopped talking, looked at her.

'Thank you.' She reddened slightly. Cleared her throat. 'I've, erm . . . I've examined the case notes from yesterday's murder and of course been briefed by Ben on today's,' she said, giving a shy smile and a nod towards Fenwick who beamed in response. 'And I have to say, it looks very definitely like the same man. And it is a man.'

Phil raised an eyebrow. 'Really?'

'Oh yes,' she said, her voice becoming stronger, more enthusiastic as she warmed to her theme. 'I believe, in this instance, we're looking for a spree killer.' She began gesturing, her handbag swinging from her wrist. 'Someone who it's clear has killed once, liked it and wants to do it again.'

'Right,' said Phil.

'And he will do it again. There's no doubt about that.'

Fiona Welch's voice trilled, like the song of an insistent bird. Phil closed his eyes. Felt a thumping behind them, in

156

his head. Wished Marina was with him. She would tell him what to do, who they were looking for . . .

'Anything else?' he said.

Another shy smile. 'I think I should look at the crime scene first. It should help to confirm my suspicions.'

'Yes, that's a good idea,' said Phil, his headache starting to intensify. 'Where did you say you were from? The Department of Wild Guesses?'

Fenwick turned to him, anger flaring in his eyes. 'Phil.'

Fiona Welch's mouth fell open. She stood, stunned, like she had just been slapped in the face.

'Sorry,' said Phil. 'But you seem very sure of your theories and you haven't even seen the crime scene yet, or the reports.'

Before she could reply, Fenwick took her arm, hurried her wide-eyed inside the apartment. 'Well, let's get a move on, then.'

Phil watched them go. And wished, not for the first time and, he felt, not for the last, that Marina was with him.

35

The latest husk had been stored away.

It would be screaming and shouting and sobbing by now. The carrier shells always did because that's what happened when the spirit left them. But the Creeper never listened. Just walked away, wondering where Rani would appear next.

He lay back, eyes closed. The slight swaying from side to side lulled him, gave him peace, allowed him to conjure up her face once more. How she had looked when he first met her. How she would look one day when he saw her again.

Her smile. That's what he had first noticed about her. The way the skin round those dark eyes crinkled at the corners as her lips turned up, her even, white teeth exposed. His heart would sing with joy when she did that. It was all he could do to stop himself jumping up and grabbing her, whisking her round and round, off her feet, taking her in his arms, hearing her laughter in his ears and seeing that smile light up her face.

And knowing he was responsible for that smile. He couldn't describe how good that made him feel.

'I'm thinking of you again.' He told her his thoughts, of picking her up and whirling her round.

I wish you had, she said. *I wish you'd said something at the time.*

'So do I,' he replied.

Not kept it till later, when . . .

He could no longer see Rani's eyes. Like a cloud obscuring the sun, the rest of her smiling face disappeared.

'No . . .' He stood up quickly, shaking his head, his eyes still closed. 'No, no . . .'

And in his mind she was taken again. One minute she was in his arms, the next she was gone, pulled away from him. He could see her getting smaller, her arm reaching out to him, screaming. Then the heat, the blackness enveloped her from all sides and, even though she fought to be free from it, it was too late. She was gone.

He sat back down. Sighed. Eyes still closed, seeing only the blackness. Alone.

He didn't want to think of all those years alone. Lost without Rani. When the pain was so great he couldn't eat or sleep, couldn't live or talk, even. All he could do was think of her. And how lost he was.

And that's how it would have stayed if her voice hadn't called to him once more, begged him to search for her. She guided him on. Told him where she was, gave him clues, instructions on how to find her. Her body had died, she said. The body he knew her in. But her spirit was too strong. It still lived on. It lived, she said, because her love for him was so great. She had to see him again. They had to be together. Forever. The way it should be.

He had thought his heart would explode when she told him that.

So he had gone looking for her. She hid clues for him to find, secret codes for him to decipher. She warned him she would look different, depending on the body her spirit was inhabiting. But not too different, she hoped. Similar enough so he could spot her.

And he did. Easily. And he thought that was it. They would be settled. But then she jumped to the next one. And he had to follow.

He didn't like that, was impatient, told her to find a body and settle down, so he could be with her. She said it wasn't that easy. She didn't have full control over the bodies yet. Sometimes, like had just happened, the shell wasn't right. It couldn't hold her. And she couldn't just jump out because the person whose body it was would know. So the hosts – the husks – had to be taken away. Dealt with. He didn't question it. Just knew that if he wanted to be close to Rani it had to be done. And that was the important thing.

Rani. He sighed again. Saw her smile.

It wouldn't be long now. She would find another host and then he would hear her voice, the secret codes she gave him, the hidden clues so he could find her again.

Yes.

It wouldn't be long now.

36

Phil watched Fenwick and Fiona Welch enter the flat then turned to his team. He noticed Rose Martin had stayed behind with him, her eyes still on Fenwick's retreating back. Phil had noticed the way Fenwick's hand had rested on the small of Fiona Welch's back, guiding her over the threshold. He was sure Rose had noticed it too.

'Right,' he said and turned to Mickey. 'We have a profiler. Happy?'

Mickey didn't seem to know what to say.

'Not what you expected?'

'Erm, not really . . .'

'Never mind,' Phil said, a grim smile playing at the corners of his mouth. 'They can't all be good. Just down to us then. Right.' He blinked, trying to ignore the headache. 'Plan of action. What have we got. Any ideas?'

'I think Ben's right,' said Rose. 'I think the two might be related.'

'I think so too,' said Phil, 'but it'll still pay to keep an open mind. Having said that . . .' He turned to the team individually. 'Anni. This was your case. Keep on it. Work on the missing girl's background and the murdered girls. They were friends, work mates, maybe there's some overlap between the two here and Julie Miller, something in their backgrounds.'

'OK.'

'Oh, and get Rose to brief you on her visit to the boyfriend last night. Make sure we're all up to speed. Mickey.'

He turned to his DS. 'The van that was seen on the quay yesterday morning. Keep on it. Eyewitnesses, ownership, number plate, anything. And see if there's been similar sightings round here. That should help to tie these two together. And Adele Harrison. Check with John Farrell for black vans.'

Mickey nodded, scribbling in his notebook.

'Rose. You're still part of this team. Julie Miller was your case and she still is. I want you to go through her background again.'

'I've done that—'

'I know you have. But this time you're looking for anything that sticks out, anything that can be flagged up. And anything that might strike a chord with Zoe Herriot and Suzanne Perry. Anything. OK?'

She nodded.

'Good.' He sighed, checked his watch. Breakfast time. But he wasn't hungry. 'I'll get Adrian to do chain of evidence, follow the body for the PM. Twice in two days. He's going to love me. In the meantime—'

'Ah, you're still here, good.'

Phil turned. Fenwick and Fiona Welch had emerged from the flat. Fenwick's face was decidedly pale. Fiona Welch looked wide-eyed, detached.

Phil felt a small pang of guilt over his earlier treatment of her. 'We were just off,' said Phil.

'Can you stay? Talk to Nick Lines?'

Phil said he could. Fenwick also asked for a gathering

later, pooling what information they had received. Phil agreed.

'Oh, Phil,' Fenwick said, putting his arm round the DI's shoulder, taking him over to one side, 'a word.'

Phil waited.

'Let's chat. Fiona. She has insights which could be most valuable.'

'Is she qualified, Ben?'

'She teaches at university. What more could you want?'

'But is she qualified?'

'Yes.'

Phil didn't think he sounded so sure. 'Good. Because if she isn't, if she's just an assistant, nothing she says will be taken seriously.'

'She . . . she . . .'

A wicked smile crossed Phil's face. 'Comes highly recommended too?'

Fenwick knew what Phil meant. He reddened. 'She's had papers published, is, is highly thought of.'

'And she's cheap.'

Fenwick's lips curled in a snarl. His voice dropped. 'Make all the jibes you want, Phil. You aren't the one who has to balance the books, provide accountability.'

'No. I'm just the one who has to get results.'

Phil turned, went to rejoin his team.

Fenwick hurried after him. Phil was about to address them but Fenwick, seeing this, jumped in first.

'Right, then,' Fenwick said. 'All got jobs? Good. Go softly on. And remember, we're a team. We work as a team.' He gave a quick glance to Phil. 'And there is no "I" in "team".'

Anni walking away, caught Phil's eye. 'No,' she said, muttering, 'but there are five in "patronising fucking idiot".'

Phil smiled. He didn't know if Fenwick had heard.

Didn't care.

37

'So . . . who, who are you? What's your name?'

Suzanne heard only the echo of her voice, then silence. The voice had stopped talking.

'Hello? Are you still there?'

Nothing.

'Hello?'

Nothing.

Panic began to rise within Suzanne once more. Stuck here on her own and now hearing voices. Or maybe it was her captor, taunting her. Pretending she wasn't alone, trying to drive her mad. Trying to get her to . . .

What? Get her to do what?

She didn't know. Nothing made any sense any more.

'Please . . .'

Nothing.

She sighed. Heard her breath trail away. Her heart felt like a huge black stone inside her. A dead, dark lump. She felt cold and empty. She felt, suddenly and totally, devoid of hope.

This was it. The rest of her life. No rescue. No Hollywood ending.

She was going to die here.

She didn't realise she was crying until she felt the tears run out of the corners of her eyes and into her ears. They tickled and she couldn't reach to scratch them. That just made her cry all the more.

'Hey . . . hey . . .'

Suzanne stopped herself crying. Was that the voice again? Talking to her?

'Hey . . . hey you . . .'

'Yes? Yes, I'm here . . .' Suzanne was shouting, her voice verging on hysterical. 'Hello, hello . . .'

No reply.

'Hello . . . are you still there?'

A silence that stretched for a hundred years, then, 'Yes I'm still here. Where would I be going?'

Suzanne could almost have started to cry again. From joy this time. Someone else there. She wasn't alone. She didn't have to suffer this – whatever it was – alone.

Questions began to tumble out of her. So fast she could barely articulate them. 'Are you . . . are you here like me? Held here . . . Are you . . . what's going on? Who are you?'

'It's best not to talk. They don't like it when we talk.'

'We? There's more than you and me here?'

A silence. A sigh. 'Not any more.'

'What happened?'

'Don't know. She went, you came.'

'Why? What's going on? Why am I here?'

Another silence. 'I cried at first. Just like you. And all the questions. But you get used to it.'

'Get used to it? How long have you been here?'

'Don't know.' Her voice faded a little. 'Try not to think of it.'

Panic began to rise in Suzanne again. 'But we'll get out, won't we? They have to let us out eventually.'

'Do they?' Another silence. Suzanne thought the person

165

speaking had disappeared again. 'That's what the other one thought.'

'The one who was here before me?'

'Yeah.'

'And what happened? Did they let her out?'

Suzanne heard a bitter laugh. Tinged with hysteria. 'Oh yeah. She got out.'

'Good . . .'

'I heard the screams. I heard what they did to her . . .' The voice broke, sobbed away into silence.

'Hello?' Suzanne felt like she was throwing her voice into a void.

'I don't want to talk any more.'

Silence returned.

Suzanne tried not to panic, not to cry.

For the first time in her life, Suzanne knew what it was like to feel totally, utterly, without hope.

38

'Oh my God . . .'

Hazel Mills, the woman sitting opposite Anni, had her hand over her mouth in a gesture of shock that would have looked caricatured if she hadn't been so sincere and upset. 'Oh my God . . .'

Speechless, thought Anni, then felt guilty at even thinking of a joke like that.

She was on Gainsborough Wing, in the office of the Head of Speech Therapy at Colchester General Hospital. The unit was as institutionalised as the rest of the building but efforts had been made to make it appear more colourful and comfortable. Anni had glimpsed primary coloured chairs and tables in the treatment rooms as she had been led along the corridor. Boxes of well-used toys were stacked and overflowing in corners where small children weren't playing with them. Charts adorned the walls, phonetics and letters in bright, bold letters interspersed with positive messages.

Hazel Mills' office was just the same: big, bright and bold. But there was little positivity at that moment. Anni had just told the head of department about Suzanne Perry and Zoe Herriot.

Anni had spoken to Rose Martin before she left the crime scene for the hospital. Asked her about her chat with Mark Turner, seeing if there was anything he had said that could have thrown some light on the situation. Given them something to work on. She had been tight-lipped about it.

'I don't think it's him,' was the first thing she had said.

Anni was taken aback by her defensiveness. 'I didn't ask that. Look, I'm sorry that Phil made you do it. It should have been me.'

Rose had said nothing, just looked at Anni as if waiting for her to finish talking. She barely blinked.

'It wasn't my decision. He's the boss.' Anni sighed. 'Look, if it's any consolation, I've just had a big bust-up with him.'

A light came on in Rose's eyes.

Anni sensed a breakthrough. She smiled. 'He's not the easiest of people to get on with. I know.' Phil was probably the best boss Anni had ever had if she was honest but if it would bring Rose Martin onside she would say what the woman wanted to hear.

Rose seemed to snap out of it then. She shook her head, gave a small smile. 'We had a bit of a . . . difference of opinion yesterday.'

'First day?' Anni laughed. 'Good going. I waited at least a week.'

Rose's turn to laugh then. Anni joined her. More out of relief than anything else. She hadn't known her long, but already she found the DS hard to get along with.

'So, I'm sorry, yeah? Apology accepted?'

Rose nodded, the hint of a smile playing at her lips.

'So what happened last night? Anything I should know about?'

Rose shrugged. 'He's a bit of an odd one. Typical student, I thought. Dull and nerdy. Not much to him. I doubt he's a serious contender.'

'Why not?'

'Well, for one thing he's got a girlfriend who he says can give him an alibi for when Suzanne Perry reckons the intruder was in her flat, and another thing . . .' She tailed off.

'Yes?'

Rose smiled. 'He's just not that into her.'

Anni laughed.

'Really. Had to be prompted to see if she was OK or not. Sounds like he'd moved on. No great loss, she can do better than him.'

'Let's hope she gets the chance.'

Rose reddened. 'Sorry. I meant . . .'

'I know.'

'We can talk to him again, if you think we should, but to be honest . . .' She shrugged.

'Not a priority.'

'I doubt it.'

So, armed with that and the hope she had made a new ally, she had gone off to the Speech Therapy Department at Colchester General.

There were other officers and uniforms taking statements from other members of staff but Anni, being of senior rank, was interviewing Hazel Mills.

She was a small woman. Compact, Anni would have said. In her late forties with short, greying hair and wearing a striped, mannish blouse, linen trousers and little make-up, she was clear-eyed and sharp-featured. But not today. Those eyes were wide and threatening tears, her featured blurred and unfocused.

'I'm sorry,' said Anni. She hated this part of the job. Seeing the carefully constructed worlds of ordinary people collapse. It always made her think of the Shakespeare she had studied at school. Macbeth. The death of Banquo, the spectre at the feast. The reminder that no matter how much people try and forget, go about their ordinary lives, follow their dreams, indulge their passions and make their wishes, it all, ultimately, stands for nothing. Because it can be taken away so easily, so arbitrarily. And where a work colleague or friend or lover should be there's now just a void. An ache. And with it another reminder: *That'll be me one day. One day there'll be a world without me in it.*

If that hadn't yet happened to Hazel Mills, if she hadn't quite reached that stage, thought Anni, she soon would.

'I'm sorry,' said Anni once more.

Hazel Mills nodded, barely hearing her. She reached for a box of tissues on the corner of her desk, pulled one out. Then another. Rubbed her eyes with them. Kept them there a long time.

Anni waited for her to look up, then continued. 'It happened quite quickly,' she said. 'To Zoe. She wouldn't have suffered.'

Hazel Mills nodded. 'Does . . . have you told her, her boyfriend yet?'

'Someone's there now.'

'And, and . . . Suzanne?'

'We don't know. Yet.' Anni leaned forward. 'Obviously we're doing all we can to find her.'

Hazel Mills nodded once more. Anni wasn't sure she had heard her. She looked at her, trying to make eye contact.

'But we need help. D'you mind if I ask you some questions, please . . .' Anni checked the woman's fingers for wedding rings, '. . . Ms Mills?'

'Go ahead.' She blew her nose, blinked the tears from her eyes, took a deep breath, sat stiff and erect, her body tensed as if ready to ward off blows.

Anni looked down at her notes. 'Did you know Suzanne had a stalker?'

Hazel Mills leaned back in her chair, thoughtful. Anni got the impression she was a very serious person although she clearly wasn't seeing her at her best. 'I . . . yes.'

'She told you?'

'Word . . . got out. There was talk so I asked her outright. And she was honest with me. Told me it was something that had happened when she was at university. All over and done with. All in the past.' She sighed and Anni thought she was about to start crying again.

'I'm sorry,' she said. 'We're a small unit here. We all have to work together. Get on. That's one of the things I look for in staff when I employ them. I like to create a . . . nurturing environment. The two girls fitted in very well with that.' Her bottom lip trembled. She bit it. 'I take a personal interest in my staff's welfare.' She sniffed, dabbed her nose. 'I'm sorry.'

Anni nodded, said nothing. There was nothing she could say.

'So this stalker problem Suzanne mentioned,' said Anni, keeping the questions going, keeping Hazel Mills' mind occupied, 'it was all over and done with by the time she came to work here.'

Hazel Mills nodded. 'She hadn't been here that long really. Just before Christmas. She wasn't long out of university.'

'I know. And she had no trouble here?'

Hazel Mills shook her head.

'Did she mention the name Anthony Howe?'

Hazel Mills frowned. 'Doesn't ring a bell . . .' She sighed again, dabbed away at her tears. 'This is awful. Especially after what happened to that occupational therapist. Like we're cursed, here . . .'

Anni's heart skipped a beat. 'Occupational therapist?'

Hazel Mills nodded. 'Julie.'

'Julie Miller?'

Hazel Mills' eyes widened. 'You know her? You know what's happened to her?'

'Let's talk some more.'

39

Rose Martin stood outside the house on Greenstead Road once more. Knocked. Waited.

She hadn't been paying attention the previous evening. She knew that and wasn't proud of the fact. If she had she would have listened to her gut instinct. She had during the night. Virtually all night. Playing back one aspect or another of the previous day. Some more times than others. Some things kept her awake longer than others. Like Mark Turner. The more she had thought about him, the more she thought there was something off about his manner. She couldn't define it, couldn't explain it. But it was there. And she should have noticed it.

But she wasn't going to dwell on that. She was going to put it all behind her – along with most of the previous day – and work on it now.

Another knock. Another wait. At least there was no level crossing siren this time.

She heard Phil's voice in her head. *Julie Miller was your case and she still is . . . go through her background again.*

Right. Again.

. . . anything that sticks out, anything that can be flagged up . . . She knew what he meant. It was just an exercise to see if she'd made a mistake, another slip-up. Find something else he could pick up on, beat her with. Like she was going to give him the chance.

Another knock, harder this time, more impatient.

Nothing.

And no mavericking.

Right. Ben would vouch for her. He was a DCI. His word mattered.

She waited. Nothing.

Then turned, walked away.

The level crossing siren just starting to ring out.

'Tell me about Julie Miller, Ms Mills.'

'She . . . worked as part of the department.'

'Here? On your team?'

'No. On this wing, though. We have a structure here in therapy management. Different branches under one heading. The OTs and the SALTs come under the same Therapy umbrella. As well as Nutrition and Dietetics, Neuro and Health Psychology—'

'Sorry? SALTs? OTs?'

Hazel Mills gave the ghost of a smile. 'Occupational therapists. Speech and language therapists. Every job has its jargon.'

Anni returned the smile. 'Don't I know it. So, would Suzanne and Zoe have worked with Julie Miller?'

'They might have done. We're a multi-disciplinary team. We use standardised assessments for our referrals. SALTs can overlap with OTs, psychologists, any AHP.'

Anni raised her eyebrow.

'Allied health professionals.'

'Jargon.' She made another note. 'What kind of work did Suzanne and Zoe do here, Ms Mills?'

'In what way?'

'Therapy-wise. What kind of people did they work with?'

'Anyone who needed it,' Hazel Mills said. 'Some therapists specialise but Suzanne and Zoe hadn't been here long enough to do that. They were still starting out.' There was a catch in her voice. 'Starting out.'

'Give me a for instance.' Anni, keeping her on track.

'Well, children, adults—'

'What kind of adults?'

'All stripes. Whoever was referred to us. Stroke victims. Cancer patients needing reconstructive surgery and learning how to communicate again. Paralysis cases. And with the garrison being nearby, a fair few soldiers suffering PTSD.'

'Post-traumatic stress disorder?'

Hazel Mills nodded. 'But, as I say, that would all overlap.'

'Could you get me a list of patients that Suzanne and Zoe saw, please?'

Hazel Mills' face darkened. She glanced quickly round the room as if being watched. 'I don't know . . .'

Anni nodded, kept her voice calm and reasonable. Hazel Mills didn't strike her as the kind of person to respond to threats. And Anni wasn't going to make them. At least not yet.

'I know,' Anni said, 'patient confidentiality. Data protection, all that. This is a murder inquiry, Ms Mills. And Suzanne's missing.'

She said nothing.

'There was a body found yesterday,' said Anni. 'Just outside Julie Miller's flat.'

Hazel Mills' hand went to her throat. 'Is it . . .'

'We don't know. But it answers her description. And now Suzanne's missing . . .'

Hazel Mills nodded. She looked even paler. 'I'll go and get the files.'

She stood up, composed herself and left the room.

Anni waited.

Impatiently.

40

' **A** nd you can see the lightship, just down there . . .'
     Phil pointed through the window of Julie Miller's flat. Fiona Welch followed his directions, looked down. She was thoughtful for a few seconds then nodded to herself, a slight smile troubling her lips, as if this confirmed something she had been thinking. She started making notes on her BlackBerry.

She was already irritating Phil. He couldn't make her out. On first impression she seemed small and timid, almost afraid to speak up for herself, content to keep her opinions safely hidden behind her glasses. But when she had spoken he felt that, behind her passive/aggressive manner, was a steely resolve. An arrogance even, in the belief that her theories were correct, no matter how unsubstantiated. And that everyone else would eventually come round to see things her way.

The lightship was still cordoned off with CSIs combing the area once again for clues. They would be there, Phil knew from experience, for days.

'So what d'you think?' he said, turning into the room and

leaning back against the window, studying Fiona, not the murder scene. 'Any ideas you want to share?'

If she noticed the low-level sarcasm in his voice she didn't acknowledge it. 'It's obviously sexual.' Nodding as she said it, confirming in her own mind. 'A sexually motivated killing.'

'Obviously.'

'The placing of the body with her legs apart on the deck, the tower of the lightship between them . . . he's sending us a clear, unambiguous message that he is a sexual predator.'

'Not to mention the mutilated genitals and the fact that he'd carved the word "whore" into her body.'

Again, she made no acknowledgement of his tone of voice. She nodded. 'Quite.'

'If this is Julie Miller, which is increasingly likely, would you say it's significant that he placed her body on the lightship in view of her flat?'

Fiona seemed about to rush into saying something but stopped herself. She glanced at Phil before continuing. 'I think so.' She smiled. 'You could also argue that the tower of the lightship is pointing towards Julie Miller's flat. Like it's accusing her in some way . . .'

'Of what?'

Another shy smile. 'I don't know. We'll see, won't we?' She shrugged. 'Or perhaps we won't . . .'

Phil felt anger rising inside him. He shouldn't have to work with someone like her, some eager little upstart trying to make a name for herself, not on a case as important as this. He wanted a profiler whose opinions he could respect, whose reasoning was sound and conclusions were reached by clear and tested empirical thinking. He wanted—

Marina.

He sighed.

'Are you OK?'

Fiona Welch was right in front of him, her hand hovering

in front of his face, as if about to touch him but unsure what the reaction would be. She stared into his eyes, concerned.

'I'm . . . I'm fine,' he said and caught her eyes. Yes, there was concern there. But was there something more? Or was he imagining it?

He stepped away from her, aware that her eyes were still following him.

'You sure?' Her voice sounded lower, huskier.

'Yeah.' He turned, looked out of the window once more. 'I'm sure.'

She was still looking at him, he could feel it.

'You look tired.' She moved next to him. He could feel the warmth from her skin, her bare arm against his jacket. She snaked out a hand. It rested on his. 'Are you?'

'Let's look at the rest of the flat,' he said, moving away from the window and crossing into the centre of the room. He knew she was still watching him, risked a glance at her.

Fiona Welch's head was down. She quickly looked up, saw he was looking at her, then cast her eyes downwards once more.

'I'm sorry,' she said, her voice small once more. 'I was just . . . we didn't get off on the right foot. I was . . . trying to help.'

Phil looked at her standing against the window, seemingly unaware of the light streaming round her, how it turned her thin summer dress translucent, obscuring her features but heightening her shape; the swell of her hips, her small breasts, the pinch of her waist . . .

She sighed and moved forward towards him, her walk fluid, flowing. She reached him. He looked at her. She looked at her watch.

'I'd better have a look around,' she said, dropping her wrist, her eyes back on him. 'See if there's anything that stands out. Anything that'll help with my report.' She moved away from him. 'This is her bedroom, through here, yes?'

'Yeah, through there . . .'

She walked away. He watched her go. Wondered what had just happened there. Had she been concerned for him? Trying to build bridges? Or had she started to come on to him? And if she had, would he have responded? She had stirred something within him, even though what he'd seen of her so far he hadn't taken to. Was it opposites attracting? Or something more? Or, if he was imagining things, less.

Phil sighed, looked at his own watch. Closed his eyes, forced himself to concentrate. The clock was ticking. He could hear it, feel it inside him. There were only two things standing between Suzanne Perry and the same fate that had befallen Julie Miller. Him. And his investigation.

But he could feel the investigation slipping away from him. In giving him Rose Martin and Fiona Welch and forcing him to work with them, Fenwick's interference in the investigation bordered on sabotage. But Phil was used to his superior officer. Normally he would have been able to work with that, found ways round it. But this time was different.

His head wasn't in the right place. Marina and Josephina were his world. And they were no longer there. Usually he compartmentalised, kept his work and personal lives separate. But not this time. One was bleeding into the other, making his head pound, his thoughts mix and swirl. He could barely think what to do next.

Fiona Welch emerged from the bedroom.

'Well,' she said, 'you lot have been thorough in there. There's virtually nothing of Julie Miller left.'

'Sorry,' he said.

'No matter. My report will just have to reflect that. Shall we?' She walked towards the door.

Phil followed her out of the apartment, closing the door behind him.

Thinking not of Suzanne Perry, but of Marina once more.

41

Marina knew she shouldn't have come here. She didn't know where she should have gone, but it wasn't here.

Another beautiful day in another park. She had pushed Josephina's baby buggy down to the play area where she now sat on one of the wooden benches, her hand resting on the handle. She knew the infant was too small to get out and join in – plus she was sleeping – but if she had gone to any other part of the park she would have felt guilty.

Something else to beat herself up over.

She closed her eyes, could still hear the sounds of children playing enthusiastically. Swings, slides, roundabouts. Children never tired of them. Backwards and forwards, in and out, up and down. Dizzy and out of breath, seconds to pause, then back in again. Shouting and laughing. The moment, everything.

Life in miniature. Or life how it should be.

And hers anything but.

She shouldn't have come here.

Bury St Edmunds, a small, market town in Suffolk. A heritage town of old shop fronts, buildings and churches.

Ruined abbeys and castles. And, more recently, an ultra-modern steel and glass shopping centre that the locals, predictably, hated.

It should have been the perfect place to escape to, to think, decide. But everywhere Marina went she saw Phil. His ghost, following her around. Here, in the park, he walked between the geometrically laid out flowerbeds. Sat on a ruined abbey wall. Walked over the wooden footbridge and watched the beautifully coloured caged birds trying to escape in the aviary.

Everywhere.

In the hotel room, at the foot of the bed as she slept, when she woke up. In the French restaurant where she had eaten dinner the previous night.

Everywhere.

She had walked past the Georgian theatre but it just reminded her of him again.

It was where they had spent Christmas. Their first together as a couple. She had said to Phil at the time that if she was ever called on to do the *Guardian* questionnaire and had to answer 'When and where were you most happy?' she would have said there and then. There were things between them they couldn't talk about, shadows cast around them, but they both tried not to let them interfere with their happiness. Thinking, they would deal with that eventually.

But they never had. And because of that she was here now, without him.

But he was with her too.

And he wasn't the only one.

She sighed, louder than she had intended, as it attracted the attention of some of the nearby mothers. She didn't look at them, thankful that her sunglasses hid her eyes and the wet sadness in them.

And for all that, she was no nearer making her mind up.

She stood up. The children's voices were beginning to

irritate her, stop her from thinking. From deciding, she told herself. She needed to move, to get away. Find somewhere peaceful, silent. Calm.

Marina turned, walked towards the cathedral. It would be silent in there.

He's behind you . . .

Oh no he isn't . . .

Oh yes he is. He's always behind her. Waiting to jump out. Or to creep up, surprise her. And Phil couldn't help. She was convinced Phil couldn't help.

They had gone to the pantomime at the Georgian theatre at Christmas, her and Phil. Held hands, laughed and even sang along. Phil had looked around at the other families, placed his hand on her growing stomach, smiling the whole time. They had felt so hopeful, so confident. So filled with the future.

It seemed a long time ago. A world away.

Then at the hotel eating Christmas dinner. Being told by a waiter that was the hotel Angelina Jolie had stayed in when she was filming in the area. Ate nothing but lettuce and boiled chicken, he had said. They had laughed, looked at Marina's stomach. Said there was no chance of anything like that happening to her.

She walked towards the cathedral gates. Thinking all the time.

Putting off her decision.

Feeling Phil with her the whole time.

Knowing someone else was, too.

42

Rose Martin hated the library lifts.

They were completely open, continuously in motion and with a gap between the floor of the building and the floor of the lift wide enough to see straight down. To get a foot caught in, even.

She took a deep breath and, cursing whoever had invented them and allowed them to be installed, stepped into one.

She had gone looking for Mark Turner. Had tried his department first, flashing her warrant card to a shocked administrator, calming her down by telling her she only wanted to ask Mark Turner a few questions about an old girlfriend of his, nothing to do with the university whatsoever. Then, once he had been located, asking her to keep this visit very hush-hush.

Mark Turner was in the library. It was a huge, square building constructed of concrete slabs and glass panels and had probably looked like the future when it was built. Now it just looked stained and grim, even more so sat opposite a brand new, award-winning lecture hall that currently looked like the future, if the future involved buildings being circular and seemingly made of tin foil.

She eventually found him on the third floor, sitting in a cubicle with a view of the lake, books piled high around him, laptop open before him. She discreetly flashed her warrant card to the student next to him, inclined her head sharply to get the student to move. She didn't need to be told twice and hurriedly escaped. Rose sat down in the now empty seat, leaned over towards him, tapped him on the shoulder.

'Good book?'

He jumped, staring at her wide-eyed. She noticed he had the white buds of an iPod in his ears. She didn't want to hazard a guess as to what he was listening to but, judging by the shabby way he was dressed and the way he had behaved the previous day, doubted it was anything fashionable.

He pulled the earpieces out, letting the tinny sound bleed out. He turned it off, looked at her. Fear and indignation fighting for dominance in his eyes.

'What d'you want now?'

'Ssh,' Rose said, 'we're in a library.'

He looked round quickly, checked that no one was watching them, dropped his head and leaned in close. 'Are you following me? This . . . this is, is harassment, you know.'

Rose raised an eyebrow.

'I could have you . . . have you . . . struck off for this.'

'That's doctors not police officers,' she said with a patronising smile.

'So what d'you want?' Resigned now. Take the pain, get it over with as quickly as possible.

'Same thing we talked about yesterday, Mark. Suzanne. Seen the papers today? The news?'

He shook his head, unsure where this was going.

'She's disappeared. Her friend has been murdered and she's disappeared.'

His mouth fell open. 'Oh my God . . .'

Rose waited.

'Did she . . . did she do it?'

'What?'

'Suzanne. Did she, did she kill her friend?'

'State she was in? I doubt it. No. She's missing. Someone broke in, killed her friend Zoe—'

'Zoe . . . oh my God . . .'

'—and took Suzanne.' Rose sat back, looked at him, trying to gauge his reactions. So far his shock and horror seemed genuine. Her questions might change that. 'Where were you last night?'

'Last night?'

'Yes. After I left you, where did you go?'

He looked around as if seeking someone to supply his answer for him. 'I . . . I was at home.'

'All night?'

He paused before answering, weighing his words carefully. 'No . . .'

A small thrill ran through Rose. 'Where were you?'

'I . . . went to the pub.'

'On your own?'

'Yes.'

Another raised eyebrow from Rose.

'Well, I mean I went on my own. But I met some people there. Some friends.'

'How many?'

'Four. No, five. Six, including me.'

'And was your girlfriend there?'

A smile played over his lips. 'No.'

'Why's that funny, Mark?'

'Just . . . because. You'd think so if you knew her. If you knew my friends.'

'And what are your friends like?'

He took a deep breath, let it out. Here it comes, thought Rose. They're paedophiles. Or worse, gamers.

'We're a . . . film society.'

She sat back a little. 'What sort of films?'

185

'Horror.'

She crossed her arms. 'Right. Video nasties, that kind of thing?'

'All sorts. The university British Horror Film Society. We just get together upstairs in this pub—'

'Which pub?'

'The Freemason's Arms. Military Road. New Town.'

Rose knew it, nodded. Motioned for him to continue.

'Well, we . . . that's it, basically. We sit and watch films on this huge video screen they've got there. Have discussions, a few drinks.' He was becoming animated, interested in what he was saying. 'Sometimes we get guest speakers. Kim Newman's been.'

He said the name like Rose should have been impressed. She humoured him.

'I'll need their names,' she said, taking out her notepad.

He gave her them.

'And what did you watch last night?'

Light was shining in his eyes. 'A double bill. *Horror Hospital* and *Killer's Moon*.' He laughed. 'It's hilarious.'

'Yes,' said Rose, 'murder always is. And you were there the whole night?'

He nodded. Then leaned back, relieved. The relief brought with it a cocky light in his eyes. 'So, you see, Detective Sergeant, I have an alibi. Once again.'

'And you also have a key.'

The light went quickly out.

'What?'

'A key. To Suzanne's flat. The one you never gave back. Where is it?'

He looked speedily round once again, head darting from side to side, appealing mutely for anyone to step in and help him.

'The key, remember?'

'I . . . don't know where it is. I . . . haven't seen it in ages.'

'Why did you keep it?'

He shrugged. 'I don't know. I just . . .' Sighed. 'I don't know.'

Rose nodded.

'I never gave it back. That's all. She never asked for it and I never gave it back.' He made an imploring gesture, desperate to be believed.

Rose looked at him, unblinkingly. She got the feeling that something was off with him but also knew she wouldn't be getting any more out of him at the moment. She flipped her notepad closed, stood up.

'That's all for now, Mark. But stay where we can find you. We'll want to talk to you again.'

She left him sitting there, pleased that she had managed to upset or unnerve him.

But her victory didn't last long. She still had to negotiate the lift.

43

Phil stood in front of the door, hand out, ready to knock. He paused, waited.

A terraced street of old houses in New Town. Front doors leading directly on to the pavement, no gardens. Windows to the left and right so passers-by could stare right in, watch other people's lives like television.

Colchester didn't have high-rises or sprawling estates. Instead it had New Town. Streets and streets of old red-brick houses, curling and narrowing and circling in on itself, and nothing new about it. Drugs, prostitution, gangs . . . all thrived in, and were controlled from, New Town. Phil wasn't naïve, he didn't think everyone who lived there was a criminal. But it was a poor area, and poverty, he knew both from studies and personal experience, created the conditions for crime to flourish. Poverty led to envy to anger to desperation. To crime. A doomed attempt at gentrification stood over the road by Aldi, a new, exclusive, gated development built right alongside the old terraces to attract a new, moneyed type of dweller, pull the area up a bit. The locals had turned and it now had the highest rates of property and car crime in the whole town.

Envy to anger to desperation.

To crime.

He looked up and down the street. Most of the houses had been quite well maintained; rotted old sash windows and wooden front doors replaced with uPVC. But some had not been touched, their doors and frames rotted away, an outward manifestation of whatever decay was housed within.

Phil stood before one of the uPVC replacements.

'Is this the right house?' said Fiona Welch.

Phil hadn't wanted her with him but she had insisted. She would just sit quietly, she had promised, say nothing. Observe. It would help with her report, honestly. All perky and smiling, eyes glittering. Phil gave in. Not because he wanted her there but because he thought her report would need all the help it could get.

'It is,' he said.

'Bet you've been round these streets a few times,' she said.

'Most Colchester police have at one time or another.'

'Not surprised,' she said, giving a small laugh. 'All crack dens and brothels round here . . .'

'Not all,' he said, irritated at her tourist attitude. 'Lot of lettings round here. Students, immigrants, some belong to elderly people. Too old to keep up the maintenance.'

'Move them into a home, then. Stop cluttering up the street.' Her voice suddenly frosty.

He looked at her, frowned. She smiled at him. 'Anyway,' she said, perkiness back in her voice, 'I do know what it's like round here. Shared a house in my second year at uni.' She pointed. 'Two streets over.'

Phil couldn't help himself. 'Crack den or whorehouse?'

She looked up at him, eye to eye. A smile slowly uncoiled on her face, like a librarian's approximation of sultry. 'Wouldn't you like to know . . .'

He turned away from her. Knocked on the door.

He waited, glancing round, watching life continue as normal. Eyes had been averted as he approached, pavements suddenly found to be interesting. If people didn't know who he was they knew what he was. That kind of area.

The door was eventually opened. A young girl answered, about two or three, pyjamaed and messy haired. She stood before them, eyes wide and staring, as if she had just woken from a deep sleep. It was nearly lunchtime.

Phil found a smile. 'Hello there. Is your mum in?' He realised his mistake, corrected it before she could answer. 'I mean your grandma?'

The girl kept looking between the two of them.

'Please,' said Phil. 'It's important.'

The girl slammed the door shut. Phil looked at Fiona. 'Probably been told not to talk to strangers.'

Fiona laughed. 'Or coppers.'

The door reopened. Paula Harrison stood there. She looked no better than the day before. If anything, she looked worse. She had both hands on the door, peering round it as if expecting to be attacked. She recognised Phil and the hope drained from her face.

'Oh no . . .' She backed away from him, legs crumpling but still clutching the door like it was the only thing keeping her upright. 'Adele . . . oh no . . . oh no . . .' The words came out in a breathless rush.

'No, Paula,' said Phil, stepping towards her, taking the door, ready to catch her if she fell, 'it's not that. We still haven't found Adele.'

'The news, that girl on the Maldon Road . . .'

'Isn't Adele. I promise you. Can we come in?'

She released a juddering breath, her strength leaving her

body along with it. Phil took her hand. Guided her inside. She allowed him to do so.

The house was small, the door opening straight into the living room where large lumps of furniture made a small room seem smaller. A huge, off-white leather three-piece fought for space with a sub-cinema-screen-size TV. An elaborately patterned rug sat on the pale beige wall-to-wall carpet. Cupboards held figurines of big-eyed porcelain children and photogenic animals. Family photos were prominently displayed on the shelves and the walls. Most of them showed herself and Adele. And the little girl who had answered the door. There were also a couple of photos of a young man in army uniform. Children's toys littered the floor, creating a primary coloured assault course to negotiate. Old, stained mugs sat on the floor, coats and other bits of clothing, dirty plates and cutlery. Paula Harrison seemed oblivious to the mess.

Phil led her to the sofa, sat her down.

From the huge TV came an oversized image of a cartoon dog running along a road with a cat and a hamster in a ball. The sound came from all round the room. Paula pointed the remote at it, silenced it. The tiny girl looked at her, uncomprehending.

'Nana needs to talk to these people, sweetheart. Go on upstairs.'

The girl looked between them but, still with an uncomprehending expression on her face, made her way upstairs.

'Is that Adele's daughter, Mrs Harrison?' said Phil, sitting on the opposite armchair.

She looked surprised for a moment, as if she didn't know who he was talking about. 'Yes, yes, she is . . .'

'Seems a nice girl.'

She nodded. 'Nadine? Yes, she's . . . she's lovely . . .'

Phil smiled in what he hoped was a reassuring manner. 'This is Fiona Welch, by the way,' he said, gesturing to

191

Fiona who was still standing. 'She's a . . . helping us with the investigation.'

Fiona Welch moved forward, hand outstretched, smiling as if being introduced to someone at a party. 'Pleased to meet you.'

Paula dazedly shook hands.

Fiona pulled away, took out her BlackBerry, sat down, started making notes.

'Why don't you go and make some tea, Fiona, while I talk to Paula? Yes?' The look on his face, for Fiona only, told her it wasn't a question.

Fiona looked up, eyes alive with unasked questions. Clearly she wanted to stay. Expected to. Phil's gaze didn't waver. Fiona's eyes dropped. She put her BlackBerry back in her bag, sloped off into the kitchen.

Phil turned his attention back to Paula. 'Did DS Farrell come and talk to you yesterday?'

She nodded. 'He did. Thank you.'

'That's OK. Family Liaison been round?'

Another nod, head down at the carpet. 'She wanted to stay with me but I told her no. As long as she kept me informed, made me feel part of it, that would do.' She looked up. 'That's all I wanted, Mr Brennan. Just to know what was happenin'.'

'I know.'

'Thank you.'

He managed another smile. Paula's face darkened once more.

'That girl, the one on the news . . . is she, are you the one dealing with that?'

He told her that was his investigation. 'And that's why I'm here. We think – and I must stress we don't know for definite – but we think that the two may be connected.'

'And Adele?'

'That's what I want to talk to you about,' he said. 'I've got some questions. About Adele.'

Paula braced herself, knowing this wouldn't be pleasant.

There came a clatter from the kitchen. Paula jumped.

The mood broken, Phil cursed inwardly, stood up. 'Excuse me for a moment.'

44

Suzanne was once again aware of nothing but the sound of her own breathing.

The other woman's voice, her fellow captor – if that's who she was – had kept her word and not spoken after her outburst. In the silence that followed, questions had massed inside Suzanne's head, fizzing and spitting like frenzied bubbles in a boiling pan. Questions, fears, screams . . . but not hope.

Anything but hope.

She tried moving around, making herself more comfortable, relieving pressure on her back and sides, stopping her muscles cramping. There was just enough room to do that but any movement was temporary. Lack of space made sure her body always came back to rest in its original position.

She didn't know how long she had been there. Could have been minutes or hours or days. No. Couldn't have been days. Because she hadn't eaten since she had been put in here. And she was getting hungry now. Not to mention wanting to pee.

As if on cue, her stomach growled.

And the pressure on her bladder increased.

Panic gripped her again as the reality of her situation took hold once more. She tried moving around, looking for a way out, throwing her tied hands against the ceiling of her chamber, hitting, hitting, breathing heavily, adding a few grunts and shouts, helping the exertion.

Nothing. She lay back, heart hammering, panting, the sound of her breathing an almost physical thing in there with her.

'It's better if you just lie there . . . makes it easier . . .'

The voice was back.

'But I'm . . . I'm hungry. I need to, to go to the bathroom.'

'Just hold it in. Hold it in.' The voice, cautious, quiet and steady. Balanced on a tightrope where a slip would involve a long, screaming fall.

'Hold it – how long? I can't . . .'

'They'll let us out at some point. Hold it in till then.'

'What? When?'

'Don't know . . .' The calmness in the voice was beginning to crack. It struggled to return resolve. 'They will. He will. Just, just hold on.'

Suzanne sighed, closed her eyes. It made no difference.

'And, and don't make so much noise.' The voice, pleading with her. 'Please.'

'Why not? Maybe someone'll hear, come and rescue us.'

'No.' The voice, strong now. 'They won't.'

'But how do you know?' The other voice talking to her, making some kind of communication, knowing she wasn't alone . . . Suzanne was starting to feel hope well up inside her. She ignored the danger of that, kept talking. 'Look, if we both do it together, shout at the same time, maybe someone will hear—'

'No.' The voice emphatic, almost shouting. 'No. We can't.'

'It's worth a try.'

The voice laughed. 'That's what the other girl said. Look what happened to her.'

'But . . . we have to try . . .'

'That's what she said.' The voice fell silent for a few seconds. Suzanne thought she had disappeared once more but when she spoke again it was clear from the quaver in her tone that she was just trying to hold herself together. 'Yeah. What she said. Exactly what she said. D'you want the same thing to happen to you?'

Suzanne didn't answer. Couldn't face giving an answer.

Silence fell again.

Suzanne couldn't bear it. She couldn't lie in the dark any longer and not communicate. She had to talk and make the other woman talk. Whether she wanted to or not.

'Look,' she said, 'please. Talk to me. I can't . . . if we're here we may as well talk. Please.' The final word echoed round her box.

Silence.

'Please . . . don't leave me on my own. Please . . .'

A sigh. 'How do I know you're not a plant?'

Suzanne almost laughed. 'A what?'

'A plant. They've put you in here to see what I'm goin' to say. You're one of them.'

She did laugh this time. There was no humour in it. 'I could say the same about you.'

Silence once more.

'Look,' said Suzanne, 'we're stuck here. Let's just talk. Please.'

Another silence.

'All right,' the voice said eventually. 'But if they say anything I'll tell them it was your idea.'

'OK.' Suzanne nearly smiled. The hunger, the pressure on her bladder were almost forgotten with this small victory. 'Good. Well. My name's Suzanne. What's yours?'

Silence.

Sadness began to envelop Suzanne. Even blacker and heavier than the darkness in the box. 'Oh, come on. Please. You said you'd talk to me . . .'

A sigh. 'I'm taking a risk here. A real risk.'

'I know. Just tell me your name. Then I know who I'm talking to.'

Another sigh.

'Julie. My name's Julie . . .'

45

'What are you doing?'

Fiona Welch turned, stopped. She was kneeling on the counter in Paula Harrison's kitchen, hands in the overhead cupboards. A jar of instant coffee lay on its side, still rolling, spilling brown granules as it rocked from side to side.

'I'm . . . just getting something . . . for the tea . . .'

Phil closed the kitchen door behind him so Paula couldn't see in. He crossed the small kitchen until he was standing directly in front of her. She turned, still kneeling, and towered over him.

Phil's hands were balled into fists at his side. He flexed, unflexed them. 'Get down.'

'I think I'll stay here, thank you. Harder for you to be angry with me if I assume a physically dominant position.'

'Get down.'

The sultry librarian smile appeared again. 'Don't you like dominant women?' She frowned, quizzical. 'Is that a police thing, d'you think? An alpha male response?'

He was shaking with anger. He managed to keep his voice

steady. 'If I have to come up there and get you down, you won't like it.'

He stared at her. She locked eyes with him.

Eventually she looked away. Climbed down.

Phil made no attempt to help her.

When she was on her feet he grabbed her by the shoulders. 'What the hell do you think you're doing? This is someone's house. Someone whose daughter's gone missing.'

'Yes, I know,' Fiona said, picking up his rage and flinging it back at him, her voice an angry hiss, 'I was looking for clues, evidence. Anything that I could find to help me build a fuller picture of Adele Harrison. I mean, that's what I'm supposed to be doing, isn't it? Putting together a profile?'

'Of whoever's taken her. Of whoever killed Julie Miller. Not . . .' – he gestured round the kitchen. The coffee had stopped spilling out now, the jar motionless – '. . . this.'

Fiona Welch looked unrepentant. 'Did you see the living room? Not a single book on a single bookshelf. DVDs, yes, but no books.'

'So? These are real people here. With real lives. Not everyone gets all their ideas from books.'

A strange smile playing on her lips as if she was filing away his words, mentally storing them for use in some future thesis. That just made him even angrier.

'I think it's best if you leave. Right now.'

She blinked. Twice. 'Why?'

'Because I don't want you with me any more.'

'But Ben said—'

'I don't give a stuff what Ben said. I'm running this investigation and I don't want you here. OK?' He gestured towards the door. 'Go. Now.'

She gave him one last look of blazing defiance and opened her mouth as if to say something then closed it again, thinking better of it. She turned and left.

*

'Sorry about that,' Phil said, putting a mug of tea down before Paula. The mug was big and looked well used. On the side it had a cartoon of a smiling woman holding a baby in one hand and a vacuum cleaner in the other and underneath was written: World's Best Mum.

'Is that your mug?' said Phil.

'Adele's,' said Paula, sipping from it. 'Got it on Nadine's first birthday. Told Adele it was from the baby.' She choked back a sob.

'OK,' said Phil, putting his mug down and leaning forwards, keeping Paula focused long enough to talk to him. 'Questions.'

She took a deep breath. Waited for him to start.

'Tell me about Adele.'

'Like what?'

'What she's like . . . how she seemed before she went missing, that kind of thing.'

Another deep breath. 'She was . . . before she disappeared she was lovely. Best I'd seen her in years.'

Phil frowned. 'Why? What happened before that?'

'Well, she was . . . wild. You know what kids are like. Her dad ran off, left us. Just me, Adele and her brother.'

Phil glanced at the photos on the wall of the young soldier. 'That's him? Adele's brother?'

Paula nodded, head down. 'Was.'

'What d'you mean?'

'He died. Just over a year ago. Helmand Province. Afghanistan.'

'I'm sorry.'

Paula kept her head down, nodded. 'Roadside bomb. IED, they call them now.' She sighed. 'Got my letter from the Prime Minister. That was somethin'.'

Her tone of voice told him it wasn't.

'What was his name?'

'Wayne.' Still looking into her lap.

'How did Adele take it?'

Paula looked up, thought for a while before answering. 'It hit her. Hard. She'd been runnin' round before then, ever since her dad . . .' She sighed. '. . . her dad left, she'd be off with boys, sometimes for days on end. Then she got pregnant and that was like a wake-up call, you know? Like an, an intervention.'

Too much Jeremy Kyle, thought Phil. He nodded.

'She settled down. Got a job.' Paula looked directly at Phil. 'I know what you think. What DS Farrell said.'

'What?'

'That Adele was a prostitute. A whore. Well, she wasn't. Maybe she liked her boyfriends to give her something, presents, and that, but she wasn't a whore. Definitely not.'

Phil nodded. 'She was a barmaid, wasn't she?'

Paula nodded.

'Whereabouts?'

'The Freemason's Arms, Military Road.'

'I know it.'

Paula gave a small smile. 'I bet you do. It's not as bad as people think, though. And, anyway, that was just temporary for Adele. She was savin' up, goin' back to college. Get some A levels first. Then . . .' She shrugged. 'I don't know. Somethin'.'

'And there was nothing to show that she was going to run away again?'

Paula leaned forward. 'Nothin'. At all. Nothin'.'

Phil talked with her a while longer, asking more questions. Adele had left the Freemason's Arms after a shift to walk the couple of streets to her home. She never arrived. Between Paula reporting the disappearance and DS Farrell's investigation starting, any possible forensic evidence had been lost.

Adele had no boyfriend. Studying too hard for that, Paula said.

Phil had a look in her room but felt like there was nothing

he could find there. Farrell had already done it and it was clear Paula had tidied things away.

He came back downstairs, ready to go. He looked at the photos on the wall. There was one of Paula's two children together. Taken at a barbecue, the young man wearing an apron and holding up a speared sausage. The young woman at the side of him holding a bottle of some violently coloured alcopop, both smiling for the camera, laughing as if they would stay that way forever. Life would always be as good as that moment.

'That's her,' said Paula. 'With Wayne. Just before he went back to Afghanistan. Just before . . .' She sighed.

Phil kept looking at them. Adele had long dark hair. Just like Julie Miller. Just like Suzanne Perry. Just like the unrecognisable corpse on the lightship.

'It's always us that gets hit worse, isn't it?' said Paula. 'The poor people. The ones who live round here. Never them in the posh houses, is it?'

Phil thought of the body he had found the previous morning, the trip to Julie Miller's parents house.

'Not always,' he said. 'Sometimes grief is grief, whatever or whoever.'

He left.

46

Mickey Philips was bored. There were people who probably enjoyed this kind of thing, scrolling through lists on screens, working their way down printouts and sheets of numbers and details. But he wasn't one of them.

He would watch TV shows like *Spooks* and *CSI* and watch the tech guys doing what he was doing, except on better computers and in more moodily lit offices, and it only took them a few seconds to get a match. Then they'd up and off, guns out, shouting and roping in the bad guy before the end credits.

How he wished real life could be like that.

Instead he sat at his desk in the incident room at Southway, cup of something dark and brown masquerading as coffee at his side, pen in his mouth, while he scrolled down a screen and cross-referenced the numbers he saw there with the list in front of him.

The incident room was in the bar. He had found that a little strange at first, but Phil had assured him it was always the way with a major case. Tables had become desks, upholstered seats, stools and banquettes office chairs. The pool table had been covered over and was now home to a scale-model cityscape made out of files and papers. The whiteboard had been placed in front of the shuttered bar itself, photos of the two dead girls and two missing ones linked by spider-web felt-tip lines and circled names. A constant reminder, should anyone look up from their desks, of what they were engaged in, what was at stake.

Couldn't have been more obvious, thought Mickey, if someone had put a ticking clock next to it.

He sighed, took a sip from the mug of brown water with grit in it, grimaced, went back to his lists. This was the part of the job he hated most. He knew that didn't make him unique but it wasn't something he'd done too much of in his previous posting. Although, considering how he was back then, this kind of thing might not have been such a bad idea. Would have kept him out of trouble, at least.

Or in less trouble, at any rate.

He had spent most of the morning printing off photos of vans, 4×4s and pickup trucks, then had headed back to see his burger van guy. Needless to say, he wasn't pleased to see him. After Mickey had left he had been questioned yet again, his alibi checked and rechecked and his background gone into, none of which had helped to improve his mood.

But Mickey had persevered, reminding him of the good business generated by the police working the scene of crime. When that didn't work he played on his conscience, saying he owed it to the murdered girl to find her killer. When that appeal fell on deaf ears he told him the way he'd been questioned up to now was nothing and that he'd hit him with everything he could, both him and his van and his family if he had to, if he didn't help. That did it. Reluctantly, the burger van guy had looked through the photos.

Mickey had watched him doing it, gauged his reaction. Eventually they had the make and model narrowed down to two: a Ford Fiesta van or a Citroën Nemo. When pressed, he had narrowed it down even further: a Citroën Nemo. Mickey had thanked him for his time and told him not to go away; he would be back if he needed to see him again. The burger van man was clearly overjoyed at that news.

So there was Mickey sitting in the office. Finding Nemo.

It was all a matter of circling round, narrowing down, moving in. He had discounted any Nemos that weren't black. Then he had discarded any that weren't registered within a hundred-mile radius. There were still more than he would have liked. Then he made a separate list of vans registered in Colchester. Again, still more than he would have liked. That was where he would start. If he drew a blank with that list, he would start again. He just hoped he struck lucky. If not he would have to try van hire and leasing companies and, if that yielded no results, go nationwide. But whatever happened, he knew he wouldn't be up and running with his gun out, shouting and roping in the bad guy any time soon.

'Hi.'

He looked up, startled out of his reverie. Fiona Welch stood before him, head on one side, smiling.

'Oh. Hi.' He turned away from the screen, rubbed his eyes. 'How you doing?'

'Fine.' She smiled. Perched herself on the edge of his desk. 'Thought I'd come back and start on my report. Think I've got enough to be going on with now.'

'Did Phil show you round everywhere?'

She smiled but something flitted behind her eyes, something fleeting and unpleasant. 'I've seen as much from him as I need to see.'

'Good. Well, I'll let you get on with it . . .'

Still sitting on the edge of Mickey's desk, Fiona Welch stretched, arching her back and in the process thrusting her breasts out. He tried not to look, glancing everywhere and anywhere rather than at her, but couldn't resist.

A quick look. And another. Nice, he thought. Very nice. Not his type, but still . . . boobs are boobs.

She finished stretching, put her arms by her side. Smiled at him.

'So what you working on, then?'

He gestured towards the screen, the printout. 'The van. Got a sighting of a black van near the quayside. Working my way through all possible combinations, trying to find the right one.'

She was still smiling. He returned the smile.

'Not like the kind of thing you do. Proper, good old-fashioned police grunt work, this.'

'Everything has its place,' Fiona Welch said. She leaned forward, looking at the list, the screen. 'So how d'you do it, then? How d'you find the right van?'

Mickey found it hard to look at her face. Once again her breasts were dominating his vision. Since she had leaned forward he also got an unimpeded view down her low-cut top. The curve of her breast, the edging of her bra – white lace – the shadow of her cleavage when she moved around . . .

'Sorry?' He looked up. 'What?'

She was smiling at him. Innocent, seemingly unaware of the effect she was having on him. 'I said how do you know you've got the right van?'

'Oh, erm . . .' He could feel himself blushing. He looked down at the screen, away from her, started talking. 'We, er, I cross-reference. Get a list of everyone who owns the van we want then check it against . . .'

He looked up again. Fiona Welch was no longer looking at him; her eyes were jumping between the screen and the printout, scanning her way down both, lips moving as she read. He stopped talking. It took her a couple of seconds but she stopped reading, looked back to him. 'And you know what kind of van it is.' she said, more of a statement than a question.

'A Citroën Nemo.' He smiled. 'Finding Nemo, eh?' He had been waiting for an opportunity to do that joke.

Fiona Welch didn't laugh, just nodded. Looked around once more, checking desks and empty spaces. 'So where's everyone else?'

'Anni's looking into Suzanne Perry and Zoe Herriot's background, Rose is checking on Julie Miller and Phil, well, you know where Phil is.'

She nodded, made to stand up. 'Nice chatting to you. Got to make my report now. But thanks. Knowing what he drives, the van, it all helps.'

She turned and, before he could say anything else, walked away from him.

He watched her go, her legs striding across the office to where a makeshift desk had been made for her.

She was an odd one, he knew that much. Probably because of all that academia, that learning. They forget how to talk to people properly in the real world. And she wasn't his type, not at all.

But the way she arched her back, her breasts . . .

He wouldn't say no.

Probably.

Mickey looked at the screen once more. Tried to get his attention back on the job in hand. Glanced across the room to Fiona Welch. She was sitting at her desk, BlackBerry in her hands, thumbs working away. Making notes or texting or something. Lips moving with the words, head cocked again on one side, smiling, nodding as she wrote.

Lucky bloke, thought Mickey. Then admonished himself. Was he really falling for a mousy little thing like her? Was he getting jealous over who she was talking to?

Her legs were stretched out, crossed at the ankles.

Nice legs, too.

He shook his head, tried to force himself away from the direction his thoughts were heading in, the feelings running through him. Tried very hard to ignore the growing bulge in his trousers.

He took a sip of the cold brown water, grimaced. Looked at the screen.

Forced Fiona Welch out of his head.

Himself back to work.

47

The Creeper was missing Rani.

Lying there, slowly rocking, the gentle sway going from side to side, should have been comforting, lulling.

But it wasn't enough. It wasn't what he had had. It wasn't back in the flat with Rani.

That was what he lived for. Planned for, worked towards. The time they could spend together. And when it was cut short like that it hurt. Especially when she hadn't spoken to him yet, given him her next location.

Maybe he should get up, go for a walk, see if he could spot her. No. He'd tried that before. Daytime made him too visible. Too obvious. Attracted too much attention. He worked better in darkness, where he could use the shadows, practise stealth. And even then he might not find her. At worst, he would just settle for someone who reminded him of her. And that didn't satisfy anyone.

He knew. He'd done it before.

So he would wait. Be patient. Lie low. Even though it was killing him.

The reason it felt so bad this time was because he felt so . . . unconsummated.

It was the third time she had appeared. Each one better than the last. Closer. And in the flat, just the two of them . . . that was the best so far. Perfect. Living with her, watching over her, looking out for her. They had eaten together, watched TV together, even slept together. Him right above her, watching over her in bed. He smiled, his heart sang again at the memory. Sure, certain people got in the way and had to be dealt with but that was nothing. That always happened. The course of true love, and that.

And then she said she was leaving. And he had to dump the husk. It wasn't right. All his plans, his ideas . . . never got to carry them out. And that upset him. He had such plans for Rani, such exquisite plans . . . she would have been screaming in pleasure at them.

But no.

Or rather, not yet.

He sighed, looked round. At least he could see Rani from where he was. He had covered the walls with pictures of her in her various incarnations. He saw her everywhere. Sometimes glimpsed only through TV and magazines. Newspapers. Sometimes tantalisingly close, near enough to reach out and stroke, but just too far away. And sometimes right beside him. With him. He had photos from all of that.

He smiled. Lost in his world, lost in Rani.

And eventually he heard her voice again.

Had you given up on me?

'Never. Always. I'm here for you always . . .'

I'll remind you of that sometime.

He heard her laugh, waited until it died away. Felt like his heart had stopped beating, waiting for her to speak again. Waiting for her to say the words he wanted to hear.

I'm back, lover . . .

He sat up. 'A new host? When can I see you?'

Soon . . .

She was being playful. He should enjoy it, play along. But

it just made him angry when she did that. Like she was mocking him. His love for her.

He said nothing, waited.

You've gone quiet. Don't you want to see me?

'Course I do. You know that . . .' He could wait no longer. 'So . . . where are you? When can I see you?'

Soon. I'll give you the new address. Might be a bit difficult, this one. You see, I don't live alone in this body.

He felt himself starting to shake. Someone else with Rani? He couldn't have that . . . 'I'll see to them.'

No, she said quickly. *Not yet. Wait for my signal. I'll let you know when. Trust me.*

'OK.' He calmed down a little at her words. Patience. That was all. No matter how much it hurt. And then there was the next question. The one he always asked. He both feared and loved the answer at the same time. 'What . . . what do you look like now?'

The same as I always do. Just a bit different. Give me time to adapt. I'll start to look like my own self soon.

And she did. Always. That was the strange thing. When he would first see her in her new body he wouldn't recognise her. But when he'd looked at her for a while, spent time with her, she started to change, resemble the Rani he knew and loved. It was weird. He wondered how it was only him who noticed, never the people around her.

'When can I see you?'

I'll let you have the address. And what I look like now.

'And your new name. Don't forget that.'

I won't. She sighed. *I have to go. But I'll see you soon, my love.*

'I can't wait. I love you, Rani.'

I know.

And she was gone.

He lay back, grinning like some love-struck teenager. Happy once more.

He ran over everything she had said to him, all her words. Over and over. Memorised them. Like always.

Then he had her new address. Easy enough to find. Then he saw what she looked like. And smiled again. Beautiful. But not as beautiful as she was going to look.

The name meant nothing to him because he knew her real one. Her secret one. But this was what the husk was known by so he would have to remember it, get used to it before he could start calling her by her real one.

He said it out loud, practising. Once. Twice. Then again, loud as he dared.

'Rose Martin,' he said and smiled.

48

'I thought we might be seeing you again . . .'

Rose Martin forced a smile. She found the man sitting before her obese and obnoxious. His suit was stretched tight over his flabby frame, as if wearing a size smaller would make him look slimmer, and he seemed to be composed of melting lard. His face so sweaty he looked like he was leaking oil, his hair stubbornly refusing to be gelled down. He had a squint and a lecherous smile and his eyes constantly addressed her breasts.

As Head of Occupational Therapy he might be good at his job, she thought, a truly gifted man in his profession. But to Rose he was a dead ringer for BNP leader Nick Griffin. And just as charismatic.

'Julie Miller . . .' He lay back in his chair, the springs and joints groaning, and furrowed his brow. 'I read about it in the papers. Terrible . . .'

'We haven't officially confirmed that it's her, Mr Laverty.'

He rolled his eyes theatrically. 'Oh come on. Why else would the whole of this wing be getting torn apart by your people?'

She frowned. 'My people?'

He ploughed on, pleased to have the upper hand. Thrilled, even. 'The police. The murdered woman whose body was found this morning was a SALT. Speech and language therapist. So was the woman who went missing.'

Rose Martin understood. And was immediately angry with herself. Ben had briefed both her and the new profiler separately otherwise she would have made the connection straight away.

If the police were here, then the connection had already been made.

'So I suppose it's all connected, then?' Laverty said, reading her mind.

'It's too early to say at the moment.' The answer trotted out automatically.

Laverty wiped his brow with the back of his hand, wiped his hand on the side of his jacket. His eyes were dancing, he was almost buzzing with excitement. Some people were like that, thought Rose. Ignoring any tragedy, horror or upset to personal relationships, just thrilled to be part of a police investigation.

'We'll need to see your files.'

He frowned. 'Why?'

'To cross-reference them against the speech and language therapists. See if any patients match up. See if we get a hit.'

A look of horror was creeping up his face. 'Patients? Our patients' records?'

Rose nodded.

'Don't you need a warrant for that kind of thing?'

'I can get one. If I need one.'

He sighed. It took some effort. 'Out of the question.'

Rose leaned forward. She wasn't in the mood for this. She was behind in the investigation, and she didn't want Brennan and his acolytes to take over. She needed to catch up quickly. 'Mr Laverty. I will get a warrant. But that takes time. However, if you wish to cooperate and willingly allow my team access to your patient records then you won't be officially blamed.'

He frowned. 'For what?'

'For the next death. Because the way things are going, there will be one. And if there is, I'll make sure everyone knows you held us up.'

Laverty looked down at his desk. Reluctantly, he nodded.

Rose smiled. 'Thank you. I'll get someone on to it straight away.'

But not me, she thought. I'm going to follow some other leads.

'Are there any of Julie Miller's colleagues here? I just want a word.'

'Haven't you done all that?' Laverty, miserable now, wanted her out of his office.

'I have but . . . let's just say I'm pursuing another line of inquiry.'

Mine, she thought.

'Julie? Yeah. She was lovely.'

Amy Hibbert was walking through the corridor on the way to see a patient. She had asked Rose to walk with her. Small, compact, with bobbed, blonde hair, she seemed the opposite of Julie Miller.

'You and her started the same time, is that right?'

She nodded. 'We kind of clung together, you know? Till we got settled. Went for lunch, that kind of thing.' She shook her head. 'Can't believe it . . .'

'It gets people that way. Amy, did Julie mention any boyfriend to you?'

She shook her head. 'She wasn't seeing anyone. Between boyfriends, she said.'

'Was there anyone who was interested? Did she mention that?'

Amy Hibbert screwed up her eyes. Rose knew what she was doing. Sometimes people just wanted to help. Even if they didn't know anything or had nothing to contribute, they wanted to help.

'No,' she said eventually, looking disappointed, 'not really.'

'Not really? What d'you mean?'

'Well, she said she had friends who were boys. But they weren't anything more than that.' A sad smile. 'She wondered whether hanging round with them was stopping her getting a boyfriend.'

'Do you know the names of these boys?'

Amy shook her head. 'Not really. We were supposed to meet them one night, all go out together. Never happened. Never will now . . .' She stared off into the distance, lost in her own thoughts.

Rose straightened up. 'Thanks, Amy. Do you think it would help looking through Julie's Facebook page?'

'Might do.'

'If I saw anyone there you know would you help me identify them?'

'If I know them.'

Rose smiled. 'Thanks, Amy. You've been a big help.'

She touched the girl on the shoulder. Amy tried to smile.

Rose's phone rang. She checked the display: Phil. She was considering ignoring it but decided he wouldn't be phoning unless it was important. She picked up.

'Where are you?' he said, no preamble.

'Doing what you told me to. Chasing down information on Julie Miller.'

'Good. Need you back here by six thirty. The profiler's done her report and wants to share it with us.' From the tone of his voice she could tell what he thought of it.

'That's quick,' she said.

'Isn't it.'

Rose put her phone away, thanked Amy, headed out of the hospital.

She needed to think. Find another connection.

Do it her own way.

49

Phil looked round the room. The last time he had been in the bar for a briefing during a major case like this Marina had been here too. And Clayton, his old DS. Both gone.

But one returning. Hopefully.

He pushed those thoughts aside, concentrated. It was still light outside with just a crepuscular hint creeping across the sky. The nights getting longer and warmer, summer on its way. The board was in front of the shuttered bar, the tables and chairs pulled in a loose semi-circle round it. Fenwick was standing to one side, discussing something in hushed tones with Rose Martin. Anni had sat down in the seat next to him, a pile of papers and files over on her desk that she kept glancing at as if it was pulling her back. She looked exhausted. Probably they all did.

Fiona Welch sat at the far end of the row, head down, making notes, her BlackBerry next to her, pen stuck in the corner of her mouth, fingers absently playing up and down the length of it. Beside her, Mickey Philips was trying hard not to be transfixed. Phil didn't know whether to be amused or angry. He didn't like the profiler. Couldn't get on with her. And that made him wonder just how accurate her profile would be.

There were others in there too. Milhouse had managed to drag himself away from the computer screen, eyes blinking behind his thick black frames, like a miner emerging into the light. The Birdies sat behind him, together, as always, the wiry Adrian Wren contrasting with the large Jane Gosling like an old variety act. Beside them were other detectives, drafted in from other teams to help out with the case. Phil knew some of them personally, some only to nod at. It didn't matter. They didn't have to know each other. As long as they got their jobs done.

Fenwick turned away from Rose, gestured for her to sit down. Then he crossed the room, stood in front of the whiteboard.

'Thanks, everyone,' he said, looking round the room. 'Let's get started. Phil?'

Phil stood up, walked to the front. He hated speaking in front of people, even his own team, preferring to just get on with the job. But he knew it was necessary and he was getting better at it. No panic attacks now.

'Right,' he said, wasting no time. 'This is what we've got so far. Julie Miller. Missing, presumed dead. Just waiting for confirmation from her PM.'

'Nick said he'd be across soon to join us,' said Adrian.

'Good. Zoe Herriot. Dead. Murdered.'

'Why do we presume it's the same person for all of this?' said Mickey. 'Isn't her death different? Don't serial killers find a way of killing and stick with it?'

Phil saw Fiona from the corner of his eye. She tentatively raised a finger to answer but he didn't want her to. Instead he answered for her. 'We're not sure this is a serial killer, Mickey. Or the work of one person. But all the other evidence would seem to point that way.' He turned, pointed to the board. 'Adele Harrison. Missing. Dead or alive, we don't know. Suzanne Perry. Missing.' He drew his finger in a line between Suzanne, Adele and Julie. 'Note the similarities. All dark-haired, all approximately the same height, same build. Same age, or thereabouts. Dark eyes. Now look at Zoe Herriot. Blonde, blue-eyed. Not the same at all.'

'But Suzanne Perry and Zoe Herriot were both speech therapists,' said Anni, 'and Julie Miller's an occupational therapist. There's a connection.'

'Definitely,' said Phil. 'So are we getting the patient lists cross-referenced?'

'Yep,' said Anni.

Phil noticed Rose didn't rush to reply. 'Good. Rose?'

Rose Martin looked at him as if she wasn't going to speak just to spite him. But he was in no mood for her games. He kept staring at her. 'Rose?'

She sensed the steel in his voice. Started to speak. 'Same as Anni. I've got some of my old team going over Julie Miller's casework, checking for overlap. I'll let you know.'

'Thank you.' He saw Fiona Welch moving about in her seat like she wanted to say something, tried to ignore her. But he knew he couldn't. She had written her report – in record time, he had to admit, not sure that was a good thing – and it was time for her to deliver it.

But not just yet.

'Mickey, how's the van hunting coming on?'

Mickey looked up from his notepad. 'It's going. We're looking for a black Citroën Nemo. There's photos coming round to all of you and the uniforms. I've narrowed it down to Colchester owners and I'm going through them now.'

'Let me know if you need any more help. Jane?'

'Nothing so far on CCTV from the quayside,' said Jane Gosling. 'Cameras don't extend to where the body was left. The door-to-door in the flats opposite hasn't given anything up either.'

'Thanks.' He sighed. Felt a slight constricting of his chest. Maybe he had spoken too soon about not getting panic attacks when speaking in public. He ignored it, hoped it would go away. 'That's everything so far.' He glanced over at Fiona Welch. She had her papers in front of her and was sitting up straight, like the teacher's favourite, ready to be called to the front of the class to show them all how to unravel some impenetrable equation. He had to let her speak. It was her turn.

'Well, if there are no questions, I'll hand over to—'

He got no further. The door opened and Nick Lines came striding in. Everyone turned at his entrance. The normally unflappable pathologist was out of breath, his tie askew, his forehead beaded with sweat. For him that was the equivalent of huge disarray.

'Apologies for the late running of this service,' he said, walking straight to the front of the group, joining Phil before the whiteboard. 'I have the results of the post-mortem. And some preliminary DNA results too.' He paused, eyes taking in all the people watching him. He didn't seem impressed by their reactions.

'Do you know what that means?' he said, loudly.

There was a general shaking of heads.

'It means I pulled a hell of a lot of strings to get the results in record time. So you should be grateful. Very grateful.'

'I'm, erm, sure we all are,' said Ben Fenwick, stepping forward, giving his politician's smile. 'And I'm sure that . . . well, I think I speak for the whole team when I say that.'

Nick Lines raised an eyebrow. 'I'm sure you think you do, Ben.'

Phil hid a smile.

Nick was soon serious again. 'But it's a good job I did get them.'

'Why?' said Phil.

Nick took his time, waited until he was sure he had everyone's full attention.

'Because the body we found on the quay, the one I've just finished the post-mortem on and received DNA samples from, is not Julie Miller.'

50

Time stood still as the whole room took in Nick Lines' words.

Phil was the first to speak. 'You're sure about that? Definitely not Julie Miller?'

'As certain as I can be about anything,' Nick said, deadpanning the room. 'No matches at all.'

'Then if it's not Julie Miller . . .' Mickey was speaking for everyone.

'Oh God,' said Phil. 'I think I know . . .'

'Adele Harrison?' said Anni.

Phil nodded. 'Looks like it. Unless there's another one somewhere that we don't know about.'

'Let's hope not,' said Fenwick. He turned to Nick. 'How soon can we get another DNA test done?'

Nick raised his eyebrows. 'Won't be cheap.'

'This is an upgraded case. High-priority. The money's there.'

Nick screwed his eyes up, thinking. 'Few days at best. Sooner you want it, the more money it costs.'

'Do it,' said Fenwick. He turned to Phil. 'Where does this leave us?'

'Revising everything we had until now. If Julie Miller's still alive we have to assume it's not for long unless we can find her. Same goes for Suzanne Perry.'

'Clock's ticking . . .' said Fenwick, unnecessarily.

'Right,' said Phil, trying not to feel annoyed at his superior's pointless interruption. 'Based on what we've seen so far, whoever's doing this seems to be following a pattern. Abduct the girl, keep them a while, torture them, kill them.'

'Let their bodies go,' said Fiona. 'Give them back.'

'Good point, Fiona,' said Fenwick, giving a smile he probably thought was charming but if he had used it on a woman in a bar or nightclub she'd have made her excuses and left.

Rose Martin was still looking at him, though, Phil noticed.

Fenwick continued. 'You were about to present us with your profile. The floor's yours.'

Nick Lines took a seat as Fiona Welch stood up from her desk, arranged her papers in a neat order and crossed over, almost skipping. to the whiteboard. She looked excited, thought Phil. An *X Factor* contestant whose big moment has come.

'Right,' she said, trying to look serious but failing to hide the excitement in her voice. 'Apologies for the speed in putting this together but, as Ben reminded us there, the clock is ticking.'

She paused dramatically, making sure she had all their attention.

'Based on the reports I've read and the evidence I've seen, the site where we found the body and the victim's homes, I'd say we're looking for a sexual sadist.'

Phil rolled his eyes, not caring whether she saw it or not.

She saw it. Flashed him a dagger look, continued. 'A sexual sadist. A predator. He's getting off on what he's doing.'

'I think we've all worked that one out,' said Phil.

Fiona reddened. Fenwick turned to him, looking cross. 'Phil, please.'

'I suppose he's white, aged between twenty and forty, lives on his own and has trouble forming relationships?' Phil couldn't resist it.

Fenwick wasn't amused. 'Phil. Either listen or get out.'

Phil was aware that others in the room were looking at him. His junior officers. His team. He needed their respect. They needed his leadership. He needed to get a grip.

'Sorry,' he said, holding his hands up.

Fiona continued. 'He's acting alone. He doesn't let anyone else into his fantasy, his scenario. He wants to control it.' She leaned forward, eyes wide behind her glasses. 'But he can't. Once the thrill is on him he loses control. The torture, that's just . . . a surrogate for sexual pleasure. That's how he gets his kicks. That's when he can let himself go, really be the person he believes himself to be.'

Phil watched Fiona. As she spoke, her whole demeanour changed. There was no trace of her earlier timidity. She was totally into her words, eyes roving the room, gesturing frantically, living them out, almost.

'He has somewhere special he goes to. A place where he does this that no one else in his life knows about. It means something to him. It's his chamber of dreams and secrets.'

'Any idea where we can find it?' said Phil.

Fenwick gave him a warning look.

'No,' said Fiona, 'it's a fair question. The short answer is no. Or not yet, anyway. I haven't had time to do a geographical profile. But there is one other thing, one major factor in his make-up.'

She paused again, making sure she had her audience.

'He's a sociopath.'

'Not a psychopath?' said Mickey.

'No,' she said. 'He can blend in. That's the difference

between them. Psychopaths can't help themselves, they just do what they do and don't care about the consequences. This man's not like that. He plans. Plots. Schemes. He knows what he's doing. He may have a good job, he may even be married. A sociopath can fool people for years.' She looked round the room again, a slight smile on her face. 'One of us, in this room, could quite easily be just like him. And the rest of us would never know.'

'Some more than others,' said Nick Lines.

Phil hid his smile.

'So how will we recognise him?' said Anni. 'What can we look for?'

Fiona glanced at her notes once more, then back up to the room. 'You were wrong, Phil, by the way. Right with a lot, wrong with one crucial point.'

Phil leaned forward.

'Age. I don't see him as being all that young. Everything points towards an older man.'

'How old?' said Anni.

Fiona shrugged. 'Could be anything up to forties, fifties, even?'

'And what would his character be like?' Anni said. 'Any pointers?'

'Arrogant, that would be the main thing. This is someone who knows what he's doing. He's intelligent. Fiercely intelligent. And that makes him confident he won't get caught.'

'Can he be caught?' said Fenwick.

'It's taken him a long time to get into this position. He's been practising, escalating his behaviour, building up to this and now that he's actually gone through with it, well . . . he thinks he's found his purpose. His calling.' She looked over at Fenwick. 'So he's not going to stop any time soon, if that's what you're asking.'

'Would he be arrogant in real life, too?' said Anni. 'Would we recognise that about him?'

'Oh yes,' said Fiona. 'He would want you to.'

Anni sat back. 'I know who it is.'

All eyes were on her.

'Anthony Howe.'

51

Suzanne lay in her box, staring straight ahead, blinking, her breathing shallow. Almost calm. She felt different. Not sure if it was better or worse. Just different.

Because she had been out of her coffin.

It started when she heard footsteps. Julie, if that was really her name, started shushing her, telling her to be quiet. Suzanne was still talking, wanting to know what was going on, but when she got no response and she listened for herself, hearing the footsteps, she did as she was told.

'Close your eyes.'

The voice was muffled, disguised, hidden by something thick and distorting.

Suzanne did as she was told.

'Don't open them. Not for a second. Or you're dead. Right?'

She nodded.

'Right?'

'Yes . . . yes . . .'

She closed her eyes tight.

There were sounds of scraping, like something heavy was

being removed from somewhere, followed by a creaking, tearing sound. Suzanne felt a change of air on her feet, her ankles. The box was being opened.

She was tempted to look, just a peek, a squint. The temptation was great, almost overwhelming.

'No looking.' The muffled voice again, threat explicit in its tones.

She kept her eyes closed.

Something landed on her chest. She jumped.

'Put that on.'

Her hands found the object. It was flaccid and rough. Working with her eyes closed, she discovered it was made of sacking or hessian, something like that. A hood. She pulled it over her head, opened her eyes again. Thinking quickly, she had expected to see something, some small amount of light between the weave, but there was nothing. It was tightly woven, thick and heavy. It smelled bad too. She didn't like to think what it must have originally contained.

'Come on.'

Suzanne just lay there.

'Come on . . .' More threat laced into the words.

She realised then that she was expected to get out. She couldn't believe it, her heart suddenly soared. This is it, she thought, I'm going, I'm being set free. She dared to hope.

Suzanne wriggled her body towards where her feet had been and found only open air. Encouraged by that, she hurried out. She put her feet down, expecting solid ground, a flat floor. And gasped. There was no floor, just water. She had put her feet straight into freezing water. Gasping at the sudden cold, she stopped moving.

A hand reached in and grabbed her, pulling her out of the box entirely. She put her feet out to steady herself and found the water only came over her ankles. She was standing in what felt like a shallow trough. The rest of her body was pulled upright.

Suzanne didn't have time to orient herself as the same hand grabbed her and forced her to start walking. She sloshed through the water until she came to a small step, stepped up. The floor here was dry and flat, cool. Concrete, she thought.

Suzanne breathed in, to see if she could recognise any smells, either from her surroundings or from her captor. It was impossible. Whatever made the hood smell overrode anything else.

She could hear something, though. A rumbling, throbbing sound like a car turning over. A generator?

She was pushed along, her hands in front of her, held together in an attitude of prayer by the plasticuffs. She kept moving at the speed at which the hand propelled her.

'Who . . . who are you? Why are you doing this?'

No answer.

'Are, are you the man I saw in my flat? In my bedroom?'

No answer.

'Please . . . talk to me, let me know what's happening . . . please . . .'

Nothing.

Suzanne kept walking until the hand grasped her harder, forcing her to halt.

'Here,' the voice said. 'The toilet.'

Suzanne was pushed forward. She put her hands up to stop herself from falling into whatever was in front of her but it was her legs that connected first. She gasped in pain as her shins slammed into the hard porcelain of a toilet bowl.

'Hurry up,' the voice said.

She did so. Suzanne thought she had had some pretty bad toilet experiences when she was backpacking round the Greek islands as a student but nothing compared to this one.

She managed to do what she wanted to. Even found paper at the side. She flushed. It made no sound.

'Finished?'

The hand grabbed her once more, pulled her away from the toilet, back the way she had come.

Her heart began to sink as realised what was happening. She was being led back to the coffin once more, made to lie down, be closed up, sealed in once more. She made one last attempt to talk.

'Why are you doing this? Why?'

She tried pulling away from the hand.

'Let me go. Now, let me go.' She put her hands up to her hood. 'I'll pull this off. I will, see what you look like. I'll do it . . .'

Literally, she didn't know where the punch came from. All she knew was that it connected with the side of her head and knocked her over. She hit the concrete floor hard, the wind knocked out of her lungs, hot wires of pain radiating out from her left knee.

'Up.'

The hand pulled her up once more.

Soon her feet were back in the water trough and she was being pushed inside her coffin once more. The same creaking, groaning sound and the box was sealed up.

She put her tied hands to her head, pulled the hood off, grateful to be able to breathe freely again. She listened for sounds outside of the box. Heard nothing.

Suzanne found her voice again. 'Is that it? What about some food? When do we eat?'

Nothing.

'Hello . . . hello . . .'

Nothing.

She lay back, sighed. And felt something at her side. Hard and round. A can. She leaned over, managed to get it between her two hands. There was a ring pull on the top. She opened it. Smelled it. Meaty, solid. But not pleasant. She had no idea what it was but had no choice. She put her fingers in, scooped a fingerful towards her mouth, ate. It tasted awful. And she realised what it must be.

Dog food.

Her first reaction was to spit it out but if she did that, she knew that would be it, no more. Left to starve. So she ate. Kept eating.

Barely aware of the tears streaming down her face, the sobs coming from her body.

She ate like it was the best meal she had ever had.

52

Phil stared through the two-way mirror, scrutinising. Anthony Howe sat in the interview room, sitting at the table, nervous, agitated. Looking round all the time, occasionally making fruitless attempts to engage the uniform by the door in conversation, fear fighting disbelief for prominence on his face.

'Sure you want to do this?' Ben Fenwick beside Phil, staring through the glass alongside him.

'Why wouldn't I?'

'Well, it's late, you've been working all hours, a new father . . . don't you want to go home?'

Phil kept looking straight ahead, his eyes, his voice, flat. 'This needs to be done.'

Phil felt Fenwick take his eyes off the glass and look at him. His body language had softened, there was nothing arrogant, adversarial about his manner. 'Is everything OK?'

'Everything's fine.'

'Look, Phil, I know we don't always see eye to eye, but if there's anything . . .'

'Everything's fine.'

Fenwick turned away, back to looking at Anthony Howe. 'Whatever you say.'

The door opened. Fiona Welch came in, arms full of files and papers. As soon as Anni had spoken at the meeting, moves had been made to reach Anthony Howe. Anni and Mickey had found him at a pub in Wivenhoe near the university, sitting with students. Taking, Anni had told Phil when she came back, special notice of one young brunette in particular. Doing all the tricks, leaning forward, appearing to be hanging on to every word, his hand 'accidentally' landing on her thigh.

When Anni and Mickey had spoken to him, he had made a scene, refused to come with them at first, but they had been insistent. Eventually, and with great embarrassment, he had left the pub.

'How's he doing?' said Fiona Welch.

'Just sitting there,' said Fenwick, turning towards her.

She nodded, as if that was what she expected. 'Good.' She turned to Phil. 'You doing the interview?'

He nodded.

'Right. Here's the plan.' She set her folders down on the desk, opened one, scanned the page.

Phil turned away from the mirror, looking directly at her. Giving her profile before the whole team seemed to have energised her. Bringing in Anthony Howe based on what she said had changed her mood to one of vindication. Consequently, Phil was finding her even more insufferable.

'I think I know what to do by now,' he said.

'Yes, but—' She held up a sheaf of papers.

Phil's eyes flashed. 'I know how to conduct an interview. Thank you.'

Fenwick was looking at him with concern. 'You sure you want to do this?'

Phil felt anger rising within him. Fenwick was right. He should have been at home now. With Marina. With

234

Josephina. As a family. But he wasn't. He was still at work about to question a suspected murderer and sexual sadist.

'I want to do it,' he said, louder than he intended. 'Let's get going.'

'Go in hard,' said Fiona. 'That's the best way with this type of sociopath.'

Phil ignored her. He had planned on that but didn't want to tell her.

'D'you want a relay from in here?' said Fenwick.

Phil shook his head. Left the room. Ready to find an outlet for his anger.

Anthony Howe looked up when Phil entered the room, nodded to the uniformed constable standing by the door, sat down opposite the university professor, stared at him, his face stone.

'I . . . I want to know why I'm here,' said Anthony Howe. 'On what charges.'

'As you know you've been formally cautioned but you haven't been charged with anything.'

'Good.'

'Yet.'

Another wave of fear swept over Howe's face. 'Now, wait a minute . . .'

Phil opened the file he had slapped down on the desk, pretended to be reading, looked up. 'You had an affair with Suzanne Perry.'

Howe put his hands up, palms out, as if in supplication or surrender. 'Look, I've explained all this to your, the other detective, the other day. It's finished. Over.'

'Why did she call you yesterday, then?'

Howe's eyes widened. 'I . . . I don't know . . .'

We've checked her phone records. She called you yesterday afternoon. You didn't answer. She left a message.'

'Ah . . . yes . . . I didn't phone her back.'

'No.' Phil looked down at the file once more. 'You were investigated for stalking her.'

Howe leaned towards Phil, looking desperate. 'That was never proved. No charges were ever brought.'

'Always the last refuge of the guilty, I find, that line. "That was never proved". Person who says that always thinks they've got away with something.'

Howe swallowed hard. 'What am I . . . what's happened that I should know about . . .?'

Phil shook his head, felt his anger rising a notch at Howe's manner. 'Don't pretend you don't know what's happened. It's been on the news, the internet, everywhere. Suzanne Perry is missing. Her friend Zoe Herriot is dead. Murdered.'

His hand went to his mouth. 'Oh God . . .'

'Yes, oh God.' Phil sat back, looked at him, squirming and sweating in his seat. 'So where is she?'

'I . . . I don't know . . .'

'Not good enough.' Phil's voice was tight, coiled. Contained. 'Where is she?'

'I don't know!' Howe was leaning across the table, pleading to be believed.

Phil leaned in also, screaming in Howe's face. 'Not good enough! Where is she?'

Howe crumbled, head in hands. 'I don't know . . .'

Phil sat back, stared at him. Either he was telling the truth and was genuinely innocent or he was the cunning sociopath of Fiona Welch's profile, hiding behind another mask. He wasn't going to take that chance.

Phil sat back, folded his arms. Stared at Howe who couldn't return the look, eyes darting about all over the place.

'Suzanne Perry. Where is she?'

Howe shook his head. 'No, no . . .'

'Zoe Herriot.'

Phil slid a crime scene photo across the table. Howe looked at it, looked quickly away, his eyes screwed tight.

'Why did you kill her?'

Howe didn't reply.

Phil slid another crime scene photo across the table. The body from the lightship. Howe acted as if he didn't want to look but couldn't help himself. Once he had seen what was there he swiftly turned away once more.

'Who is she, Anthony? What did she do to you? Did you stalk her first? Or was that never proved?'

Anthony Howe didn't answer. He was slumped forward on the table, head in hands, sobbing.

Phil leaned back, stared at the ceiling, sighed.

'Interview suspended,' he said.

53

Rose Martin hadn't gone home. Still in the station, away from the rest of the team, she was following a hunch.

And Phil and his 'no mavericking' rule could go to hell.

Fenwick had given her his office and she sat at his desk, opening up Julie Miller's laptop, hoping she was going to be right. She waited for internet connection, opened up Julie Miller's Facebook account. Went to the photos, paged through.

And eventually found what she was looking for.

The jolt, the spike she felt when she saw it was almost physical. An adrenalin rush like no other. They could do all the cross-referencing they liked, but this was going to put her far ahead of the rest of them, bring all the glory to her.

She closed the laptop, sat back, smiled.

Time to go home. Deal with it tomorrow.

But she knew she was too wired for sleep.

Wonder what time Ben was planning on leaving?

Anni Hepburn flopped backwards on to the sofa, bottle of beer in hand, sighed. Exhausted.

She had spent most of the afternoon going through

patient files at the hospital, looking for possible matches with Fiona Welch's profile. So far she hadn't found any. But there was always tomorrow.

If Anthony Howe didn't confess, that is.

She flicked the remote at the TV, stared at it for a few seconds, thinking about maybe running a bath, lying in there for an hour or so with another beer and this week's *heat* magazine. Then her mobile rang.

She answered it.

'Hi, it's, er, it's Mickey. From work, you know?'

She was surprised but managed to hide it well. 'Yeah, I know. Hi, Mickey, what can I do for you?'

'Well, I was just wondering . . .'

She smiled, waited.

'There's a couple of things about the case I was . . . I just wanted to talk through. And, well, to be honest, you were the only one that I thought would listen.'

She almost laughed out loud. That was the lamest chat-up line she had heard in a long time. Or at least from one of her colleagues.

'I'm sorry, Mickey, I'm exhausted.' It wasn't a lie. 'I just need an early night. Maybe we could talk about it tomorrow, yeah?'

She heard the disappointment in his voice. 'OK. Tomorrow. See you then. Sorry to, you know, bother you.'

She smiled. He might look and sound like some alpha male wannabe at work but on his own he was quite sweet. And cute, too, now that she thought of it.

She said goodnight, hung up the phone, smiled.

'Yep, girl,' she said out loud, 'you still got it.'

Then went to run herself a bath.

Mickey Philips put the phone down, sighed. Snow Patrol playing in the background, singing about her being the only thing right in all he'd done.

He hadn't done anything right at all. In fact, he'd done that all wrong. Now she would think he fancied her. Well, yeah, he might, but that wasn't the point. He had suspicions about this case. Suspicions he wanted to share with someone. Talk through, see if he was just imagining things. Or not.

Hopefully the former.

But now it would have to wait. He doubted he would have the time or the opportunity to talk to Anni alone tomorrow. Not without her thinking he was after her. He would just have to keep his suspicions to himself for now.

And having an early night? Yeah, right. How lame was that excuse?

He sighed. Sat back on the sofa. Flicked the remote at the stereo, silencing it. No longer in the mood.

On the one hand, he thought, things used to be much more complicated when he was in the Drugs Squad. But in a way, much simpler.

He got up, not wanting to stay in the flat any longer.

He would find a bar, have a couple of drinks.

Drown his suspicions at least.

And hopefully not bump into Anni, not having an early night.

He closed the door behind him.

54

'Now, where were we?'

Phil sat down opposite Anthony Howe once more. The professor looked like he was in pieces. He had dried his tears but his face looked like it had aged ten years in the time Phil had been out of the room.

The crime scene photos were still in front of Howe, exactly where Phil had left them. He hadn't even touched them.

'Had a good look?' said Phil. 'Pleased with your handiwork? Because no one ever is, really, are they? There's always something they could have done better. Something that seemed like a good idea at the time but just doesn't look right once it's finished.' He leaned across the table. 'Is that how it is with you, Anthony? Was there something here' – he pointed at the photo of the woman on the lightship – 'that maybe you could have done better? Hmm?' He sat back, arms out, hands on the table. 'What would that be, then? You tell me.'

Howe's voice was tremulous, small. 'I . . . I've never seen her before. I didn't do it . . . I didn't do it . . .'

During the break in the interview he had gone into the observation room. Fenwick and Fiona Welch had been watching. They both turned to him as he entered.

'That's it,' said Fiona. 'Keep at him. He's going to crack, I know it. Just keep at him.'

Fenwick looked slightly concerned. 'Can I talk to you outside a moment?'

Phil followed his boss into the hallway. It had the same institutional smell that every police station had. Phil had often thought there must be a spray somewhere, sitting in boxes in some store cupboard in the Home Office. Eau de Nick.

'Are you OK?' said Fenwick.

'Fine.' Phil's eyes, face, gave nothing away.

'Really? Because I saw you in there with that suspect and I'm not so sure.'

Phil said nothing. Fenwick continued.

'You're the best interviewer in the station, Phil. You know that. I've seen you get inside that room, get to work on someone and get them to confess while they still think you're their best mate. I've seen you demolish villains that no one else could crack. But in there . . .'

Phil's defences were up. 'What about in there?'

'You're off your game. You're going for him hard, why? Because she says so?'

'No. Because . . . because . . . because it's my job . . .'

Fenwick shook his head. 'Phil . . .'

'Look, Ben. If he's guilty, he'll crack. If he's not he won't. Simple as that.'

From the look on Fenwick's face, he had realised he would get no further with Phil. 'Fine. Do it your own way.'

'I will.'

And Phil went back in the room.

'So you didn't do it,' said Phil, looking at the top of Howe's head, resting on the table.

The head moved slowly, side to side.

'But you admit to stalking Suzanne.'

He nodded.

'Good. That's progress. We're getting somewhere.'

Howe looked up. 'We were in a relationship . . . She ended it and . . . and . . . I couldn't bear it . . . I wanted to see her, talk to her . . . that's all, just to talk to her, tell her I . . . I . . .' His voice trailed off once more. He sighed. 'She phoned me yesterday, yes. And I didn't call her back.'

'Why not?'

'Because she would have . . . shouted at me . . .'

'And you don't like being shouted at?'

He shook his head.

'Right,' said Phil. 'What about Julie Miller?'

He shook his head.

'Adele Harrison?'

Another shake of the head, eyes tightly closed.

Phil's voice was rising. 'Zoe Herriot. Why'd you kill her? Was she in the way? Was she a barrier to you being with Suzanne again? Is that it? Would she have shouted at you?'

No response.

'Is that it?'

Howe started to cry again.

Phil sat back, stared at him. And a moment of self-doubt crept into his heart. A thought took shape: *Fenwick's right. I don't know what I'm doing.*

Was Howe guilty? Phil realised he didn't know. And he didn't know why he didn't know. He should have been on top of it, looking for the signs, interpreting them, basing his next set of questions on those interpretations. Instead he had gone in shouting, breaking the man before him and still not knowing whether he was guilty or innocent.

He thought once again of Marina. Wished she was with him.

And that was it. He knew it. The reason he couldn't operate.

He stood up. 'Interview terminated.'

Howe looked up, hope daring to dance at the corners of his eyes. 'That's it? I can go home?'

Phil looked down at the broken man sprawled across the table and didn't know the answer.

'No,' he said. 'I'm going to charge you with the abduction of Suzanne Perry and we're going to keep you here overnight. We'll talk again in the morning.'

Howe recoiled as if he'd been hit. 'No . . . no, you can't . . . please . . .'

Phil gestured to the uniform by the door to take over, turned away from him.

'Please, you can't . . . I can't go in a cell, please . . .'

Phil said nothing.

'I'm . . . I'm claustrophobic, please . . . please . . .' And then shouting. 'I'm scared . . .'

Phil left the room. Hands shaking, unfocused.

He had a phone call to make.

55

Phil sat on Marina's side of the bed for the second night in a row. Staring ahead, seeing nothing, eyes focused inwards not outwards.

Thoughts focused once more on his partner and daughter.

He shook his head, lifted the beer bottle to his mouth. Empty. He couldn't remember drinking it. He sighed. His head wasn't where it should be. He should have been in the case, right in the thick of it, on top of it, surfing it like a wave, but he wasn't. He just couldn't bring himself to concentrate on it. And that both worried and scared him.

Anthony Howe. Innocent or guilty?

Julie Miller/Adele Harrison.

Suzanne Perry/Zoe Herriot.

And Fiona Welch. Why did he dislike her so? Why was he listening to what she said? Why were any of them?

There was something he was missing. Something he couldn't see. Like there was fog all around, inside and out. Something . . .

The phone was in his hands. He didn't remember putting it there. He looked at the floor. Must have let the empty beer bottle slip to the floor.

He dialled a number he knew off by heart.

Waited. Not breathing.

Marina saw the phone light up, vibrate. It was on the bed next to her. She had carried it with her all day, in her hands all night. She just looked at it. Let it ring.

Josephina was asleep in the travel cot at the side of the bed. The TV was playing softly in the corner of the hotel room. From the window in her bedroom she could see the night. It seemed barely dark, the lights of Bury St Edmunds twinkling and shining. Safe and enticing.

She sighed.

The phone kept flashing, vibrating.

Josephina stirred.

She had told herself she would answer it when he rang. Talk to him. Explain.

Because she would have made up her mind by then. She would know what she was going to do.

But she didn't. She hadn't made up her mind. In fact she was no further forward. So she couldn't talk to him. Didn't trust herself.

The phone kept flashing, vibrating.

Her fingers were right next to it. Reaching . . .

It would be so easy, just pick it up, talk to him . . .

So easy . . .

It stopped.

She sighed. Sat back. Looked at it.

She felt empty once more, alone.

She could pick it up, call him.

She could.

But she wouldn't. Because she didn't know what to say.

So she sat there looking at it.
Her heart breaking.

Phil put the phone down. He didn't leave a message. He lay down on the bed, eyes wide open, staring at the ceiling.
He tried to sleep.
Couldn't.
Added it to the list of things he couldn't do.

56

The Creeper stood outside the house. Smiled.

It was a large house but, crammed into a small street with other large houses, it just looked small. Old, with grey and red brick and big bay sash windows with stained glass in them. Nice. The sort of place that looked welcoming. The sort of place you could call home.

Rani had done well for herself this time.

The Creeper would never have dreamt of calling a place like this home. It was a different world. But he might. Soon.

He had watched it for a long time. A man had driven up, parked down the road in the first available space and let himself in. Suited and carrying a briefcase, he was young, confident looking. Like he knew what he was worth. Or thought he knew.

The Creeper had smiled. The man would soon find out.

He had waited longer. Eventually another car had pulled up, parked in the road. There were two people in it, a man driving and a woman in the passenger seat. His heart skipped a beat. There she was. He knew it as soon as he saw her.

Rani.

He couldn't stop smiling. It was all he could to stop him-self running out to meet her. But he did. He would be patient. He would wait. Bide his time.

He watched them talk. The driver looked like an older ver-sion of the man who had entered the house. He saw them hold hands before she left the car. Felt a sharp pang of anger when that happened. The car drove away. He watched it go, saw Rani enter the house.

Went back to waiting.

It wasn't perfect where he was but it was good. It would do. It wasn't as good as the last place, where he lived with Rani, was together with her all the time, but it would do. He wouldn't be disturbed. The owner of the house he was in would be no more trouble. He could see her leg sticking out from the spare room where he had left her body.

All he had to do was wait.

And he was good at that. He could be a patient man. Because he had something to wait for. Someone.

Rani.

PART THREE

57

Phil knew what he must look like. But he didn't care.

He had made an effort to smarten himself up, sort himself out. Clean shirt and a shave. Wash and brush up. But his eyes were black-rimmed, broken capillary fractals, gazing away when they should be staying focused, clouding over when they should have been clear.

He sat at his desk in the bar, waiting for the briefing to start. Caffeine-alert, telling himself to pull it together, compartmentalise. Shut off his home life, live only in his work life. But whether he was actually listening was another matter.

He had tried Marina again last night. And again and again. A different message every time. Inquiring about her safety and wellbeing, their daughter's too. Then telling her how much she was missed, just to talk to him if something was wrong. She didn't need to come back home. Even asking for her opinion on his case. Different every time, something he hoped would attract her to pick up, make it impossible not to. She didn't. Eventually he stopped leaving messages. Eventually he stopped calling.

He must have slept at some point. But he couldn't remember when. Woke up on Marina's side of the bed once more. Several more bottles at his feet. He couldn't remember those getting there either.

He had formulated a plan for contacting Marina. Really simple, wondered how he hadn't thought of it earlier. He would do it later. First he had the briefing to get through.

He pulled his eyes on to the whiteboard, took another hit of pitch-black coffee, forced himself to concentrate on the case.

The team were assembled. The same faces as the day before looking marginally refreshed and rested. Anni would catch Mickey's eye then turn away with a private smile while Mickey would look anywhere but at her. He didn't know what was going on there, didn't want to know either unless it affected their work. Rose Martin seemed to be humming with some kind of energy, ready to go. Either that, thought Phil, or she'd just had another fight. Fenwick was at the end of the room, trying not to look at her. Fiona Welch sat at her desk, straight-backed, pen poised. Face unreadable. She still unnerved Phil. Nick Lines had come over, armed with more findings from the post-mortems.

Fenwick moved to the centre of the room, ready to go.

'Thanks for coming in early, people. Appreciate it. Let's get started. Phil?'

Phil stood up, took centre stage. 'As you know, we've got Anthony Howe downstairs in the cells. He's been charged with Suzanne Perry's abduction. Progress report, Adrian?'

Adrian Wren stood up. 'He's got no alibi for the night of the abduction and murder. Says he was out on his own, walking. Stopped in a pub for a drink. Can't remember which one.' He checked a sheet of paper in front of him. 'Took a call from Suzanne Perry in the afternoon, tried calling her a few times that night. No reply.'

'Left a message?' said Phil.

Adrian shook his head. 'No. But called her three times up until ten o'clock. After that, nothing. Says he went home. Wife's left him so there's no one who can say yes or no to that one. Got the CSIs going through his house now, though.'

'Thanks, Adrian.' Phil turned to the rest of the team. 'So that's where we are with him.'

'Gut feeling, Phil?' said Fenwick, his usual question.

Phil thought. He was the one who had interviewed him and charged him but he honestly didn't know if he was guilty. Usually he got a feeling, a copper's instinct. It wasn't infallible but was accurate about 90 per cent of the time. But this time, no yes or no, nothing.

But before he could answer, Fiona Welch jumped in.

'He fits the profile perfectly,' she said. 'Textbook. Just a matter of breaking him down, I would say.'

Fenwick stared at her. Phil knew he didn't like profilers, only paid lip service to the idea of them for the sake of workplace politics and personal advancement. A win/win situation for him – able to take the credit if they got it right, providing someone to blame if they got it wrong. But he certainly didn't like them interrupting when it wasn't their turn. Fenwick blanked her.

'Phil?'

'Yeah, he fits the profile, but . . .' He shrugged. 'I don't know.'

'You mean whether he's guilty or innocent?'

'Yeah. I just . . . don't know.'

Fenwick waited for him to expand on that. He didn't. Instead, Phil turned to Nick Lines.

'Nick. Good to see you again. What you got for us?'

Nick Lines got slowly to his feet. 'Quite a bit since yesterday, actually. Nothing more on the DNA front yet, unfortunately, and there won't be for a while, I don't think. So I took a journey down some other avenues. I checked the physical description we had of Adele Harrison against the body we've got. Looked for any distinguishing features.'

'And?' said Phil.

'Well, we didn't find anything at first. So I persevered. Adele Harrison had a tattoo on the base of her spine. You know what I mean. Popular among a certain type. Some kind of curlicue. Arse antlers, I believe they're called.'

Despite or perhaps because of the tension in the room, everyone laughed.

'Tart tats, you mean,' said Mickey.

'If we were less politically correct,' said Fenwick, glancing quickly at Rose Martin to gauge her reaction.

'Please,' said Phil, 'can we?'

The laughter died away. Nick Lines continued.

'It wasn't an easy match. There wasn't much of her lower back left.'

Silence, tinged with guilt for the earlier laughter.

'The skin's been flayed off. Whether that was deliberate to stop us identifying her or whether it was just frenzy, I don't know.'

'Maybe both,' said Phil.

'Perhaps,' said Nick, continuing. 'But they hadn't done a complete job. There were still traces of the tattoo left. I was able to reconstruct a partial impression from that.'

'Julie Miller doesn't have any tattoos,' said Rose.

Nick nodded.

'So you think that confirms it?' said Phil.

'As I said, we won't have the DNA back for a while, but . . .' He shrugged. 'Maybe we should think about bringing her next of kin in for an identification.'

A depression settled over the room. He had all but confirmed what they suspected. But there was no sense of triumph or even achievement at it.

'I found something else, too,' said Nick. 'Stomach contents analysis. Her last meal. As far as I can tell, dog food.'

'Oh Jesus,' said Phil, vocalising what the room must have been thinking. 'It gets worse.'

'Can we get a match on that?' said Fenwick. 'Find the brand, the make, maybe even the batch?'

Nick Lines nodded. 'We're already ahead of you. We've contacted all the major pet food manufacturers. Shot in the dark and may take a while, but stranger things have happened. Also. Suzanne Perry's blood sample. They phoned me with results. Traces of pancuronium.'

'That's not good, right?' said Phil.

'Not good at all. It's a muscle relaxant. Taken in large doses it paralyses the body. They can still feel but not move. It's given to death-row inmates in lethal injections in the States.'

'Charming,' said Phil. 'Well, let's follow that up. See where a supply could be found. Check—'

The door burst open. A uniform rushed in.

Fenwick was first to react. 'This is a—'

'Sorry, sir,' said the uniform, out of breath, 'but this is urgent.'

'What?' said Phil.

'The prisoner, sir, Anthony Howe . . .'

'Yes,' said Phil.

'Tried to kill himself.'

58

Anthony Howe had managed to rip his sheets up to make a rope. Then, knots tested, pulled strong and tight, he had looped it round the light fitting. Lassoed in place it hung there, a hangman's noose. He had placed it round his neck, pulled the slipknot tight. Stepping off the bed, the sudden jerk expelled what air there was from his body, forcibly denied access to any more. The jolt and drop weren't sufficient to break his neck so he had hung from the ceiling, legs thrashing and air-cycling, hands grabbing at his throat, dangling and strangling. His face had turned purple and his bladder and bowels evacuated.

The makeshift gallows hadn't held for long, his weight being too much for the electric cord, and it had given way, the noise of his body hitting the floor and alerting an on-duty uniform.

'Get the paramedics in here!'

Phil ran into the cell. A uniform had removed the noose from Howe's neck and was attempting CPR on him. His body was in a state and there was no trace of the cultured, arrogant university lecturer.

'What's happening?' said Phil.

The uniform looked up, fingers locked together, hands pressing down hard, rhythmically, on Howe's chest. 'Still breathing, sir . . .' Breaking off to count the presses. '. . . just trying . . . to revive him . . .'

And back down to breathe more air into his lungs.

Phil stood up, looked around, felt impotent rage inside him. The light fitting was on the floor in pieces, bulb and casing shattered. The noose was lying in a corner where the uniform had thrown it, a venomous snake, once dangerous, now dead.

The doorway was full: the whole team from the briefing room having followed him down, now crowding round, trying to get in, winning the world record for most number of people crammed into a door frame at one time.

'Who was looking in on him?' Phil said. 'Who was checking him?'

Another uniform, standing by the door, keeping the press of bodies back, glanced nervously at him. 'We did, sir, we checked in on him regularly. Looked like he was sleeping.'

'Well, he wasn't, was he?'

The uniform recoiled. 'No . . . but we weren't given any special orders. No suicide watch or nothing . . .'

Suicide watch. Phil looked down at the body, thought of Howe's words in the interview room the previous night:

I can't go in a cell, please . . . I'm claustrophobic . . . please . . . please . . . I'm scared . . .

Phil hadn't listened to him. Ignored him, in fact. He heard stuff like that all the time, thought nothing of it. Looked again at the mess on the floor.

I'm losing it . . .

At that moment the paramedics arrived, ushering everyone out of the way, taking over. Phil allowed himself to be led from the cell along with everyone else. Now the corridor was full of bodies.

Fenwick pushed his way over to Phil, placed an arm round his shoulder. 'A word.' He separated him from the rest of the group, walked him away to a quiet spot round a corner.

As Phil went he turned, saw Fiona Welch's face. She was staring into the cell, her eyes lit up, a smile on her face. Fascination? He didn't know. Didn't have time to think about her now. He turned to Fenwick.

'What the fuck just happened here?' Fenwick's voice low, angry.

Phil shook his head.

'Where was the risk assessment? Why wasn't this flagged up? Why didn't you do that?'

Anger was still swirling around inside Phil, looking for an outlet. It had just found it. 'Me? This is all my fault, is it?'

'You interviewed him.'

'You observed.'

'Yes,' said Fenwick, finger jabbing in Phil's face. 'And I said you didn't look up to it. You were off your game in there, not thinking for yourself, doing whatever she told you too.'

Phil's anger jumped up a gear. 'Don't make out this is my fault. Don't you try and make me take the blame for this.'

'Whose fault is it, then? That profiler's?' Fenwick sneered. 'We all know you do whatever a profiler tells you, don't we? She the next in line?'

Phil couldn't stop himself. His fist was coming towards Fenwick's face before his brain had a chance to stop it.

It connected. Fenwick's head snapped back and round, taking his body with it. His legs went too, tangling and tripping over each other, taking Fenwick to the floor.

He lay there, looking up at Phil who just stared down at his superior officer. Shocked, stunned and amazed at what he had just done. His mouth was open, flapping with words that wouldn't emerge.

Fenwick's hand went to his mouth where Phil's fist had broken the skin, blood pooling there. He stared upwards, as shocked as Phil was.

Anni appeared in the hall behind Phil. 'Boss—' She stopped dead at the scene before her.

Phil, aware that she was there, put his arm out to help Fenwick to his feet. Fenwick accepted.

'It's all right, Anni,' said Phil. 'Everything's OK.'

Fenwick made it to his feet, staggering slightly. Phil couldn't meet his gaze, turned to Anni.

'Yes.'

'I, uh, just wanted to tell you that the Super's on his way. From Chelmsford. Said he wants to speak to you.'

'Thanks, Anni.'

She looked between the two men, wide-eyed, then turned and rejoined the rest of the team in front of the cell door.

Phil looked at Fenwick. 'Sorry,' he said, eyes hitting the floor.

Fenwick nodded.

'I'll go.' Phil turned to walk away.

'Wait.'

Phil turned. Fenwick was still rubbing his jaw. Mouth working, trying to find words that wouldn't come easily.

'Go and lead your team. We'll deal with this later.'

Phil nodded, turned, walked away.

He rounded the corner, back to where everyone else was. The paramedics were taking Anthony Howe out on a stretcher. Fiona Welch was still staring, fascinated, as his body went past her.

'Fiona,' said Phil, 'geographic victim profile. Can you do that?'

She looked up at him. 'Of course I can.'

'Then do it, please.' He looked at the rest of the team. 'Right, upstairs. Back to work. It's our job to make sure there aren't any more deaths. Come on, excitement over.'

He turned, walked away. Thinking about what Fenwick had said, that this mess was all his fault.

Thinking that he might be right.

59

Excitement over.

Phil was off, taking the stairs two at a time. Mickey walked back up the stairs to the bar along with the rest of the team. With a day of looking through vehicle registrations to come, that phrase went doubly for him.

He bumped into Anni. She looked up, startled.

'Sorry,' she said, 'miles away.'

'Don't blame you,' said Mickey. 'What just happened . . .'

She looked sharply at him. 'You saw—' Her features changed. 'Oh. Right. Yeah.'

They walked together in silence.

'Look,' said Mickey.

A ghost of a smile played round Anni's lips. 'Is this going to be an "about last night" thing? Don't worry. It doesn't matter.'

'It wasn't like that.' Even as he spoke he felt himself reddening. 'I didn't mean it that way.'

She gave him a quick look, eyes mischievous. 'What way did you mean it, then?'

He glanced round, seeing who was listening. Jane Gosling

was right behind him, behind her Rose Martin and Ben Fenwick, deep in conversation, Rose's face angry.

'Not here,' he said.

'Man of mystery,' she said, smiling again. 'Giving me a key to your house of secrets then, are you?'

Mickey sighed, shook his head. He thought he could trust Anni. Out of all of the team she seemed the most approachable, the one with less of an agenda, the most honest.

They reached the top of the stairs, turned the corner. Anni put a hand on his arm. He stopped, turned.

'Sorry,' she said. 'Just winding you up.' She looked at her watch. 'I've got to go out, follow up those client list leads of Suzanne and Zoe's from the hospital. But I'll be around later.' She smiled again. 'Or you could phone me.'

Fiona Welch came past, walking double time, self-importantly, like she was in an episode of *The West Wing*.

'I'll talk to you later,' he said and turned, went back to the bar.

Hoping he wasn't blushing too much.

He reached his desk, sat down. Sighed. Looked round. Fiona Welch was at her desk on the other side of the room, looking at her screen, energised, lips moving in a dialogue only she could hear.

He just might give Anni a ring.

He looked at his own screen, at the scrolling numbers, the lists. Knowing in theory why his work was so important but wishing there was a more exciting way to do it.

Fiona Welch laughed to herself, went on staring at the screen.

He hoped the thing he wanted to talk to Anni about would keep, hoped he was right.

But hoped more that he wasn't.

60

Anni stood on the doorstep and rang the bell.

The house was way out in Coggeshall, one of the most photogenic villages on Essex. Anni had always had a problem with the place and others like it, though. Because its main street and offshoots consisted of the kind of old, beamed, uneven houses, thatched roofs, Regency-windowed pubs and quaint, red-brick cottages that spoke of a certain kind of intractable tradition and held a natural attraction to a certain kind of reactionary mindset, being black, female and a non-*Daily Mail* reader made her feel uncomfortable there.

The bell she rang was only comparatively modern, 1970s as opposed to the rest of the house that looked like it belonged more in the 1870s. It was slightly less well maintained than the rest of the row, the paint round the windows chipped and peeling, the door needing a fresh coat of varnish, the front garden less manicured. She checked her list. It belonged to a writer.

Suzanne Perry and Zoe Herriot's list of clients from the hospital. In need of speech therapy. Luckily, they hadn't been there for a long time so the list wasn't huge. But it was extensive and far-ranging. Socio-economically and geographically. Anni had ruled out the children. She didn't regard them as a priority and would only start looking at them if the adult list didn't pan out. There might be a vengeful parent or family member involved somewhere but she doubted it, really. So the adults were where she was starting.

She had cross-referenced the ones that she had flagged up with Julie Miller's list. There were three that stood out and she was calling on the first one now. He had been referred to a speech therapist following a stroke. Anni had the bare essentials of his medical notes. Writer. Early fifties. Heavy drinker, heavy smoker. Mild to medium stroke. Responded well to treatment, discharged after three months of regular sessions, expected back for a check up in three months time.

She waited for the door to be answered.

The scene in the cell earlier that morning had stunned her. Horrible. Awful. She had heard of things like that before but never witnessed it for herself. Especially to someone she herself had questioned and fingered as a suspect.

Anthony Howe. When Fiona Welch read out the profile his name had jumped out at her. A perfect match. There had been such a sense of jubilation when she had brought him in, the exhilaration of a job well done. Or a good job about to be done. And then this. A total unravelling. Had he done it because he was guilty or because he was innocent? She didn't know. She hoped he came round so they could ask him.

But the real shocker had been the follow-up she had witnessed. Her boss striking a superior officer. Their superior officer. She had seen arguments before, differences of opinion, sure. On an almost daily basis. Strong personalities clashed all the time when under pressure, no big thing, part of the job. But to actually go so far as to take a swing at a superior officer and to see Phil Brennan be the one to do it, that was unprecedented. Admittedly, there had been times she had felt like doing that to Fenwick herself, but still . . .

She hadn't said a word. Knew she shouldn't, it wasn't in her best interests to. Knew Phil wouldn't want her to either. And no matter what had gone on between them recently, she was still loyal to her boss.

And then there was Mickey. With his spiky hair, cocky smile and sharp suit she had dismissed him as just another ambitious young officer, thinking he was a master of the universe and a shag magnet because he had put away a couple of villains, won a few fist fights and made it to DS. That was how she had taken the previous night's phone call at first, but the way he had behaved on the stairs earlier was different. He seemed serious, intense, even. Worried. In fact, she was beginning to think she had misjudged him.

And the way he had blushed when she had touched his arm. Sweet. She smiled at the memory.

But not too much. She didn't date guys she worked with. Not after last time.

But maybe he did have something important to say to her. Maybe he would ring her.

The front door opened, putting all further thoughts of Mickey Philips out of her mind. In front of her was a man. Small, grey-haired, portly. He looked old enough to be the father of the man she was calling on. He looked at her, warily.

'Keith Ridley?' she said, folding out her warrant card.

'Yes?' His voice held a tremor that matched the one in his hand holding the door open.

'Detective Constable Anni Hepburn. Can I have a few words?'

He slowly stood aside to let her in, closing the door behind her.

She entered and all thoughts of her fighting bosses, Mickey's tongue-tied attempts to talk to her and the condition of Anthony Howe were forgotten and pushed from her head as she concentrated on the job she had to do.

Forty minutes later she was back out in the sunshine, striking him off the list.

He was a writer of crime fiction, she had discovered, although she hadn't read any of his books. However, it would have been more accurate to say his real calling was self-destruction as he had sat in front of her chain-smoking cigarette after cigarette with a can of lager on the arm rest of his chair while she questioned him, his shaking hand alternating what he put to his lips.

He told her he didn't know why he had suffered a stroke, must have been something hereditary. His wife was out at work teaching and he was home alone. Working on a new novel, he said, although he had turned off *Homes Under the Hammer* when they entered the living room.

He had nothing but praise for the work of Suzanne and Zoe, though. And, Anni thought, genuine shock and regret when he saw on the news what had happened to them. And, most importantly, a verifiable alibi. She had thanked him and left.

Walking to her car, feeling the kind of imagined, malevolent eyes on her that all outsiders were treated to in remote villages, especially black ones, her phone rang.

She answered it. Mickey.

'Hey,' he said. 'How you doing?'

'Fine,' she said. 'Working through the therapy list like I said I was going to.'

'Any luck?'

'Not so far. Got an ex-soldier next. Post-traumatic stress disorder. That'll be a laugh. See what he comes up with.'

'Right.'

'You?'

He sighed. 'Losing the will to live. Rapidly.'

She laughed. 'Still hunting for Nemo?'

'Yeah . . .'

'Dory was my favourite. And the sharks.'

'What?'

'The film. Don't say you haven't seen it?'

'No. You have kids, then?'

'Nephews. Two of them.'

'Right.'

Mickey fell silent. Anni waited. Eventually she decided to prompt him.

'What was it you wanted to talk to me about, then?'

'Yeah. When are you free?'

She told him she had an address for the soldier on a houseboat by the quayside at the Hythe.

'Where we found the body,' said Mickey.

'Probably,' she said. 'D'you want to meet up there?'

He did. They made a time, rang off.

She drove away, glad to be heading back to the town. Feeling much safer there than in the country.

61

The Super sat behind the desk in Fenwick's office. Stared at him, unsmiling.

'Jesus Christ. What a fucking mess.'

Phil said nothing.

Fenwick was sitting next to him, a red welt over the side of his lip, his cheek puffed up, face turned away from the Super, eyes still on him. Phil kept the swollen knuckles of his right hand covered with his left.

The Super was never known by his full title, Chief Superintendent Brian Denton, at least not throughout Colchester Division. Just the Super. He wasn't a physically imposing man but he had the confidence and presence that comes from knowing whatever he said was going to be listened to and acted on. With his swept-back grey hair, impeccable uniform and artfully concealed broken veins on his nose, Phil was always reminded of an ageing matinee idol who thought he was bound for Hollywood but somehow ended up in daytime soaps. Not everyone can run the Met.

But he was a first-class copper and he still retained a thief taker's instinct, no matter how many years he had spent behind a desk.

Usually on a case like this Phil reported directly to the Super at Chelmsford, the DCI at the station, his direct superior, taking more of an office management role. The Super had mentioned Fenwick before. Phil got the impression he didn't rate him much.

'Heads should roll for this.'

Phil again said nothing.

Fenwick, however, leaned forward. 'Well, sir, I . . . I've covered all bases adequately. Perhaps if the . . .' – he risked a sly, angry glance at Phil – '. . . shall we say lower-ranking officers had done their jobs properly, we wouldn't be in this mess.'

Phil's vision turned red. His hands began to shake. *Bastard.*

He still said nothing.

The Super stared at Fenwick. 'Surely as senior officer the blame should lie with you, DCI Fenwick?'

Fenwick went red. 'Well, yes, perhaps . . . but I'm not out on the front line. I'm here, coordinating. I can't be held responsible for everything that goes on.'

'So you're . . . what? Just a glorified office manager, is that what you're saying?'

It was Fenwick's turn to shake. Phil suppressed a grin.

'I . . . I . . . no . . .'

The Super cut in. 'This is a bloody mess. You've got more resources and bodies on this one than any other case in Essex. I want results. And I want this kept quiet, the press out of. If I see one word of this in the papers I'll have both your jobs, clear?'

They both nodded.

'Good. Right.' He turned to Phil. 'DI Brennan. Did you get a confession out of the suspect before he was taken to hospital?'

Phil shook his head. 'No, sir.'

'Pity.' He looked at his watch. Sighed. Clearly on his way

271

to another appointment. He looked between the two of them irritably. 'Can I trust you both to carry on with this? Without one blaming the other for failings either real or imagined? Or the other feeling the need to express his feelings physically, no matter how deserving the recipient may be of them?'

The Super's eyes twinkled. Phil caught it. He didn't know if Fenwick had.

He knows. He knows what's happened.

Phil nodded. 'You can, sir.'

Fenwick was more hesitant.

'Problem, DCI Fenwick?'

Fenwick risked a sly look at Phil, eyes lit by a vengeful light. Here it comes, he thought.

'Yes? I'm waiting.'

Fenwick shook his head, dropped his eyes to the floor.

'Good. DI Brennan, you're still in charge of this investigation. Move it forward, get results. The whole world and his bloody wife are looking over our shoulder on this one. DCI Fenwick, you're in charge of damage control here. Like I said, not one word of this to the press. Or heads will roll.'

The Super stood up, bid them good day, let himself out.

Fenwick breathed a sigh or relief.

Silence in the room.

'Not one word, Ben,' said Phil eventually, 'or heads will roll.'

Fenwick turned to him, quickly, angrily. 'You won't get away with what you did.'

There were plenty of retorts that came into Phil's mind then but he kept his mouth shut. Instead he stood up, left the office and walked back to the bar.

The investigation was in full swing. Phones were being worked, keyboards pounded, voices raised, bodies all over the room. But there was something Phil was interested in more than the investigation at the moment. All to do with the plan he had thought up on the way to work.

He walked across to Milhouse, crouched at the side of his desk.

'Milhouse,' he said, 'need you to run a check on someone for me.'

Milhouse looked up, pushed his glasses back up his nose. 'Who?'

He handed him a folded slip of paper. Milhouse opened it, read it. Then looked up, his mouth a perfect 'O' of shock.

'This is—'

'Marina.'

'Right.' Milhouse frowned. 'What kind of check?'

'Financial, mainly.' He gave him another sheet of folded paper. 'Here's her account details. Debit and credit cards. I want to know if you can find a trail, see where they've been used.'

'But, this is . . . this is against the law.'

Phil tried to act casual. 'Strictly speaking, without a warrant and all that, yes. But please. As a favour to your superior officer? A discreet favour?'

Milhouse looked between the computer and the paper. Eventually he nodded.

Phil managed a smile. 'Thanks. This means a lot to me. And let me know as soon as you find something, yeah?'

Milhouse said he would.

He stood up, crossed to the door. Fenwick was just walking through it.

'Where are you going?'

'To do some policework.'

He swept through the doors before Fenwick could say anything else.

Rose Martin looked up from her desk. Ben was standing by the double doors, watching Phil Brennan walk away. She knew the look on his face by now – angry enough to do some serious damage.

She stood up, walked towards him.

'Ben? You got a minute?'

She walked outside, knowing he would follow her into the corridor. Knowing he would follow her anywhere. Aware also that Fiona Welch had looked up, was watching them go.

'That bastard . . .' As soon as they were alone, the anger was vented. 'The Super knows what happened, knows what that bastard did and condones it, bloody condones it . . . oh, he didn't say it in so many words but I know what he meant. It was clear whose bloody side he was on . . .'

'Ben.' She placed her hands on his shoulders, looked directly into his eyes. They were flailing around, avoiding her gaze, but she kept at him, waiting for them to settle, like startled crows following a gunshot.

'D'you want to get back at him? D'you want to get even?'

'You're bloody right I do. I want to see the look on his face when—'

She jumped in quickly. 'D'you want the glory for this one? Want Brennan to come in looking clueless?'

He looked at her. Said nothing.

'I've got something that no one else has. And it's gold.'

His anger stopped. She knew it was still there, though, like a stationary train at a platform or cancer in remission.

'What?' he said.

She smiled. 'Calm down first, then I'll show you.'

He smiled. It was a struggle. 'You always know the right thing to say to me.'

'I know,' she said. 'Come on.'

She led him back into the bar, aware that Fiona Welch's eyes were still fixed on the pair of them.

Rose smiled to herself. *Hands off, spod*, she thought. *There's only one person going to get the glory on this case and shag the boss.*

And that's me.

62

Paula Harrison's face registered a range of emotions that Phil hoped he would never have to experience.

She stood in the doorway to her house, clutching the door. She stared at him, round-eyed. If she blinked, Phil thought, the tears would start.

And might never stop.

'Adele . . .'

'Can I come in, Paula?'

She let him in. It was the same as his last visit only more so. The mess was messier, the cartoons on the TV louder and more vivid, the sense of lost hope more palpable.

She chased Nadine upstairs, waited until the door closed, perched on the edge of the sofa. Looked at Phil. Preparing herself.

'We . . .'

She cut him off. 'It's her, isn't it? The body. Adele . . .'

'I think you'd better prepare yourself for the worst.'

And she broke. Not just tears but her whole body seemed to crumple as if her bones had dissolved, leaving her unable to move, to stand.

'I'll . . .' Phil went into the kitchen to make tea. Let her sob in peace.

He returned to find her dabbing her eyes and blowing her nose with a paper tissue. She kept dabbing, kept blowing until the tissue was too sodden to function then, seemingly forgetting about it, just let it drop to the floor.

'How . . . how did . . .'

'We believe the body we found is Adele. We still need to do other tests to be sure but I just wanted to warn you.'

She nodded absently.

'You'll be asked to make a formal identification of the body once we've confirmed it's her. Is there anyone you'd like to come with you?'

She shook her head.

'A family member? Friend?'

'Adele was my family. All the family I had left . . .'

'What about her father?'

A dark wave passed over Paula's features. 'He won't be back . . .' She glanced up at Phil, glanced away. 'And, anyway, Adele hated him. She wouldn't . . . wouldn't . . .' The tears started again.

Phil said nothing.

'She was all, all I had . . .'

Phil looked at the pictures on the wall. Adele when she was younger with her brother. Both smiling, both looking like the summer would never end.

Both gone.

Phil didn't know what else to say. He had no words that would make things better for her, no actions that could help. He phoned FLO, asked them to send Cheryl Bland round. She was on her way. Phil hung up, told Paula.

She nodded.

'I think . . .'

But he never got to tell her what he thought. His phone went again. He answered.

'Adrian here, boss. I'm with the CSIs in Suzanne Perry's flat. Found something I think you should see.'

He looked across at Paula. Didn't want to leave her alone. 'Right now?'

''Fraid so.'

'What kind of thing?'

He hesitated. 'I think you should come and see for yourself, boss.'

'OK.' He checked his watch. 'On my way.'

He turned to Paula. 'I have to go.'

She looked up at him sharply, as if she had forgotten he was actually there.

'Cheryl Bland'll be here soon. She'll help you.' He handed her a card. 'Call me if you need to.'

She took it. Let it slip through her fingers to join the used tissue.

Phil saw himself out.

63

'Up here, boss,' said Adrian Wren. 'And, like they say in *Star Trek*, set faces to stun.'

Phil didn't correct him, knew the misquote was intentional. He was standing in the hallway of Suzanne Perry's flat, a two-person CSI still working their way through, Jane Gosling supervising.

The flat was well on its way to looking like no one had ever lived there. The careful accretion of Suzanne Perry's life – not to mention Zoe Herriot's body – had been removed, broken down and analysed. It was something that always depressed Phil. Not for the first time did a murder scene remind him of a stage set when the actors had finished. This time it went even further. The play was over, the set being torn down. There was only the hope that another one would take its place.

Phil looked away, looked up towards Adrian's voice.

The hatch to the loft was open. His DC was leaning over, looking downwards. 'Get a chair, boss, and I'll pull you up.'

Phil did so, struggling to be hauled into the square loft opening. Adrian, despite his scrawniness, was surprisingly strong. Phil knew he was a runner. Must have helped to build him up.

Phil reached the edge of the opening, let Adrian help him to his feet.

'Watch your head,' said Adrian. 'And your feet. It's been boarded over a bit, but not too well.'

On the floor were several old doors laid across the rafters, thick, wadded insulation sticking out between the gaps. Above his head, the ceiling was covered in cobwebs. Dust and dirt caught in the webby strands, strung like filthy grey hammocks between the beams.

Adrian gestured with his hand, pointed. 'Along there.'

Phil looked. At the far end of the loft where the wooden beams ended in a triangular brick wall, there were no cobwebs, no dust, no dirt. It had been cleaned and cleared. The old doors had been moved together making a floor. Phil noticed now that the other doors over the rafters mirrored the layout of the flat below. A walkway.

Someone had been living here.

'Christ . . .'

Adrian nodded. 'I know.' He moved forward slightly. 'Don't want to disturb it too much, the CSIs haven't been along there yet. But, look, you can make out what's been happening . . .'

He pointed again.

'We became suspicious when we found some tiny cameras in the living room downstairs. Fibre-optic, good ones. Never know they were there if you weren't looking for them. Well hidden.'

'So you checked the other rooms?'

Adrian nodded. 'Same in every one. Bedroom, bathroom, kitchen. Tiny, with a wireless transmitter. So we checked the range, realised it wasn't very far, looked around to see where the likeliest place to receive them would be. Traced them up to here. In that corner there, specifically.'

'So . . . what? A bank of TV screens, or something?'

Adrian gave a grim smile. 'It's the twenty-first century, boss. All you need is a laptop and the right software.'

'And our man had that.'

'Oh yes.'

Phil shook his head. Adrian Wren loved a gadget. He would be in his element with this line of inquiry. 'So,' said Phil. 'This was planned. Premeditated, yes?'

'Meticulously, I'd say.'

'Would we be able to trace him from the equipment? Find him from where he bought it? I'm assuming this is specialised stuff. You won't get it at Currys.'

'You're right there. It could be government-issue. Army. I'll be looking in to it.'

Phil frowned. 'Why did he leave it behind? Didn't he know we'd find it?'

'I don't know. He's taken his laptop. Maybe he's got another set of cameras and can start again. Maybe he got what he wanted here and didn't need them any more. But that's not all.'

Phil's stomach flipped. He didn't like the tone of Adrian's voice, the look in his eye when he said that.

'There.' Adrian moved forward. Phil followed.

Two rows of bottles, the kind of specimen jars a doctor provides, were displayed neatly along the last door before the wall. All of them containing something off-white and viscous.

'We've had a look at one of them. Human semen. He's been knocking one out and saving it. Collecting them till he's got the set. Don't know what for, though.'

'Tributes?' suggested Phil. 'Saving it all up for the woman he loves?'

Adrian grimaced. 'Happy Valentine's Day. Lovely.'

'Get them analysed. Might get a DNA match.'

'Already doing it.' Adrian sighed. 'He was living here, too.

Bottling and boxing up his waste, leaving it under the floor. It looks like he had a sleeping bag here too.'

'Food?'

'Few remains. Wrappers from energy bars, that kind of thing. Red Bull cans. Maybe he went downstairs if he wanted anything else, helped himself when Suzanne was out.'

'And there's no trace of him now.'

Adrian shook his head. 'Place is cold. My guess is he took Suzanne and headed out with her. Got what he wanted, no need to come back here.'

Phil stood staring at the scene before him, saying nothing, thinking.

Working out what to do next.

'The others,' he said eventually.

Adrian listened.

'Julie Miller. Adele Harrison. Was he watching them?'

'He might have been . . .'

'I'd say he definitely was.' He looked round, suddenly anxious to be out of the loft, on the move. 'Can I leave you with this?'

Adrian nodded.

'I'm off to check the other women on the list, see if he's been there.' He sighed.

'Just what we need to be looking for. An obsessed survivalist. Brilliant . . .'

64

'Hello? Mr Buchan . . .'

No reply.

Anni could see the crime scene on the lightship from where she stood. King Edward Quay on the Hythe stretched away from the Colne Causeway Bridge with the upscale apartments either side of it to a series of newly installed mooring points. The walkway had been block-paved with new trees planted in specified circular areas at regular intervals. Each mooring point had a heavy metal tie for the rope to be looped round and a power-point post providing an electricity supply for each berthed vessel. The electricity substation hummed behind a spiked metal fence over the road behind her.

The boats varied. Some were narrowboats, freshly painted and decked out in traditional livery and colours. One was a larger boat, part home, part business, with a sign on the deck offering river tours alongside plant pots and chained-up bikes. Some were old fishing vessels extended into houseboats.

Eventually the pavement, the trees and the power-point

posts ran out. On one side of the narrow road the businesses faded away leaving only piles of greening timber and full skips behind spiked metal railings and rusting 'Keep Out' signs. Piles of rubble formed small mountain ranges on old, cracked, weed-infested concrete forecourts. What buildings there were were single-storey, over forty years old. Like an idea of the future from a sixties Gerry Anderson puppet series and just as accurate. Next to them was a huge, old, square building, the Colchester Dock Transit Company announced on the side in faded, peeling capital letters. It was all rusted and mildewed corrugated iron cladding with an ancient crane and cabin outside. The walls were covered in graffiti bringing unexpected, surprisingly welcome bursts of colour to the drab, depressing surroundings. Boarded-up doors carried warnings that inside was unsafe and to stay out.

The boats moored along this section mirrored their surroundings.

No mooring posts or power points or trees here.

Just old rusting wrecks, mostly unserviceable, superannuated fishing boats, their water-going days long behind them. Now left to rust away to nothing, float, piece by piece, out to sea on the tide.

It was one of these that the next contact on Anni's list had given as an address.

'Hello . . . Mr Buchan . . .' She called again. With more trepidation this time.

Still no reply.

There was nothing on the deck to show that the boat was lived in or even habitable, apart from a hand-painted sign hanging at an angle on a death trap of a boarding ramp: 'Rani'.

She looked round. No one about. Even though it was another hot, sunny day with a cloudless blue sky, she felt a damp chill run through her because of her surroundings.

The boarding ramp was open. The door to the hold looked unlocked. She gave another quick look round, stepped on to the boat.

The tide was out and it was pitched at an angle on a mudbank. Anni crossed the deck, careful of her footing as some of the wooden planks felt soft and rotten beneath her feet. She reached the wheelhouse, leaned across and pulled on the small wooden door. Unlocked. It opened slowly on creaky, horror-movie hinges. Before her was darkness, a steep set of stairs leading down.

'Mr Buchan?'

Nothing. Just an echo.

She took another look round. Then went slowly and carefully down the steps.

The only illumination in the hold came from gaps in the wooden ceiling and rusted walls. Jacob's ladders of light criss-crossed in front of her, dust motes dancing in the rays.

She looked round. Grimaced.

On the floor were a sleeping bag, some old newspapers, dirty underwear and T-shirts. Opened and emptied food cans lay about, with varying degrees of fungal growth attached to them, looking like an Al-Qaeda chemical weapons breeding lab. It stank of waste, decay. Scratching, scuttling noises sounded underfoot as Anni moved.

That was bad enough. But it was the walls that really made her gasp.

Pictures, everywhere. Dotted around randomly, culled from different sources. Some cut from newspapers, grinning topless models and celebrities. Others, their open legs, naked bodies, faked ecstasy and even more fake breasts betraying porn mag origins. Some actual photos. Anni took out her mobile, used the lighted screen for illumination as she examined them more closely.

She recognised some of the surroundings. Colchester's main shopping centre. Maldon Road. The hospital where

Suzanne Perry and Zoe Herriot had worked. All blurred, grainy. As if they had been taken without the subject's knowledge. Like surveillance photos.

Something a stalker would do.

Her heart skipped a beat. She knew who the women in the photos were.

But that was only an educated guess. She couldn't make a positive identification. Because all the pictures, whether from newspapers, magazines or those taken in the street, all had one thing in common.

The eyes had been scratched out.

She recoiled from them, her heart hammering in her chest, suddenly wanting to get out. She stepped on the sleeping bag, gave a small cry.

Then stopped dead.

A noise from the deck above.

Someone was up there.

Anni froze, looked quickly, desperately round. Shining her phone display everywhere. Finding no other exit but the stairs.

Another footstep, then another from above.

'Oh God, oh God . . .' Her breath was coming in short, ragged bursts.

She looked round frantically.

Another footstep, getting nearer to the wheelhouse.

Her phone was in her hand, ready to dial. She just hoped that someone could get to her quick enough.

The doorway above her opened. A voice called down.

'What you doing down there?'

Anni closed her eyes. Froze.

65

Phil had struck lucky. The building that Julie Miller lived in had a doorman.

'Awful business,' the doorman said. He was a small man, in his fifties, Phil guessed. Everything about him was round. Bald head, long-sight glasses that curved and emphasised his eyes, portly figure, even bow legs. He was polite and deferential but the tattoos that covered his hands – home-made, blue ink – spoke of a different past. Phil wondered whether he had had a run-in with him before. He couldn't place him. Which was fine. He was all for second chances.

'Julie Miller . . .' The doorman brought his brows together in concentration. 'Awful . . .'

'I just wondered whether you'd seen anything else unusual in the flats.'

His frowned intensified. 'Unusual? What d'you mean?'

'You know.' Phil tried to spell it out him. 'Different people coming and going. The same people disappearing, maybe not coming back. That kind of thing.'

'Hmm.'

More brow furrowing, like he was really trying to be

helpful. Phil gave him the benefit of the doubt. Maybe he was. Part of putting his past transgressions behind him.

'Have you got a description? Of this person I should have been looking out for?'

'Afraid not.'

'Then how am I supposed to know who he is?'

Phil smiled. Fair point. 'You're not. I'm just looking for anyone who sticks in your mind.'

'Hmm. Not easy. Kind of people who pay to live in a block like this tend to want a bit of privacy. Bit of blind-eye turning, know what I mean?'

'I do. But if you could just think of anyone, anything.' Phil had an idea. 'Somewhere near Julie Miller's flat.'

Again, more brow furrowing. Then, like a light bulb going on, his eyes widened. 'The Palmers. Christopher and Charlotte.'

'What about them?'

'They went away. Long holiday, apparently. Short notice. Had a win on the lottery, apparently, so I heard.'

Phil's pulse quickened. His fingers tingled. 'Where do they live?'

'Near Julie Miller. Flat above her, in fact.'

The doorman's pass key let Phil into the apartment.

The doorman himself had wanted to accompany him but Phil had put him off. He was well-meaning and the last thing he needed was hand-holding a well-meaning amateur.

Phil closed the door behind him, looked round the flat. He didn't need to be a detective to know something was wrong.

The flat hadn't been lived in but it had been occupied. And he could guess who by. Empty Red Bull cans littered the floor, interspersed with energy bar wrappers. Just like Suzanne Perry's loft. Opened food cans joined them, some with spoons still sticking out. Like someone who had no respect for their surroundings had squatted here.

He checked the bedroom. More of the same. Sheets, duvet left all over the place. He went back into the living room, scanned it once more. He had been here. Phil was sure of that. He must remember to tell the CSIs to check Julie Miller's flat for hidden cameras. He was sure they would find some.

He had one more room to check. The bathroom. He found it, walked inside. The shower curtain was pulled across as if someone was in there. He pulled it back.

And stood back, gasping.

'Oh shit . . .'

Phil took his phone out, hit speed dial.

'It's Phil Brennan here. Listen, we've got a situation.' He looked again, looked away quickly.

'A hell of a situation . . .'

66

Anni was too terrified to move.

She stood stock-still. She was sure he could hear her hammering heart, her ragged, shallow breaths. She wanted to move, scream, or at least take in a full breath. But she didn't dare.

The voice laughed. Footsteps started on the stairs.

Oh God . . .

A figure blocked out the light, came slowly towards her.

She had to do something, buy herself some time.

'My name is Detective Constable Anni Hepburn,' she said, feeling sure her breath wouldn't carry her to the end of the next sentence, 'please identify yourself.'

Another bout of laughter. 'You sounded so formal there.'

What? Then she recognised the voice. Mickey Philips.

'And I know who you are, Anni.' He moved into one of the beams of light, laughing. 'Should have seen your face . . .'

She hit him. And again, and again, slapping him on the chest out of fear, frustration and relief. 'You . . . bastard . . . fucking bastard, Mickey Philips . . .'

'Hey, hey, stop.' He put his hands up and, still laughing, caught her wrists.

She managed to regain some semblance of composure. 'What are you doing here, anyway?'

'Said to meet you here. Remember?'

She dropped her hands. Looked round, took in the walls once more. 'Glad you did.'

Mickey followed her gaze, took in what she had seen. 'Jesus Christ . . .'

'I know. Think we might be on to something here. Fiona Welch and her profile . . .' She shook her head.

'That's what I wanted to talk to you about,' he said. 'Last night.'

Anni raised an eyebrow. Waited.

He looked round once more, took in the photos and pictures, seemed clearly unnerved by them. 'Can we go outside? Think I've seen as much of this place as I need to.'

They made their way back on to the quay. Anni was amazed that the sun was still shining. After being down below in that boat she thought she would never see the sun again.

Mickey seemed to be feeling it too. 'Fancy an ice cream?'

'I fancy a gin and tonic. Bloody huge one.'

He laughed. 'Don't blame you.'

Her smiled faded. 'So. About last night . . .' She attempted a smile but what they had just seen didn't make it easy.

'Fiona Welch,' said Mickey. 'What d'you think of her?'

Anni shrugged. 'Haven't had an awful lot to do with her. Can't say she's the best profiler ever to work in the department.'

'I can't make her out. One minute she doesn't want to talk to me the next she's all over me.'

'Must be your aftershave. Is that the Lynx effect?'

'I'm serious. She's really starting to bug me. I was thinking about this last night. And then this morning when Anthony Howe tried to kill himself, I was watching her again.'

'And?'

He looked around, suddenly uneasy about speaking his mind. 'She seemed to be, I don't know, getting off on it. Like this was all some great day out that she was having.' His eyes dropped. 'Like . . . it was all going according to plan.'

Anni stared at him. 'What d'you mean?'

Mickey's hands became restless. 'I . . . look. I checked the logs. She went to talk to him last night, Anthony Howe. Down in the cells after Phil had finished.' He sighed. 'And sometimes I've watched her in the office when she thinks no one's looking at her and she's smiling.'

'Very rare. Especially in our office.'

'Don't mean just that. It's like she's, I don't know, laughing at us. All of us. Like it's some big secret joke.' He sighed. 'Oh, I don't know. It seems really stupid saying it out loud. I'm probably making something out of nothing. But . . . she doesn't feel right.'

Anni looked at him. Mickey's discomfort seemed genuine enough. And he didn't seem like the kind of person to make up false accusations for the sake of it.

'So what d'you think she's done?'

'I don't know.'

'And what are you going to do about it?'

'I don't know that either. I just wanted to . . . I don't know. Tell someone.' He looked away down the quay. 'Someone I could trust.'

Anni smiled. 'Thank you. Maybe a background check wouldn't go amiss.'

He nodded. 'Thanks.'

Anni's phone rang, startling the pair of them. She answered.

'It's Phil Brennan here. Listen, we've got a situation . . .'

67

'Julie? Julie . . .'

No reply. Suzanne's fellow captive had drifted away from her again.

Suzanne no longer knew whether it was day or night or how long she had been there. She had tried counting from when she had been allowed out, given that can of disgusting food, trying to give structure to time, but it hadn't worked. The counting had slowed then speeded up. She lost count several times, going over the same numbers twice, three times. Sometimes she forgot to keep counting, her mind drifting off. A couple of times, like counting sheep at night, she nodded off. All sense of time was gone.

Even her panic, her anger, had abated. In its place was a dull acceptance, her body slipping into a kind of fugue state, shutting down everything but the most basic of life-support systems. Even her ability to dream, to imagine, was gone. She just lay there, enveloped in nothingness.

'Julie . . . Julie . . .'

Suzanne hoped she would answer. She had a question. But she doubted there would be a reply. She was just saying the name out of habit, a quickly established ritual. Something that kept her going. Or maybe if she could work out Julie's sleep patterns it might help to synchronise.

'Yes . . .'

A reply. Suzanne's heart quickened.

'What d'you want?' Julie sounded drowsy, just pulled out of a deep sleep.

'I've been thinking,' said Suzanne. 'You're Julie, right?'

'Yes.'

'You're not Julie Miller, are you?'

Silence. Eventually, she spoke. 'How . . . how do you know my name . . .?'

'You disappeared. It was all over the news. The police were on the wing for days.'

'On the wing?'

'Gainsborough.'

'But . . .' Julie's voice sounded animated, urgent. 'How do you know that?'

'I think we know each other. I'm Suzanne. I work there as one of the SALTs.'

'With Zoe?'

'That's me.'

Silence, while they both took the information in.

'God . . .' said Julie eventually. 'Really?'

'Yeah.'

'But . . . who's done this, then? Do we know them?'

'We must. We'll have to think.'

There was the sound of a body moving. Julie must have been excited, turning in her box.

But another sound followed the noise Julie made in turning and moving. A different kind of sound, yet one that was also familiar. The ripping, tearing sound Suzanne had heard earlier, the one that accompanied the box being opened. Just small, fleeting, like an echo of the earlier sound, but unmistakeable.

'What was that? Julie? What was that?'

The sound came again. Slightly louder, longer this time.

'Julie? You there? What's happening? What's going on?'

Silence. Suzanne thought Julie must have disappeared again, but her voice came back eventually.

'Suzanne?'

'Yeah?'

'I think . . .' Her voice was no longer sleepy, she was wide awake now. Energised. 'I'm not sure, but I think I've just found a way out . . .'

68

'In here,' said Rose Martin, ushering Ben Fenwick into his own office, closing the door behind him.

He looked round, nervous. Not wanting to be seen by other officers, going against years of accepted procedure. Whatever he was, he was a copper who did things properly. Followed the rules. Made them work for him. This was completely new territory to be in.

Rose guessed from the look on his face what was going through his mind. She smiled, unable to resist the urge to toy with him. As he crossed to his desk, sat down behind it, she put down the laptop she had been carrying, stood with her back against the door. Her hands went to her breasts, opening the buttons on her blouse. She threw her head back as if the touch of her own fingers were sending her into ecstasy.

'I want you, Ben. Here. Now. In your office. Your lovely, shiny, DCI's office.'

The look on his face was, she thought, priceless. He wanted her, too, no doubt about it. Here. Now. But it went against every action he had ever done, everything he had ever believed in.

She slid a hand between her denimed legs. She moaned, sighed. 'All this power in here. And it's all yours. God, I'm so horny . . .'

'Rose . . .' He looked like he was about to go into cardiac arrest.

Indecision played across Ben Fenwick's face, so easy to read. Like he had a cartoon angel on one shoulder, a cartoon devil on the other, and he was listening to each argument put forward, weighing them both up. Rose almost laughed out loud.

Mind made up, he got up from his desk, came towards her.

Immediately she stopped what she was doing, dropped her hands, straightened up.

'Later,' she said, pushing herself off the door, picking up the laptop and walking across to the desk. 'We've got work to do. Come on.'

She sat down in the chair he had recently been sitting in. Spun herself from side to side. Smiled. 'Nice, though. A DCI's chair in a DCI's office. I could get used to this.'

'I thought . . . thought we had work to do . . .'

Poor Ben, she thought. Didn't know if he was coming or going. Put him out of his misery, get down to business.

She reached for the laptop, opened it, powered it up. 'This was Julie Miller's.'

'Past tense?'

Irritation flashed in her eyes. '*Is* Julie Miller's. I entered her Facebook account. Found this.' She flicked through some pages, scrolled up and down a screen. 'Here. Look.'

Fenwick came round the side of the desk to join her. 'What am I looking at?'

'Photos. Julie Miller posted her life on here. There's over a hundred of them. I went through all of them. Found a few coincidences. Well, more than coincidences, really.'

She moved the laptop over, pointed to the screen.

'What am I looking at?'

The photo was of a house party. Students from the look of it, or at least all young people. Julie Miller was in the centre of the picture, tumbler of wine in one hand, a young man with his arm round her, clamped to her.

'Him. There.' She looked at Fenwick, triumph in her eyes. 'That,' she said pointing to the screen, voice raised higher than necessary, 'is Suzanne Perry's ex-boyfriend. Mark Turner.'

Fenwick frowned. 'And he's . . .'

'Looking very friendly with our girl Julie, yes.'

'So . . . they knew each other?'

'I did some digging. It would have come up eventually. Julie Miller was at university the same time as Suzanne Perry and Zoe Herriot. Here in Colchester. The same time as Mark Turner. Well, he's still there. Doing a Ph.D.'

'And did he say he knew her?'

She shook her head. 'Denied it.'

Fenwick straightened up. There was light dancing in his eyes now. 'We might be on to something . . .'

'I remembered something Mark Turner said to me. He's part of a horror-film society that meets in the Freemason's Arms on Military Road in New Town. So I did a bit more digging.' She sat back, smiling. 'Guess who the barmaid was there?'

Fenwick frowned once more.

'I'll tell you. Adele Harrison.'

'So . . . Mark Turner is connected to all the women in this case?'

She nodded. 'He is. And that's something Phil Brennan doesn't know.'

Fenwick stood up. 'Then we'd better tell him.'

Rose didn't move. 'After the way he spoke to you earlier? Why?'

'Because it's procedure. Everyone's so bloody accountable

these days if proper procedure isn't followed then heads will roll. Jobs will be lost.'

She turned to face him, stopping him leave just with her eyes. 'But not your job, Ben. Phil Brennan's perhaps, but not yours.' She stood up, pushed her body against him. 'We know something he doesn't. If we act on it, bring Mark Turner in, while he's off running round chasing non-existent leads, then we might well have cracked the case.' She pushed right close against him. 'What d'you think?'

Before Fenwick could reply, her phone rang. She ignored it.

She smiled. 'Feeling hard, Ben?'

The phone kept ringing.

He was breathing heavily. But looking irritated. 'Look, please answer that. It might be important.'

She sighed, took the phone from her pocket, glanced down at the display.

'Phil Brennan. I'll ignore it.'

She switched it off.

Fenwick looked slightly nervous. 'I think you should . . .'

She put her hands round his neck.

'Now, where were we?'

69

'They've been dead a while,' said Phil. 'Both of them.'

'I can see that . . .' Mickey Philips tried to back out of the bathroom, only to find Anni blocking his way. Reluctantly, he stayed where he was.

'You OK, Mickey?' said Phil. 'Not going to have a repeat of the other day?'

'I'm fine, boss. Yeah . . .'

Phil wasn't so sure. And he couldn't blame his DS. The bathroom looked like the aftermath of a particularly violent, drunken party in an abattoir. Blood spray covered the white tiles from floor to ceiling, almost like a caricature of slaughter. But there was nothing caricatured about the bodies in the bath. A man and a woman, both fully-clothed, their necks slit open, the wounds deep and fierce, their bodies just dumped without any ceremony.

'We know he likes a knife,' said Phil. 'That's how he got rid of Zoe Herriot too.'

'Weapon of choice,' said Anni. 'What's that stuff they're covered in?'

'Quicklime, I reckon,' said Phil. 'Helps to break down the bodies faster. Hides the smell too.'

'Lovely,' said Anni.

'Good job you were both nearby,' said Phil.

'Yeah,' said Mickey, still trying not to look at the sight before him, 'wouldn't have wanted to miss this.'

Anni had told him all about Ian Buchan, the soldier she was tracking down, the boat he lived in. Seeing what had been done to Julie Miller's neighbours in such close proximity, he had just jumped to the top of their prime-suspect list.

'I'll call it in, get a CSI team over here. I'll just try Rose first.' He dialled a number.

'So what d'you reckon?' said Mickey to Anni while Phil was on the phone. 'He moved in here, kept Julie Miller under surveillance, then took her off somewhere.'

Anni nodded. 'But why? Why take her away? Why not just keep watching her or if he wanted to, move in on her?'

'Don't know,' said Mickey. 'Maybe it's, I don't know, the next stage? Whatever he's got in mind?'

'But why one after the other?'

'I don't know. But I know one thing. That profile from Fiona Welch was a piece of shit. Either she's not much cop or . . .'

'She did it deliberately,' finished Anni.

Phil put his phone away, clearly not happy. 'Not answering. She's bloody useless . . .' He turned to the other two. 'Right. We'll get a team over here, go over the flat. I'm sure they'll find surveillance stuff. In the meantime, I want you two to get over the river, keep watch on that boat for anyone coming back. Don't go after them or try to take them on your own, just keep watch and let me know soon as. I'll get an armed response team down there straight away.'

Anni and Mickey both nodded.

'I'll seal this place up then get back to the station. Brief everyone on what we've found. Things are picking up speed, let's keep on with it. Any questions?'

Mickey looked uncomfortable. 'Boss . . .'

'Yes, Mickey.'

'Fiona Welch. That profile . . .'

'Was awful, I know. Fenwick got her on the cheap. His usual tactic, covering his arse, trying to make savings while paying lip service to what he considers good practice. She's useless. I'll get shot of her when I get back. Anything else?'

Mickey seemed to want to say something further but hesitated.

'OK. On you go. Keep in touch.'

They left the flat.

Phil got on the phone again.

The case was moving.

It felt good.

70

Fenwick's phone rang. He was still in his office, zipping up his trousers, Rose Martin sitting on the desk beside him, head back and smiling, like a cat that had just been particularly well fed.

Fenwick looked at the display, saw who it was. Phil Brennan.

'Don't answer it,' said Rose, rearranging her clothes, running fingers through her hair.

He looked conflicted once more, his post-coital mood dropping away to reveal his earlier doubts.

It kept ringing.

Rose leaned across, placed her hand on his. 'Don't answer it.'

'I can't just . . . I'm the superior officer on this case. It might be important.'

Fire flashed in Rose's eyes once more. 'Ben, what have I just showed you? What links have I just made for you? I've just given you a lead that's going to blow anything Phil Brennan's got right out of the water. Now you can either answer that phone, go running after him or you can come with me.'

Fenwick said nothing. Kept his eyes averted from hers.

'What'll it be?'

The phone stopped ringing.

Fenwick sighed. 'Come on,' he said.

She smiled. 'Good call, Ben. That's the right decision.' She gave a sly smile, thrusting her breasts out as she did so. 'And besides, you might just get another reminder of my awesome blow-job technique if you come with me.'

Despite having come only moments earlier, he felt himself stiffening once more. She knew how to press his buttons. And he loved to have them pressed.

'Come on then,' he said, unlocking his office door and stepping into the hall.

As he did so, Fiona Welch was walking towards him.

'There you are,' she said, 'I've been looking for you.'

He stopped walking. As he did, Rose emerged from the office, bumped into him. Fiona looked between the two of them, a smile spreading across her face.

Fenwick felt himself reddening. 'I've just been . . . We've been looking at a new lead that's . . . that's just come in. That we've just discovered. That Rose – that DS Martin has just shown me.'

'Right.' Fiona Welch nodded, kept her smile controlled. 'There's been a phone call for you in the bar. I took it. DI Brennan. Says he's got a new lead. Lot of them about.'

Fenwick nodded. 'Right. Right. Well, I've just – we've just got to pop out for a bit. Got a lead of our own to follow up.'

'Oh, whereabouts?' Fiona's question was sharp, quick. She smiled. 'I'm only asking because I'm . . . doing the geographic profile DI Brennan asked me to do. If you've got something I should know where it is, factor it in.'

'Greenstead Road,' he said. 'Now, if you'll excuse me . . .'

Fenwick, with Rose in tow, squeezed past Fiona Welch. She watched them go. Then went back to her desk. Keyed the information Fenwick has just given her into her BlackBerry.

71

The Creeper had stopped noticing the smell.

He was used to being surrounded by death. Years of living with it on a daily basis had done that to him. There were tricks he used, ways to make them smell less, or to make him not think about them being there so much, but that's all they were. Just tricks. The actual death, of stopping someone's heart, seeing the light go out in their eyes, that didn't bother him at all. In fact, he enjoyed it. And having their bodies around him, the empty husks that had once housed their spirits, just lying on the floor or in another room was nothing. Just more rubbish lying about.

It hadn't always been like that. Or at least he didn't think it had. If he thought back hard enough he could remember a time when things were different. Before the fire.

Before the nightmares and the monsters.

In those memories and dreams it was always summer. The colours so vivid, alive. There were swings and laughter. And a girl. Always a girl. Small, smiling. At him. In a kind way.

Not Rani. Not like her.

And yet . . . not unlike her.

And she would laugh and he would smile and the sun would make the soft downy hairs on his arms tickle. Those dream memories.

And he would open his eyes. And the world would be as it was now. With no colour in it. And there would be no sun tickling his arms. No heat. No fire.

And the girl with her sunny smiles would be gone.

And he would think some more and there would be Rani. Only Rani.

The old woman's body had started to smell. It had gone through being stiff and impossible to move, like bodies did. And now it was starting to loosen up. Soon it would be nothing more than an old sack of fluid, fat and bones.

The Creeper didn't care. It was nothing to him.

He was still watching. Waiting. Practising being patient. Willing Rani to appear again.

Rose Martin. That was the name she was going by. But it wasn't important. He would call her by her real one. Make her answer to it.

He didn't like that man being around, though. Felt a shaft of something hard and icy hot lance through him when he thought of that man with her, touching her, talking to her . . . He wished he were nearer to her than across the road. In the house with her where he should be. Living together as lovers.

Soon, though. Once he'd worked out how to go about it. Soon.

He closed his eyes. He could feel her, trying to get through, trying to talk to her.

And there she was.

'Hello, Rani.'

Hello, my love.

'I . . . I'm watching you. Can you see me?'

Yes, I can see you. I always know when you're there.

He grinned, let out a little giggle. 'Good.'

Listen, she said, *d'you want to come and meet me?*

He was too shocked to talk for a few seconds. That wasn't what he had been expecting to hear her say. 'Wha— . . . when? Where?'

She gave him directions.

As for when . . . Why not right now?

'Really? You mean that? I don't need to watch the house any more, I can come and meet you?'

I'd love you to.

He heard the yearning in her voice. No mistaking it. Yearning for him. He giggled again.

But there is one thing. I have to tell you this and you've got to know. It's very important.

'What, Rani? Anything. You can tell me anything . . .'

Well, there's this man. He's been bothering me. Wanting me to . . . well, I couldn't say. But I'm sure you can guess.

And there it was, that hard, icily hot shaft spearing him once more. Making him angry. 'Is it the one from the car last night?'

She was silent for a few seconds. *Yes. That would be him. I want you to deal with him for me. Get rid of him. Would you do that?*

'Of course I would. You know that. I'd do anything for you. Anything.'

She laughed. *I know. He'll be with me. Get rid of him and then . . .*

He waited. 'Yes?'

You can have me. I'm all yours.

'I can't wait.'

Me neither. Isn't this great? We can be together again . . .

72

'You got a minute?' Milhouse grabbed Phil as soon as he entered the bar. He was trying to be secretive about it, but since he was standing by the door looking shifty and suspicious, he couldn't have been more obvious if he'd been wearing a trench coat and a trilby with the word 'spy' written across the hatband.

Seeing Milhouse, he realised that he hadn't thought about Marina for hours. With the case moving the way it was, and at the speed it was, that was understandable but he still felt guilty over it.

Milhouse led him over to his desk. 'Those cards,' he said quietly, 'the ones you asked me to trace . . .' His voice dropped to a stage whisper. He sat down at his computer.

Phil stood over him, waiting. Anxious once again. 'Yeah?'

Milhouse waved his hands over the keys. 'Bury St Edmunds,' he said. 'Hotel, restaurant, supermarket.' He looked up, compassion in his eyes. 'That's where she is.'

Phil managed a smile. 'Thanks, Milhouse, I owe you one.'

'My pleasure.'

'Could I ask you another favour, though?' Phil gave a quick look round to make sure no one was in earshot. 'Could you keep this quiet?'

Milhouse gave what he supposed was an enigmatic smile. 'I am a keeper of many secrets.'

'I'll bet you are,' said Phil, and crossed the room.

Bury St Edmunds. That made sense. So obvious when he thought about it. Where he should have looked first. It was almost like she wanted him to come, to find her. Suddenly his mobile felt hot in his pocket.

He took it out, ready to call, when he saw Fiona Welch enter. He quickly put it back, crossed to her.

'Fiona,' he said.

She stopped walking, looked at him. Her lips had been moving, deep in conversation with herself. She looked up, surprised to see him, startled, as if she had just woken from a dream.

'Yes?'

'The geographical profile,' he said.

'Yes.' Her eyes flickered like she was running through her mental Rolodex, working her way round to what he was talking about. 'Right. Been working on it all morning. Nearly done.'

'Don't worry about it.'

Fire flashed in her eyes. 'What? What d'you mean?'

'We have a suspect under surveillance that we favour very strongly.' He smiled, trying to play the diplomat. 'So we won't be needing it after all. But thanks.'

Her eyes began moving quickly from side to side, like she was scanning something, reading it quickly. 'What? Who? Who is he?'

'An ex-squaddie. Burns victim, apparently. Was being treated by both Suzanne Perry and Julie Miller.'

Her features became unreadable. 'How did you . . . how did you find him?'

Phil shrugged. 'Police work. It's what we do. So, anyway. Send in your invoice and we'll get it sorted.'

She stepped closer to him, got right in his face. 'No.'

Phil stepped back, looked at her, frowned. 'I'm sorry?'

'I said no. I'm not going. I won't go.'

'Why not?'

'Because you need me. I'm an integral part of this investigation and you need me. So no. I won't be got rid off so easily.'

Phil felt anger rise inside him. He had never liked Fiona Welch, never rated her, never even wanted her on the team in the first place. And he was tired of being polite to her.

'Listen,' he said, letting his voice be as angry as he could considering where he was, 'your contribution so far has been to give us a profile that was so inaccurate, so inept, that an innocent man is now on life support because of it.'

'Innocent?'

'Well, it's looking that way, isn't it?'

'That's not my fault.' Her voice was low, hissing. 'I provided you with the best profile I could on the information provided. Anyone else would have done the same.'

'No they wouldn't. Not anyone. Certainly not anyone competent.'

Her eyes were dancing with anger. It seemed it was all she could do not to physically assault him. 'Don't you dare. Don't you dare say that about me . . .'

Phil was matching her. 'Good job we didn't get your geographic profile. Might have sent us looking for someone in Cardiff.'

She stared at him. 'How dare you.' Her voice low, ominous. 'You. A copper. An uneducated copper talking to me like that. How dare you.' She spat the word 'uneducated' at him.

Phil stared at her, struggling to control his temper. 'Send us an invoice,' he said and walked away.

*

Phil walked outside into the car park. He sat on a wall. Sighed.

That went as well as expected, he thought and shook his head, tried to calm himself, clear Fiona Welch out of it. He was shaking, wanting to do something physical to take her memory away. A heavy workout in the gym or a five-mile run.

He didn't remember getting his phone out, but there it was, sitting in his hand. Then he found himself dialling the number. And waiting.

And waiting.

Answerphone.

He sighed. 'Hi, Marina, it's me. Listen, I know where you are. Bury St Edmunds. It wasn't hard to work out, I am a detective. And I should have known. Somewhere special. Special for us.'

Another sigh. He kept going.

'I don't know what else to say. I'm here. For you. Whatever. I . . . Whatever. Just . . . just call me.'

He hung up. Sat back. Looked at the sky. That beautiful, robin's egg blue again.

Thought of what to do next. How to move the case along.

He stood up, making his way back inside. Stopped. His phone was ringing. He checked the display.

Marina.

He answered.

'Hey,' she said.

73

'Is this the one? Are you sure of that?'

Rose Martin sighed. 'Yes, Ben. Stop being such an . . .'

He summoned a smiled. 'Old woman?'

'I was going to say arse, but that'll do.'

They were standing before Mark Turner's house on Greenstead Road, Rose knocking once more. They waited.

'I don't think he's in,' said Fenwick, clearly uncomfortable with what was happening and wanting to walk away.

'I hope not,' she said. 'In fact, I'm counting on it.'

Fenwick's heart skipped at the words. 'What d'you mean?'

Rose smiled. 'I've spoken to Mark Turner before. A couple of times. If I speak to him again he's going to get lawyered up. He threatened to do it last time and then we'll get nowhere. So we need leverage.'

She dug into her jacket pocket, brought out a memory stick. 'Let's make sure he's got the same photos on his computer.' She then brought out a lock pick. Held it up to show to him. Smiled.

Fenwick physically recoiled, frantically looked round to see if anyone was watching. 'Oh no . . . oh no . . .'

'Oh yes.'

'But this is . . . this is wrong. If we do this then any evidence we find, any confession we make on the basis of that evidence, is inadmissible in court. It's tainted. We have to follow compliance . . .'

She turned to him, no longer smiling. 'D'you want this collar, Ben? Really want this collar?'

'Yes . . .'

'Or do you want Phil Brennan to get all the glory? Again?'

Fenwick shook his head. 'No . . . no . . .'

'You sure? Maybe I chose the wrong man.'

'No, no you didn't. You didn't . . .' Fenwick swallowed hard, eyes never leaving the lock pick. 'No, I want it . . . I want . . .'

She smiled, nodded. Clearly in control. She knew what he wanted.

'Good,' she said, and began to pick the lock.

It didn't take long. She pushed. The door opened.

Fenwick was still nervously looking round.

Rose smiled at him. Reassuringly this time. 'If anyone asks, we heard a cry and had to break in. Got that?'

He nodded.

'Sure?'

'I'm . . .' He took a deep breath, swallowed hard. 'We heard a cry. Right. I'm sure.'

'Good. Then let's go in.'

Rose stepped inside first. The house was as dark as she remembered it, the curtains still drawn, the light hardly penetrating. Fenwick followed, closing the door quietly behind them. He looked round. Stepped into the centre of the room, head going from side to side. 'Should I—'

He didn't get to finish his sentence. A dark shape emerged from behind the sofa and, before Fenwick could react, was on him.

Rose turned. Gasped. The figure was all in black, looking

like a moving, angry shadow in the darkness. She watched as the figure pulled back its arm and thrust towards Fenwick's stomach. Fenwick crumpled. And again.

'Oh God, oh God, I'm bleeding, oh God . . .' Fenwick staggered, holding his stomach.

'Ben . . .' Rose cried out, moved towards him, but the figure turned. She stopped moving, frozen, saw the blade in its hand. She looked at Fenwick who was swaying, now falling to his knees. Heart hammering, she turned and ran for the door.

The figure was on her. Arms holding her tight, pressing round her like the grip of a huge anaconda.

She tried to get her hand inside her pocket, reach for her pepper spray. Her fingers touched but didn't connect. The figure saw what she was doing, loosened his grip with one arm, knocked her hand away, leaving it stinging from the blow.

Taking advantage of the loosened grip, Rose twisted her body round, trying to pull away.

That was when she saw his face.

'Oh God . . . oh God . . .'

His mouth opened. Some kind of awful sound emerged.

'Hahhneee . . . Hahhneee . . .'

He seemed to be saying the same word over and over. She didn't know what it meant, didn't want to think about it. Just wanted to escape.

'Hahhneee . . . Hahhneee . . .'

But it was too late for that. She saw him bring his arm up. But didn't feel it come down.

74

'Hi,' she said.

'Hi yourself,' said Phil. He knew he was grinning like an idiot. Didn't even try to stop it. 'How are you?'

'Been better.'

Silence.

'Bury St Edmunds,' he said. 'Should have guessed.'

'You did.'

'Right.' He looked round the carp park. Saw Fiona Welch walking out of the building. She glared at him. He looked away.

'I'm . . . sorry.'

He nodded. Then, realising she couldn't see it, said, 'That's OK. How's Josephina?'

'She's fine. We're . . . we're both fine.'

'Good.'

Silence.

'Look . . . d'you want me to come and get you?'

Silence. Phil could hear the world turning through the phone but not Marina.

'OK,' she said eventually.

He exhaled, not realising he had been holding his breath waiting for her answer. 'Good.' He looked at his watch. Weighed things in his head. 'I'll be right up.'

He heard her gasp. 'Aren't you in the middle of a murder inquiry? You can't just . . . just leave everything and run off.'

'You did.'

Silence. Phil thought he had lost her again.

'OK. But we need to talk.'

'I'll be right up.'

He hung up, got in the Audi.

'Yeah,' he said aloud. 'They can do without me here for a couple of hours.'

Still smiling, Doves coming out of the stereo, he headed off to Bury St Edmunds.

75

Suzanne heard more tearing, more creaking.

'What's happening?' she said. 'What are you doing now?'

'Just . . . a bit . . . more . . .'

Julie had been working away. Suzanne didn't know exactly what at, just that she said there was a way out and she was trying to do it. The tearing noise was the same as the one she had heard when she was let out of the box earlier. Suzanne was terrified. If their captors came back when she was trying to escape, she didn't know what they would do to her. Didn't even want to think about it. Didn't dare.

'I can see . . . daylight. It's day outside.'

Suzanne felt her heart beating faster. That forbidden emotion, hope, welling up inside her. Daylight. And Julie nearly out. And once Julie was out, she could help Suzanne out and then they would both be free. She found herself smiling uncontrollably at the thought.

The noise stopped. Suzanne could hear her own breathing once more, feel her heart beating so fast it threatened to leave her body. She almost didn't dare speak. Almost.

'What's . . . what are you doing now?'

Silence.

'Julie? You there?'

'I'm here.'

Relief flooded through Suzanne.

'I've got the bottom of the box open. I don't think they closed it properly when they let us out. It's a bit . . . bit tight, but . . . if I can just, just . . . wriggle down . . .'

Suzanne listened, heart in her mouth. 'Keep talking, Julie. Keep telling me what's happening . . .'

More tearing and creaking.

Then silence.

'Julie . . .'

Suzanne heard a sigh.

'I've done it.' She laughed, disbelieving. 'Suzanne, I've done it . . .'

'Brilliant! Yes!'

'Yeah, now all I've got to do is . . .'

And then she screamed. Julie screamed, loud and long and hard.

Suzanne's eyes were wide, staring. 'Julie . . .' She tried to block the noise, cover her ears with her hands but couldn't manage it. So she had no choice but to listen.

'No, Julie . . .'

The screaming died away.

Silence.

'Julie . . . Julie . . .'

Nothing.

'Julie . . .'

No response.

'Oh God, oh God . . .'

Suzanne started sobbing. Hope. That bastard emotion hope. Suzanne kept sobbing.

Feared she would never stop.

PART FOUR

76

Brasserie Gerard was a French restaurant on the corner of Lower Baxter Street and Abbeygate Street in the old English town of Bury St Edmunds. Sunny, airy and light inside, it had a courtyard-like quality where a spring or summer's lunchtime meal could easily slip into a leisurely afternoon of French hors d'oeuvres, good company and plenty of wine. How Phil wished he could be doing that right now. He imagined Marina felt the same.

They sat opposite each other, more distance between them than just the restaurant table. Both eyeing each other nervously, trying to smile, not sure whether to touch or not touch. Two tightrope walkers trying to keep their balance.

This is ridiculous, thought Phil. I should be at work, on the case. I shouldn't be here, pulling a domestic. Then he looked at Marina, her perfect, dark features, her beautiful face, and their daughter lying asleep in her buggy at the side of the table, arms up, perfectly contented. And he knew why he had come.

'You're looking well,' he said.

'I look about as good as you do.' Marina managed a smile, concern in her eyes. 'But it's nice of you to say so.'

She did look well, he thought. Yes, there was fear and worry etched in all her features but she still looked good. She always looked good to Phil.

Marina looked away, down at her menu. Wavering, her balance going. She sighed. 'This is a bad idea. Maybe we should do this later.'

Phil kept his eyes on her. 'Marina, if we don't do this now, there may not be a later.'

She sighed once more, looked down at the table. The waitress chose that moment to arrive. Phil was about to wave her away but Marina was already ordering herself sea bass with a spinach and tomato salad. He quickly scanned the menu, ordered the first thing his eye rested on, the duck. And a large bottle of water. The waitress disappeared once more, leaving them alone with their silence.

Phil waited.

'There's . . . something between us,' Marina said eventually. 'Or, rather, someone.'

Phil forced an intake of breath to his body, steeled himself. He had imagined everything he could think of on the drive up, everything awful that Marina could possibly want to say to him, in the hope that whatever it was he would be prepared for and it wouldn't feel so bad. Her finding someone else was the worst thing he came up with. And no amount of preparation made hearing those words any easier.

Phil just nodded, waited. Kept nodding.

The waitress brought the water. The bottle stood there on the table, untouched.

Marina looked away from Phil, down at the table. 'It's Tony.'

Tony. Marina's ex-partner. Bludgeoned nearly to death by a killer Phil and Marina had been hunting. Just before Marina had a chance to tell him she was leaving him. So that was it, he thought.

Phil blinked, startled. 'Tony?'

'Tony. I . . .' Another sigh. 'I . . . he's just lying there. And I keep . . .' Her fingers began working on the napkin. 'I just . . . I have to make a decision, Phil. He's lying there on that life-support system and they want me to make a decision. They want me to turn it off.'

Phil's voice was quiet, calm. 'Is this why you ran away from me?'

She nodded, fingers now shredding the napkin.

'But . . . surely we could have worked this out together . . .'

Marina looked up, directly at him, eye to eye. Hers were red-rimmed, wet, only the public place holding back full on tears. 'No. I have to do it. It's my decision. D'you understand?'

'You tell me,' he said.

'I can't do it,' she said. 'I just can't bring myself to switch off that life-support system, to, to . . . acknowledge he's dead, really, finally dead, once and for all.'

Phil leaned forward. 'D'you think there's a chance he could come back? Is that it?'

She wiped her eyes quickly with the back of her hand, determined not to let any tears fall. She shook her head. 'No. No, that's not it. At least I don't think so, no . . .' She shook her head once more. 'It's the guilt. It's . . . it's . . .' Her voice dropped. 'Crippling me.'

And that was just how her voice sounded, he thought. Twisted, crippled. 'The decision?'

She shook her head once more. 'Not just . . . no. It's . . . eating me away, gnawing inside me . . . the guilt. I can't . . . can't move forward, can't . . . enjoy . . . myself, my life, or allow myself to enjoy life, until I make that decision. Until I let him go.' Her head dropped once more, shoulders heaved, like she was bearing a huge weight. She kept her gaze on the table. 'And I can't let him go . . .'

Phil said nothing, taking in her words. He picked up the bottle of water, unscrewed it, poured it into the two glasses.

Neither drank.

Phil kept looking at her. When he spoke his voice was still calm and controlled, the opposite of the emotions raging inside him. 'OK,' he said. 'What about this. If Tony hadn't . . . if he wasn't where he is now, if he had never been attacked, if he was still . . . I don't know, with us . . . what would you do?'

She frowned. 'What d'you mean?'

'Just that. What would you do? What would you be doing?'

'I'd . . .' She sighed, shook her head, looked away once more.

'You were going to leave him, Marina. Tell him you didn't love him any more and leave him. Weren't you?'

She nodded, head still bowed.

'For me?' He made it a question.

She nodded once more.

'Why?' His voice was even quieter, calmer. The kind he used in interviews, the one that made people open up to him, trust him.

'Because . . . I love you . . .'

He risked a small smile. 'That it? That's all?'

She shook her head once more, looked up. 'No. Because I wanted to spend the rest of my life with you. Because I've never loved anyone like I loved you. Because I'd never met anyone like you.'

'Who was so like you, you mean.'

She nodded. 'And because I was pregnant with your child.'

'Our child.'

'Our child. And you're the love of my life.' She turned away, words choked off by sobs.

Phil waited until she had composed herself. 'Tony knew you'd leave him, Marina. He was older than you. He was your teacher, what you needed at that stage in your life. He

324

knew you weren't going to stay with him forever. That you'd go eventually. He expected it. Might not have welcomed it or been looking forward to it, but he expected it.'

Marina wiped her eyes, her nose, with the crumpled and torn paper napkin, her head still bowed. Phil reached across the table, took her hands in his.

'Isn't that the problem?' he said. 'The fact that you never got to say that to him? That you never gave that relationship closure?'

She pulled her hands away. 'It's not just that,' she said, sniffing. 'He's in a coma because of me.' She looked up, directly at him. Her eyes raw with emotion. 'And you too, Phil.'

'How?'

'Because if we had never met, if I'd never come to work with you, if none of that had happened, Tony would still be alive.'

'And you'd still be unhappy.' He leaned forward again. Reached out for her hands once more. Held them tight. 'I understand you, Marina. That's not arrogance on my part. I understand you because you understand me. More than anyone I've ever met. I know your mind because it's like my mind. I know what's in it. I know the damage in there.'

She flinched at his words, but didn't interrupt.

'That damage stops you from thinking you're worth anything. Worthy of happiness. Well, you are.' He held her hands tighter. She didn't pull away. 'And this might be the only chance we get. And we have to take it.'

She looked straight at him, no tears, listening to everything he said.

'What was that you once said to me?' he said. 'All psychologists are just looking for a way home? I'm offering you that way home, Marina. It might not be easy, we've got tough decisions to make, but it's real. It's there.' He sat back, still holding her hands. 'D'you want to take it?'

Marina said nothing. Just looked at him.

'Say no and I walk away,' he said. 'Forever. From you and our daughter. Forever. It'll hurt like hell but if that's what you want, that's what I'm prepared to do. But say yes and we go home. Today. And face whatever we have to face together. Up to you.'

He let her hands slip from his. Waited.

He hadn't intended to say all of that. Or even half of that. And he wasn't the kind of person who would come out with something like that normally. But he had never met anyone like Marina before. She was special. She was worth fighting for.

She said nothing. He wondered if he had gone too far.

He sighed. Waited.

The food arrived. The plates were placed before them. Neither took any notice, not even looking at the waitress.

Phil waited. Could feel his heart breaking.

Eventually Marina spoke. 'Yes,' she said, her voice small but strong. 'Yes. I'm coming home with you.'

Phil reached across the table, grinning, grabbed her hands and squeezed. He hadn't felt so happy in ages.

He inhaled. The food smelled delicious.

'I'm starving,' he said. And smiled.

Marina smiled back. Looking as happy as he did.

77

Outside the restaurant, Phil switched his phone back on. And the happiness he had been feeling dissipated.

Message after message piled up in his phone. He played them. Marina stopped fussing with Josephina and looked up, becoming aware of the hardening in his features, concern spreading over her face in response to the changes to his. Eventually he took the phone away from his ear. Marina waited.

He looked at her. 'Oh God . . .'

'What?'

'I've got to go. Now.'

'Need me to come with you?'

Phil looked between the baby and Marina. 'Can you?'

She nodded. Phil caught the look in her eye, fleeting and sharp, but unmistakeable. She was as hooked as he was.

'I'll fill you in on the way.'

They went to find the car.

Greenstead Road was a crime scene.

The road was entirely closed off, from the supermarket at

the far end to the roundabout at the top of Harwich Road to the level crossing at East Street. Yellow and black tape fluttered in the slight, warm breeze, making a gentle, lapping sound that would have been calming and summery in any other situation.

Phil showed his warrant card as he stepped under the tape, uniforms closing in to block the cameras that tried to follow him. He kept a protective arm round Marina's shoulders as he walked from the level crossing and round the corner to the house itself.

They had phoned ahead to Don and Eileen, asked if they fancied spending a bit of time with their granddaughter. They jumped at the chance. Although Phil kept the tone light, they sensed something was wrong but, from years of experience, knew better than to ask what.

Phil saw Nick Lines enter the house, his pale blue suit clashing with the colours on the tape. Anni was standing on the opposite pavement, waiting for the signal to enter the house. She saw Marina and him approach, crossed over to them.

'Where've you been, boss?' Conflicting emotions were running behind her eyes.

'I . . . went to get a better profiler.' He turned to Marina who said hello to Anni.

Anni returned the greeting.

'So what we got?' Phil tried to appear professional, speaking as if this was any other crime scene. But he didn't pull it off.

'Well . . .' Anni looked round, herself struggling to keep it together.

'From the beginning, Anni. I got your calls but catch me up.'

'Call came in over an hour ago. Someone staggering about on the pavement, blood all over the place. Called for an ambulance.' Her eyes involuntarily went to the pavement in front of the house, now dried brown against the grey. A mundane stain barely reflecting the enormity of what had actually happened.

'Where is he now?'

'The General. Thought we'd lost him at first. But he's hanging on in there, apparently.'

'That the latest?'

She nodded. 'They're operating now. Lost a lot of blood.' Her eyes back to the pavement. 'Hell of a mess.'

Phil nodded, looked around. The Birdies were there, notebooks out, coordinating uniforms. 'Where's Mickey?'

'Keeping watch on the boat. Didn't want to leave that lead in the wind. Thought he might be the best one for that.'

'And Rose Martin?'

Anni shrugged. 'Dunno, boss. Not answering her phone.'

Phil's pulse quickened. 'When was she last seen?'

'At the station. Talking to Ben Fenwick.'

'Fuck . . .'

Anni said nothing. She knew what he was thinking.

He rubbed his face, his eyes. Trying to think, concentrate. He glanced at Marina. It felt good to have her back on the team. To have her back beside him.

'Right,' he said. 'Looks like I'm acting DCI now for this case. Let's get on. Any witnesses? Anyone know what happened?'

'Person who called it in, neighbour opposite. Saw the DCI come out of the house and stagger into the street clutching his stomach, waving something round. Turned out to be his warrant card.'

'Clever man,' said Phil, a sadness in his voice. 'Identifying himself.'

'It worked. Someone called an ambulance straight away. Saved his life.'

'What about the people who live in the house? Any sign of them?'

329

'None.'

'Who lives there, do we know? Looks like a student's place.'

'It is,' said Anni. 'I had a little root around before. Mark Turner, Suzanne Perry's ex, lives there. Renting.'

'The guy Rose Martin questioned the other night.'

'That's the one. And said she thought he was harmless.'

Phil sighed. 'She's good, isn't she?' Not bothering to hide the sarcasm in his voice. 'Does Mark Turner live alone?'

Anni shook her head. 'With his girlfriend.'

'And neither of them are there.' It wasn't a question.

She shook her head again. 'But we're on the lookout for them. Got their descriptions out straight away.' Anni looked uneasy. 'And you're not going to like this, boss.'

Phil waited. Eyes hard.

'The girlfriend. Like I said, I rooted round in the house before. Found some photos, paperwork . . .'

'You're stalling. Tell me.'

Anni sighed. 'It's Fiona Welch.'

78

Mickey was keeping watch. And he wasn't happy. Just over the river from where the action was, stuck watching a boat just in case its occupant returned at any time soon. When he and Anni had received the call telling them of Ben Fenwick's attack he had experienced that old Drugs Squad adrenalin rush straight up his spine, making the hairs on the back of his neck stand on end. He was ready. Two-fisted, lip curled and ready. And he and Anni had discussed and it and, yes, in his head he understood that him staying behind and Anni going to the crime scene was the right decision but his heart was telling him something different. He was a copper. A detective. And he should have been down there, getting stuck in, finding the villain, hauling him in, making him sorry.

But he wasn't. And that adrenalin was still there, charged up, pawing around inside him like a caged beast, just waiting for an outlet.

It wasn't long in coming. And, when it did, he could barely believe it.

He was sitting in the car, fidgeting and uncomfortable. At

least when Anni was there he had someone to talk to. All he had now was the radio and that was tuned to Radio One, spewing afternoon inanities and songs he was embarrassed to admit he didn't recognise. He was contemplating turning over to Radio Two but something within himself wouldn't allow it. It was comfortable. It was set in the past. It had DJs he had grown up with playing songs he had grown up with. To listen willingly would be like acknowledging he would never again embark on a four-day coke and alcohol bender, go straight from clubbing on a Friday night to the football on a Saturday afternoon, pick up a girl in a bar and stay with her for the whole weekend, coming in to boast about his stamina and prowess on a Monday morning.

He sighed. The truth was that part of him, an increasingly large part, didn't want to do that any more. There was more to him than that. Use his brain again, remind himself why he had gone to university in the first place. That was why he had transferred out of the DS. He was concerned about himself, his future. But another part of him wanted to keep on living like that and damn the consequences. He had successfully managed to keep it controlled for now but he wasn't sure he could do that indefinitely.

Maybe Radio Two would help, he thought, reaching out to change the channel, hating himself for it at the same time. Some anonymous eighties hit came on. He settled back in his seat.

He was glad he had confided in Anni. He felt he could trust her. And that was something, because for all the hard as nails fun he had had in the DS, there were none of them that he considered his lifelong friends. That all seemed to go when he went. But Anni . . . yeah. She was a good one.

His thoughts were stopped from wandering any further down that particular avenue because something had caught his eye. And he couldn't believe it.

A van had pulled up in front of the boat. And not just any old van.

A black Citroën Nemo.

Mickey couldn't believe his luck. The dormant adrenalin powered up inside him once more. He wanted to open the car door, run over and collar whoever was driving, pull them out, slam them against the bonnet old-school, making sure their head bounced off a couple of times as he did so, then loudly proclaim, 'You're nicked, my son.' See what Anni made of that.

But he didn't. Instinct kicked in, reluctantly overrode the adrenalin. Watch, he told himself, learn.

He did so. And saw the driver side door open, someone get out. Any hopes of a clean identification were dashed because the driver was wearing green army camo gear, buttoned up to the neck, a black wool watch cap pulled down tight on their head and a pair of big, face-obscuring aviator shades.

'Bastard.'

The driver came round the side of the van, went to the back doors. Mickey tried to take in what he could. Medium height, male. That was it. Didn't walk with a limp, have any particular distinguishing features. Nothing.

Then the passenger emerged. Walked round to the back. The van was parked so that the passenger was further away and Mickey's vision was obscured. And this one was dressed identically to the driver. Army fatigues, boots, wool hat and sunglasses. But that was where the similarity ended.

The passenger was taller, walked more slowly than the driver. And there was something not quite right about the gait. Throwing his left leg out as he walked, a definite limp.

Mickey smiled.

He focused on what he could see of the passenger's face. His smile widened. The man's face wasn't as he had expected it to be. What Mickey could see of it was red and blotchy, smooth – nearly flat – in parts, pitted and cratered in others.

A burns victim.

He watched as the two men opened the back of the van, leaned in, brought something out. They struggled with the object, a heavy bundle wrapped in a rug. He looked closer. The rug was discoloured, darkened in places. Mickey's heart flipped. He knew what that was.

Blood.

And he knew what was in the rug. It didn't take a genius to realise it was a body.

He sat back, as far down in his seat as he could, trying desperately not to be noticed. Heart hammering out Motörhead drum riffs, breath in short supply. The two men carried the bundle on to the boat, went below deck. Mickey let out a breath he didn't know he had been holding.

He watched, waited. Nothing happened.

He picked up the radio, ready to call for back-up, for the armed response team Phil had promised would be there when he wanted it, when there was movement on the boat.

Mickey put the radio down. Watched again.

One of the figures, the driver without the limp, came back up on deck, walked across the gangplank and left the boat. He walked over to the Nero, got behind the wheel, turned over the engine.

Mickey looked between the van and the boat, torn.

The driver revved up the engine.

Another look between the two. Mickey weighed it up. The scarred man had a body inside the boat. But no transport. And whatever he was doing down there, not going anywhere would be top of his list. Whereas the driver of the van was clearly leaving and there might not be another chance to get him.

Mickey's mind was made up. He waited until the van turned round and headed up the road, counted a few seconds, set off after it.

Once on the road he picked up the radio, gave the call sign.

'Am in pursuit of a suspect. He's driving a black Citroën Nemo, registration number . . .'

He would tell them what was happening in the boat. Get Phil's armed response team on to it. Whoever this was in the van was his.

He smiled, switched back over to Radio One.

Thrilled to be giving his adrenalin a workout.

79

'Ah . . .' the Creeper sighed. 'Alone at last . . .' He was, for the first time in a long while, almost happy.

He looked at the bundle in front of him. The rug had been unrolled, its cargo disgorged on to the floor of the boat. Rani. She lay there, unmoving but awake, looking round, her eyes wide.

He crossed to her, knelt down beside her. 'You awake, beautiful?'

He was giddy with excitement. Here she was. After all this time. Alone together. At last. His heart was hammering with excitement, stomach flipping with expectation. He wanted all his senses to take her in. He looked her over first, his eyes devouring her whole body. Then he closed his eyes, leaned in close, smelled her, fragrance, sweat, everything. Nothing was bad, all was good. All was Rani. He wanted to taste her, too, put his lips on her, his tongue, kiss her, lick her, all over . . .

There would be time enough for that later. For now he would be content to just start slowly. He reached out his hand, began to stroke her hair. She didn't pull away or recoil, just lay still, eyes wide, breathing heavily.

He laughed. 'Nearly awake. Good.' Another sigh, his breath ragged. 'Well. Face to face. After all this time, all these years . . .' He knelt in closer, his hand stroking her face now, down her cheek. 'We've got . . . we've got . . . a lot of catching up to do, my darling . . .'

His hand stopped stroking. He studied her face closely, eyes falling on every feature, memorising it as if he would never see it again, taking her all in once more. Seeing not Rani as she used to be but Rani as she was now. She looked different. That was to be expected, of course; there was no way she would be able to find a perfect match. She would in time, though, once her spirit settled in and began to change things. But even now he could see the similarities, make out what was to come. He touched the features he recognised. Her eyes, yes, he thought, fingers playing over them, and the curve of her cheekbone . . . and her mouth, her lips . . . so soft . . . oh, so soft . . .

He felt himself beginning to harden. Stopped stroking her. Not now. That was for later. Now they would just talk, get to know each other once more. Cuddle, even, like lovers were supposed to do.

He looked at her face again. Laughed, shook his head once more.

'All the things I'd planned to say . . . years, you know, years . . . Years of stuff just built up, all those conversations I'd had with you in my head, when you couldn't answer and I had to make it up . . . and then when I saw you again and we did talk for a bit, all those secret words when no one else was listening, but not proper conversations. Not like now.' He laughed again. 'It's funny, but I've got all those things to say, all those things I've stored up and . . .' He shrugged, almost apologetically. '. . . they've all gone out of my head. Isn't that funny?'

She said nothing, just lay there, breathing heavily, eyes wide open.

'So much to say . . .' He shook his head once more, like he could barely believe his luck. 'I suppose . . . we should go back to the beginning, shouldn't we? Start with the fire. And I should say sorry for that. Because that was the start, wasn't it? The cause of everything.' He sighed. Stroked her face once more. 'Sorry. For what happened.' He leaned in even closer. 'But it was all your fault. You did it. You've got to take the blame. If you hadn't come on to me in the first place, pushed yourself against me, flirted . . .' The last word was almost spat out.

He sat back, eyes never leaving her, his gaze hardened, his breathing quickening. Eventually his features softened. He smiled once more, laughed. Giggling like he was on a first date. Because that was how it felt. How it was. They had been apart so long it was like meeting for the first time.

'You see, I knew you fancied me. All that time, you tried to hide it. Leaving the room when I came in, trying not to talk to me, all of that . . . But I knew. I wasn't stupid, I could tell. And I know you knew I liked you.' He leaned forward again, hand back on her face. 'But you were shy, weren't you? Just needed a bit of a push, that's all. Get you to like me.' He wagged his finger in her face. 'Playing hard to get, you were. I know.' He cocked his head on one side, stopped wagging his finger. Smiled again, moved in closer. 'All I had to do,' he said, voice dropping low, 'was tell you how I felt. In my heart. How deep my love for you was. Then I knew you'd fall in love with me too.'

He dropped his hand from her face, sighed, his memories taking him down a dark, sad street. 'And everything would have worked out just fine, if there hadn't been that fire . . .' He sat completely still, memories overtaking him.

No longer in the boat, no longer in the present. He felt heat on his face once more, panic in his heart . . . Then pain, all over, starting at his skin then lancing through him, trapped in a cabinet of flaming swords all slicing through

him at once, pushing nerve-deep inside him . . . no way
out . . .

And the smell . . . roasting pork . . .

'I still hear the screams . . . they're in my head. Always.' He
closed his eyes. 'Trapped there, no way out . . . I close my
eyes and hear you screaming, Rani, screaming . . . and the
flames are, are . . .' He sighed. 'Fire is power, Rani, fire is
power . . . it scares people . . . and the screams . . . you
and . . . and me . . . there's always this screaming in my
head . . .'

He screwed his eyes up tight, curled his hands into fists,
began to punch himself in the temples.

'Screams . . . make the screaming . . . stop . . . No . . .
no . . . Out of the cleansing fire . . . I was born . . .'

Black.

He opened his eyes. Blinked. He was lying on the floor of
the boat. He looked round quickly, sat up. Rani—

She was still there. Lying exactly as he had left her. He
breathed a sigh of relief. Allowed himself a small smile.
'Thought I'd lost you again . . .'

He shook his head, clearing it of the screams, or at least
quietening them down. For now. He didn't know how long
he had been out but it couldn't have been long. Sunlight still
streamed through the slats of the boat, the air was tipped
with warmth.

'You're still there. Good. I'm not going to lose you again.'
He sighed. 'Because I did, you know. Well, of course you
know. That's how I found you again, isn't it? Because you led
me to you . . .' He giggled again stroked her chin. 'But you
led me a merry old dance, didn't you? Popping up here and
there, different bodies, hopping from girl to girl, teasing me,
hoping I'd find you . . .' He smiled, kept his hand cupping
her face. 'But still. All worth it. Because now you're here.
And here to stay, aren't you?'

He looked round the boat, seeing where he lived through

her eyes. He felt a sudden stab of shame. It wasn't much. And he hadn't kept it good. The place was a tip. She deserved better.

'I know what you're thinking,' he said. 'This place. Not much, is it? Well, not at the moment. But you know what it's like. Needs a woman's touch, doesn't it? You know what us men are like, living on our own . . .

'I know you should have better. And we'll make it better.' He moved in closer, lay down next to her, slid one arm round her shoulder. She didn't resist. 'I know I've got to be patient because you told me I've got to be patient, but still, you don't have to do it all today, do you? Haven't seen each other for a long time. Not properly, anyway . . .' His other hand began touching the front of her top, stroking her stomach, his grip tightening, his breath quickening.

'Got a lot of catching up to do . . . haven't we?'

80

Another incident room, thought Phil, another bar.

They had moved over to the Rose and Crown hotel on East Street at the other side of the level crossing. It was an old restored pub with black and white Tudor outer work, uneven floors, roof and ceilings, wooden beams and small leaded glass windows. The façade of authenticity stopped at the contemporary dining-room furniture and the modern hotel block at the rear. But first impressions were good.

Phil wasn't there for that, though. He had commandeered the restaurant as a temporary incident room, flashing his warrant card and claiming that a murder inquiry took precedence over dinner preparations. The chairs and tables had been arranged in a semi-circle, and those with laptops had them open. Phil's was open in front of him, a video link to Milhouse back at the station.

Phil hadn't wanted to stop the team working, finding Fenwick's attacker and Rose Martin's abductor. But he felt it was important that they all got together before they set off. All singing from the same hymn book, he thought, echoing Ben Fenwick in the cliché stakes.

He also needed to find something inspirational to say, something to rouse them, drive them on. Saw Marina sitting at the back. Knew he'd manage somehow.

'This is what we've got so far,' Phil said, standing up to address the room. 'Suzanne Perry and Zoe Herriot. Both SALTS. Both worked at the Gainsborough Wing at the General Hospital. One missing, one dead. Julie Miller. Occupational therapist. Again, working in the same hospital wing as part of the same team. Missing. Hopefully alive. Adele Harrison. Barmaid. Deceased. No connection to the others that we can find. Yet.' He paused, letting the toll of the dead and the missing hit home.

'Christopher and Charlotte Palmer. Julie Miller's upstairs neighbours. Both deceased. Killed, we imagine, because they were in the way. Because our killer wanted somewhere to watch his victim from.'

Phil sighed. 'And now a couple of our own. DCI Ben Fenwick, the DCI of this unit, severely wounded, in hospital now. DS Rose Martin, missing.'

'And Anthony Howe,' said Anni, 'don't forget him.'

Phil nodded. 'Any news on him?'

'Stable, apparently,' said Jane Gosling. 'Hospital talk for not alive but not dead yet.'

'Right.' Phil suppressed the urge to sigh again. 'Any ideas so far? Any theories about links? Leads?'

'Adele Harrison, Julie Miller and Suzanne Perry all look alike,' said Anni. 'Or, rather, all share similarities. Tall, white, dark-haired. Same bone structure and features. Same ages, just about.'

Phil nodded. 'And Rose Martin too. On that basis you can add her to that list. It looks like that's his type, his trigger.'

Nick Lines put his hand up. 'I think you're right.' He said. 'Compare the way Adele Harrison's body was attacked and mutilated as well as killed with the way Zoe Herriot was murdered. Like she's been dispatched. She doesn't fit the profile so she's cut and dumped as quickly as possible.'

Several of the team flinched at his words. Nick didn't elaborate or apologise.

'We have to make Mark Turner and Fiona Welch our top suspects at the moment.'

'What about the boat, boss? The soldier?' said Anni.

'There's a lot of pieces that aren't in place yet. We keep our options open at the moment. But since Ben was knifed in Turner and Welch's house, we have to assume they're a big part of it. The university are looking out for them. They've been told to call us the second they set foot there. Although I doubt they will. Nick, anything you can tell us from the house?'

'Not much,' said Nick Lines. 'From the stains and the blood spray patterns, it looks like everything happened in the living room. It also looks like a rug's been removed recently.'

'How recently?'

'Since Ben Fenwick was stabbed.'

'Wrapping Rose Martin up in it?' said Phil.

'An educated guess,' said Nick.

'Adrian, any neighbours have anything to say?'

Adrian Wren stood up. 'A woman opposite does say she saw two men loading a carpet into the back of a van in The Beijing car park.' The house was next to a Chinese takeaway with a piece of waste ground between that the fast food outlet liked to call a car park.

'That sounds like our team. Make? Model?'

He shook his head. 'Just something dark. Quite small. Not a big one. No descriptions either. Both in some kind of work clothes, apparently. Woolly hats and sunglasses.'

'Comedy Blues Brothers,' said Phil, no humour in his voice. 'Brilliant.'

'The van fits with what Mickey's been following up, boss,' said Anni. 'Black Citroën Nemo.'

'Get some photos, Adrian. Ask her again.'

He nodded, made a note.

'Fiona Welch,' said Phil. 'One of Ben Fenwick's innovations, I'm afraid. I never rated her, never liked her, never wanted her here. And after that profile, never trusted her.' He looked round the room. 'Please feel free to join in with her character assassination.'

'Mickey felt the same way, boss,' said Anni. 'Spoke to me about her earlier. Said there was something about her he didn't like.'

'Why didn't he mention it to me?'

'Because you'd said you were going to get rid of her. So that, he probably thought, was that. But he did say something else interesting about her, though.'

Phil listened.

'He said she went to see Anthony Howe last night. After you'd finished questioning him. In his cell.'

Phil frowned. 'What about?'

'Don't know. No record of that. Only of her visit.'

Phil thought for a moment, glancing round the restaurant. It looked comfortable, the kind of place you'd be happy to spend a few hours in if you were away from home. The bar looked the same. It was yet another glimpse into that other world, the safe, comfortable one, the one he could never inhabit.

'I don't think,' he said, 'we're jumping to conclusions to say that whatever she said to him contributed to his suicide attempt.'

Anni frowned. 'Why, boss?'

He shrugged. 'Maybe he taught her at university. Maybe he made a pass at her. Some grudge or other.' He sighed. 'Why wasn't her background checked into? Why wasn't she properly vetted?'

No one answered. The only person who could was fighting for his life in hospital.

'OK,' said Phil. 'In the meantime we keep an eye on the Greenstead Road house. It's a long shot, but they may return. We're also still going through it looking for any clue as to where they might be now.'

'Don't forget the boat, boss,' said Anni.

'I'm not.'

Anni's phone rang. Phil stared at her, clearly unhappy with the interruption. She checked the display. 'Mickey,' she said. 'I'd better take it.'

She got up from her seat, crossed into the bar.

Phil wanted to keep talking but knew as well as Anni that Mickey wouldn't be phoning unless it was something important. 'We'll just wait a moment,' he said. 'This might be urgent.'

Anni returned, pocketing her phone. She sat down. Phil could sense the energy, the adrenalin, coming off her.

'What you got?'

'That was Mickey,' she said, 'he's at the boat. There's been developments.' She told the team what he had seen, relaying it in almost as breathless a fashion as he clearly had to her.

'Oh, lucky,' said Phil, feeling that familiar tingle pass through him. He knew the others would be feeling it too. 'A breakthrough. Anni, phone him back and tell him to keep tailing and we'll get back up to him as quickly as possible. I'm guessing that's Rose Martin on the boat. We'll get an armed response unit down there as quickly as possible. Even if it's not Rose, whoever it is we need to get them out safely. I'll get down there right now.' He looked round the room. 'The rest of you get back to your jobs.' He sighed. 'Most of you, if not all of you, know that Ben Fenwick and I didn't always see eye to eye. Or hardly ever, if I'm being honest.'

A small amount of laughter could be heard, breaking the tension.

Phil continued. 'But that doesn't mean I wanted this to happen to him. Or anything like it. It's awful. What's happened is absolutely, bloody awful. So let's get out there and avenge him. Let's do this for him.'

The meeting broke up.

81

R ose was terrified.

She lay on her back, on the filthy floor of some falling apart boat, eyes wide open, not daring to move or even to breathe. Like an animal freezing before a predator, hoping that if she stayed still long enough she would be ignored.

His hands were on her. His breath in her ear, raw, ragged grunts. His hands getting faster, moving quickly over her body, roughly tugging at her clothes . . .

She closed her eyes, trying to expel the vision of his face from her mind, take herself to somewhere she could think. Tried to make some sense of what had happened to her and how best to deal with it, thought back to how she had ended up in this situation.

She hadn't seen him coming. That much was obvious. If she had, she would have been prepared. And then seeing what happened to Ben, watching him collapse like that. Was he dead? Oh God . . . All that blood, so much blood . . .

And now this. She had lain there, terrified, while he spoke to her. At least, she assumed that was what he was doing. She could barely make out any of his words. But that was no surprise. His mouth – his face – was ruined. She had studied him in close up all the time he was 'talking' to her. Clearly not Mark Turner. This man had suffered. His face was smooth in parts, pitted and wrinkled in others. Sometimes dead white, sometimes pink and red.

Burns, Rose thought. Bad ones.

As he moved closer she could see veins and arteries below the surface. They looked like fiery little red lines, networked, red hot pipes ready to burst and burn and spray at any moment.

His eyebrows were gone, as was half of his mouth. His teeth were pulled back in a perpetual, grimacing snarl. No wonder she couldn't understand what he was saying. She understood why he wore the woollen cap, too. When he took it off his head had the same kind of smooth and uneven look as his face. What hair there was left had been razored down to nothing, leaving him looking like an angry, red skull.

He reminded her of a character in one of her little brother's comics that he used to read. Ghost Rider, a demon biker with a flaming skull. He had terrified her then.

This one terrified her now.

And then that voice . . . deep, raw and wasted, all breath and pain, but with attempts at precision and diction. Like a horror-film zombie trying to articulate enough to get a job in a call centre.

He grunted loudly. She opened her eyes.

And wished she hadn't.

He was on top of her now, pulling at her jeans, trying to get his lumpen, misshapen hand down the front. Grunting even more, his other hand pulling at the waist of his army trousers.

Oh God . . .

She closed her eyes tight shut once more, lay completely still, hands by her side, legs as rigid as possible.

And then she felt something. Her handbag.

Still on her shoulder from when she had been grabbed, it had been tight to her body when she had been wrapped in the rug and was with her now. And in the front pocket . . .

Oh please, please, let it be there . . . please God, let it still be there . . .

It was.

Rose couldn't believe her luck. She almost shouted out aloud, punched the air, even. But she did neither. Just lay there as if nothing had happened, nothing had changed. But it had.

She had found her pepper spray.

Keeping her breathing as shallow as she could so as not to alarm Ghost Rider. Although the way he was twisting and grunting in his efforts to remove her jeans, she thought he would be beyond noticing any changes in her breathing.

She tried to disconnect from what was happening to the rest of her body, just concentrate on what her fingers were doing. Touching the can of spray, finding the front, fitting her fingers round the container, getting her grip in the right place, readying herself to shoot . . .

She brought her arm up as far as it would go. Held the can right in his face.

Sprayed.

The effect was immediate. As the pepper hit him in the eyes, he reared back off her, hands going to eyes, clawing at them. She took advantage straight away, pushing herself off the floor, making for the stairs, the exit.

But he was quick. Even half-blinded he knew the boat better than her. His hand clamped round her ankle, pulled. His grip was too strong. Rose's leg was pulled out from under her.

She fell to the floor, landing awkwardly, feeling something pop in her left knee.

She screamed, tried to rise once more.

Too late. He was on her.

Still clutching the can of spray, she brought her hand up but he was ready, knocking it out of her hand. She heard it land uselessly, somewhere on the far side of the boat, in the mess and shadows.

She tried to rise again. Felt pain arc from her knee all the way up her leg.

She gasped.

Saw his malevolent, red skull in her face once more. Eyes streaming.

Heard him scream in pain and rage.

Glimpsed his fist coming towards her face.

Felt nothing.

82

Suzanne still hadn't moved. Had barely breathed.

She lay there, eyes wide, staring, straining to hear anything, something that would give her a clue as to what had happened to Julie. Just a scream and then silence. She didn't know what had happened, but she knew it wasn't good.

She closed her eyes, the better to concentrate, the better to hear.

Nothing.

She let out a breath. After the scream she had tried calling but received no response. She had tried again. Nothing. Eventually she accepted the fact. Something bad had happened to Julie and she wouldn't be talking again.

The easiest thing would have been to give in to panic. Scream, shout, pound the sides of the box, kick out . . . and it was so easy . . . she had felt it build inside her, a volcanic eruption of emotion looking for an outlet, a screaming, shaking outlet, but she had managed to stop it. Keep it dormant, keep it down. It would get her nowhere. Accomplish nothing.

She had to think. Work out what happened to Julie. Make sure it didn't happen to her.

Suzanne controlled her breathing once more, kept her mind focused. Thought back to what Julie had said, what she was doing.

I've got the bottom of the box open. I don't think they closed it properly when they let us out. It's a bit . . . bit tight, but . . . if I can just . . . wriggle down . . .

Then tearing and creaking . . .

Then silence.

Then she was out and laughing then . . .

The screaming. Long and hard.

Suzanne shook her head, shaking loose the image that had stuck there. The darkness just made her imagination worse. Seeing something so horrible, no true, real-life scene could ever match it.

Or at least she hoped not.

She focused. The box, the tearing and creaking . . . that was the noise it made when opened. And Julie had said their captors mustn't have closed it properly.

Think, think, process . . .

What about her trip out of the box? Her toilet break? Anything to be gleaned from that?

She retraced it in her mind once more. The door had opened, she'd been given the hood to wear. Nothing there. What about the feel of things when she was out? The sounds?

The first thing she had experienced had been water up to her ankles. What could that tell her? It was still. And there was no smell. Not tidal, then. Not on the seafront, then.

The water had ended and she had stepped out. So a small amount of water. A pool, maybe? Ditch? Concrete underneath. A trough of some kind? But why?

Leave it. On to the next part. She had been guided over a cold concrete floor. Hard and dirty, with small, sharp bits sticking in her wet feet as she went.

Was there anything about the walk itself . . .

Nothing. Except . . .

That sound. Like a humming or churning. Power lines, pylons . . . or a generator.

A shudder ran through Suzanne, jack-knifing her body with its suddenness.

She knew what had happened to Julie now. And it didn't make her feel any better.

A generator. And a trough of water. And a scream from Julie as soon as she wriggled out of the box.

Booby-trapped. Even if they managed to escape the box itself they couldn't escape from where they actually were. The water must be too wide to cross. And electrified.

Suzanne sighed.

Felt more alone and abandoned, more hopeless than ever.

83

Mickey was following the Nemo. Out of King Edward Quay and on to Haven Road. Over the roundabout and down the Colne Causeway. Heading towards the Magic Roundabout.

At first he had thought it was just a nickname, a less than affectionate term everyone used. He was surprised to learn that was its official name too. He was less surprised to learn that the rest of Colchester despised it as much as he did.

It comprised one main roundabout with several mini ones orbiting it, plus a lot of irritated motorists. And that was where the Nemo was headed.

Mickey thought he had managed to shadow the van without being seen so far but he was winging it on his own. Following was a delicate operation, usually carried out in tandem with at least one, possibly two other vehicles. That was how he was used to doing at. On his own he was just improvising.

And the Magic Roundabout could be where his luck ran out.

He was two cars behind and no other unmarked cars had

come to join him yet. So he had to be careful. Too close and he would give himself away, too far back and he would lose him. He watched, waiting for him to indicate.

Right. Mickey did the same.

The Nemo pulled out. Mickey tried not to be too impatient with the car in front, concentrate on not losing the Nemo, keeping it in visual contact all the time. The car in front went left. Mickey went right.

The Nemo was just in front of him.

Mickey allowed himself a small smile. Kept his eyes on it.

Right at the next mini roundabout. Mickey did the same.

And off down St Andrews Avenue, signalling and moving over to the right.

Mickey kept smiling. He knew where the Nemo was headed.

He thought about getting back on the radio, giving his location and where he thought they were going but, since his car was directly behind the Nemo on the dual carriageway, he didn't want to do anything that could be seen in the wing mirror, something that might tip the driver off, make him suspicious.

Off to the right down Brightlingsea Road.

Yes. Mickey knew where he was going.

The university.

He had heard on the radio that the house in Greenstead Road had belonged to Fiona Welch and her boyfriend. This confirmed that they were involved in this.

The Nemo turned into the grounds of the university, then into the car park. Mickey followed. The Nemo parked. Mickey drove round until he found a space nearby. He found one in the next row, facing the van. He watched, the engine running.

The driver was definitely male, thin. The wool hat was removed revealing longish, unkempt hair. Typical student, Mickey thought.

The driver shucked out of his army jacket leaving a sloganed T-shirt beneath. It looked like he was pulling something down over his hips. Getting rid of his army trousers too, Mickey reckoned. He got out of the van, leaned back in, grabbed a canvas bag from behind the seat, slung it across his body. Ready for class.

Mickey smiled. Mark Turner. He knew it. And there was virtually nothing on him. This would be easy, he thought.

Turner set off in the direction of the campus. Mickey got out of the car and, at a discreet distance, followed.

Essex University campus was a textbook design in sixties neo-brutalist modernism, with each subsequent architectural feature either an accompaniment or an apology to the original. It was laid out as a series of squares and quadrants with concrete steps and walkways joining them. Turner walked towards the main quadrant through the car park, going past the gym and down the steps, trees on either side. Mickey followed him easily.

He should have radioed for back-up but, again, he didn't want to risk losing him or letting him see the radio. Instead, Mickey opened his phone, called Anni. She answered immediately.

'It's Turner,' he said.

'Where are you?'

'University. He's just got out the van, walking towards the campus. I'm on foot. Looks like he's trying to behave as normally as possible.'

'Give himself an alibi, more like.'

'Anyway, back-up would be appreciated.'

Turner didn't look back, which was helpful as most of the people Mickey's age were much less formally dressed. Turner didn't seem hurried or stressed, just walking along casually. Either that, thought Mickey, or he was affecting to look casual just in case anyone was watching him. Which meant he really was nervous.

Which meant . . .

Turner turned round. Saw Mickey. It was clear from his reaction that he didn't know who Mickey was but certainly knew what he was.

Turner ran.

Mickey, no longer needing to pretend any more, cut his call short, gave chase.

Along a concrete walkway, the Student's Union bar on one side, opening out to a main quadrant. Windows all round and, in the floors above, coffee shops and a general store on the ground.

Turner ran to the right, up a flight of stairs, under over-hanging buildings. Knocking students, teachers and administrators alike out of the way. A cluster of smokers in one corner jumped as Turner came barrelling towards them.

Mickey ran at full pelt, his chest burning, legs pumping. He tried to match Turner for speed, knowing how difficult it would be to slow down and stop if Turner took an unexpected route.

Turner ran into the nearest building, up a small flight of stairs, down a corridor, Mickey right behind him. Students jumped out of the way when they saw the pair of them coming.

Turner slammed open a set of double doors, took the stairs before him two at a time. Mickey still chased. At the top of the stairs he went through another set of doors, then left down another corridor. Through another set of doors and into the main cafeteria.

People turned, initially puzzled but then rooted to the spot with fear as the two men came their way. Turner took advantage of the situation, grabbing a pile of trays as he passed, throwing them behind him. They scattered and clattered, fanning out and hitting Mickey in the legs. He did his best to jump over them, not lose speed, not let them slow him down.

357

Turner hit the double doors at the other end of the cafeteria, slamming them open, knocking the people before him out of the way. Mickey didn't give up.

Down another flight of stairs, out on to the upper quadrant. Then left and away, past the library, heading towards the lake.

It seemed like Turner had no real idea where he was going, his only thought to get away. Mickey didn't know where the lake route led to but, if it was outside the campus, Turner could escape. He powered on, finding extra strength from somewhere, pushing himself as fast as he could go.

He was gaining on Turner . . .

Faster, faster, pushing harder and harder . . .

Stretching out, almost able to touch him . . .

Turner risking a glance over his shoulder, seeing how close his pursuer was.

Then, looking forward again, Turner missed his footing, hit a pothole in the grass, stumbled.

And Mickey was on to him. Rugby tackling him to the ground, both his hands on Turner's back, pushing him into the earth.

'Get off, let go . . . bastard . . .'

Turner struggled, tried to kick, to punch. But Mickey, adrenalin ascendant, ignored him. He twisted the student's arm up his back until he cried out in pain. Then twisted it further.

'Get off me . . . bastard . . .' Another cry of pain to accompany it.

Mickey didn't care. Fed on that pain. Ate it up. Smiled. There would be time for the full reading of Turner's rights soon enough. But there was something else he had to say now. Something more important.

He laughed. 'You're nicked, my son.'

And there was Mickey triumphant. His old self back again.

84

The Creeper looked down at Rani lying there still, eyes closed.

And then she spoke to him.

Is that you? Are you there?

The Creeper frowned, confused. How could Rani be talking to him if she was lying there, right in front of him?

'Rani . . .?'

Yes. It's me. She sounded impatient. Hurried. *Come on . . .*

'But you're . . . you're there, on the floor . . . with your, your eyes closed . . .'

Never mind about that now.

He was genuinely confused. 'But how . . .'

Never mind.

What was wrong with her? Was she upset with him? Because of what he had done? 'Have I . . . have I done something wrong? I didn't mean to hit you that hard. I'm sorry . . . I should have, should have . . .'

I don't have time for that now.

He had to tell her, make himself understood. Plead, if he needed to. 'But you did a bad thing to me first. I only hit you after that, you made me do it . . .'

Stop it.

'I wouldn't have done it otherwise . . .'

Stop it! Now shut up and listen.

'But . . .'

Listen. She took a deep breath, stopped talking. He listened. *I'm not mad at you. You did . . . It doesn't matter what you did to me.*

He smiled. Felt relief wash through him. 'Thank you . . .'

Don't interrupt. I don't care about that now. You have to listen to me. You need to be prepared.

'I am prepared . . .'

Good. Listen closely. You need to get out of there. And you need to make it so that no one can follow you. Understand?

He frowned, confused once more. 'No . . . what, what d'you mean?'

There are people coming for you.

'I don't . . .'

I told you. Listen. Closely. Right? Good. You need to get out of where you are now. Quickly. Now we discussed this, remember? What you had to do if something like this happened?

The Creeper thought hard. This was difficult. This didn't feel right at all.

Remember. What we discussed. People are coming to the boat. You need to get out of there and not leave anything behind. What we talked about. What we planned. Remember?

He sat down beside the inert body of Rani. Tried not to look at her. He closed his eyes, forehead furrowed. Thinking. It took some effort, but, yes, he remembered. He told her so.

At last. That wasn't so hard, was it? We got there eventually, didn't we?

He laughed, thinking that was what she wanted him to do. She ignored him. *You remember what to leave?*

'Yeah, no problem.' He wanted to please her once more, make her happy again.

Good. Now—

'What about you?'

What d'you mean?

'You. Lying here, on the floor. With your eyes closed. You're talking to me and you're not talking to me. What am I going to do with you?'

Just . . . just leave, leave me there.

'Like a husk? Another husk? You mean put it with the others?'

No, no time. Just leave it there.

He felt a sharp stab of pain in his heart. 'But, but you said this would be the one. The one body you were going to stay in. Forever . . .'

Well, plans change, don't they?

Her words, harsh. He didn't like that. It upset him. Made him feel like crying.

'I'm sorry . . . I didn't, didn't mean to . . .'

It doesn't matter. Just leave the husk there and do what I told you. Can you do that?

'I won't let you down. Promise.'

Good. Now, when you've done that, there's somewhere I want you to go to.

He listened. She told him. Asked him to repeat it back to her until she was sure he understood.

Good. I'll talk to you soon.

And she was gone.

He looked down at the husk. Sighed. Felt that stabbing in his heart once again. What a shame. He had thought that this was it. This was them back together forever. He should have known better. Should have known things wouldn't work out.

Oh well.

He looked round the boat, knowing this was going to be the last time he would ever see it. It didn't feel like home. Not really. But then nowhere ever did. Not any more. No place felt like home. Not if Rani wasn't in it.

Felt tears well up. Swallowed them down. Wouldn't give in to them. Not again.

But he was going to meet her. She had said so. Would this be the real Rani? No more husks? He hoped so. But then he had thought so before and been disappointed.

Still.

His eyes fell on the box in the corner. He smiled. That would help. That would be something to look forward to.

Fire. He liked the fire. It was power.

And he liked having power.

No longer caring about the husk on the floor, but checking it didn't need another punch to keep it quiet, he crossed over to the box in the corner, opened it. Looked in.

Everything just as he remembered it.

Yes.

Fire was power.

And he was going to use it.

85

The circus had arrived.

The armed response unit had been hastily assembled in an old abandoned warehouse at the far end of Haven Street, along from King Edward Quay where Ian Buchan's boat was moored.

It reminded Phil of the kind of desolate, empty, run-down place – all rusting metal supports, crumbling walls, rubble-strewn floors and partially destroyed roofs – that he imagined spies being exchanged in during the Cold War. Or the kind of location in which producers of TV spy dramas held end-of-episode shoot-outs. As he watched the armed response unit check, lock and load their weapons, he hoped that was just fanciful thinking.

He refused to carry a gun. Wasn't even firearm trained. He disliked guns intensely, in any shape or form. Knives were worse, he knew that, but if he couldn't disarm a potential aggressor with his mind and wits, or at the most with his hands and stick, he wasn't being truly effective as a police officer.

He disliked the armed response unit. Thought the whole

of CO19 – the Met's supposedly elite force responsible for training all armed officers in the country – were a bunch of macho, fascist cowboys who hid behind the uniform while committing acts of barely licensed villainy. He was also intelligent enough to know that wasn't a popular opinion for a serving officer to hold, never mind express, so kept it to himself. Most of the time. But he did admit there was a time when they were needed, a necessary evil. And this was one such occasion.

He snapped the Velcro tapes shut on his stab vest, pulled it down, making sure it fitted snugly but not tight enough to restrict his movements. He turned to the team, saw a bunch of hard-faced men standing there, in the kind of mental and emotional zone reserved for sportsmen and cage fighters. If they were superheroes, aggression would be their superpower and it would explode from their fingertips like lightning.

Their senior officer, Joe Wade, was addressing them.

'Right,' he said. 'Here's the objective.'

He gestured at his laptop, placed on a folding table that had been brought along specially.

'This boat. King Edward Quay. Out of here and to the left. About two hundred yards along the quay. The target is on the boat. He may be armed. He is certainly dangerous. He may also have a hostage with him.'

'Detective Inspector Rose Martin,' said Phil. 'She was with DCI Fenwick when he was stabbed.'

Wade nodded, acknowledged the interruption, continued. The team were well drilled, well organised. While Wade marshalled his team into sections, Phil tried to calm his nerves. Anni had given him a description of the layout, which he had passed on to Wade. He wouldn't be entering the boat until Wade's team had secured it and brought Ian Buchan out. And, hopefully, Rose Martin. Then, with the area secured, he would enter.

Wade finished his address, looked at Phil.

Phil nodded. 'Right,' he said. 'I just want to emphasise once more that this man is dangerous. He's an ex-soldier who brought his training home with him. And he's been making full use of it in this town recently. Be aware. Oh, and one more thing. This is also a missing persons case. We need him to tell us where they are. So please, don't kill him.'

A few of them laughed, thought he was joking.

He wasn't.

'OK?' said Wade, putting on his helmet, 'let's go.'

86

'You've had some real cowboys in here . . .'

Marina was sitting at Anni's desk back in the bar, looking through the reports Fiona Welch had made. She wasn't impressed.

'Did no one check this?'

Anni looked at her, uncomfortable. 'Phil wasn't happy.'

'I'll bet he wasn't. And he shouldn't have been the only one. What was Ben Fenwick thinking?'

'I don't know,' said Anni, 'but he was doing it with another part of his anatomy.'

Marina looked at her, open-mouthed. 'What?'

Anni turned away. 'Sorry. Said too much.'

Marina looked at the files before her, back to Anni. 'Tell me.'

Anni pulled up a chair beside Marina, leaned in, dropped her voice. 'Rose Martin, the missing DS? Ben and her were getting it on.'

Marina nodded. 'And that impeded his judgement?'

'He's a man. You know what they're like. Especially at work.' She saw Marina's reaction. 'Sorry. I didn't mean—'

'That's OK. I know you didn't.' Since Marina and Phil had initially got together during a case she had a right to be cagey about criticism.

'He paid too much attention to her. Allowed her to influence the investigation. Same with Fiona Welch.'

'Didn't anyone see this? Try to stop it?'

'Phil did.' Anni smiled. 'He ended up punching the DCI's lights out.'

Marina smiled. 'Good for Phil.' Then she thought of the situation Ben Fenwick was in, felt immediately guilty. 'Anyway. Moving on. This profile. A child of nine could have come up with something better.'

'We think now she did it deliberately,' said Anni. 'To lead us to Anthony Howe.'

'I know Anthony Howe. Taught by him and worked with him. He was an arrogant letch but he wasn't capable of this. Where does Fiona Welch work?'

'The hospital. But she's also doing a Ph.D. at the university. This allowed her to teach, she told us.'

'And Ben Fenwick found her.'

Anni nodded.

Marina wasn't impressed. 'He should have asked for a forensic psychologist. And if he got a clinical psychologist he should have had a qualified one otherwise their opinion won't be recognised. Fiona Welch must be an assistant, right?'

Anni nodded again. 'Looks like it now. Maybe she told him she was qualified.'

'I wouldn't be surprised. She's clever, though. Inserted herself right at the heart of the investigation, tried to influence it, control it even. I'm surprised Phil went along with it.'

'He didn't seem to be on the ball.'

'Why not?'

Anni was reluctant to speak but knew she had to. 'I don't know. Something was distracting him.'

Marina nodded, not wanting to say anything further.

'Well, whatever. He saw through her eventually.' She sat back, ran her hands through her hair, thinking. 'Let's see what we've got. She's manipulative, she's controlling. She fed you a false profile that pointed to Anthony Howe. Who was someone she knew, someone who taught her.'

'Someone she held a grudge against?'

Marina nodded. 'I'd say that was very likely. Especially if she went to talk to him alone. And the suicide attempt followed. She's manipulative all right.'

Marina rifled through the files on Anni's desk. Brought over the post-mortem report on Adele Harrison. 'And then there's this . . .' She looked through it. 'I get a completely different feeling from the profile she gave based on this. Maybe it's because I'm just looking for something different but it doesn't feel right. Not at all.'

She picked up the phone, called Nick Lines. He answered.

'Hi, Nick, Marina Esposito here. Listen, this PM on Adele Harrison . . .' She looked through it. 'I've read it and got a couple of things to run by you. Just a theory, but here you go. These injuries. Do you think there's any chance this wasn't sexually motivated?'

She listened to his reply.

'I'll tell you. Because they strike me as overkill, done to make us jump to conclusions. Mislead us. All this genital mutilation . . . it doesn't seem consistent with the rest of the injuries. I mean, clearly they're sadistic and there's a lot of hatred there that's been acted out, but . . .'

She listened again. For quite a while. Her eyebrows raised.

'Interesting. Very interesting. Thanks, Nick.'

She put the phone down. Anni was looking at her, expectantly.

'Well?'

'He agrees. Thinks the sexual mutilation could have been done as a cover-up. No sign of actual penetrative sex, just aggression. And he did tell me something else.'

Anni leaned forward, irritated she was being made to wait.

'He's got the preliminary DNA results back from Adele Harrison's body. Three sets.'

'Three?'

Marina nodded. 'And there's something very interesting about one of them.'

But she didn't get a chance to say what it was. Because at that moment Mickey Philips strutted into the bar looking flushed but exultant, and told them Mark Turner was in an interview room, ready to be cracked.

He looked between Anni and Marina.

'So what d'you reckon?' he said. 'Good cop, bad cop or what?'

'Let's have a little chat,' said Marina.

87

The sun was beginning to wane, getting paler, lower, more distant. The home-time traffic trying to escape Colchester was well into its gridlock of the Colne Causeway all the way through to the Avenue of Remembrance, drive-time radio of one sort or another soundtracking the long journey home. The other world going about its daily business while, down on King Edward Quay, Phil stood behind a rusted metal fence watching the armed response unit, weapons ready, take up their positions around the target houseboat.

Wade gave the signal. The team moved swiftly and silently into place. Phil found he had stopped breathing. Forced himself to start again.

The takedown was smooth. One team surrounded the boat, giving back-up and support if needed, the main team boarded. Over the gangplank, on the deck, down the stairs. A battering ram of testosterone, muscle and metal knocking down all before it. Screaming, shouting, creating noise and confusion for the target, years of training making them able to operate with clinical clarity of thought and precision timing within that confusion.

Seconds. That was all it took.

Seconds.

Joe Wade made his way back up on deck, looked over at Phil, shook his head. Phil ran over to him, joined him on the boat.

'Gone,' Wade said, unable to hide the disappointment in his voice. 'But he left his hostage.'

Phil was straight down into the belly of the boat.

Rose Martin was being propped up by an officer, his gun at his side. Her hands were tied behind her body, her eyes wide with fear, pain and shock. Phil crouched before her.

'How you feeling?'

She just stared at him, eyes roaming and pinwheeling in terror, like the rescue was just another weapon in the armoury of pin to be inflicted on her.

'Rose, it's me, Phil Brennan.' He took her face in his hands. 'Rose . . .'

She flinched from his touch but he kept his hands there. Tender but firm. Eventually she managed to bring her eyes back into focus, look at him. No words, but definite recognition.

'Yeah, it's me. You're safe now.' He smiled, emphasising the point.

She nodded, going along with him.

'Good. There's an ambulance on its way. We're going to get you to the hospital now. You're OK. Everything's OK.' He turned to the officer at her side, pointed to the plastic cuffs attached to her wrists. 'Can we get these things cut off?'

The officer took out a knife, cut them through.

'Not standard issue, but I'm glad you brought it along,' said Phil. He took over from the crouching officer, helped Rose to her feet.

'All right?'

She nodded once more, rubbing her wrists. 'He . . . he . . .' Her mind slipped somewhere else, somewhere unpleasant. 'I tried to stop him, but he . . . oh God . . .'

'Never mind that now,' said Phil, wishing that just the act of saying those words could make things better but knowing that it couldn't.

'I'm sorry . . . I'm sorry . . .' She grabbed hold of his vest, clung to him.

'Don't worry. You're safe. Let's get you out of here.'

He started to move her, walking her slowly across the floor. As he did so, he took in the walls. The photos, magazine clippings, images of women with their eyes scored out.

Nutter, he thought, using the kind of technical term he was sure Marina would approve of. He scrutinised the images as he walked, taking Rose to the stairs.

Then froze. He had seen one of the pictures before.

And he knew where.

He began to move her with more of a sense of urgency. There was somewhere he had to be.

'DI Brennan.'

He turned. The officer who had freed Rose was standing at the far end of the boat, looking down. He had flipped the lid on an old, wooden box, scarred and battered, and was staring inside.

'What is it?' said Phil.

The officer looked up. 'Get out now, sir.' Then louder, more generally, 'Out now. Everyone off this boat, now. Go go go . . .'

Phil didn't need to be told twice. He hurried Rose, who had jumped hearing the officer's voice and started sobbing, up the stairs as fast as he could. On the deck and over the gangplank. He hurried her away. Behind him, armed officers were running for cover.

Phil just managed to make it back to the fence he had been behind at the start of the operation. He didn't have time to settle because a huge wave of heat, forceful and strong, knocked him face down into the road.

He lay there, panting for breath, eyes closed. Not daring

to move, wondering whether his legs were broken, his head still had hair, his back still had skin or whether it had been ripped off in the explosion. His ears more than ringing, sounding like he was stuck inside a tunnel with two high-speed trains passing each other at the same time.

He opened his eyes. Moved his legs. They still worked. Pushed himself up to his elbows. No real pain in his back. Got slowly to his feet.

He had managed to get outside the blast radius and was, apart from cuts and aches and gravel burn to the side of his face, relatively unharmed. He looked round. The warning had been given in time. No one had been caught in the blast.

The boat was belching out oily black smoke, flames licking their way up to the sky. On the Colne Causeway, the other-world inhabitants were staring out of their cars. People in the opposite flats coming to their windows, doors.

'We need a fire crew here ASAP,' Phil shouted, then looked round for Rose Martin. She was lying on the ground, curled up in a foetal ball. Unharmed.

'Bastard was waiting for us,' said Wade, walking up to Phil. 'Must have been tipped off. We'll get him.'

'See she gets to a hospital,' said Phil, walking off.

'Where you going?' said Wade, clearly not happy at the paperwork he was being left to face alone.

'I'll be back,' said Phil. 'Just have to go talk to the person who can tell us where he is.'

88

Mark Turner looked like an unremarkable man sitting in an unremarkable room.

His longish, dark hair was swept to the side in an identikit student indie manner, his clothes – jeans and a T-shirt – were dull, boring and uniform. Even the nonsensical slogan on his chest was nothing but a regulated attempt at individuality.

The room matched its inhabitant. Office surplus chairs and table. Grey scratched metal and worn, pitted and scarred wood. Depressing overhead strip lighting made Turner's eyes look hooded, his face gaunt. A still, empty vessel waiting to be filled. A doll waiting to be wound up.

And that was just what Mickey Philips intended to do.

'Look at him.' Marina stood in front of the two-way mirror in the observation room, watching him sit there. Unmoving. Barely breathing. 'Was it Flaubert or Balzac, which one?'

Mickey, standing next to her, gave her a blank, confused look.

'What is it?' she said. 'That quote. I will live like a

bourgeois so my art will be revolutionary? Something like that. Do you think that's an accurate description of our friend Mr Turner?'

Mickey frowned, genuinely puzzled. 'What? You think what he's been doing is art?'

Marina shook her head, her eyes compassionate, like she was explaining something complex to someone who spoke a separate language. Not patronising, just different.

'No,' she said, 'I don't. I just mean that he's been giving the impression of a normal, boring life, you know, studying, his film club, all that . . . while really he's been saving all his energy to live out this depraved fantasy life of his. You agree?'

'You mean he's been showing the world one face and living another?'

'That's it.'

'Yeah,' Mickey said. 'Definitely.' Put like that, he agreed.

Marina, learning Mickey was to be conducting the interview, had pulled him into the observation suite to prep him. Explaining that was usually how she worked with Phil, she had asked him if he wanted two-way communication with her in his ear. He had never done that before and was unsure whether to do it this time. He'd done interviews before and knew how to go about things. Even had his first questions in mind for this one.

Where's Suzanne?

Where's Julie?

What have you done with them?

Where are they?

Take it from there. But he hadn't made his mind up yet. He would see how this conversation went before making a decision.

Marina looked at the file in front of her. 'There's one question that's never been asked in this case. At least, not that I know of. And I think it's the most important one. The one that the investigation should have hinged on. Why do men hate women so much?'

'What?' Mickey felt himself getting angry. Was she talking about him? 'You mean me?'

'I mean all men. Or at least all men who act on it.'

'I hope you don't include me in that,' he said. 'I don't hate women.'

'You never wanted to hit a woman? Punish her?'

'I've wanted to hit lots of people. And I have done. But they deserved it. I've never hit a woman, though.'

'Good.' She smiled, nodded to the glass once more. 'I'll bet Mr Turner has. In fact, I think he's done more than that.' A quick glance down at her notes, then back up to Mickey. 'Stalkers fall into two categories. Psychotic and non-psychotic. They're usually sexual obsessives. The worst kind of women haters. And while our Mr Turner is not the best example of the male species, he doesn't fit into that category. I'm not getting him as our stalker. That, we think, is the other one. On the boat.' She pointed at the glass. 'So what does he get out of it? Where does he fit in? Turner . . .'

Marina turned away, head back, eyes closed. Thinking, Mickey presumed. He watched her. She was completely different from Fiona Welch. That was a given. Older, certainly and better looking, although knowing she was the boss's partner he pushed any such thoughts from his head. But there was something else. A conviction. Like she knew what she was talking about and said it in such a way that you could see what she meant. That, he knew from past experience, was rare in profilers.

'I think . . . yes, I think our Mr Turner has a different motivation,' she said. 'Yes . . . It's connected to Fiona Welch.' She nodded as if confirming the thought to herself. 'All bound up with her.' She opened her eyes, turned back to the glass. Watched him intently. Turner was sitting there, looking like he was almost asleep.

A sure sign, Mickey knew, of guilt.

'They're Brady and Hindley, Bonnie and Clyde,' said Marina. 'Leopold and Loeb.' She smiled, eyes alight with electricity. Turned to Mickey, gestured with her hand as if addressing a seminar. 'Yes. Yes. That's why they've . . . yes. That's how they think of themselves. Nietzschean supermen. Yes . . .'

She paced the small room, gesturing to herself, alive with her theorising. Mickey watched her, wondering if she was like this at home.

She turned to him. 'That's the approach to take. Go for his vanity. His ego. Remember, this is someone who lives a rich inner life and a poor external one. Everything's in his head.'

'So why's he acted it out?'

'Because he met Fiona Welch. Classic pair. One leader, one follower. An enabler, allowing the other to become the person they imagine themselves to be.' She turned to him. 'Is that the approach you were going to take?'

Mickey just stared at her. Thought of his opening questions.

'Er, yeah . . .'

He thought for a few seconds. Marina said nothing.

'That link up, in my ear and that.'

'Yes?'

'I think I'll take you up on that, thanks.'

Marina smiled. 'Let's go.'

89

'Why didn't you tell me, Paula?'

Phil stood in the doorway of Paula Hamilton's terraced house. She held on to the door frame, swaying, fingers trembling. She looked terrible. Clothes askew, like she'd just won first place in a dressing in the dark contest. Hair greasy and unkempt, sticking out at odd angles, as if she'd just woken up and the sleep and the dreams were still stuck in it. Her eyes roved, not settling until she realised who he was. Then he wished they hadn't. They looked like two open, ragged wounds.

She moved slowly aside, swaying insubstantially, a ghost, and allowed him to enter.

The living room matched its owner. A mess that wouldn't be straightened out for quite some time. Phil saw empty rectangles on the wall where some of the photos had been removed. He could guess which ones. They must have been taken down after his last visit.

After he'd looked at them.

He moved debris from an armchair, sat down.

'Why didn't you tell me, Paula?' he said again. 'You knew, didn't you?'

Paula slumped rather than sat on the sofa, crumpling. She nodded. 'Yes.'

'Then . . .'

'What?'

He sighed. Same question again. 'Why didn't you tell me?'

Her turn to sigh. Phil saw the vodka bottle lying on its side on the floor. Knew that whatever answers he received – if any – would be filtered through it.

'I . . . I just . . .' Another sigh.

'He didn't die in a roadside bomb, did he, your son?'

She shook her head. Looked at the carpet.

'What happened?'

'He . . . he was, was injured.' She kept her eyes on the floor. 'Badly injured. They . . .' She trailed off.

'They what, Paula? Tell me.'

She said nothing, just sat there deflated as if all the air, the fight, had left her body.

Phil leaned forward. 'Paula, your daughter is dead. And it looks like your son is responsible. And that's terrible. Horrible. One of the worst things that could ever happen to you. But there are two other women out there. Missing. That your son has taken. And if you can help me find them, if there's anything you know that can help me find them, that can stop another mother going through what you're going through, then do it. Please.'

She sat silently for a while, then she began to shake. 'There's no one . . . no one knows what I've been through, no one . . .'

'Then tell me,' said Phil. 'Make me understand. Tell me about your son. Tell me about Wayne.'

She sighed, picked up a glass from the side of the sofa, put it to her lips, realised it was empty. She sighed again, as if even that was conspiring against her, replaced it. Looked at Phil, resignation in her eyes. She began to talk. 'He was trouble, Wayne. Ever since he was little. Trouble. At first we thought . . . you know. Just bein' a boy. But no. There was something in there.' She pointed to her temple. 'Something not right.'

Phil waited. Knew there would be more.

'His dad didn't help, neither. Ask me, his dad was the problem. Always wantin' him to grow up. To be a man. Do the things Ian wanted him to do.'

'Such as?'

'Fightin'. Taught him how to box when he was tiny. Was always throwin' punches at him. Wanted him to harden up, he said. Stand up for himself. Made him play rugby because he said football was for poofs. Took him into the woods. Said he was gettin' him to hunt for things.' A shadow passed over those dark, ravaged eyes. 'That's what he said. But there must have been somethin' else going' on.'

'You mean he was abusing him?'

Paula nodded her head slowly. A ghost image wavering on a badly tuned TV.

'Yes. For years he was . . . he was doin' that. Years . . .'

'Is that why you left him?'

'He left us, I told you.' Sharp, a weary kind of fire in the words.

'Where did he go?'

She didn't answer. Just returned her head to the floor. Not soon enough. Phil saw what flitted across her face.

She's said too much, he thought. And knew just what had happened to Ian Harrison.

'You killed him, didn't you?' Phil's voice was quiet, non-judgemental. Encouraging her to continue.

She sat completely still for a while until she eventually nodded.

'Yes,' she said. 'I killed him.'

90

Mark Turner looked up when Mickey entered the interview room. File under his arm, walk purposeful, expression confident. He just hoped he could be as efficient as he looked.

He sat down, opened the file. Studied it for a few moments. Turner sat opposite him, slumped in his chair, resolutely resisting the urge to sit up, lean forward or even acknowledge Mickey's presence. Mickey kept his head down, apparently reading.

The curiosity became too great for Turner. He just had to see what Mickey was reading. Slowly he leaned forward, surreptitiously trying to get a glimpse of what was in the file. Mickey snapped the file shut, looked up.

'So who'd win in a fight, then?' he asked.

Turner looked puzzled.

'Dracula or Frankenstein, who d'you reckon?'

Turner's eyes widened, mouth gaped. It wasn't the question he had been expecting.

'Er . . .' Turner began to speak, give an honest answer. Then a smug smile appeared on his face. 'It's not

Frankenstein. It's the Frankenstein monster. Frankenstein was the name of the man who created him.' He sat back, triumph in his eyes. 'You don't know anything.'

'That's what I said,' said Mickey, not missing a beat. 'Who would win in a fight, Dracula or Frankenstein? Not the monster. The Baron. The Peter Cushing Baron. And the Christopher Lee Dracula.'

He waited. Turner's eyes widened again.

'Oh. Right. Dracula. Obviously.'

'You sure? I mean, yeah,' said Mickey, leaning forward, arms on the table as if it was just two mates in a pub having a chat, 'physically, yeah. Dracula. No contest. But the Baron . . .' Mickey shook his head. 'Tricky. He wouldn't play fair. He'd have traps and things waiting. Devices. Gizmos. I reckon it's him.'

Turner leaned forward too. 'I still reckon Dracula. He doesn't get to live that long without learning a thing or two.'

'Yeah, but a bit of garlic, sunlight, crucifix . . .' He shrugged. 'You think the Baron won't take all that into account? Lay some traps for him to fall into?'

Turner nodded, giving the matter serious thought.

'Anyway,' said Mickey, 'just thought I'd ask because I heard you're a real horror film fan. The old stuff. The good stuff, yeah?'

'Yeah.' Turner looked incredulous. 'Why? Are you too?'

'The old stuff. Seventies, all that. British stuff. Love it. Could sit here all night talking about it. But . . .' He looked at his watch. 'Better crack on. Right.' He opened the folder again. Looked at it. Closed it. Looked back at Turner. 'Why did you run away from me, Mark?' Asking the question in the same tone of voice he had used for the pub discussion.

Turner looked at him, seemingly trying to find an honest answer for him. 'I, I . . .'

Mickey waited, watched. Checked the way Turner's eyes went. Marina had briefed him, told him how to start the interview, get him onside, ask him questions, see which way his eyes went when he answered them. Up to the left for thinking and truth, down to the right for lying. Or was it the other way round? What had she said?

He scratched the back of left hand with the middle finger of his right.

'Up to the left for the truth, down to the right for lying.'

He gave a small nod. Marina had spotted the signal, spoken to him.

Turner tried to stonewall, shrugged. 'Just running,' he said. 'Didn't know who you were. What you wanted. You'd have ran. If it had been you. Someone chasing you.'

Mickey nodded. 'So where's your girlfriend, then, Mark? She done a runner too?'

Turner shrugged.

'Didn't share your taste in films? Her idea of an evening in wasn't sitting down to watch *Killer's Moon*?'

Turner's eyes widened in shock. 'You've seen *Killer's Moon*?'

'Great film,' said Mickey. 'Not what you'd call a horror film, though. Comedy classic, more like.'

He heard Marina give a small chuckle in his ear. 'Good old Milhouse, knew we could rely on him . . .'

Mickey leaned across the table. Speaking again like they were two mates in a pub, about something more important this time. 'She's left you, Mark. Gone.'

Turner shook his head. 'No . . .'

'Yeah.' Mickey nodded his head in sympathy. 'She has, mate. Gone. Sorry, but she's abandoned you. Left you here to take the full brunt of it.'

He kept shaking his head, more vehemently now. 'No, no, she wouldn't, never, no . . .'

'She has. So you may as well tell us what happened.'

Nothing. Just Turner shaking his head.

'You see, with her gone, there's just you. And everything

gets pinned on you. The murders, the abductions, the misleading of a police investigation, everything. All down to you.'

No response.

'But if you start talking, tell me things . . .' Mickey shrugged. 'It'll make things a lot easier for you. Help you in the long run.'

Turner stopped shaking his head. Sat completely still, staring at the desk. Mickey waited.

Eventually Turner looked up. Smiled. It wasn't pleasant. 'You nearly had me there. Copper.'

Mickey frowned. 'What you talking about?'

'The films, all that. Dracula, Frankenstein, God, *Killer's Moon*, you've done your homework . . .' He laughed. It held as much humour as the smile did. 'And all for this. All to be my mate' – he spat the word out – 'all to get me to talk. No.'

Mickey said nothing.

'She said this is what you'd say to me. What you'd try to get me to do if I ended up here. She knew that, course she did. She's a psychologist, for fuck's sake.'

'Not a very good one,' said Marina in Mickey's ear.

Mickey scowled. He didn't need that. Marina apologised.

Turner sat back, folded his arms. 'Anyway. It's done.'

'What's done, Mark?'

'It. Everything. What we set out to achieve. It's all complete. Really, it doesn't matter what happens to me now because it's over. Finished. We've done it.'

'Done what?'

'Proved our point.'

'Which was?'

Again, that smile. 'That we are superior to you.'

'To who?'

'All of you.' Turner stretched out his arms, put his hands behind his head, relaxed. 'And that's all I'm going to say.'

Mickey stared at him.

Lost.

91

Phil exhaled. Felt no sense of triumph at guessing correctly. 'What happened?'

Paula sighed once more. 'It was . . . Adele. Adele and me. We just couldn't bear it any more. He was . . . hurtin' me. And starting to look at Adele in a way I didn't like. I couldn't have that. I wouldn't have that.'

She stopped talking, reached for the empty glass once more. Sighed. Continued.

'So one day I . . . hit him. With a shovel. From the back garden. And he fell. And that was that.'

'So where is he?'

'We—' She corrected herself. '*I* buried him. In the back garden.'

'And you weren't worried about getting caught?'

'I did it at night.'

'I mean about the murder. You weren't worried about people finding out?'

She thought for a moment. 'I went over that in my mind. Over and over. For ages afterwards. Ages. No. Because I'd done the right thing. He was a monster. I hadn't killed a man. I'd killed a monster.'

Phil looked at her, the sad, defeated woman before him. He didn't know what she had gone through, could only guess at that. But he did know one thing. Police officer or not, there were times when the law just wasn't enough.

'I got my story straight, stuck to it. People asked. But not much. They knew what he was like. Most people round here were relieved for me when he'd gone.'

'Did you do this all yourself?'

'Yes.' A fast answer.

Too fast, thought Phil.

'No, you didn't. Adele helped you, didn't she? And you want to protect her.'

Paula looked at him, straight in the eye for the first time since he had arrived there. Then she dropped her gaze. Nodded at the floor.

'That's OK,' he said. 'I can understand you wanting to protect her. You did it for her. You didn't want her to suffer for it.'

She nodded again.

'And Wayne? How did he take it?'

'He didn't know. I told him his dad had gone. Run away. Left us. I thought that would be it, you know? The end of it. That would be fine. I'd get my son back and we'd all be happy. A happy family.' She sighed. 'Wrong.'

'What happened?'

'He . . . he blamed me. For what had happened. For his dad running away. Said I was a, a bitch. And a cow. That it was my fault he'd gone. I'd driven him away. My fault.' She swallowed back tears.

'And then what?'

'He joined the army. Wanted to get away. Said what his dad always said. The army makes a man of you. Well, it makes a certain kind of man out of you . . .'

'And his name?'

'Changed it. Ian was his . . . his dad's name.'

'Buchan?'

'I went back to my maiden name. Adele too.' Another sigh. 'Ian didn't.'

'Did you keep in touch with him?'

'Not really. No, in fact. And then the army got in touch. Told me he'd been burnt in a fire. Badly burnt. Well, I went to see him. You have to, don't you? I mean, he is my son, after all. So they sent him back here, to the garrison. And I went there.' Another sigh. 'My God. What had happened to him . . .'

'What had happened to him?'

'He'd . . . he'd raped a woman. A translator. Afghan. A local, civilian, working with the army. He'd been, been pursuin' her. Stalking her. They didn't actually say that, not to me, but that's what they meant. And this woman, Rani, they said her name was, she kept turning him down. Anyway, one night he followed her home, got her on her own. Tried to . . .' Another sigh. 'Like I said. His father's son.'

Phil waited, impatient for Paula to continue but knowing he had to let her do it in her own time.

'He raped her. I mean, not just, you know, had sex with her. It was bad, what he did to her. They told me.'

'His father taught him to hate women. He was just acting out.'

She nodded. 'But he made his own mind up to do it. He was a man. Anyway, then, I don't know exactly what happened next. Neither did they. Did he get upset when he realised he'd gone too far with her? Had he killed her? Did he want to hide the evidence? I don't know. But he started a fire. He was always startin' fires when he was a kid. Loved them, he did.'

Still does, though Phil, but decided it was best not to say it.

'Anyway, he got caught in it. Couldn't get away. Couldn't get out. It . . . it . . . they let me see him. There's . . . not much of him left now.'

387

'Was he invalided out of the army?'

She nodded. 'Came back to Colchester. Didn't want to come and live here, though. They covered it up, arranged for therapy, treatment. All sorts of stuff. Tried to put him back together again.' Another sigh. Her voice became bitter. 'Needn't have bothered. There's nothin' left of him. His mind . . . Should have left him where he was.'

'So what happened with Adele?'

She sighed. Steeled herself for the pain to come. 'He . . . tracked her down. And, and took her.'

'Why?'

'He's not right, is he? He's . . .' She sighed.

'Did you know it was him at the time?'

She shook her head. 'Only afterwards. It only made sense afterwards. I didn't know what to think at first. I knew she hadn't run away. She wouldn't. I mean, she'd had her wild years, but she'd come through that. And then, then I thought about it. Guessed it might be him. Comin' for her first. Then me next.'

'Why didn't you come to us? Say something?'

She gave a harsh laugh. 'Yeah, you'd really put yourselves out to find my Adele, hadn't you? And how could I? My son's after my daughter and me because we killed his father? Yeah. I can see that goin' down well, can't you?'

Phil said nothing. She had a point.

'Did you recognise the names of the other women? When you'd heard they'd gone missing or been killed? Did you not connect them with your son?'

'I might have . . . I don't know. No.' Shaking her head, closing her eyes, saying the words without conviction, as if to confirm it to herself.

So she didn't have any more guilt to carry around, thought Phil.

'You should have talked to me,' said Phil. 'To me.'

She didn't answer. Couldn't answer.

'So what now?' said Phil. 'He's not on the boat he's been living on. D'you know where he would be?'

Paula shook her head.

'Don't protect him, Paula. Not now. If you know, tell me.'

She looked up. Fire in her eyes. And tears. 'I'm not protectin' him. D'you think I really would? After all he's done? All he's taken away from me? You think so? His mind's gone, Mr Brennan. All he's got left is hate. If I knew where he was I'd tell you. I'd lead you to the bastard myself . . .'

She trailed off, tears overtaking words.

From upstairs came the sound of a baby crying.

'Our Adele's,' said Paula.

The baby kept crying. Paula didn't move. There was nothing more Phil could say, no more questions to ask. He stood up.

'I'll have to bring you in.'

She nodded. The baby kept crying.

'But not tonight. We'll do it later.'

Paula didn't nod this time. Phil walked to the door. Turned back and looked at her. Sitting alone in the wrecked room. The baby still crying upstairs. He wanted to say something, give her some encouraging words, tell her something that would make it better, help her find a way out of her pain, make the loss more bearable.

But there was nothing. Nothing at all.

He left her there.

Closed the door behind him. Stepped out into the darkness.

92

Mickey didn't have to wait long for something to happen. There was a knock on the door. He got up to answer it, went into the corridor, shutting the door behind him. Hoped it was something or someone to help him.

Anni.

'Here.' She handed him a sheet of paper. 'Preliminary DNA results from Adele Harrison's body. Like Nick said, there's something funny about one set.'

'What?'

'There.' She pointed to the relevant section.

Mickey read it. Smiled. 'Thanks, Anni. This might be it.'

She returned the smile. 'Good luck.'

Marina appeared. 'Good work, Mickey.'

His smile faded. 'You think so? I've lost him.'

'You'll get him back. I think he's the follower. Fiona Welch is the leader. If he'd never met her, come under her influence, he wouldn't be here. I don't think he's all that bad. Not really. Play on that. Use it. Appeal to his good side. Be his mate.'

'Be blokey?'

'Worth a try.'

He waved the sheet of paper. 'And if that fails, there's always this to fall back on.'

'Absolutely.'

He went back inside. Sat down again.

'Sorry about that.' He smiled at Turner. 'Where were we? Oh yes. You were telling me how superior you were.'

Turner smirked, said nothing. Accepting the words as if they were due praise.

Mickey scrutinised Turner. 'You used to go out with Suzanne Perry, didn't you?'

'You know I did.'

'Nice girl. Why'd you ditch her?'

'Found someone better.'

'Really?' Mickey shook his head. 'You mean Fiona Welch? Listen, mate, you backed a wrong 'un there.'

Turner just stared at him.

'I mean, there's Suzanne. Good-looking, intelligent, good company . . . And Julie Miller. You were with her before Suzanne, yeah? Same. Real looker. And then you go from them to Fiona Welch.'

'So?'

'So it's like trading in a Rolls-Royce for a Mondeo. She must be a good shag, mate, because there's nothing else going for her.'

Turner's face reddened, his eyes narrowed. He struggled not to rise from his chair. 'And what would you know? Eh? Mr Thick Policeman? *Mate?* Nothing. That's what. Nothing. "All things are subject to interpretation. Whichever interpretation prevails at a given time is a function of power and not truth".' He managed a smile. 'Know who said that? Course you don't. Because you're thick. Thick thick thick thick thick.'

Mickey said nothing.

'I'll go and look it up.' Marina's voice in Mickey's ear. He shook his head. Hoped she caught it.

Turner was still talking. 'That's your interpretation. Because you think you've got power. But it's not. It's nothing like that.'

'Then tell me what it is like.'

Another humourless laugh. 'You wouldn't understand. You're not intelligent enough to understand.'

'Then make me. Because I'm all that stands between you and a life sentence for four murders. Make me.'

Turner sat back. 'All right then.' Closed his eyes. 'What Fiona and I have is so, so much more than anything I have ever felt in my life. Suzanne, Julie, even Adele were nothing. Boring little nobodies. But Fiona has shown me things, made me realise what I am, what I'm capable of . . .' He sighed, a happy, cruel smile on his face. 'I've never felt so alive. All because of her.' He opened his eyes. Fixed Mickey with a direct gaze. 'I pity you. Really pity you.'

'Why, Mark?'

'Because you'll never feel what I've felt. Experience what I've experienced. Your life will always be boring. And you will always be stupid. "Every man takes the limits of his own field of vision for the limits of the world." And that's you. Bet you don't know who said that, either.'

'Would it matter if I did?'

Turner laughed, shook his head. 'Course not.'

Mickey sighed, sat back, folded his arms. Fixed Turner with a direct look. 'Mark, I'll be honest with you. No bullshit now. You can sit here and come out with all these quotes and all these insults and it doesn't make a blind bit of difference. No any more. Not to you. Because, like I said, you're looking at a life sentence for four murders. At least. That we know of. And it looks like your girlfriend's dumped you. Left you to take all the blame.'

Turner flinched at that.

'Good one,' said Marina.

Mickey leaned forward once more. The last few minutes

forgotten, mates again. 'So why don't you tell me, Mark? Eh? Tell me everything. You're not going anywhere.'

Turner stared at him, mouth moving, chewing the inside of his lip.

Nerves, thought, Mickey. Good. Getting there.

'Tell me the whole thing, Mark.'

Turner sighed.

'All right.'

Mickey managed to hide his smile.

93

The boat was almost gone. It hadn't been much to start with, but the fire and explosion had rendered it down to a black, rusted skeleton. A charred, blurred representation of what had once been moored there. A smudged after-image.

Phil stared at it, wanting it to give him answers. He looked round.

Fire teams had handled the blaze, stopped it from spreading. But King Edward Quay had been evacuated along with the apartments on the opposite side of the river, the house-boats and businesses sealed off, no access to anyone.

TV crews had been kept at a distance and the crews working the lightship murder site and Julie Miller's neighbours had also been stood down until the area was declared safe. Uniforms were keeping watch, stopping any trespassers, so Phil had the place to himself.

He had phoned Marina, tried to tell her what was going on, but got only her voicemail. So he had left a message telling her about his conversation with Paula and for her to phone him back as soon as possible.

He closed his eyes, listened. Tried to get a feel for the area, for the space inside Ian Buchan's head. For where he had been, where he would go next. He turned round. The old Dock Transit building stood behind him. Huge and hulking against the orange sodium darkness, holding shadows and secrets behind its boarded-up doors and windows. The corrugated, rusted metal along its roof making it look like the crenulated top of an old, haunted castle. Phil found a uniform, showed his warrant card.

'Has inside there been checked?'

The uniform was middle-aged, greying hair, well-built. Time-serving but sharp-eyed. Doing his job but counting up the overtime. 'A few hours ago,' he said. 'Didn't get far. Place is a death trap. Doubt he'd be in there. Didn't look like it. Could barely get it opened.'

Phil turned towards the building, back to the uniform. 'Got a torch I could borrow? Just have a nose round for myself.'

The uniform handed it over. Phil thanked him.

Worth a try, he thought. From the way the officer had spoken, he doubted the building had been seriously searched.

He crossed the rubble-strewn, broken concrete forecourt, walked under the huge, rusting metal arm of the crane, approached the building. He could imagine it as it once was, a working building, the crane moving constantly, grabber sliding back and forth along the overhead beam, containers being emptied, filled and transferred, loading and unloading cargo from Europe, the dock alive with bustling activity. A confident place, making a serious challenge to Harwich.

And now. A rusted, wrecked shell. As much of a ghost as the burnt-out husk of a boat in front of it.

He walked up to where the door used to be. Now just several huge sheets of thick plywood decorated with 'Danger – Keep Out' signs, gang tags and graffiti art. He felt round the edges for some purchase, something to pull at, saw the rusting imprint of well-hammered-in heavy-duty nails.

Maybe the uniform was right, he thought. Maybe there hadn't been anyone here.

Maybe.

Phil knelt down, felt all along the bottom of the wood.

Something gave.

Just a little bit, a slight movement accompanied by the creak of old wood against rusted nail. Not much, but enough to give him hope. He pulled, wondering which part of the building the uniforms had entered from. Or even if they had.

The wood didn't want to give. At least not without a fight.

And Phil was in the mood for a fight.

He edged his fingers beneath, prising the wood away, catching his fingernails, feeling splinters embed themselves in his palms as he did so. He ignored everything but the need to pull the wood off.

More creaking, more straining as the wood reluctantly pulled away from its surrounding. Phil screamed with the exertion, fell backwards as the corner of wood came away. He sat up, looked at it. There was a big enough hole for him to squeeze through.

Just.

He put his arms through, managed to pull his body along.

As he did so, he was reminded of a similar crawl through a restricted space he had made several months before. He hoped this one turned out better than that.

He made it through to the other side. Lying on the floor, he looked round. Pitch-black, he saw nothing. The air was damp and cold. Fetid. He listened. Heard the wind playing through the rust-eaten walls, ghosts drifting.

He felt for the torch, took it out of his jacket pocket, switched it on. Swung it round. Saw small black shapes scurry away from the beam. The walls were mottled, discoloured, crumbling. The metal struts holding up the roof rusted and flaking. The floor pitted and broken concrete, a pile of old rags in a far corner, with a stack of old, stained cardboard next to it. Empty cans, bottles. Someone had been living there at some point. Not recently, though.

He stood up. Walked towards the centre of the building, looking all round all the time. Checking the dust on the floor as he walked. This place hadn't been searched. Uniforms had probably decided to leave it for the morning.

Lazy bastards, thought Phil.

He swung the torch. The building had another floor towards the back, a metal staircase leading the way. He looked up to the ceiling. A metal walkway ran along the length of the building leading to the crane outside. No one up there. He walked on, towards the back of the building, ready to mount the steps to the next floor.

Stopped dead.

Something wasn't right.

Tucked away in a shadowed corner were two large black boxes. Phil moved in closer. Wooden packing crates, rectangular. A concrete block, the kind used in roadworks, in front of each one. And before that a trough of water.

There was something in the water.

Phil moved quickly, fearing the worst.

His fears were justified. In the water was a body. Charred and burnt. Electrocuted, he guessed.

He looked round. Saw cables snaking into the water. He traced them with the torch. Saw that they connected to a generator in the corner. He crossed over, made sure the generator was switched off. Turned back to the trough of water, reached in, turned the body over.

A young woman, tall, brunette. Julie Miller or Suzanne Perry, he was guessing.

Too late. Damn.

He stood still, listening. Heard a sound. Scratching. Moving. Not the rats, too big for the rats.

Looked round. One of the crates was open, the end pushed out against the concrete block. The other block was still in place. Phil moved round the side of the water, bent down beside the end of the box.

'Hello?' he said.

The scratching stopped.

'Hello?' he said again. 'Is there anyone in there?'

Nothing.

'My name is Detective Inspector Phil Brennan. Essex Police. Is there someone in there?'

He waited. Eventually he heard a voice.

'How . . . how do I know you are who you say you are?'

A woman's voice. Phil felt a rush of adrenalin course through him. 'Are you Suzanne Perry or Julie Miller?'

'Suzanne . . .'

Relief flooded through him along with the adrenalin. He smiled to himself. 'Thank God,' he said. 'I'm going to get you out.'

She started to scream.

He tried to calm her down. 'Hey, hey it's OK. It's fine. You're safe now. You're with me. You're safe. Don't worry. I'm going to get you out, OK?'

He waited. Nothing.

'OK?'

A sigh, then sobbing. 'OK . . .'

'Right . . .'

He pulled away the concrete block, slowly. It was heavy. Then, when there was space enough, he prised open the bottom of the packing crate.

'Come on, Suzanne, out you come . . .'

'The water . . .'

'Don't worry about that. It's taken care of. Just come on out.'

He heard movement, shone the torch in. Slowly, Suzanne made her way towards the light.

He smiled, encouraging her.

She emerged. Blinking, shaking. He reached out a hand for her, helping her to the side of the trough, so she wouldn't get wet.

'Come on . . .'

She froze. He frowned.

'It's OK, Suzanne. Come on. You're fine, you're safe . . .'

'No,' she said, backing into the crate, 'no . . .'

'Suzanne?' Phil looked after her. 'Come on, Suzanne, it's fine, I'm here . . .'

'And so am I.'

Phil froze. Turned quickly.

Saw something come towards him. Fast.

Saw the world explode.

Then, finally, blackness.

94

'**H**ow did you meet Fiona Welch?'

Turner sat staring straight ahead, arrogance exuding from him in waves like cheap aftershave. 'University. She was Psychology, post grad, I was doing an M.Sc. in Biological Science. We were friends. Hung around in the same groups.'

'So what made you leave Suzanne Perry for her?'

He smiled. The arrogance waves increased. 'Nothing. She just told me how much better I could be.'

'In what way?'

Turner gave a laugh that he probably thought went with his arrogant smile but made Mickey think of camp villains in old James Bond movies. He said nothing.

'You know what transgression is?' Then, without waiting for an answer, he continued. 'It means stepping over your limit. Violating your laws and codes. Being what you would call wrong. That's what Fiona offered me. She took one look at my life, my boring, ordinary little life, and she changed it. Get with her and it could be so much better. I did. It is.'

He sat back, arms folded, as if waiting for applause.

'So what does this transgressing involve? How did you go about it?'

'By doing what we wanted. Nothing is real. Everything is permitted.' Another laugh. 'That's what we did.' He leaned forward, eyes blazing. 'Everything.'

'Right. Specifics?'

He put his head back, laughed. Trying to look superior, but Mickey caught a glimpse of his eyes before he did it. They looked uncertain. Fearful. His arrogance, Mickey was learning, wasn't very convincing.

'Too many to name.'

'Just one instance. Of your superiority. Your transgression. Go on, Mark. Just one.'

Turner sat forward. Again, that fear flashed in his eyes. 'It's enough that you know that that's what we are.'

Mickey sighed. 'Fair enough, Mark, if you say so.'

Turner felt Mickey's disbelief, felt he needed some qualification. 'We plotted, that's what we did. Planned. To find a way to transgress, to make everyone see we were serious. Show people what we were all about.'

'So . . . what? You kidnapped Adele Harrison? Why? How does that demonstrate your superiority? Or that you're transgressing anything?'

Turner's voice rose. He slapped his arms down on the table. 'Don't you understand? That was the point. Take a life, any life, someone worthless, some nobody, and do with her what we want.'

He sat back, pleased with himself.

'What you want.'

Turner nodded.

'What did that involve?'

'Anything.'

'What, killing? Torture? Maiming? What?'

'Anything.'

'And you did that, did you? What you wanted? Anything you wanted?'

He smiled. 'Sort of.'

'What d'you mean, sort of?'

'That's when the experiment moved into it's next phase. Because we didn't just do that ourselves. That would be too simple. No.'

'What did you do, then?'

'Obvious. Got someone to do it for us . . .'

95

Phil opened his eyes. Felt pain lance through his head. Closed them again, groaned.

'Ah. He's awake.'

Phil tried opening his eyes again. It hurt, but he managed it this time. He tried to move. Couldn't. His hands were behind his back, his legs curled beneath him. He blinked, letting his eyes get accustomed to the darkness.

A light went on. He shut his eyes quickly, the sudden glare burning him.

He opened them slowly. Looked down. Gasped. He was high off the ground, still in the old Dock Transit building. On the metal walkway that ran along the roof of the building.

The light was coming from a hastily rigged arc light that had been positioned next to him. He saw chains hanging from the ceiling. With huge hooks on the ends.

He remembered Adele Harrison's body. Took a deep breath. Shuddered.

Phil moved what parts of his body he could, checking himself for damage. His head hurt, his vision was blurred.

Concussion, probably, from the blow that had knocked him out. He flexed his arms, his legs. Moved his torso. No damage that he could feel. Good. That was something.

A groan from behind him.

He tried to turn to the source of the sound, twisting his body as far as it would go. Suzanne Perry was curled up on the walkway next to him. She wasn't tied to the railing. From the look of her she didn't need to be.

'Suzanne?' he said.

She looked up. Her eyes signalled that she was exhausted, totally beaten. She didn't speak, just stared.

He shook his head. 'I'm sorry,' he said. 'I should have been more careful. But don't worry, I'll get you out of this.'

'Oh will you, indeed?'

The voice was familiar. He looked round. There, ahead of him, standing on the edge of the lamp's beam, was Fiona Welch. She was smiling. It wasn't pleasant.

'Hello, Phil. Fancy meeting you here.' She held out a piece of paper in her hand. 'I've got my invoice. Do I give it to you or send it to accounts?'

Phil said nothing. Just stared at her.

She laughed, crumpled it up, threw it over the side. It took a long time to reach the bottom. Made only the slightest of sounds when it did.

'Ooh,' she said. 'Long way down.' She crossed towards him, crouched down beside him. Stretched out her hand, touched his cheek. 'Wouldn't want anything to happen to you now, would we?'

Phil tried not to flinch, to pull away from her touch. He just about managed it. She kept her hand where it was, kept stroking.

'Let it go, Fiona.' He kept his voice calm, reasonable. It wasn't easy. 'Let it end now before you get into more trouble.'

She just smiled at him. It wasn't a smile connected to sanity.

'And let Suzanne go. She's done nothing wrong.' No response. 'Please, Fiona. Let her go.'

She kept stroking, moved in closer to him. When she spoke, he felt her warm breath on his cheek.

'How does it feel, Phil? Hmm? How does it feel to lose?' Her eyes looking directly into his, fingers playing along his cheekbone. Her smiled widened, showing him her teeth. White and sharp and wet.

Phil tried not to look at her. He looked away, into the shadows she had come from. And saw something.

Or someone.

A hulking presence, a shadow against shadows. Breathing raggedly, deeply. Waiting.

Phil guessed who that was.

He turned his attention back to Fiona Welch. 'Is that what you think, Fiona? That I've lost?'

'Of course you have, darling.' In close to him, whispering, her breath on his ear, tickling. 'I'm not the one chained up and . . . *helpless.*'

He could feel an involuntary erection coming on. Hated his body, himself, for allowing it, fought to keep it down.

He pulled his head away, looked at her face. Steel in his eyes. 'No,' he said. 'You might not be. But there's a nation-wide manhunt going on for you. Your description is in the papers, on TV, the internet, everywhere. You can't get away. They'll find you.'

She smiled.

'Maybe they will.'

She laughed, moved her body in close to his.

'But not just yet . . .'

96

Marina sat back, waiting to see what Mark Turner would say next, waiting to see where Mickey's questions would guide him.

He was good, she thought. Getting the information out of him in his own way at his own pace. He was surprising her. She had thought on first meeting him that he was just a typical copper: boorish, macho, problems with women, especially those with authority over him, the usual. But he was proving himself to be different. There was a slight glitch when she saw his response to Turner's goading of him, calling him thick, throwing quotes at him he didn't know, but he handled himself well, recovered quickly.

Her eyes caught her mobile on the desk. She had put it on silent when the interrogation started. She checked the screen: two messages. One from Phil, one from Nick Lines. She looked back at Mickey, thought he could handle himself for a few minutes, took out her earpiece and hit voicemail.

Her eyes widening as she listened.

*

'So who was this person?' said Mickey. 'The one you got to do things for you?'

Turner shrugged. 'Nobody. A real nobody. Even less important than our targets.'

'Really? I'd have thought it would be someone quite important if you wanted to get them to do all that for you.'

Turner shook his head. 'Well you'd be wrong. As you have been about everything else, thick copper.'

Mickey said nothing. Waited.

'He was just a squaddie. Some damaged, war-traumatised squaddie. Completely mind-fucked. Piss easy to manipulate.'

'Why?'

'He'd killed this translator. Woman in Afghanistan that he got obsessed over. Big cover-up about it. Threatened with a court martial, everything. But instead they invalided him out, on the quiet.' He laughed. 'Didn't want the embarrassment.'

'Can't blame them,' said Mickey. 'Already in enough trouble over there.'

Turner nodded, back to being mates in a pub, then checked himself. Remembered where he was, who he was supposed to be. Worked the arrogance back into his features once more. 'He burnt this woman to death. Raped her then killed her. Burnt himself pretty badly in the process too.'

'So how did you come across him?'

'Fiona did. At the hospital. He'd been sent for therapy.'

'What kind?'

Turner shrugged. 'Don't know. Speech, psychology, occupational, all sorts, I suppose. Whatever he needed.'

'And he met Fiona Welch.'

Turner nodded. 'She said he so easy to manipulate it was laughable. She could tell him anything she wanted, anything at all. And he'd believe it. Didn't matter what kind of stupid, twisted shit she said, he believed it. She used to come home telling me what she'd said and how he'd believed it.' He smiled, shaking his head. 'We used to laugh about that . . .'

Mickey was about to speak when he heard Marina's voice in his ear. Fast urgent. 'Can you talk?'

'Give me a minute, Mark.'

Without waiting, Mickey stood up, exited the interview room.

Marina was waiting for him in the corridor outside. 'I wouldn't have interrupted you unless it was something important,' she said. 'I've had a couple of phone calls. There's something I've got to tell you.'

She told him.

When Mickey went back into the room he could barely keep the smile off his face.

'Sorry about that,' he said. 'Where were we? Oh yes. You were telling me about your squaddie.'

'The Creeper, we called him.'

'Why?'

He shrugged. 'Because he's a creep.'

'And Fiona chose him because he was easy to manipulate?'

Turner nodded. 'Like a retarded little kid.'

'No other reason?'

'No.' He saw the half-smile on Mickey's face. Doubt crept into his features. 'Why? What d'you mean?'

'She didn't choose him for another reason?'

'Like what?' Very uneasy now.

'Like, the fact he was Adele Harrison's brother?'

Turner's mouth fell open.

Stayed open.

Mickey kept his smile controlled.

Got you, he thought.

97

'I'm going to tell you a story,' said Fiona Welch to Phil, still up close to him, almost sitting on his lap, moving her hips rhythmically, grinding slowly against him.

Phil swallowed hard, tried to look – move – away. He couldn't. 'What about?' he said. 'Anything interesting?'

'Me,' she said, the words whispered breathily, Marilyn Monroe-like. 'How naughty I am.' She traced her finger down his chest. 'And what drives me to do . . . what I've been doing.'

'Oh,' said Phil. 'Nothing interesting, then.'

She drew back from him, teeth bared. Hissing. 'Just another thick copper. Like all the others.' Leaned into him again, her finger back on his chest, joined by the others, dug the nails of her left hand into him this time. Hard.

Her nails were sharp. Strong. They hurt. Drew blood.

'OK,' he said. 'Tell me. Why you do what you do.'

She took her finger away. Smiled. 'That's better. Much more fun when you play along with me, isn't it?' A sigh of contentment. 'Now. Where were we? Yes. Why I do what I do.' She stuck her hands out, together at the wrists. 'Because

409

I'm a bad girl, Mr Policeman. You'd better take me in your big strong arms and handcuff me.' She giggled. 'Oh, I forgot. You can't.'

Venom in the final words.

'You're so funny,' said Phil. 'See how I'm laughing?'

Her eyes blazed. 'You think you're clever? Do you? Really?'

Her hands were on him, slapping his face, tearing at him.

'Do you? Do you?'

More slaps, more scratches. Digging her nails into the side of his face, deep, sharp, dragging them down to his chin.

Phil wanted to scream, to shout right into her face. But he managed to stop himself, despite the searing pain in his face. He wouldn't give her the satisfaction.

'Do you?' The words screamed in his face.

'No,' he said, gasping for air, 'No. I . . . I don't . . .'

She took her hands away. They were bloodied, parts of his face beneath her nails. She examined them like they had just gone through an expensive manicure. She nodded, pleased with the results. Turned her attention back to Phil.

She smiled. 'Good. I'm glad to hear it.'

'So,' Phil said, his face burning with pain, 'why are you . . . are you doing . . . what you're doing . . .'

'Good boy. Doing what you're told.' Whispering again. 'I like that in a man. In fact, I demand it. So why have I done all this?' She swung her arms round, as if taking responsibility for their surroundings. 'Simple. To prove a point.'

'Which is?'

'How superior I am,' her voice sing-song.

'You mean to me?'

'Oh, certainly to you. But to everyone else, too. *Everyone*. I am the Nietzschean concept of the Superman made flesh. Or, rather, Superwoman.'

'And how do you . . . do you go about that, then?'

'I . . . bend people to my will. Make them do my bidding.

Make them do . . .' A gesture, a theatrical flourish of the wrist. 'Anything I want.'

'Even murder?'

She knelt in close to him again. He felt her hot breath on his ruined face. 'Oh yes,' she said, licking his blood off her nails, 'especially murder . . .'

98

'What . . . what d'you mean?' Turner looked confused, scared even. 'He was . . . he was just a squaddie. Just a squaddie that Fiona found. That we could use.'

'No he wasn't, Mark. He was Adele Harrison's brother.'

Turner shook his head. 'No. You're lying. Her brother died in Afghanistan. Roadside bomb. IED. She told me.'

'She told everybody that, Mark. Because it's easier to believe than what, or who, he really is.'

'A murdering rapist,' said Marina in Mickey's ear. He nodded.

'A murdering rapist,' he said aloud.

'No . . . no . . . you're lying. She said you would, Fiona said you'd, you'd try something like this. Play mind games, try to get inside my head . . .' He put his elbows on the table, head down. Hands balled into fists, rubbing his temples.

Mickey leaned forward, his voice, calm, quiet. No need to shout or scream, just let the authority of his words carry over. 'Mark. I'm telling you the truth, mate. She's lied to you.'

'No . . . no . . .'

'Yeah.'

'She wouldn't . . .'

'He's going,' said Marina, 'don't lose him, keep him talking. If he goes into himself now we'll have lost him. Bring him back, Mickey.'

Mickey nodded. 'Well, let's come back to that. Tell me what you wanted him for.'

Turner looked up, confused once more. 'What?'

'The Creeper, as you called him. Tell me what you wanted with him. What you did with him.'

'We . . . we programmed him.'

'Why?'

'To do what we wanted. To prove we could do it.'

'And what did you do? What did you make him do?'

'We turned him into . . . anything we wanted, really.'

'A weapon?'

The sneering smile made a small reappearance. 'The British Army had already done that to him.'

'You just refined the process, yeah?'

Turner shrugged.

'So, this programming. How'd you do it?'

'Told him . . . told him what he wanted to hear.'

'And what was that?'

'Rani. That was the translator he killed. The woman. We told him she was still alive. Still . . . still in love with him.' Another laugh. 'And he believed it. Stupid bastard.'

'How did that work?'

'She spoke to him.'

'How?'

'Through her BlackBerry. She texted him. We told him it was the spirit of Rani speaking to him. He had to imagine that the words that appeared on his phone he could hear in his head. And he could text back to talk to her.'

'And he believed that?'

'Yeah. Soft bastard.'

Mickey sat back, sighed. This wasn't what he was expecting. This was too much. He didn't know how to deal with it. He gave a quick glance to the screen, hoped Marina saw the signal.

'Oh God,' said Marina in Mickey's ear. 'He must be some kind of . . . let me think . . . borderline personality? Psychopath? Certainly with psychopathic tendencies. Something like that. I don't know enough about him. Ask him how they made it convincing.'

'How did you convince him it was actually Rani talking to him? Could have been anyone pretending to be her.'

'He did it because there's not much left of him and he wanted to believe. She's all he had left.' He thought for a moment. 'And she told him what he wanted to hear. That she was coming back to him. He just had to find her.'

'Find her? How?'

'She would be in different bodies. He'd be told where she was, what she looked like. And that Rani's spirit would be inside some woman. He had to watch her until we told him otherwise.'

'And then?'

Turner shrugged. 'We didn't want them any more. Got rid of them.'

Mickey sat back, letting the information sink in. He couldn't believe it. Didn't see how someone would fall for it, no matter how mentally damaged they must be.

'I don't believe you,' he said. 'No one would fall for something as lame as that. No matter what condition they were in.'

Turner just laughed. 'You haven't seen the Creeper. You wouldn't say that if you had.'

'Messed up?'

'Totally.'

And even more messed up by the time you two had finished with him, thought Mickey, but decided not to say it aloud.

'So . . . help me here, Mark. I'm trying to understand. You've got this guy to . . . what? Kill for you?'

Turner shrugged.

'What does he do? Talk me through it.'

'We give him a target. He stalks them, we get him going, tell him things about them, what they feel for him. He gets obsessed, goes mental over them. Then we tell him the spirit's gone, jumped to another body.'

'And . . . what then? He kills them?' A feeling of dread went through Mickey as he waited for the answer.

Turner shook his head. 'We tell him they're husks, the bodies. Just husks. No use any more. Then we get him to put them away somewhere.'

'Where?'

'Somewhere safe.'

'And leave them there?'

He nodded.

'Why?'

'Because we might need them again. That's the next stage. Programming someone who's not a nutter like him. Someone normal. See what we can do with them.'

'And because they might tell.'

Turner shrugged. Casual. 'Yeah. That too.'

Mickey sat back, his head spinning from all the information. He shook his head, tried to clear it. 'But why? Why, Mark? Why do all this?'

Turner leaned forward, eyes alive with a sick, dark light. 'Because we can, that's why . . .'

'Keep focused, Mickey.' Marina in his ear again. 'Ask him about the victims. Who chose them, how they were chosen. He's not telling us the whole story. And I don't know why. Either he doesn't know it all or he's holding something back. Find out which it is.'

'Who chose the girls, Mark?'

'Fiona.'

'All Mark's ex-girlfriends,' said Marina. 'Interesting.'

'So you didn't mind that they were all your ex-girlfriends, Mark? That Fiona was targeting them?'

Turner flinched, a sharp, quick stab of pain showed in his face. Then nothing. In control again. He forced a shrug. 'Why? I'm above all that now. Doesn't matter, does it?'

'No he's not, Mickey, he flinched. They're his old girlfriends and it still hurts, no matter what he says.'

Mickey looked at him, listened to Marina.

'It's his weak spot. We've got him,' she said in his ear. 'Go in for the kill. Finish him off.'

99

Phil stared at Fiona Welch, tried to ignore the pain in his cheek, just concentrate. Talk to her.

'So . . .'

A wave of pain ran through him. He tamped it down, breathed deeply. Fiona Welch's head was cocked to one side as if she was an animal, listening. Or an anthropologist, observing. Her face was serene, sweet.

Phil tried again. 'Fiona,' he said, 'what's this going to prove? You can't get away with it.'

She shrugged, smiled sweetly. Didn't answer.

'The rest of the team are going to be looking for me. I told them where I was going. When they get here, they'll get you too.'

Another shrug. 'So?'

'So you'll be caught. Prison.'

'So?'

Phil shook his head. She was beyond reasoning with. 'What d'you hope to get out of this?'

'My Ph.D.'

Phil wasn't sure he had heard her correctly. 'What?'

'My Ph.D. It's in Victimology and Coercion. It examines how a subservient personality can be totally controlled by a dominant one. It also examines the mindset of the victim, the methodology needed to create that particular mindset in the first instance.' She smiled. 'With examples.'

Phil couldn't believe what he was hearing. 'So, you mean . . . you did all this, the murders, the abductions, everything . . . just for your Ph.D.?'

She looked affronted. 'Why not? I told you I had a point to prove. This was it.'

'But . . .' Phil didn't know whether to laugh or scream. 'You're going to spend the rest of your life in prison for this.'

'So?'

'So? What's the good of your Ph.D. if you're going to be in prison?'

She shook her head slowly, grinned patronisingly, as if explaining a very obvious point to a very thick child. 'The Ph.D. is still a Ph.D. In prison or anywhere.' Her eyes glittered in the dark, like stabbing razor flashes. 'And just think . . . I'd be famous.'

Phil couldn't believe what he was hearing. 'Famous.'

'Yes. Famous.' She looked away, thinking, lost in her words, her mind. 'No. I won't just be famous, I'll be notorious. No. That's not right either. I'll be . . . adored.' She nodded. 'Yes. That's the right word. Adored. I'll get letters. Visitors. They'll write books about me. Serious, proper works, not just cheap lurid paperbacks. I'll have my own acolytes. Disciples.' She turned to Phil. 'Do you know Charles Manson never killed anyone? He just made others do it for him. Yet he's still locked up. And he's just some stinking, addled old hippie. He's nothing next to me . . .'

That's when Phil realised she was completely insane. He had only suspected it before but now she had confirmed it. And in that moment another thought struck him.

I may not get out of here alive.

He had thought up to now there was a chance. He could reason with her, keep her talking until his team arrived, carted her away. And, yes, she had said she expected to be caught. But she was insane. There was no telling what she would do next. Did she have one last trick, a final twist of the knife . . .

He saw Marina in his mind's eye. Josephina next to her. Had he just got them back for him to be taken away from them? Permanently?

100

Suzanne was awake. And listening to every word.

She lay curled up on the walkway, not daring to move, hardly daring to breathe. It was something she had perfected in the box. Her eyes were half open, darting back and forward between this policeman, Phil Brennan, and the mad woman who had captured him. She recognised her from the hospital. Fiona something. A psychologist. She was behind this? Why? They had hardly exchanged two words.

But it was the presence behind the mad woman that eyes kept being drawn to. The hulking, mute presence, silent except for his rasping breathing. He was mostly in shadow but not totally, and as he moved from foot to foot she recognised him.

He had the face of a nightmare.

She tried not to look up, for fear of attracting attention to herself – because she had seen what the madwoman's attention had done to Phil Brennan's face – but she couldn't keep her eyes off the man in the shadows. The Creeper, the madwoman had called him. That made sense. Considering what he had done to her. In her own home.

Her own bedroom.

But she had been following the conversation. Or as best as she could. The madwoman had made the Creeper think that she – Suzanne – was the spirit of a dead woman? And that's why he was stalking her? If someone else had said that to her, told her that it had happened to them, she would have said they were lying. That she had never heard anything more insane in her life. But it wasn't someone else. It had happened to her. And she had never been through anything more terrifying in her life.

And she still wasn't free of it. She was still here.

She gave another surreptitious glance round. Directly ahead were Phil Brennan and the madwoman. Behind them was the Creeper. No escape there. She slowly moved her head, pretended it was a random gesture. Looked the other way down the walkway.

Darkness.

She squinted. She was sure she could see a set of stairs among the shadows, leading down from the gantry to the floor. But not sure enough to make a run for it. Along the gantry hung chains, clanking in the breeze, or when anyone moved. Some with huge hooks on them, some with heavy counterweights. Could she grab one, swing down to the ground? Would that be the best way to get down? Would that be faster than someone coming down the stairs after her?

She checked herself. What was she thinking? Was that how desperate she was to escape? That she was willing to risk her life that much just to get away?

Yes. It was.

So how could she do it?

She hadn't worked that out yet. She still didn't have enough strength in her body to make a move. The walk up the stairs to the walkway had given her a chance to exercise her legs, get her circulation moving again. Probably helped more than they realised. But not yet. The time wasn't right yet.

So she lay there. Faking unconsciousness. Or something near to it.

Biding her time until it was time to go.

Time to break free.

101

Mickey looked at Mark Turner sitting slumped down in his seat. Aiming to look like a slouching student at a boring lecture, Mickey knew better. It was a posture of defeat. Turner was on the way to being broken.

I'm going to have you, Mickey thought. Time to take you down.

'So,' Mickey said, leaning in once more, 'Fiona chose all the girls. The victims.'

He nodded.

'Why those in particular?'

'Because they all looked like that dead woman, the one the Creeper was obsessed with. Rani.'

'All dark-haired and brown-eyed?'

'Yeah.'

'And it was just coincidence that they were all your ex-girlfriends?'

Turner, without moving in the chair or changing position, shrugged.

'Is that a yes?'

'Yeah.'

'And you were happy with that?'

'Yeah.' Eyes down, gaze averted. Something there he didn't want Mickey to see.

'Fiona Welch knew you'd had other girlfriends. I'll bet she asked you about them. She probably saw you with them. That's why she wanted you.'

Turner said nothing.

'You went out with the popular girls at uni and at work. Must have made her jealous. Must have made her want you.'

Again, Turner didn't speak.

'And what if you still had a thing for one of them? Or all of them? She wouldn't have liked that. Better get them out of the way. Remove the competition. So she did. One by one. And got you to help her.'

Turner remained silent.

'Why did that not bother you, Mark?' He waited. 'Mark?'

'Told you why.' His posture more withdrawn, his voice more sullen.

Getting to an uncomfortable truth, thought Mickey. Making him face up to demons he's been trying to ignore.

'That you were superior to all that. That you were superior to human emotions.'

'Yeah.'

'All human emotions.'

'Yeah.'

'Like love.'

'Yeah.'

'Liar.'

Turner shot up like he'd just been slapped, shocked and wide-eyed at the sudden change in Mickey's tone.

'You fucking liar.'

Turner's eyes widened. 'You can't . . .'

'What? Talk to you like that? Why not? You're a lair.'

'No I'm not . . .'

'Yes you are. You still had a key for Suzanne's flat. Why?

To pop back there one day? Just in case you started up again? Or could you just not let it go . . . because deep down inside, whatever Fiona Welch was feeding you, you knew it was bullshit, knew it was wrong. Knew that, no matter what she said or did for you, you'd never be as happy with her as you were with Suzanne. Is that it?'

Turner clamped his eyes tight closed. 'Stop it . . .'

'Stop it . . . why? Why should I? Let's look at them. Julie Miller. She was the first.'

'I wasn't . . .' His protestation was weak, his expression said that even he didn't believe his own words.

'Don't try to deny it, Mark, we've seen the photos of you both together on Facebook. If you weren't seeing each other then you were very close friends. Unnaturally close. Close enough to make someone else jealous.'

He didn't reply.

'Then there was Suzanne. But where does Adele fit into this? When were you seeing her?'

'On and off . . .'

'When you were seeing Suzanne?'

He nodded.

'Two-timing and a murderer. And you didn't know she was the Creeper's sister? Didn't Fiona tell you? Not like her to forget something as important as that, is it? In the New World Order of your relationship.'

Tears welled in Turner's eyes.

'Did you kill her, Mark? Adele?'

He paused, his head forward. Like a condemned man reluctantly reaching for the noose.

'What happened?'

He sighed. Stared straight ahead, seeing something Mickey couldn't. Didn't want to. 'I'd been talking to Adele . . .'

'Talking?'

'Well . . . a bit more than that . . .'

'You had sex.'

Turner looked away, nodded.

'So you'd kidnapped Adele Harrison—'

'The Creeper did that.'

'Right. The Creeper did that. But you helped. You went along with it.'

Turner said nothing. Mickey continued. 'You had her captive and then . . . what? You had sex.'

Another shrug.

'Why?'

'Because I still . . . had feelings for her.' He leaned forward, arms on the table, hands out expressively. 'I saw her there, scared and, and . . . and I wanted her.'

'So you had her.'

'Yes.'

'You raped her?'

'No . . .' He looked shocked at the thought.

'But . . . what? This rekindled feelings for her? You felt something for her again, is that it?'

'Yes . . .' Sounding like it was painful to have the word dragged out of him.

'And you . . .what? Promised to let her go?'

'Yes.'

'Tell me, Mark. Tell me what happened. Your own words.'

Turner sighed. Mickey saw the conflicting emotions fighting for dominance on his face. In the end, resignation won out and Turner, sighing and shoulders heaving, started to talk.

426

102

The Creeper was confused. Confused and getting angry. This wasn't how he'd imagined it. Not at all.

When he heard Rani's voice in his head once more, talking to him, telling him to come and meet her, he was almost too excited for words. Couldn't wait to get there and see her, leave the husk on the boat, rig the charges just like she said. He'd watched it go boom, seen the flames streak up to the sky. Huge they were, the policemen running away tiny by comparison.

He had smiled watching that. Giggled.

He had done that. Made that happen. All that power, all his . . .

And then the anticipation, meeting Rani, face to face, at last . . .

And then the disappointment.

When he had agreed to meet her after the fire he had been excited, thrilled, shaking with anticipation. And what a letdown. She wasn't Rani, wasn't anything like Rani. She was that psychologist from the hospital, the one they had made him go and see.

So where was Rani? He had started to ask her that but she had just waved him and his questions aside. Literally, her arm waving at him dismissively, then walking away, getting him to follow her. Saying Rani had left her with a list of things for him to do. And despite the fact that she made him feel unsure, uneasy, he had followed her, had done the things she asked him to.

But still the questions were rolling around inside him. Not going away, stuck there in his head. Was this Rani? After all that, was this actually Rani? And if it wasn't, then where was Rani?

These thoughts were going through his head while he was standing on the walkway watching the psychologist talk to the man on the floor. She had sat on him, tried to turn him on, then, when that didn't work, hurt him.

The Creeper had enjoyed watching her do that.

Maybe this was Rani after all.

He looked at the body lying next to the man on the walkway. He remembered that one. She had been Rani for a while until the spirit left her, until she became a husk. So what was she doing here now?

So many questions . . .

It hurt him to think. And that made him angry. He could feel it, building up inside him. That snake uncoiling, spitting out its venom. And when he got angry, when that snake got going, he wanted to get it out of him . . .

But not yet. He would wait. Be patient. See what happened.

And then do something . . .

103

Phil looked at the prone figure of the woman lying next to him, then back to Fiona Welch. He had no idea how things were going to work out, just had to hope his team would be on the way soon.

Because if not . . .

He put the thought out of his mind. Concentrated on Fiona Welch. Keep her talking. Stop her getting any other ideas.

'So how did you get to be profiler on the investigation, Fiona? How did you manage that one?'

She smiled again, that smug, unbalanced smile. 'Simple. Because Ben Fenwick is easily impressed.'

'With what?'

'Credentials. He didn't have a clue what to ask for. So I just . . . guided his hand when he phoned up. All he knew was that he should have a profiler. And I knew the police would investigate. So I made sure I was in the right place at the right time. That he would choose no one else but me.'

'And you lied to him, of course.'

'Naturally.' She laughed. 'And I'm a much better profiler

than you thought I was. Because I read him straight away. Manipulated him from the off. Easy.' She moved closer to Phil once more. 'And a much better psychologist, too. Because I read you all. Played you all. Brilliantly. Which wasn't hard. Because you were all so stupid. You allowed me into the centre of your investigation, let me control things, keep . . . I don't know, I was going to say one step ahead of you but, let's be honest, I was streets ahead. I could have kept going for months.'

'If I hadn't wised up to you and shipped you out. Not that stupid.'

A flash of anger in her eyes, her hands became claws once more, moved towards Phil's face. She stopped herself. Forced a smile. She nodded, as if to a joke only she could hear, or at a decision she had made. One whose outcome she was going to enjoy.

Phil looked down at Suzanne Perry, then back to Fiona Welch. 'So why her, Fiona? Why Suzanne?'

Fiona Welch shrugged. 'Why any of them?'

'I don't know. Julie Miller. Adele Harrison. What makes them so special? You tell me.'

Her eyes slipped away from him. Down to the right. 'Because I could. Because they were there.'

Liar, he thought. 'Nothing to do with Mark Turner?'

She flinched, like a chink in her armour had been exposed and he had pierced it.

'Nothing. Nothing at all.'

'No?' He had to keep pressing, work that sword into her. 'You sure about that? The fact that they're all ex-girlfriends of his is just a coincidence, is it?'

'Shut up.' She slapped him. 'You don't know what you're talking about.'

Phil didn't shut up. He ignored the pain in his face, kept going. 'What's the matter, Fiona? Didn't you like the competition? Was that it?'

'Shut up . . .' screamed at him.

'What, his exes made you jealous? Not very master race that, is it? Jealous of a barmaid?'

'Shut up!' Another slap.

Phil recovered quickly, looked at her face. Saw something there, something she hadn't shown before. Fear. Insecurity. He smiled inwardly. He had hit a nerve. Found her weakness.

He pushed that sword further in.

'That why you killed her, is it? Because you were jealous? What was it, did he still think of her? Talk about her? Call out her name at the wrong time?'

'Shut up, shut up, shut up . . .' More slaps, out of control. Her voice strident, pleading.

'Or was it more than that? Did he have second thoughts, not like what you were doing to her, try to let her go?'

'No . . .'

'Maybe he still liked her?'

'Stop it . . .'

Phil picked up the undertone of her words. He knew what had happened. 'That's it, isn't it? He had sex with her. And you didn't like it, did you?'

She put her hands over her ears.

'Maybe he liked the power he had over her and forced her, maybe she wanted it too. Doesn't matter. They did it. And it hurt you. How am I doing?'

Phil laughed. His bitterness almost matched hers. 'Fiona Welch, homo superior. Jealous of a student and a barmaid . . .'

Her hands flailed, face contorted. She didn't know what to do, how to respond. She screamed.

'And you killed her.'

She looked round, eyes wide, staring, like a trapped animal.

'No,' said Phil, putting it together, 'you didn't kill her. Or you didn't mean to. It was an accident. Something done in anger. Nothing to do with proving a point, showing how

431

superior you are. That's all just justification after the fact, isn't it? You accidentally killed her then panicked. Messed up her body so we would think there was a sexual sadist on the loose.'

Her hands were back over her ears, eyes screwed tight shut. Tears were running down her face.

'Isn't that right?'

She took her hands away. 'Shut up! Shut up . . .'

Phil knew he had broken her so, not waiting to see how she would respond, he turned his attention to the figure standing behind Fiona Welch.

'That you over there, Ian? Or should I call you Wayne?'

A ragged intake of breath that Phil took for surprise.

'Did she make you do it? Fiona here. Did she make you kill all the women?'

He stepped forward. Phil saw his face in the light for the first time.

And gasped.

It was ruined. Burnt beyond any kind of reconstructive surgery, red and angry, white and dead. His teeth bared like an angry, vengeful skeleton.

Phil focused, kept going. 'What did she tell you, Ian? How did she get you to do it? Did you know you'd killed your own sister? Did you not recognise her?'

The hulking figure looked between Fiona Welch and Phil. Phil didn't know what he was thinking because there was so little of face left and what there was couldn't express emotions. He opened his mouth. And a sound came out that Phil never wanted to hear again. Like the dying of a wounded animal.

He came forward, screaming.

And that was when Suzanne Perry made her move.

104

'It was my job to . . .' Mark Turner sighed. 'To . . . look after her. I used to come in every day to see that she was all right. That she had something to eat and drink and, and went to the toilet.'

'Where was this?'

'In . . .' He hesitated, corrected himself. 'Where she, where we kept them.'

'So there was just Adele there at this time?'

He shook his head. 'Julie came to join her soon after.'

'Keep going.'

'And Adele and I . . . I just saw her there and I . . . I wanted to . . .'

'Help her?'

His voice was tiny, fragile. 'Love her . . .'

Mickey struggled to keep his face as straight as possible.

'And I . . . I . . . it built up over a few days. I wanted to say something, let her know it was me, but I . . .' He sighed. 'I couldn't.'

'Frightened of what Fiona would say,' said Marina in Mickey's ear.

'One day I built up courage. I knew I was taking a risk but I . . . I couldn't help it. When I was getting them out of their, of their . . . and I was helping her to the toilet I stopped her, spoke to her. Showed her it was me.'

'And what did she do?'

'Well, she was . . . it was . . . she cried.'

He fell silent for a while. Then continued.

'And then I . . . I told her how I felt.'

'And what did she say?'

'That she felt the same as me.'

I'll just bet she did, thought Mickey. Anything to get out. 'So what did you do?'

'We . . . started having sex. And . . . and plotted.'

'Her escape?'

He sighed. Nodded.

'Or both of your escapes?'

Another sigh, heavier this time.

'And Fiona found you.'

'Yeah.' Tears welled again in Turner's eyes. 'And she . . . stopped it.' He looked away. Looked at anything but Mickey.

But Mickey wasn't letting it go. 'Stopped it? How did she stop it, Mark?'

'She, she . . .' The tears fell. 'Told me that if I didn't . . . if I didn't . . .'

He couldn't say the word. Mickey wanted to hear it. Mickey wouldn't say it for him.

'If you didn't what, Mark?'

'If I didn't kill her . . .' The words blurted out, sprayed like projectile vomit all over the table. 'Kill her . . . then Fiona would, would kill me . . .'

'So you killed her.'

He nodded, shoulders heaving with his tears.

'And all the . . . mutilation?'

Turner grimaced. 'She did that. Fiona did that. I wouldn't, couldn't . . .'

434

Mickey waited.

'She got the Creeper and me to drop off the body, told us where to leave it, how to position it. Said you'd think there was a sex killer on the loose. Then she said . . .' Another heavy sigh. 'Said that I was hers now. Forever.'

Turner said nothing more. Just sat slumped.

Mickey sighed. Mopping up time. 'She used you, Mark.'

'No . . .' He shook his head.

'Yes, she did. Just like she used Ian Buchan.'

Turner frowned. 'Who?'

'The Creeper. Used you. Kept you under her control. She made the Creeper kidnap his own sister. She used him like she used you.'

'But we were a partnership . . .'

'No you weren't. You were just like the Creeper to her. Someone to be controlled. Another experiment.'

Turner sighed. And the tears came again.

'So where are they, Mark? The girls?'

He kept his head down, stared at the table.

'You may as well tell me, Mark, I know everything else.'

Nothing.

'Everything. Even the fact that the two quotes you threw at me when I came in here were from Schopenhauer and Nietzsche.'

Turner looked up, shock and surprise in his eyes.

'Anyone can read a book, Mark. So tell me, where are they?'

Turner sighed, saw that he had nothing else left to hang on to.

'At the Quay. The old Dock Transit Company building . . .'

Mickey was straight out of the door.

105

S uzanne screamed.

It was enough to startle the Creeper, divert his attention away from Phil.

Phil could only watch as Suzanne kept the momentum going. While the others were still staring, she got to her feet, grabbed one of the huge, chained hooks hanging from the runner along the ceiling and swung it towards the other three.

Phil, being on the ground already, didn't have to duck. The other two did. Fiona Welch ducked to the side but she wasn't quick enough and the hook swung at her, catching her on the side of the head. She fell, crumpling in a heap.

The Creeper was faster to react. The hook, which, having hit Fiona Welch, slowed its momentum, was much less of a threat by the time it reached him. He put up a great, solid hand, all muscle and gristle, and stopped it, the impact forcing him backwards, air huffing from him.

Phil knew what was coming next, shouted a warning.

'Get out of the way, Suzanne . . .'

The Creeper pulled back the hook and, giving a roar of effort as he did so, let it fly towards her.

Phil pushed himself even further into the rusted metal of the walkway as it rattled along the track, gaining speed from the traction as it passed him. Suzanne however, couldn't move. She just stood there, watching it come towards her.

'Run!' shouted Phil.

It broke the spell. Suzanne turned and ran.

Along the walkway and into the shadows. Phil lost her then. He turned back to the scene before him. Welch was still on the floor, eyes screwed up in pain, hand to the side of her head, blood seeping between fingers. The Creeper's face had, if anything, turned even redder. Phil didn't know much about burns and scarring but he was sure this wasn't a positive development.

He was right. With an angry roar, he set off after Suzanne, his limping, shambling frame surprisingly fast, and was soon lost to sight in the shadows, the only sounds the heavy clang and clatter as his boots came down heavily on the metal floor.

Phil pulled himself to his feet, looked down at Fiona Welch. There was nothing he could do for her at the moment. He pulled at his wrists behind his back. But it was no good. The cuffs were tight. He needed something sharp, an edge to cut them with. He looked round. Couldn't see one.

The Creeper had reached the ground and was bellowing once more.

Wrists tied or not, thought Phil, I've got to stop him.

Treading as carefully as he could and trying desperately to keep his balance and remain upright, Phil ran along the gantry into the same shadows that had claimed the other two.

Suzanne was getting out of breath. The sudden exertion after so much enforced stillness was beginning to take its toll. Her lungs were starting to burn, her legs shake. Her breathing was coming hard and fast and she was sure he would be able to track her just from that alone.

She had no idea where she was going. She was trying to find a way out but there didn't seem to be one. The light from above cast faint rays on the ground, more than she had expected. Perhaps too much if he was following her.

And he was. She could hear him.

She ran.

The Creeper was angry. Very angry.

He didn't know what was going on but he knew he didn't like it. The husk had tried to hurt him. It was time for the husk to stop.

He reached the bottom of the steps, looked round. Listened. Heard movement to his left, breathing and fast footsteps. Bare feet slapping on the concrete floor.

He smiled.

Easy.

But just in case, he had something that would give him an advantage.

The night-vision goggles were still in his pocket. He had used them earlier when he came to meet Rani – or thought he was coming to meet Rani – to get into the building and dodge the police. He always used them at night. Something else he loved that gave him power.

He put them on, activated them. The world turned ghost-green and he could see.

And there she was. Almost to the far wall, by the boxes and beyond them, the water.

The electric water.

She disappeared from view. Hiding. Or so she thought.

He smiled.

Too easy.

106

By the time Mickey had emerged from the interview room, the whole station was in action. He found Anni.

'Did you hear?' he said. 'The old Dock—'

She cut him off. 'The circus is ready to go. We had an idea it might be there. The last call from the boss came from there. We haven't been able to reach him since so there was a squad already being put together.'

'Right,' he said, disappointed that his thunder had been stolen.

Anni sensed that. She managed a smile. 'You were good in there. Well done.'

'Thanks.' Was he blushing?

'Come on,' she said, 'let's go.'

He didn't need to be told twice.

The team left the building. Marina was still in the observation room, watching Mark Turner.

She had seen the same patterns of behaviour before. When a suspect had given a full confession, got all their crimes out of their own souls and into a police report, they often slept. Turner, with his drooping eyes and lolling head, looked to be no exception.

Marina was curious. She left the observation room, crossed to the interview room. Stood outside, poised. Should she go in? Would that violate his confession in any way? Speak of harassment, coercion? She didn't know. But it was a good opportunity to talk to him before he was taken away.

'D'you mind?' she said to the uniform on the door.

He stood aside, let her enter.

The room smelled of sweat. Hardly surprising, considering the way the two men had being going at it. Turner sat, barely registering her as she sat down opposite him.

'Hello,' she said.

He didn't reply.

'I'm . . . the new profiler on this investigation. Can we talk?'

He shrugged.

'It's just,' she said, 'that this is such an unusual case, I feel someone should be writing it up. Would you let me do that, interview you with that in mind?'

He looked up, seeing her for the first time, she thought.

He smiled.

'They're too late, you know.'

She frowned. Not what she had been expecting. 'What d'you mean? Who's too late?'

'They are. The *police*.' He said the word like he was describing a virulent, hateful illness.

'Too late for what?'

'To save them, of course.'

Her heart flipped. 'What d'you mean? Has he killed them? Is that it? Are they dead already?'

He shook his head. 'Not yet . . .'

'Then . . . what?'

'The building. The Dock Transit building.'

'What about it?'

If things got too bad, too out of hand. There was a plan in place.'

'What kind of plan?'

'Remember what he did to the boat?' Then, just in case Marina didn't get the picture, he gestured, his fingers exploding slowly in the air, like a gently opening flower. '*Boom . . .*'

Marina ran out of the room as fast as she could go.

107

Phil reached the bottom of the steps. It hadn't been easy. There were times he had had to steady himself with both hands to stop himself from either going over the side or tumbling down the metal staircase. But he had managed it.

At the bottom he looked round. Pulled at the cuffs tying his hands together. Searching for something sharp enough to cut through.

Wind was blowing through the gaps in the rusted corrugated sheet metal walls. That gave Phil an idea. He crossed over to one wall, going slowly in the dark, watching his footing, until he came to the outer wall and, putting his back to it, felt along for a gap.

There were plenty. He eventually found one at waist height with a rusted, jagged edge.

Perfect.

He found the sharpest point, put his wrists over it, worked the plastic up and down as hard and as fast as he could.

His arms ached, shoulders burnt with the exertion, chest heaved. But eventually it started to give. Encouraged by that, he rubbed all the harder, ignoring the growing pain until he could feel it coming and started to pull. It stretched and sharpened, digging in as it got thinner and eventually came apart. He was free.

He fell to his knees, gasping, rubbing his wrists.

Looked around, searching for any sign of the Creeper or Suzanne.

None.

He set off into the shadows, listening, watching, hoping his eyes would soon be acclimatised.

Hoping he wasn't too late.

The Creeper felt the thrill of the hunt coursing through him. This was what it was about. Never mind all that is she/isn't she Rani, this was the real thing. What he lived for.

Stalking, hunting down, trapping his prey. He loved it. Came truly alive then.

This was when he remembered his father, could honour the man's memory. Even if he had run away and left him.

Not that he blamed him. Not with those bitches in the house.

He thought of all those holidays camping in the woods, tracking an animal, hunting it down and killing it. That, his father had told him, is what a real man does. How a real man lives.

The Creeper couldn't have agreed more.

Then there was the other stuff, the things that happened afterwards . . . he didn't like them so much. In fact he hated them. The pain, the hurt, being made to do things with his body he didn't want to do.

At first, anyway. Eventually he got to tolerate it. Expect it, even.

Because it came along with his father's words, words he had taken to heart, always lived by: 'Women are whores, son. All of them. And you've got to treat them like that. Every one.'

And he had.

And he did. The snake within him uncoiling, ready to strike.

He scanned the area. Saw nothing, no movement at all.

Then his eyes fell on the boxes in the corner. The trough of water beside them, the blocks before them. There. Quick, fleeting. Just a movement.

He smiled. He had her.

Kept looking. There she was again, thinking she was hiding but showing herself at the far end of one of the boxes, beside the water.

This was so easy. In fact he wished it could be more of a challenge, more of a struggle. But it didn't matter. A hunt was a hunt.

He moved in slowly, stealthily.

He was going to enjoy this.

At first, Suzanne was terrified. Full-on terror: heart hammering, legs wobbling, teeth chattering. Repeating the same thing to herself as she ran: 'Oh God, I'm going to die . . . oh God, I'm going to die . . . oh God, I'm going to die . . .' Over and over in her head, her own personal mantra.

And then she reached the boxes. Saw Julie's body lying in the water.

'Oh God . . .' Whispered, under her breath, but no less heartfelt. No less urgent.

He was after her. Somewhere, in the dark, he was there. Coming for her. To kill her. Or . . .

Worse.

She stood still at the water, looked down at the other woman's body. Still breathing heavily, still gripped by fear. And then something happened. A kind of serenity descended on her. All the things she had been through these past few days, the things she had witnessed, the things she'd been through and, most horrific of all, the things that had been done to her . . . It all tumbled out of her mind.

444

So she stood there, looking down at the once-electrified water and the body of someone who could have been her friend, at the box that had imprisoned her, robbed her of hope, left her welcoming death, and she found such a clarity of thought within her, a stillness. And that stillness gave her the ability to think. And, more importantly, to plan.

To make sure she didn't die after all. But lived.

Because that was what she wanted more than anything else in the world now. To live. To hope.

And she knew what she had to do.

She looked down at the water once more, no longer panicked, and thought that the old Suzanne, the one of a month, even a week ago, wouldn't believe what she was about to do next. But the new Suzanne, the one who not only wanted to live but also to punish the person who had hurt her so much, robbed her of hope, could understand it perfectly.

She knew he was coming.

She got to work.

108

This is easy, thought the Creeper. Too easy. No skill required.

He could see her from where he was, her head poking out from in between the two boxes. Beside the water trough. Thinking he couldn't see her. Thinking the dark would hide her.

Wrong.

Even allowing for his damaged body he could still hunt. He crept up slowly, scanning the area through his goggles, using all his surveillance and tracking skills. Making himself silent. Invisible.

A deadly, moving shadow.

He reached the water trough. Smiled to himself. She was still there, crouched and unmoving between the boxes. Probably frozen with terror, he thought, made immobile by the thought of him, of what he would do with her.

And so she should be.

Because, freed of thinking of her as Rani, as the woman he loved, he could do what he liked.

And there was so much he would like to do with her. She

wouldn't go easily, or quickly, and he would enjoy every moment. All the anger and uncertainty he'd been through the last few days, here was his chance to just have fun.

He unsheathed his knife, kept the blade covered. Didn't want her to see the razor-sharp metal glinting in what light there was. Didn't want her to feel it on her until it was too late.

He moved forward, deciding which side to approach from. The far side, next to the generator by the wall. Yes. That would maximise the biggest shock for her. Scare her the most.

He advanced.

Faces danced before his eyes. Women. His mother. His sister. Whores, all of them. Any woman he had ever met in his life. Whores.

Rani.

The serpent twisted, writhed.

Especially Rani. The way she avoided him, laughed at him, even. Then spurned him. That had made him angry. Brought it all back to the surface again. Whores. All of them.

So he had taken her. She had struggled, tried to fight him off, but it was no good. He was stronger than her. His hunger to have her greater than her hunger to get away.

And he had her. Any way he wanted.

Afterwards, he had cried, feeling guilty, hating himself. Then came the anger. At her for leading him on, at himself for the self-loathing.

And then came the fire.

And the rebirth.

He smiled. Nearer to this one now. Nearly on her . . .

He edged round the corner of the box, crouching, moving stealthily, in his mind's eye a panther. A sleek, remorseless killer.

She was just in front of him, lying full length on the ground, head round the corner, expecting him to come at her from the front.

He nearly laughed. She was in for a surprise . . .

He crept up right behind her, knife in hand, arm out-stretched . . .

Then stopped. Something wasn't right.

The woman on the ground, she was . . .

'Bastard!'

Pain, sharp, on the back of his head. His knees buckled, his hands went to the source of the pain. He fell to the floor, dropping the knife.

'Bastard!'

Again, another dose of pain, bigger this time. He felt his skull crack, heard it in his head, tearing open.

He tried to turn. Saw the woman from upstairs, the one who had been Rani, standing behind him with one of the breeze blocks used to jam the doors of the boxes closed.

She had tricked him.

The whore had tricked him. *Him*.

Anger welled. He screamed, tried to get up.

She brought the block down again, hitting him in the face this time. He felt something break, hot liquid squirt in his eyes.

His hands went to his eyes, wiped them. Opened them.

Just in time to see what she was doing next.

She held the two cables from the water trough, hooked up to the generator. They were fizzing and sparking where drops of water hit the exposed ends. Holding them by their insulated sides, she thrust them towards him.

'Die, fucking die, you bastard . . .'

She held them to his chest as the current coursed through him.

He tried but couldn't pull away, couldn't get his hands up to stop her, to rip the cables away. The current was too powerful.

She held them there, his chest sparking and arcing, his body vibrating and shaking.

448

He looked at her face. Saw Rani, grinning. Not as she had appeared to him in the other bodies but as she was first. Grinning, watching him die. Vengeful and happy.

He reached out for her but it was too late. She was gone. And then so was he.

109

'Right,' shouted Wade, 'you know your places . . .'

Mickey watched as the armed response unit surrounded the Dock Transit building. He and Anni had come
straight out when the circus was mobilised. Wade's team had
barely had time to get changed from their last assignment.
They were all in place, just awaiting Sergeant Wade's order
to move in. His arm was raised.

'We'll wait until they've gone in,' said Anni, fastening the
straps of her vest, 'then we follow, yeah?'

'Yep,' said Mickey, doing the same. 'We just—' His phone
rang. He shook his head in irritation. 'Probably my mother.'

'Answer it,' said Anni. 'Might be important. Might be the
boss.'

He checked the display. The station. He answered it.

'Mickey? Marina. Is that you?'

'Yeah, Marina.' He looked at Anni, rolled his eyes. 'Look,
we're a bit busy at the moment. We're on the quay, just
about to—'

'Yes, yes, I know.' She cut him off. 'Listen. This is important.
Has anyone gone in yet?'

'They're just about to.'

'Then tell them to stand down. Now. Do it . . .'

'I can't just—'

'Turner says the whole building is wired. Just like the boat. If they go in they'll be killed . . .'

Mickey took the phone away from his ear. Anni saw the look of urgency on his face.

'Sergeant Wade,' he shouted. 'Get your team to—'

Too late. The front of the building exploded into a wall of flame.

110

Phil heard the screams, saw the lights. Went running over to the boxes.

He never made it.

At that moment the far wall of the building burst into flames.

He was blown on to his back, overwhelmed by the blast, the heat. Once he got his breath back he pulled himself up to his elbows, squinted ahead.

It was as if daylight, violent and flaming, had been brought into the night-time. The front of the building was ablaze, the flames spreading.

No way out.

Phil looked round, saw Suzanne Perry staggering over by the right side of the building, pulling herself slowly along the wall.

'Suzanne . . .'

She heard him, saw him, crossed over to him. Slowly, as if in a daze.

Has she been hit? he wondered. He ran towards her.

'You OK?'

She nodded, her face devoid of expression, mouth open. 'You sure?'

Another nod.

'Where's . . .' He pointed towards the boxes.

'He's . . . gone . . .'

Shock, thought Phil. That's what it was. He needed to get her out of there. Both of them needed to get out of there.

'Come on,' he said. 'We can't go out that way, let's look for somewhere at the back.'

He put his arm round her, turning her away from the flames, the boxes. Numbly, she let him guide her.

They made it back to the metal stairway leading up to the gantry. Phil looked up. Fiona Welch had come round, was staring down at him, her face a mask of pure hatred.

'Get out of here,' Phil shouted. 'It's not safe.'

'Fuck you, copper . . .'

She turned and ran along the gantry, away from him.

There was another explosion behind them. Phil turned.

'Christ, the whole building must be wired . . .' He looked round. If the front was wired, would the back be? He couldn't take the chance. Seeing no other alternative, he started up the stairs.

'Come on, Suzanne, up here . . .'

With his arm around her, they made their way back up the gantry. By the time they had reached the top, Suzanne seemed to be more aware of what was going on. Phil didn't feel like he had to hold on to her all the time.

'You OK?' he said. 'Can you make it along here?'

She nodded. 'Yes . . .'

'Come on, then . . .'

Fiona Welch had run away in the opposite direction to them. They had no alternative but to follow. Phil and Suzanne ran along the gantry, dodging the swinging metal chains. At the far end of the walkway he could see the night sky. He tried to get his bearings.

They were facing the side of the building with the crane on it. It was a huge metal frame with a crane mechanism that moved along the heavy metal horizontal bar at the top, controlled by an operative in a cabin on the ground. There was a maintenance opening from the gantry on to the top of the horizontal bar. He doubted that had been rigged to explode. If they could get out there, edge their way along, they could climb down the other side, away from the flames.

He was sure Fiona Welch had had the same idea.

'This way . . .'

He pulled Suzanne along towards the opening.

They reached it. He looked round. No sign of Fiona Welch.

She must have already gone ahead, he thought. Got away. She wouldn't get far.

'Come on . . .'

He opened the door, stepped out. The metal was rusted, not too wide. And a long way down. Might be better to sit on it, edge their way along that rather than run. That was a sure way to fall.

Phil swallowed hard. Felt his legs begin to shake, vibrate. He had a huge fear of heights. Always had a panic attack whenever he was up high. Someone had once told him that it wasn't the heights he feared but what he would do when he was up there. What he wanted to do. He had laughed at that, said his friend was talking rubbish, but it had played on his mind ever since. And now that he was up high and unsafe once more, it came back to him.

But this time he had an answer.

He wanted to get down safely. Because he had a wife and daughter waiting for him.

He corrected himself. *Partner* and daughter. Had he really just said wife to himself?

Really?

He didn't have time to think about that now. And he

454

certainly didn't have time for a panic attack. He looked back at the doorway, ready to tell Suzanne to sit down, pull herself along, but the words never left his mouth.

Fiona Welch was standing there. He could see the body of Suzanne lying behind her, on the gantry inside.

'Have you killed her?' he shouted.

She shrugged. 'What do you care?'

She stepped outside, on to the beam. Phil tried to move backwards, away from her. He felt himself slip, his foot go over the edge. His body lose its balance.

Oh my God, he thought. I'm going to fall.

I'm going to die.

111

'Look up there,' shouted Anni. 'It's the boss . . .'

Mickey followed her arm. Saw Phil Brennan standing on the top beam of the crane mechanism. 'What's he . . .'

'No . . . he's going to fall . . .'

Phil brought his foot round. Placed it securely on the beam. Steadied himself. He didn't fall. His breathing was heavy, chest heaving.

And then he felt it. The tightening bands round his ribcage, squeezing, tightening . . .

No. Not now. Ignore it. Not now . . .

Fiona Welch smiled at him. 'One push. That's all it takes . . .'

'Give it up, Fiona,' he shouted. 'You're going nowhere.'

'Oh really?'

'Look down there. That's my team. They've got this place surrounded. You can't get away.'

She laughed. 'One push. And you'll be seeing your team sooner than you think . . .'

'Don't be a fool, Fiona. You've got nowhere to go.'

'Apart from the history books. I'm going to be famous, Phil Brennan. You're not. You're just going to be the latest in my list of victims.' She laughed. 'So I suppose you'll be famous, too, in a way. Isn't that exciting?'

The wind was getting up. If it got too strong the argument would be meaningless. They would both go. And there was the pain in his chest . . .

'Fiona . . . don't. Give up. Please.'

Another laugh.

Phil didn't think he could hang on much longer.

Suzanne opened her eyes. Sat up. She saw two sets of everything, had a sharp, shooting pain in the back of her skull. She could guess what had caused that.

She looked round. Saw that woman, Fiona something, outside on the gantry. The way Phil had gone. She looked beyond the Fiona woman. Saw Phil standing there.

And from the looks of him, he wouldn't be there long.

She had to do something. Stop her.

She looked round, trying to find something – anything – that could be used as a weapon. Nothing.

Did another sweep with her eyes. Looked back into the building. Looked up, looked outside.

She had an idea . . .

'You a religious man, Phil? You look the type.'

He didn't answer.

Fiona Welch edged forward. 'Only, if you know any prayers, I'd start saying them now . . .'

He tried hard to keep his balance, keep his breathing in check.

'You'd better start believing in the afterlife. Not that there is one – I know because I'm a psychologist – but it might make your last few seconds more comfortable.'

She edged closer.

Phil felt himself begin to totter . . .

Then Fiona Welch flung her arms out wide, a preacher beseeching her flock. Her eyes widened, her arms began windmilling.

'No, no . . .'

She flung out her arm, fingers extended, grasping only air.

'No, not me . . .'

Her eyes were wide with terror, with the realisation of what was about to happen.

Fiona Welch screamed. And fell.

To her death.

Phil looked at the entranceway. There was a hook on a chain swinging backwards and forwards through it. Suzanne Perry standing beside it. He smiled.

Suzanne returned it.

He edged slowly back towards her.

Ready to get down.

Ready to go on living.

PART FIVE

112

The only sound in the room was the soft bleeping of the life-support machine. Regular and rhythmic, it had a soothing quality.

'That noise,' said Marina quietly, like she was in a church and didn't want to talk above a whisper, 'I always thought . . . always used to think . . . as long as it was going, everything would be all right. There'd be hope.'

Her final word was choked off by a sudden sob.

Phil, standing beside her, tightened his grip round her shoulder.

'But that's not always enough, is it?' she said, still whispering. 'Sometimes you need the truth. Stop dreaming.' Another sigh. 'Start living.'

She stepped forward, looked down at the figure lying in the bed. Phil stayed where he was, behind her. There if she needed him.

Tony seemed to be shrinking. Every time she saw him he seemed to get smaller. She thought of that old black and white science fiction film she had seen when she was a child, a man shrinking, getting so small he eventually becomes a microscopic organism, an atom at the heart of the universe.

This was different, though. He wasn't shrinking, just wasting away.

And he wouldn't be falling into the heart of the universe. And he wouldn't be coming back.

Marina bent down, made to kiss him. Then straightened up, turned to the nurse, panic on her face.

'What if he can see me? Or hear me? That happens, doesn't it? People in comas for years suddenly come back to life, say they can hear everything that's been going on . . .'

The nurse, standing silently at the side of the room, stepped forward. 'Sometimes,' she said, her hushed tone matching Marina's. 'In some instances. It depends on the kind of injuries the patient has sustained. The state they're actually in.'

'And Tony . . .'

The nurse shook her head.

Marina knew that. They had had this conversation over and over. But she hadn't heard what the nurse had actually said.

Until today.

Marina leaned over Tony, kissed his forehead. He didn't flinch, didn't smile or frown, gave no indication that he felt anything.

She straightened up. Mouthed one word: 'Goodbye.'

She stepped back, looked for Phil. His arm was straight back round her. She drew strength from his touch. She nodded to the nurse who then stepped forward to the machine at the side of the bed.

The noise stopped.

She turned into Phil's chest, started to cry.

His arm strong around her, it felt like he would never let her go.

113

The sun was high, the beach flat. She could see for miles and miles. If anyone approached, she would know.

And that was just how Suzanne wanted it.

She sat on the wall of the house, looking out to sea. The house behind her was well protected. No one knew who she was, just a tourist renting a secluded beach-front house in a Norfolk village.

She had been advised not to go away alone, to always have someone with her, but that wasn't what she needed. Newspapers had been on the phone to her constantly, wanting her to tell her story, offering prices that started off ridiculously high and just escalated. They gave her no rest, no respite. She had been tempted to choose one, the highest bidder, tell all and take the money. But once she had decided on that she hadn't been able to go through with it. Didn't want the whole thing opened up again in a way she had no control over, didn't want to become public property, be stared at in the street, talked about in the supermarket. She just wanted to get away from all that. Run.

So she had.

And she couldn't blame herself for doing it. Her best friend had been murdered. She had been stalked, kidnapped and imprisoned. And she had killed two people. The fact that it was in self-defence was something she was glad about in legal terms as it meant she wouldn't have to stand trial or go to prison. But she, herself, had taken two lives. And that was just as hard to live with as everything else that had happened.

It had been five weeks since that night on the quayside and the nightmares still hadn't stopped. They weren't as frequent as they were at first, but they still came along, jumping out and surprising her when she thought she was healing, her life getting back on track. Claiming her day, her night, stopping her from moving forward.

It was something she imagined she would be living with for years to come.

Suzanne had been referred to the psychologist, Marina Esposito, for counselling. She was proving a great help, but most of it, Suzanne knew, she would have to face alone.

'You don't have to,' Marina had said to her. 'You're not the only one to go through something like this, you know.'

Suzanne had looked at her, wary. What did she mean?

Marina had looked down at her knees, crossed over, smoothed out an imaginary wrinkle in her skirt. 'I shouldn't be telling you this. Because it isn't professional in any way and, I should think, violates what we're doing here. But I think it'll help for you to hear it. Something similar happened to me last year. I was . . . kidnapped, taken prisoner by a brutal, unhinged madman. And I had to . . . fight my way out, shall we say.'

Suzanne hadn't known what to say, how to respond. 'And . . . you got out? Well of course you did. Stupid question. But you . . . you had nightmares? All those fears?'

Marina had nodded. 'Oh yes. Loads.'

'And . . . and what happened?'

'They . . . went away. Eventually. Mostly. The body heals. The mind does too, with help. Would you like my help?'

Suzanne had nodded.

Then burst into tears.

She still had regular sessions with Marina. Looked forward to them, because she felt that whatever she was unloading, she was doing it with someone who wasn't just sympathetic or empathic, but someone who genuinely, sincerely, understood what she was going through. Because she had been through it herself.

She looked out at the sea, the waves rolling into the beach, waves that look so huge and threatening from a distance becoming smaller and smaller the nearer they got to her, eventually fizzing out to nothing on the sand. Harmless.

She smiled.

Determined not to let the nightmares claim her.

Determined to make this a good day.

114

Phil sipped his pint of lager, looked out along the front of the river. Wivenhoe waterfront was crowded, the Rose and Crown overspill sitting on the picnic tables eating Sunday lunches, drinking beer, enjoying the sunshine.

Next to him, Marina was feeding Josephina. They were waiting for food and had both brought things to read. Marina had given up on *Double Indemnity*, gone back to Jane Austen. Phil was wrestling with the Sunday papers. As perfect a family scene, he thought, as could be imagined.

Enjoying one another's company, he thought. Like it should be.

Six weeks after that night at the old Dock Transit building. Enough time for wounds to heal, things to change.

Or not change.

Ben Fenwick had pulled through. He was less his gall bladder and some other internal organs had been shredded and rebuilt but he was starting to mend. However, he was out of the police force. An internal investigation and inquiry found that he had made a number of fatally flawed decisions in what was his final case and his conduct had been found to be less than exemplary. It had been decided that, given the circumstances, early retirement with a full pension was the best thing all round.

Rose Martin had, of course, blamed Fenwick for everything. He had led her on, promised her promotion in exchange for sexual favours, asked her to do things in the course of the investigation that she knew were wrong or, at best, misguided. But in light of what she had been through – the kidnapping and the rape she was currently in counselling for – her version was believed. Ben Fenwick even went along with it which, Phil thought, was either an act of uncharacteristic self-sacrifice on his part, or guilt.

He knew which one he believed.

Mark Turner was being held awaiting trial. He was going to be charged with murder. He had been judged sane. Marina had seen to that.

Paula Harrison had also come forward, confessed her part then tried to commit suicide. Phil's heart went out to her. And even more so to her granddaughter. He hoped that poor child wouldn't have the kind of upbringing he had gone through.

Fiona Welch's death had left a great deal of unanswered questions, mainly of the 'How did she manage to slip through the net undetected for so long?' variety. The ghouls had come out in force. Newspaper and magazine articles and profiles, anyone and everyone who had ever had contact with Fiona Welch were wheeled out and interviewed and there were books in preparation about her.

Maybe she was right, thought Phil. Maybe she was going to be famous.

Things were improving between Phil and Marina. But the time immediately following Tony's death had been difficult. Phil remembered stepping out of the hospital, walking to the car park.

'Are you OK?' he had asked her.

'No,' she had said and then not spoken all the way home.

But during the days that followed, things had improved. Marina began to get on with her life again, rediscover her joy at being Josephina's mother, Phil's partner.

Like the wounds on Phil's face, healing had begun.

The sun was still high in the sky. Phil took another mouthful of beer, looked at Marina. The sun was shining round her profile, giving her a halo. He smiled. She looked so beautiful.

He took another sip of beer.

She drank her gin and tonic.

Josephina closed her eyes, went to sleep in Marina's arms.

'Marry me,' he said.

She didn't look at him, just kept her eyes straight ahead, looking at the water, her head haloed in the sun. She sat there silently for a few seconds.

'Yes,' she said.

A tear fell from her eye down her cheek.

Phil leaned across, wiped it away.

The sun, hot and bright in the sky.

The Surrogate

Tania Carver

A shocking double-murder scene greets Detective Inspector
Philip Brennan when he is called to a flat in Colchester. Two
women are viciously cut open and laying spreadeagled, one tied
to the bed, one on the floor. The woman on the bed has had
her stomach cut into and her unborn child is missing.

But this is the third time Phil and his team have seen such an
atrocity. Two other pregnant women have been killed in this
way and their babies taken from them. No-one can imagine
what sort of person would want to commit such evil acts.

When psychologist Marina Esposito is brought in,
Phil has to put aside his feelings about their shared past
and get on with the job. But can they find the killer
before another woman is targeted?

'Tania Carver delivers a dark, sexy thriller in her relentlessly
suspenseful debut. If you haven't discovered this talented
newcomer yet, hurry. She's on her way to the top'
Richard Montanari

978-0-7515-4228-8

Bloodline

Mark Billingham

When a dead body is found in a North London flat, it seems like a straightforward domestic murder until a bloodstained sliver of x-ray is found clutched in the dead woman's fist – and it quickly becomes clear that this case is anything but ordinary. DI Thorne discovers that the victim's mother had herself been murdered fifteen years before by infamous serial killer Raymond Garvey. The hunt to catch Garvey was one of the biggest in the history of the Met, and ended with seven women dead.

When more bodies and more fragments of x-ray are discovered, Thorne has a macabre jigsaw to piece together until the horrifying picture finally emerges. A killer is targeting the children of Raymond Garvey's victims. Thorne must move quickly to protect those still on the murderer's list, but nothing and nobody are what they seem. Not when Thorne is dealing with one of the most twisted killers he has ever hunted …

'A well plotted thriller featuring a very human detective'
Choice

978-0-7515-3994-3

Fever of The Bone

Val McDermid

Meet Tony Hill's most twisted adversary – a killer with
a shopping list of victims, a killer unmoved by youth and
innocence, a killer driven by the most perverted of desires.

The murder and mutilation of teenager Jennifer Maidment
is horrific enough on its own. But it's not long before Tony
realises it's just the start of a brutal and ruthless campaign that's
targeting an apparently unconnected group of young people.
Struggling with the newly-awakened ghosts of his own past
and desperate for distraction in his work, Tony battles to find
the answers that will give him personal and professional
satisfaction in his most testing investigation yet.

'Everything a great detective novel should be: pacy, gripping,
clever and stylish and, most of all, a fantastic read'
Sunday Express

978-0-7515-4321-6

Other bestselling titles available by mail